WELC...
◄ TIME ...

The Warhammer world is founded upon the exploits of brave heroes, and the rise and fall of powerful enemies. Now for the first time the tales of these mythical events have been brought to life in a new range of books. Divided into a series of trilogies, each brings you hitherto untold details of the lives and times of the most legendary of all Warhammer heroes and villains. Combined together, they will reveal some of the hidden connections that underpin the history of the Warhammer world.

◄ THE BLACK PLAGUE ►

The tale of an Empire divided, its heroic defenders and the enemies who endeavour to destroy it with the deadliest plague ever loosed upon the world of man. This series begins with *Dead Winter* and continues in *Blighted Empire*.

◄ THE WAR OF VENGEANCE ►

The ancient races of elf and dwarf clash in a devastating war that will decide not only their fates, but that of the entire Old World. The first novel in this series is *The Great Betrayal*, and is followed by *Master of Dragons*.

◄ BLOOD OF NAGASH ►

The first vampires, tainted children of Nagash, spread across the world and plot to gain power over the kingdoms of men. This series starts in *Neferata*, and carries on with *Master of Death*.

Keep up to date with the latest information from the **Time of Legends** at *www.blacklibrary.com*

TIME OF LEGENDS™

Book Two of the Black Plague

BLIGHTED EMPIRE

The Black Plague

C L Werner

BLACK LIBRARY

To Lindsey, Christian, Graeme and Nick – my overworked editors who endure
the frustrating eccentricities of the artistic temperament.

A BLACK LIBRARY PUBLICATION

First published in Great Britain in 2013 by
Black Library,
Games Workshop Ltd.,
Willow Road, Nottingham,
NG7 2WS, UK

10 9 8 7 6 5 4 3 2 1

Cover illustration by Fares Maese.
Map by Nuala Kennedy.

UK ISBN: 978 1 84970 310 9
US ISBN: 978 1 84970 311 6

See Black Library on the internet at
www.blacklibrary.com

Find out more about Games Workshop
and the world of Warhammer at
www.games-workshop.com

Printed and bound by CPI Group (UK) Ltd, Croydon, CR0 4YY

It is an age of legend.

It is a dark age, a bloody age, an age of unspeakable pacts and powerful magic. It is an age of war and of death, and of apocalyptic terror. But amidst all of the flames and fury it is a time, too, of mighty heroes, of bold deeds and great courage...

At the heart of the Old World lies Sigmar's Empire. Over a thousand years after the god-king's passing, it is a land in turmoil. The corrupt and incompetent Emperor, Boris Goldgather, has bled the common folk of the Empire to keep himself in comfort, leaving his people to starve. The border forts, the Empire's first line of defence against the many foes that threaten Sigmar's lands, lie unmanned and the Imperial armies struggle to repel the barbarous northmen, savage greenskins and monstrous beastmen that rampage through the provinces.

None know that the gravest threat to the realm lies not in the darkness of the forests or the mountain passes, but beneath the feet of men. The sinister, ratlike skaven, long believed to be a myth, plot to destroy the Empire. Untold armies lurk in dank caverns deep below the earth, unnumbered skaven from the warrior clans ready to spread across the lands of men and wipe them out. And in the deepest vaults, the demented plague priests of Clan Pestilens brew a noxious contagion that will bring the men of the Empire to their knees.

The Black Plague.

GEOGRAPHICAL MAP OF THE EMPIRE

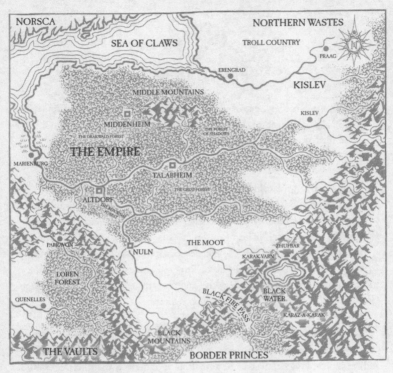

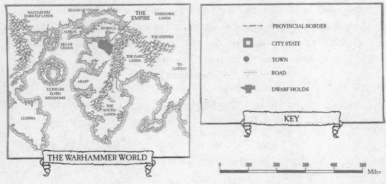

THE WARHAMMER WORLD

– – – –	PROVINCIAL BORDER
☐	CITY STATE
●	TOWN
....	ROAD
	DWARF HOLDS

KEY

0   100   200   300   400   500 Miles

⤙ PREFACE ⤚

That period of Imperial history preceding the stability brought by the ascension of Magnus von Bildhofen as Emperor in the year 2304 is a confused and frustrating time for the serious scholar. Many of the records from that era that have survived consist of accounts recorded by monks and friars and, by consequence, are couched in such a manner as to reflect and magnify the religious dogma of the author's temple. Most secular works relating to this period were destroyed over the course of the centuries of warfare that gripped the Empire in what has been termed the 'Age of Three Emperors' and the Vampire Wars which briefly interrupted that vicious civil war.

What is left for the historian, then, is a large body of myth and legend. How much veracity there may be in accounts of Underfolk is debatable at best; however, in compiling this treatment of those years when plague decimated the Empire, it has been constructive to adopt an attitude of credulity.

In the first volume of *A Folkloric History of the Black Plague and the Wolf of Sigmar*, the conspiracy of Prince Sigdan of

Altdorf and his allies against the despotic corruption of Emperor Boris I was detailed. Due in no small measure to the despicable Adolf Kreyssig, commander of the Emperor's secret police, the conspiracy failed. In the course of their invasion of the Imperial Palace, Captain Erich von Kranzbeuhler of the outlawed Reiksknecht absconded with Ghal Maraz, depriving the Emperor of the ultimate symbol of his authority.

The Black Plague's depredations across the Empire were nowhere as marked as in the region of Sylvania. In that ill-omened land, a distraught priest of Morr turned against his faith when his family succumbed to the disease. Frederick van Hal, drawing upon forbidden texts, resorted to necromancy in a desperate effort to reconnect with those he'd lost. By employing the dark art, van Hal opened himself to eldritch forces beyond his comprehension. Christening himself 'Van-hal', the terrible necromancer turned against his neighbours, unleashing the undead against the town of Bylorhof and slaughtering its populace.

Middenheim, the famed City of the White Wolf, was spared the brunt of the plague in those early years. Graf Gunthar, ruler of Middenheim, imposed harsh measures to protect his city, refusing refugees from other provinces sanctuary on the Ulricsberg. These draconian policies offended the ideals of his son, Prince Mandred, who struggled to help those he felt his father had abandoned. Ultimately, after a heroic charge to relieve the refugee camp at the foot of the mountain when it was attacked by beastmen, the young prince came to under-stand the cruel wisdom behind his father's edict.

No account of the plague years would be complete without delving into the Underfolk, the rat-like skaven of many a nursery fable. The ratmen are often credited as the instigators of the Black Plague, and anecdotes about their treacherous manipulations can be found in dwarf records of the time. A plague priest named Puskab Foulfur is often associated with the genesis of the plague. After concocting this dread disease, the skaven were emboldened enough to make direct attacks on the cities of men. Displaying the cunning depravity of his breed, Puskab contrived to place himself on the Council of Thirteen, the villainous Grey Lords, by first allying with and then betraying one of the sitting Grey Lords. Together with his own leader, Arch-Plaguelord Nurglitch, the pestiferous Clan Pestilens possessed two seats upon this Council, allowing them even greater influence over the verminous Under-Empire. At their instigation, the despotic Warmonger Vecteek commanded an ever-increasing deployment of the Black Plague.

In the grim year of 1111, the Black Plague was unleashed. Before it was finished, three of every four men in the Empire would be dead. In the midst of such widespread decimation, old evils stirred to take their place in the sun.

This second volume details the aftermath of that original dead winter.

– Reikhard Mattiasson,
*A Folkloric History of the Black Plague
and the Wolf of Sigmar Vol. II*

Altdorf Press, Vorhexen, 2513

Suppressed by order of Lord Thaddeus
Gamow, Jahrdrung, 2514

Skavenblight
Geheimnisnacht, 1112

The pungent smell of smouldering warpstone wafted through the blackened chamber, the corrupt fume slithering into every nook and cranny, oozing between the crumbling bricks, burning into beams of oak and ash, discolouring glass and tarnishing bronze. It was the stench of darkest sorcery, and this was its night.

Resplendent in silver robes woven from the scalps of man-thing she-breeders, Seerlord Skrittar perched atop the dais, his claw stroking the silky texture of his finery. The wealth displayed by such a garment! He could smell the envy in the scent of his subordinates whenever he donned it. It was a considerable expenditure to abduct the she-breeders, bear them back alive to Skavenblight and confine them in the blackest burrows beneath the city. They had to be kept in darkness, nurtured on a rich diet of glow-grubs and swamp maize for many seasons before their hair assumed the correct hue, scent and texture. It was a sad reality that only the smallest amounts of weirdroot could be used to keep the she-breeders tranquil or the drug would affect the desired properties in their hair. The breeders of the man-things were eccentric, excitable animals, entertaining pretensions of intelligence the Horned Rat had thankfully spared the brood-mothers of the skaven. They were given to crazed moods and had to be constantly watched lest they kill themselves in an unguarded moment.

Skrittar's whiskers twitched in amusement as he pondered the perfection of the skaven mind. The Horned Rat had blessed his children with the divine spark, had created the ratmen in his own image and invested in them all the craft and guile of his own black spirit. The skaven were destined to dominate and rule over all others. It was a holy imperative. To do less was to betray their sacred duty. From the very first time the Shattered Tower's bell had tolled the thirteenth note, the skaven had known it was their destiny to inherit the world.

The seerlord's whiskers became still. His furred lips pulled back to expose his yellowed fangs, his naked tail lashed in annoyance against the cold stone floor. If not for the petty squabbling and bickering amongst the clans, the skaven should have dominated the world long ago. Short-sighted despots and craven-livered tyrants who could think only of their own pretensions of power and greatness. The Grey Lords had squandered the resources of the mighty Under-Empire on their internecine feuds and rivalries. If they could only put the welfare of skavendom ahead of their own ambitions, nothing could keep the ratmen from rising up and overwhelming the surface world. There was no force among gods or men that could stand against a united skavendom!

Skrittar shook his horned head, his nose crinkling in a sour expression as though a foul scent had filled his nostrils. There was a real prospect of skavendom uniting now. The past winter had seen Clan Pestilens unleash their hideous

Black Plague against the man-things. The disease had run rampant, decimating the humans in numbers that were truly astounding. Virtually the entire Council of Thirteen had rallied behind Arch-Plaguelord Nurglitch, even permitting a second plague priest to assume a position among the Lords of Decay, the diseased Poxmaster Puskab Foulfur, creator of the Black Plague! First Among Equals, Warmonger Vecteek the Murderous had showered the plague monks with gifts and honours, indulging them as the vicious warlord of Clan Rictus had never indulged any clan before.

If things persisted, all would march together under a single banner. But it wouldn't be the divine light of the Horned One and his living prophets, the grey seers, who would guide the united hordes of the Under-Empire. It would be the pestilent minds and heretical creeds of the plague priests!

Skrittar stamped his paw against the floor, spinning around and scurrying to the gigantic mess of copper tubes and pipes that dominated one end of the vast, cavernous hall high within the holy confines of the Shattered Tower. The ancient stained-glass window that had been left behind by the original human builders of the city had been broken up and sold as scrap. It had been a necessary defilement to allow the great crystal lens of the hulking warpscope to focus upon the black tapestry of night.

A fabulous creation, that mountain of copper and bronze, glass and crystal. There were plates of polished warpstone deep inside the housing, sheets of the stone that had been ground so thin and fine as to be translucent. Exploiting a network of silver mirrors, the warpstone lenses would draw down the image of the night sky into the eye of the observer, permitting him such a view of the moons that it seemed he might reach out and grab them.

The seerlord chittered as the humour of such a thought

occurred to him. Reach out and grab the moons? That was precisely what he had done. Not through the arcane technology of Clan Skryre; all their foolish contraption – itself shamelessly patterned after similar instruments developed by the dwarf-things – could do was offer a view of the moons. With his magic, Skrittar had done much more. Much, much more! He had stretched forth his tyrannical will and gouged his sorcerous claws across the face of Morrslieb, tearing great chunks from the dark moon's surface. Chunks of raw, pure warpstone!

For a full cycle of seasons those boulders of warpstone had circled across the sky, becoming like little black stars, waiting for the moment when he, Skrittar, Voice of the Horned One, would draw them down to earth.

Skrittar's paw brushed across the focusing mechanism, manipulating the little flywheel as he pressed his eye to the observation port. Supposedly the Skryre tinker-rats had insulated the viewing plate against the harmful energies of the warpscope's lenses, but just to be safe the seerlord hissed a quick prayer to invoke the Horned Rat's protection. Ordinarily he would leave the hazards of using any of Skryre's contraptions to an easily replaceable underling or an overly ambitious subordinate, but at the moment there was no one to indulge such caution.

Looking away from the observation port, Skrittar cast his gaze across the long chamber with its arched ceiling high overhead, and its stone walls black and hoary with age. The floor was marked with a bewildering array of protective talismans and circles, each figure drawn with exacting precision in the blood of elves and griffons and even more dangerous beasts. Bronze braziers cast a fume of smouldering warpstone into the air, saturating the chamber's atmosphere with the stuff of raw magic.

Skrittar had bided his time for a full year, waiting for the cosmic conjunction of moons and stars that was Gnawdawn. It was only during such a conjunction that the black energies of dark magic were magnified to their full. Even then, even with his abilities bolstered and heightened by warpstone elixirs and vapours, his spiritual aura strengthened by obscene rites to the Horned Rat, Skrittar had known the sorcery he needed to perform was beyond his ability alone. As he had one year ago, Skrittar had summoned a cabal of his underlings, a coven of twelve of his ablest and most wicked grey seers.

They had been wary and suspicious when they had submitted to Skrittar's summons, calling them to the grand observatory. The entire Order of Grey Seers had been shaken by the deaths of twelve of their number exactly one year previously. Outwardly, none of them had been so foolish as to doubt Skrittar's claim that their comrades had expired in a failed magical experiment. He didn't think anyone had managed to ferret out the true nature of their deaths – Clan Eshin had a most un-skavenlike propensity for discretion. Still, there had been an inordinate number of assassination attempts on Skrittar's life since that Great Ritual one year ago.

Skrittar ground his fangs together in irritation. Even among the grey seers, prophets of the Horned One, there was a woeful lack of vision. Any of them should be happy to become a martyr, to give his worthless life in the name of his god. Their sacrifice would be the stuff that would blot out the heathen taint of Clan Pestilens forever! Their blood would be the first waters of a tide that would sweep through the Under-Empire and establish a theocracy that would dominate skavendom for all time! Their deaths would bring supreme power to their master, Seerlord Skrittar!

There were twelve more martyrs to the cause now. Twelve

grey-cloaked bodies strewn about the floor. All the protective wards and talismans they had carried, the spells and arcane safeguards they had evoked, hadn't been enough to save them. The grey seers had lent their magic to Skrittar's ritual, each of the greedy fool-meat imagining the wealth that would soon belong to them, presuming themselves a share of what belonged to the Horned Rat and his supreme servant Skrittar alone! Greed formed a chink in their defences, made their caution falter for just a brief moment.

It was the only moment Skrittar needed. The twelve had died in an especially agonising fashion as they inhaled the poison. The seerlord had been too crafty to use Deathmaster Silke as he had the previous year, just in case someone had learned of their connection. Instead, he had engaged the Deathmaster's disciple Killmaker Nartik to dispose of his unwanted, untrustworthy minions. Nartik had been crafty too, tossing the pungent packet of poison into one of the braziers the instant the ritual was over and the cabal had out-lived their usefulness. Skrittar had been told the effects would resemble the Black Plague to such a degree that only the most adept assassins in Clan Eshin would be able to tell the dif-ference. The rest of Skrittar's Order would be convinced the massacre had been the work of the heathen plague monks this time!

Skrittar turned back to the warpscope. Through the view-ing lens he could see the chunks of orbiting warpstone, each of them radiating a faint nimbus of green light now. Before his gaze, he could see them being drawn downwards. Soon, the magic Skrittar had conjured would have the warpstone plummeting into the earth, smashing down as a rain of mete-orites. He had been very careful in his calculations. He knew where the warpstone would come smashing down, a section of land barren enough to be shunned by most skaven yet not so distant as to make a journey there noteworthy. He'd already picked one of the less powerful warlord clans to provide the labour he would require, a clan with sufficient dread of the grey seers and enough pious terror of the Horned Rat that the slightest twitch of Skrittar's whisker would have them scurrying to carry out his commands.

The seerlord leaned away from the warpscope, rubbing his lucky cat's foot over the eye he had pressed to the observation port just in case. He bruxed his teeth as he consulted the rat-skin map laid out on a bench atop the dais. The trajectory of the warpstone would draw it down to the bleakest backwater in the region of the man-thing Empire. When the warpstone shower struck, Skrittar would not be far behind. His lackeys would harvest the biggest bonanza of warpstone the Under-Empire had ever seen, wealth that would make even Vecteek and Nurglitch bow to Skrittar and kiss the tip of his tail!

With the man-things sick and weak, with the dwarf-things hiding in their mountains and the green-things fighting among themselves, there was no one who would oppose Skrittar's invasion of Sylvania.

⟨ CHAPTER I ⟩

Altdorf
Pflugzeit, 1114

Slivers of agony raced through his arm, searing through his very bones. There was a sensation of scalding cold, the gnawing bite of hoarfrost sinking into his skin. Before his eyes, the hairs on the back of his hand turned brittle and crumbled into little motes of ice. He clenched his teeth against the torment, refusing to scream. *This time I will not scream*, he vowed to himself. It was a promise he had made many times. A promise he had always failed to keep.

As the pain became too great, Adolf Kreyssig spat the wooden block from his mouth and gave voice to a torturous cry. He screamed until he thought his lungs must burst and his throat would be stripped raw. He screamed and screamed, but there was no respite. He knew there would be none. There would be no relief until the ordeal had accomplished what it needed to accomplish.

Just as he felt consciousness slipping away, as black oblivion began to wrap its welcoming folds about his brain, Kreyssig felt the pain begin to abate. Gradually, the chill evaporated from his bones, the frost melted on his skin as blood coursed back into his arm. He watched as a cold mist rose from his warming flesh. Layers of frozen skin sloughed away as he flexed his muscles.

Through the lingering agony, Kreyssig smiled. He could feel his muscles respond, see the fingers of his hand clench and open. True, there was a certain lethargy about the motion, but it was less pronounced than before. Improvement! Reward for the torture he had been submitting himself to for over two years.

Two years! It had been two years since he'd pursued the traitors Baron Thornig and Captain Erich von Kranzbeuhler into the sewers trying to recover the relic, the Holy Hammer of Sigmar, which they had stolen from the Imperial Palace. In the very moment of his seeming triumph, tragedy had struck him down. Cornered, the two rebels were at the mercy of Kreyssig's Kaiserjaeger when events had spiralled out of control. The disgusting, verminous mutants Kreyssig had been exploiting in secret as spies had also been hunting the rebels and rushed into the subterranean gallery. Before Kreyssig could stop them, his startled men attacked the monstrous creatures. The resultant fight had destabilised the ancient masonry, bringing the building above crashing down on all their heads.

Kreyssig had been fortunate to survive. None of the others did. Crushed beneath tons of brick and stone, he'd been more than half dead when some of his men discovered him lying in a cellar of the Courts of Justice. Some of the mutants must have pulled him from the rubble and taken him to where he would be found and given help. Even with the best attention, however, he had hovered at the Gates of Morr for several months. The attentions of priests, herbalists and even the Emperor's personal physician had preserved his life, but his body had been left a broken shell. It had required stronger measures to make him whole.

Slowly, the Commander of the Kaiserjaeger, the man who was feared throughout the Reikland as 'the Hound of Boris', raised himself from the cold stone slab he rested upon. Dried weeds and the moist foulness of animal entrails fell to the floor as he moved. With a trembling hand, he started to wipe away the ghastly symbols that had been inked upon his naked flesh.

'Your strength returns, commander,' a soft voice purred. There was amusement and superiority in that voice, but also an alluring suggestiveness that sent a shiver rushing through Kreyssig's body.

It would have taken more willpower than even he possessed to keep from looking at the possessor of that voice. Kreyssig felt the shiver rise as he stared at his benefactor. The little chapel built into the side of the Lindenhaus was a shadowy, vault-like hall, a place of nigh perpetual cold and gloom. Even the head of the Emperor's secret police wasn't entirely sure what might be hiding in the murky chapel. There were some secrets even he was shy of uncovering. For now, it was enough that the darkness disgorged the one person in all Altdorf who had the ability to heal his ravaged body.

She stalked from the shadows, her slim body draped in crimson folds, smooth milky skin bared by the scandalous cut of her raiment. Flowing tresses of fiery hair fell about her shoulders, more vibrant in the darkness than her red gown. A beautiful face, so fair it might have been carved from alabaster, smiled at him. There was a coy, teasing quality in that smile. The grin of a cat toying with its prey.

'It does not hurt so much to move the arm,' Kreyssig told her. He flexed the muscles again, managing not to wince as another tingle of pain rushed through him. There had been

times when any betrayal of pain on his part had been cause
to undergo a second regimen straight away. He had learned
to hide his pain after a few such extended treatments.

'That is good,' the flame-headed woman said. She
approached the stone table, her eyes straying to give an
almost mocking look at the cobweb-shrouded statue of Verena standing beside the wall. 'In time, you will be as strong
as ever.'

'How soon?' Kreyssig asked, a quiver of uneasiness in his
tone. He was both excited and revolted when the woman's
slender finger stroked his injured arm. Her beauty was enough
to set his heart pounding whenever she was near. At the same
time, he felt the very core of his being sicken at her approach.
No man encouraged the attentions of a witch lightly.

Even when that witch bore the title of Baroness von den
Linden.

The witch stopped pacing around the table. She fixed her
intense gaze upon Kreyssig. 'Your hurts are many,' she said.
'Even I cannot say how long it may take to heal them. You
are lucky to be alive.'

Kreyssig turned his head as he heard something creeping
among the dead weeds. Glancing down, he was revolted to
see one of the witch's cats chewing at a piece of intestine
he'd knocked from the table. He'd given up trying to count
the filthy creatures – every time he visited the baroness there
seemed to be at least one cat he hadn't seen before. This one,
a great bloated beast, he was reasonably certain she'd called
Grimalkin.

'Man makes his own luck,' Kreyssig retorted. He used his
irritation to find the strength to pull away from the witch's
touch. The effort seemed to amuse the baroness. Laughing,
she reached down and drew the great fat cat into her arms,
cradling it against her breast.

'An interesting perspective,' Baroness von den Linden mused, scratching the brute's head until a loud purr rumbled from its furry body. 'Would you say that my decision to render aid to you was also of your own creation?'

It was Kreyssig's turn to laugh. 'If you didn't think I was useful, you would have let me rot,' he stated. 'If I wasn't the Emperor's strong right hand, I think you would have let me wither and die.' He flexed his own right hand, feeling the dull ache of old wounds. 'I do not blame you, of course. Your family has a history of acquiring those who are useful. Your mother, as far as my investigators can determine, was a simple Nordland peasant who seduced your father when he was hunting in the Middle Mountains. Curious how he died so soon after their wedding.'

'Perhaps he was no longer useful,' the baroness suggested. 'Perhaps his ambitions were too short-sighted.'

'And what are your ambitions, Kirstina?' Kreyssig wondered. 'How far are you trying to go?'

The witch shook her fiery tresses as she laughed. 'As far as I can go! As far as my magic will take me!'

'Your magic?' Kreyssig asked, strangely stung by the thought.

The baroness laughed again. 'My magic brought you to me,' she said. 'It has protected both of us from the plague that runs amok through the city.'

'I have wondered about that,' Kreyssig confessed. 'How is it that you have warded off the plague when even the priestesses of Shallya are powerless?'

'They try to save too many,' the witch said. 'The greater the effort, the more power the spell demands. The priestesses don't know how to make such magic. They would shudder at what such rituals require.'

'But you aren't afraid,' Kreyssig observed.

The witch dropped the cat to the floor. The beast dashed

back to the entrails lying about the table. 'To work magic, one must be afraid,' she said. 'Those who do not fear the power are soon devoured by it. To master the dark arts, there must be a balance of respect and fear.' She threw back her head. 'I have found that balance,' she announced proudly.

'Every shield has its weakness,' Kreyssig warned, thinking of the way Kranzbeuhler and Ghal Maraz had slipped through his fingers.

'Wisdom lies in finding the limits of your strength,' the baroness said. 'The plague, it is said, is spread by swarms of black beetles. Long have I guarded myself with spells to drive away any insect, so already I am guarded against the plague beetles.'

'And what is the limit of your strength?' Kreyssig asked as he strode to where his clothing lay piled on the chapel floor. He pointed to the cobwebs shrouding the statue of Verena. 'It seems the spiders don't share your respect for magic.'

The baroness frowned. 'The spell afflicts only the six-legged vermin,' she said. 'Though it has a peculiar effect upon ants. They flee from me, but if I trespass too near an ant hill, the brutes come trooping out in a frenzied swarm.'

'Protecting their home,' Kreyssig said. 'Any man would do the same when threatened by a witch.'

'Would he?' wondered the baroness. In a few gliding steps she crossed the vault and plucked the breeches from Kreyssig's hand. She laid her hand on his chest, running her fingers through his hair. 'What would you do if threatened by a witch?'

Baroness von den Linden laughed as Kreyssig took hold of her and crushed her against him.

'Kreyssig-man late-late!'

Adolf Kreyssig scowled at the scrawny, rat-like creature as it scurried out from behind a pile of rotten timber. With most of the river trade dried up because of the plague, the once bustling shipyards along Altdorf's riverfront had become derelict and abandoned, shunned as reminders of better, more prosperous times. They made a perfect site for clandestine liaisons, even with bestial mutants. During his long convalescence, he had come to dislike the subterranean haunts these brutes preferred. Better by far to draw them out into more accommodating conditions.

'You forget who is master here,' Kreyssig snarled at the creature, his hand dropping to the sword at his side. The rat-creature's head drooped as it followed the motion, then the beast leaped back, raising its paws in a warding gesture.

'Calm-peace,' it whined. 'No harm-hate! Know you take-need time for breeder-witch.'

The sword left its sheath as Kreyssig stormed towards the retreating mutant. He had engaged these creatures to spy *for* him, not *on* him! His liaisons with Baroness von den Linden were a carefully kept secret, something that could explode into a ruinous scandal if it were made known. Married to a baroness himself, involvement with another noblewoman would be bad enough, but there were already enough rumours about Kirstina to make such talk doubly dangerous.

'You've been spying on me,' Kreyssig snarled at the retreating rat.

'No-no!' the creature whined as it crawled away. 'Not follow-see!' The creature lifted a paw and tapped its long snout. 'Scent-smell cat-devil on Kreyssig-man!'

The abject terror in the mutant's voice as it mentioned cats added a note of such absurdity to the scene that Kreyssig returned his blade to the scabbard. What possible menace could such cringing vermin pose? Even if they knew more than they should, they could hardly make it public. Even in the best of times, the men of the Empire would hang them as abominations… And these were far from the best of times.

'What do you have to tell me?' Kreyssig asked the mutant.

The beast came slinking forwards, paws folded before it. 'Listen-learn much-much,' it said. The creature's voice dropped to a conspiratorial hiss. 'Boris-king leave Altdorf-nest soon! Hide-stay in Carr-o-burg!' The mutant's chittering voice stumbled over the unfamiliar name.

Kreyssig's blood froze as he heard the report. He owed his rank and position to the favour and indulgence of Emperor Boris. As a peasant, he was held beneath contempt by the nobles of Reikland and Altdorf. Without the Emperor's backing, Kreyssig's authority would be compromised, perhaps even supplanted entirely. The despot's courage would pick this time to desert him! Not for an instant did he doubt the mutant's report. Droves of nobles had already quit plague-ridden Altdorf to go into seclusion in country estates. It stood to reason that Boris would follow their example. With the execution of Baron Konrad Aldrech, the Emperor had inherited the holdings of the Grand Count of Drakwald, including the immense Schloss Hohenbach. No, the only surprising thing about the report was that Boris had waited so long to go into hiding.

The mutant's next words, however, did come as a shock. 'Boris-king leave-hide! Make-declare Kreyssig-man Protector when king-man is gone!'

He could only stare at the verminous mutant in disbelief. Kreyssig, for once in his career, was dumbfounded. Emperor Boris was abandoning Altdorf and making him, a peasant, Protector in his stead?

Adolf Kreyssig, Commander of the Kaiserjaeger, would soon be Adolf Kreyssig, Protector of the Empire. He would become, in effect, surrogate emperor, the most powerful man in Altdorf!

* * *

Drakenhof
Brauzeit, 1112

Wine dripped from the nobleman's thick moustache, staining the ermine collar he wore and trickling down the sleek steel plates of his armour. He lowered the ivory chalice, jiggling it in an irritable fashion. Timidly, a young servant girl glided forwards to refill his cup. Despite her best efforts, she wasn't nimble enough to transfer the wine from the jar to the moving cup without spilling some of it on the ground.

Immediately, the nobleman's eyes were fixed on her, blazing like living coals within his swarthy face. His hand whipped out, smashing the chalice across the girl's jaw, shattering the cup and gashing her cheek. The girl crumpled to the ground amid the broken ivory, sobbing more from terror than pain.

Count Malbork von Drak sank back in his chair, sneering at the woman's fear. Imperiously, he stabbed a finger at the wine-soaked dirt. 'Clean it up, wench,' he snarled. When the still crying servant leaned forwards and started to sop up the mess with her skirt, the nobleman brought his armoured boot cracking against her skull, sending her sprawling.

It was an ugly, sadistic sound that bubbled up from Malbork's throat as he congratulated himself on his callous brutality. Then he turned away from the bleeding servant and turned his vicious gaze on the courtiers gathered about the mouth of his tent.

'A fine jest, your excellency,' a fat, piggish man with foppish curls in his hair and a lisp to his voice whined.

Malbork ignored the man's fawning admiration. With an irritated gesture, he waved him aside. 'You are blocking my view of the castle,' the count said. With indecent haste, the courtier scrambled away.

It was well that he did, for the vista that was visible from the opening of his tent wasn't one conducive to an improvement in Malbork's humour. Voivodes of Sylvania, the von Draks had administered their domain from the walls of Castle Drakenhof for generations. The brooding vastness of the fortress loomed over the green hills and rolling fields around it like some slumbering monster, casting its menacing shadow across the villages clustered about its foundations.

They were deserted now, those villages. Devastated by the cataclysm that had struck Sylvania, the disaster the simple peasants were calling 'Starfall'. The night sky had, for a terrifying moment, become ablaze with eerie green lights, an uncountable multitude of ghoulish flames that winked down from the heavens. The length and breadth of Sylvania had been pelted with noxious green-black stones, the toxic embers of those ghoul-fires. The whole of the land had been afflicted by the dark sending: crops smashed flat, pastures poisoned, creeks turned foul with glowing scum, homes enflamed as the smouldering stones crashed through thatch roofs.

Nowhere had the destruction been greater than at Drakenhof. Elsewhere, the Starfall had consisted of tiny rocks, seldom bigger than a man's hand. Drakenhof had proved the exception. Here the stones had been far larger. In one village the mill had been obliterated by a rock the size of an ox-cart, in another a watchtower had collapsed under the impact of a stone bigger than a warhorse. Even these star-sent missiles were insignificant beside the stone that had ploughed through the face of Castle Drakenhof to embed itself in the very heart of the Drakenfelsen, the great rock upon which the fortress stood. With grim humour, some of Malbork's courtiers had christened the stone 'the Jewel of Morrslieb' after a superstitious rumour that it had been flung down at the castle by an angry moon.

The count took small amusement from such prattle. Several of those aristocratic jesters were even now labouring alongside the conscripted inhabitants of the stricken villages, working to clear away the rubble and repair the damage inflicted upon the castle by their 'moon-stone'. It was hard, unrelenting and dangerous work. A relay of corpse-carts made a constant circuit of the Drakenfelsen, retrieving the corpses overseers tossed from the broken battlements. Fires yet burned unchecked in some of the galleries, and falling debris had turned some of the lower vaults into veritable ovens. Poisonous dust waited wherever the 'Jewel' had scraped the walls and floors. Unstable halls were prone to collapse, spilling tons of stone and masonry upon the peasants desperately trying to shore them up. To all of these had to be added the biting cold of the Drakenhoehenzug, the mountain winds whistling through the broken fortress like hungry wolves.

And above all the rest, there was the Black Plague. It cut down the workers by the bushel despite the best efforts of Malbork's Nachtsheer to dispose of the sick as soon as they were discovered by the soldiers. The disease was unforgiving and insatiable, slaughtering the workers by the hundreds. The count was only thankful that it confined its depredations to men rather than more valuable things like horses and oxen. Even so, the mortality of his workers was becoming tiresome.

Staring up at the castle from his camp on the other side of the River Draken, Malbork frowned as he watched a peasant slip from the scaffolding that framed one of the towers. For an instant, the man clung to one of the gargoyles glowering from the edges of the tower's sharply angled roof, then he lost his grip on the statue and went plummeting to his doom. It would take a judicious amount of whip-work to get more labourers into the tower after this accident. Malbork didn't mind the violence, but peasants were less efficient after a beating.

He could almost find it in himself to envy that rebel maniac rampaging across the heart of the county. Some crazed priest unable to cope with the plague. The man had turned to black magic, and wielding such profane power he'd started drawing the dead from their tombs, creating an army of skeletons and corpses. By all reports, the madman's legion was unstoppable, tireless and unquestioning. They marched across the heaviest snow, through the darkest forest, into the most pestilential marsh in obedience to their master's murderous whims. With workers like that, Malbork would have Castle Drakenhof rebuilt in a month. Why, with an army like that he would deny his oaths to Stirland and make Sylvania a province in its own right, answerable to none save the Emperor – and perhaps not even him!

The smell of blood intruded upon the count's daydreams. Irritably, he turned his gaze from the castle to regard the piggish Clucer Scarlat. The foppish courtier was holding a pomander under his nose, taking deep breaths to inundate his lungs with sweet-smelling air. Scarlat, like many of the boiers of Sylvania, subscribed to the theory that the plague was brought about by foul vapours and the surest defence against them was a healthy regime of pungent perfumes. It was a theory Malbork held in as much contempt as he did the peasant belief that the disease represented the punishment of the gods.

Irritably, Malbork snapped his fingers at Scarlat, motioning for the clucer to drop the pomander. Other courtiers hurriedly followed the clucer's example, fear of their count far outweighing even their fear of the plague. 'I believe I smell his grace,' Malbork stated, not without some condescension in his tone. 'Go and admit the prayer-peddler into our presence.'

Clucer Scarlat grimaced, but bobbed his head and scrambled down the slope. As a precaution, Count Malbork's tent had been pitched behind a timber palisade, putting a wall between his personage and any sick enemies who might seek to deliberately infect him. He'd dispatched too many plague-ridden messengers to the grand duke's court in Stirland to allow himself to be victimised by his own strategy.

The clucer returned presently, leading not one but two men. Malbork was mildly surprised to see the armoured figure of Dregator Petru Mihnea. The man was supposed to be leading a Nachtsheer expedition into the Haunted Hills to round up the peasants that had escaped there from their fiefs. Fear of the plague had stirred up a great many curious ideas in the heads of peasants, not the least of which was giving survival precedence over their obligations to the boiers who owned them.

The other man with Scarlat was no surprise at all. The stink of blood announced him as loudly as any crier. Armand Caranica, Arch-Druid of the Blood Circle, high priest of Ahalt the Drinker. The druid's black robes stank of blood and death. The sickle tucked into the rope belt about his waist was stained with gore, for one of the strictures of his faith was that sacrificial blood was holy and must never be washed away. Armand's face was lost behind the deer-skull mask he wore, only his thin lips and tapered jaw projecting beneath the yellowed teeth of the mask. From behind the sockets of the skull, fanatical eyes gleamed.

'The plague still decimates my peasants,' Malbork growled at the druid before he could finish bowing before him. 'You promised me that this sort of thing was going to stop.'

Armand leaned upon his oaken staff, hands clenched tight.

'The might of Ahalt flows through the sacred tree,' he said in a confident tone. 'Very soon the tree shall grow strong enough to shield the whole of the castle from the plague.'

'That doesn't do me any good here,' Malbork said, waving his hand to indicate the camp. 'Maybe you could conjure up a sacred shrubbery to protect me while I'm on this side of the river? Just to bide the time while we wait for the tree to take root.'

A bit of the fanatic gleam left the eyes behind the deer-skull. 'Your... your excellency must allow the great god time to work his beneficence. Even Mighty Ahalt doesn't–'

The count raised his hand, cutting off the druid's explanation. 'I am no credulous supplicant coming to you on bended knee, Caranica. I am Count von Drak! Everything in this land belongs to me, right down to the robes you wear and the prayers you mutter!' He rose from his chair, stalking out from the shadow of the tent. Without turning around, he pointed over his shoulder, indicating a long line of stakes flanking his tent. 'Others have made the mistake of trying to exploit religious gullibility.' Malbork smiled as he saw Armand's eyes dart towards the bodies impaled upon those stakes, bodies that still wore the tattered rags of Sigmarite, Shallyan and Morrite clergy. One corpse, arrayed in the leather and furs of a priest of Taal, was still fresh enough that a pair of ravens were pecking at it.

'I hope you aren't repeating the mistake of your predecessors,' Malbork declared. 'I am acquiring quite a collection of gods. It might be amusing to add yours.'

Armand bowed his head again. 'The divine protection of Ahalt will preserve your excellency from the plague. It just needs more time to bear fruit, more nourishment to quicken its growth.'

Malbork chuckled at the druid's words. 'You are more

murderous than an orc,' he laughed. Spinning around, the count's glove caught the hair of the servant girl who had spilled his wine. Brutally, he pushed her into Armand's arms. 'Here's one to water your tree!' he barked as the crying girl fell to the ground. 'But I want results. Not at the turn of the tide or the dark of the moon, but now! Sacrifice and pray, but you had better pray hard. My indulgence has reached its limits.'

Mustering what authority he could, Armand made his retreat, one bony arm coiled about the girl's waist as he dragged his screaming victim away with him. Malbork watched the druid for a moment, then turned his attention on Dregator Petru.

'Shouldn't you be in the hills?' Malbork asked, his voice striking out like a lash. The dregator blanched at his master's tone, but held himself with more dignity than Scarlat, who took the opportunity to slink back into the company of the other courtiers.

'There are no peasants hiding in the Haunted Hills,' Petru reported. Hurriedly he added an explanation. 'They are gone, your excellency. They've either fled into Grim Moor or they've… joined Vanhal.'

'I understood this madman didn't take prisoners,' Malbork said.

Petru's voice was an audible shiver. 'He doesn't. Where his army marches, nothing lives. He leaves neither the quick nor the dead behind him. Those he kills he raises from their graves to join his unholy army. I have seen it. Thousands upon thousands, marching across the fields, silent but for the rattle of bones and the croaking of crows. Even with the whole of the Nachtsheer at my command, I could do nothing against such power.'

Count Malbork lowered himself into his chair, drawing the wine cup to his lips. He'd heard many such reports in the

years since this sorcerer had risen to bedevil his land. Every
force he'd sent to confront Vanhal had come back beaten and
afraid.

Smoothing his moustache, Malbork waved at his body-
guards. The warriors advanced through the ranks of his
courtiers, seizing Petru's arms. The count was deaf to the
dregator's assurances of loyalty and pleas for mercy. He'd
heard them all before. Petru Mihnea was almost beyond his
usefulness. Now he would join the priests and the other generals who had failed their count.

Plague, gods, star-stones or sorcerers, the people of Sylvania
had to understand that there was only one thing they had to
fear: the displeasure of Count Malbork von Drak.

Sylvania
Brauzeit, 1112

Cries of terror rose from the village as its slumbering inhabitants awoke to their doom. Panicked knots of humanity
scurried out into the road, shrieking as they turned their eyes
to the fields beyond their wattle-and-daub huts. Frantically,
the peasants raced to the far side of the settlement, thinking
to flee from the annihilation that threatened them only to
discover that it waited for them there as well. Like a flock of
birds, the people surged from one direction to another, each
effort at escape balked by a grinning circuit of fleshless death.

Standing atop a palanquin of fused bone and wormy flesh,
Vanhal could appreciate the pathetic futility of their struggle
for survival better than those within the village. There was no
escape. Long before the first scream tore the night, he'd moved
his army into position, locking the village within a ring of the

undead. Only the slightest exertion of the necromancer's will and that army would stir, would march down upon the village and release its inhabitants from their suffering.

Such power over life and death and that strange world beyond death! When he had been a priest of Morr, Frederick van Hal had never dreamed such power could exist. Certainly there had been the tales of the ancient necromancers, of Nagash the Black, who had been vanquished by Sigmar a thousand years past, but even after studying the forbidden work of Arisztid Olt, he'd still thought such stories to be nothing more than exaggerated myths. He had never imagined the true magnitude of such power. If he had, he would have cringed away from such study, terrified of the forces he sought to command.

But did he truly command them? That was a question that had troubled Vanhal's mind since that day two years ago when he'd brought death to the people of Bylorhof. Then, he had believed what he was doing to be justified in the name of vengeance. Justice for his brother's family, slain by the cruel deceptions of the plague doktor Bruno Havemann. Recalling the charlatan's torturous death, Vanhal lifted a thin hand to the bone mask he wore, touching the splintered fragments of Havemann's skull.

Vengeance had been his purpose then, vengeance against Havemann and Bylorhof, vengeance against the soldiers who cordoned off the town and left its inhabitants to die. But it was something darker than vengeance that drove him after that, a terrible compulsion that moved him to destroy village after village.

He had evoked powerful forces to work his magic, but the necromancer wondered, did he command them or did they command him? Was he the musician or the instrument? Sometimes, in the dead of night, when he closed his eyes, he could sense something just beyond his awareness. Something ancient and dead and in its death dreaming. Dreaming of a world quiet and still, devoid of pain and fear. A world as tranquil as the grave.

Vanhal exerted a small fragment of his power and the skeletal mound he stood upon shuffled forwards on the bony legs fused around its base. Like some monstrous beetle, the palanquin skittered towards the village. The necromancer's black robes whipped about him in the night wind, a nimbus of witch-fire crackling about his lean body as he drew upon his magic.

He could spare this place, Vanhal reflected. He could show mercy to these poor wretches. On his command, the horde of skeletons and zombies surrounding the village would withdraw as silently as they had advanced. No one needed to die. He would be able to prove to himself that he was the master of the power that flowed through him, not merely its pawn.

Vanhal's gaunt hand dropped to his belt, withdrawing the ugly black stone from a leather pouch. He stared at it, feeling its malign energies. The fields around the village were littered with these things, each one transmitting its aethyric poison into the earth. This place would soon become a twisted blight, a splotch of diseased horror.

Even if he hadn't come here, this village was doomed. The true path of mercy was to spare these people a lingering death of diseased starvation.

Vanhal closed his eyes and the ring around the village began to close. As a single creature, skeletons and zombies marched across the fields, rusty swords and splintered spears at the ready.

It would be over quickly, the necromancer mused. The villagers would only know a moment of pain and fear, then they would be spared those agonies for all eternity. They would know the tranquillity of that grey kingdom beyond the grave.

A tranquillity Vanhal would bestow upon all of Sylvania. One village at a time.

CHAPTER II

Middenheim
Sigmarzeit, 1118

Looming far above the loamy earth, the ancient trees of the Drakwald blotted out the sun with their intertwined branches, casting the forest in perpetual shadow. The only sunlight that filtered past their leaves was what snuck past as the boughs groaned and swayed in a cool spring breeze.

The men who rode beneath the trees did their best to avoid those rare patches of sunlight. The least reflection off a buckle or an exposed bit of armour would shine like a beacon in the darkened forest. The fell things that called the shadows home already had enough ways to detect strangers in their domain without making them a gift of still another.

They'd done their best to conceal their presence, limiting their numbers to half a dozen riders rather than a stronger company of horsemen. Under the guidance of Mad Albrecht, a trapper who had made his living off the Drakwald for decades, the riders had stained their leatherworks with the musky scent of forest buffalo and banded the hooves of their steeds with fur to muffle their steps. Anything that might make noise, from scabbards to loose bridles and straps, had been carefully secured lest they rattle against a bit of armour or a kicking spur.

Despite his attention to detail, Mad Albrecht didn't think their chances of going unnoticed were very high. It truly was in the hands of Grim Grey Taal, Lord of the Forests, and the trapper whispered a constant prayer to his god as his eyes roved the forest, and his ears strained to catch every sound.

Watching the trapper from the saddle of his courser, Prince Mandred felt guilt pull at his heart. Mad Albrecht was the best woodsman in Middenheim barring one or two acolytes of Taal. A refugee from the Drakwald province, the man had an almost preternatural affinity for the forest. There was no better guide a patrol could ask for.

Which was why Prince Mandred felt the flesh behind his trim black beard flush with shame. Middenheim had lost several patrols to the forest, patrols that hadn't been so fortunate to have a guide like Albrecht along. Patrols that hadn't been so fortunate as to have Graf Gunthar making sure they had a man like Albrecht to guide them.

Mandred raised his eyes skywards, watching the branches rustle far overhead. He appreciated his father's concern, was moved by his paternal devotion. At the same time, he resented being treated any differently from the brave men who risked their lives to keep the countryside surrounding the Ulricsberg secure. It was vital that the rural raugrafs and their peasants be protected. Without them, Middenheim and the refugee settlement of Warrenburg would starve. The patrols' importance was why Mandred had insisted on leading some of them himself, as a gesture of solidarity with the rangers. But with his father showing him extra consideration, he was finding his presence to be detrimental rather than beneficial to morale.

The prince shifted in his saddle, glancing back at the other riders, catching them in a hushed conversation. They threw him a guilty look and quickly fell silent. A sense of regret tugged at him. He was an outsider to these valorous men, a pampered noble who could only play in their world, never actually share it. Mandred could almost curse his breeding, the vast fissure that separated noble from peasant, prince from dienstmann. The Black Plague hadn't shown such distinction in its depredations. The turmoil and confusion left in its wake were similarly shared by all men regardless of class. Yet instead of drawing men closer, uniting them against the common adversity, it was rendering society ever more fractious and resentful.

'I'll report them to the graf,' the stern voice of Beck growled, provoking a warning hiss from Albrecht up ahead. The burly knight just scowled at the wiry trapper. Quickly he turned his attention back to Mandred. 'They have no cause talking about you.'

Mandred shook his head. Beck had been his bodyguard for six years now, ever since Franz had ridden with the prince to relieve the massacre of Warrenburg by marauding beastmen. Dear old Franz had contracted the plague in that expedition. He'd died down in the refugee camp, never again to set foot upon the Ulricsberg. Mandred was ashamed that it had taken the death of his friend to appreciate the meaning of sacrifice, of what it meant to put loyalty above one's own life. A leader could command such loyalty. A good leader was one who would never abuse it.

Beck was a very different sort of man than Franz. He was a grim, hardened warrior, a veteran of the Knights of the White Wolf. He was a man of constant vigilance, ready to see threat in the most innocuous things. A surly look, an unguarded word, and he was ready to condemn a man as a traitorous dog. Right now, Mandred could almost see his bodyguard formulating the report he would give Graf Gunthar denouncing the three *Dienstleute*.

'Let it be,' Mandred told Beck. He forced a tone of levity into his voice. 'A soldier who doesn't complain is one who doesn't understand his job.'

Beck frowned back at the horsemen. 'As you will, your grace,' he said.

'I mean it, Beck,' Mandred warned. With all the other problems afflicting them, he found it absurd that so much attention was still devoted to custom and propriety. The Empire was tearing itself apart, decimated by disease, brought to its knees by warfare. Barbarians still held Marienburg and much of Westerland. The province of Drakwald was an abandoned ruin, her countryside ravaged by beastmen, her great cities exterminated by the plague. Nordland was ablaze with civil war after the death of her grand count, grasping barons striving with one another to expand their own petty interests. Ostland was much the same, and the Ostermark was teetering on the brink of annihilation after a goblin horde descended upon the weakened land. As bad as things were in the north, Mandred had heard it was even worse in the south.

The Empire was in its death throes, and the scavengers were already gathering about the carcass.

Middenheim had withstood the worst of the plague, a fact that Mandred wasn't too proud to attribute to the draconian policies of his father. Graf Gunthar had sealed the city against the tide of refugees, preventing the disease from gaining a foothold on the Ulricsberg. It had been a cruel, inhuman thing to do. Mandred still considered it vicious and villainous. At the same time, it had spared the people of Middenheim untold death and misery. Once, the prince had excoriated his father for such brutality. Now, he understood it, hoped that if such hideous necessity ever arose again he would have the strength to make the same decision.

Alone among the great cities of the Empire, Middenheim had emerged from the plague stronger than before. As the disease abated, refugees were accepted into the city. Warrenburg evolved from a shabby camp into an organised settlement. Regular patrols were dispatched to bring order to the surrounding country, stabilising much of Middenland and extending to its scattered villages the protection of the Ulricsberg. Something approaching normality had settled upon the province.

The price for that fragile peace was vigilance. Patrols such as this one constantly ranged through the forest, watching for signs of bandits, goblins and the ever-present threat of marauding beastmen. The abominable creatures had been beaten back time and again, but with small bands of refugees still braving the forest to seek the safety of Middenheim, the lure of easy prey kept the monsters creeping back. No man, even Graf Gunthar, could cleanse the Drakwald of all the evil hiding in its shadows.

A flash of white among the dark tree trunks brought Mandred's head snapping around, his hand flashing to the sword at his side. As his eyes focused upon the shape loping out from the forest darkness, his grip on the sword faltered, his breath caught in his throat.

Trotting out from the trees was a great white wolf, the biggest Mandred had ever seen. It moved with a boldness, a nonchalance he'd never witnessed in a wolf before, as though it were completely indifferent to the armed riders less than a dozen yards away from it. The animal loped to within a few yards of the trail, then sat on its haunches and turned its head towards the prince. Mandred was struck by the piercing gleam of the wolf's pale blue eyes, eyes that were like chips of frost cut from the peak of the Ulricsberg. There was more than an animal's understanding in those eyes.

For a moment, man and wolf simply stared at one another, locked in each other's gaze. Mandred felt his pulse quicken, his chest grow heavy. He felt the primal yearning for wild places, the howl of the wild primitive that lurks beneath the thin veneer of civilisation. He knew the thrill of the hunt, the ecstasy of the kill. The devotion of the pack...

In one smooth motion, displaying a lithe grace, the white wolf rose and dashed across the trail. Though it sprinted directly ahead of Mad Albrecht and caused the trapper's horse to shy, the Drakwalder didn't see the animal. Beck and the soldiers likewise gave no shouts of alarm or surprise. Mandred alone, it seemed, had seen the wolf.

'Turn to the left,' Mandred called out, an eerie feeling rushing through his body. The men with him directed questioning stares his way, wondering what strange impulse had come upon the prince. Mandred barely acknowledged them. Raising himself in the saddle, he peered into the forest, spotting the white blur of the running wolf.

'You heard his grace,' Beck snarled at the others. The knight did not know what reason Mandred had for his strange order, nor did he care. It was enough that the prince had issued a command. 'Into the trees.' Beck spurred his horse from the trail, charging into the forest.

Mandred smiled at the man's unquestioning loyalty as he turned his own mount and left the trail. He could hear Albrecht and the others following close behind. Ahead, drifting between the trunks, its white pelt shining in the shadows, the wolf seemed to beckon.

For what seemed leagues, the rangers maintained their silent pursuit of a quarry only the prince could see. Several times, Mandred had despaired of the hunt, but always the white wolf would suddenly reappear, tantalisingly near yet frustratingly far away. He was reminded of old nursery fables about the hunter who had dared to pursue the sacred stag of Taal and been cursed by the god to forever pursue a quarry he would never catch. He thought of tales he had heard of the haunted Laurelorn forest and the fairy creatures that lurked within its borders.

Mandred felt the urge to pull rein, to stop this reckless hunt before he led his followers into disaster. There was magic here, try as he might he couldn't dismiss that frightful realisation. Even as the decision to call off the chase came to him, he saw the wolf turn its head, stare back at him with its uncanny gaze. The prince's determination faltered. He was reminded of another legend, one that wasn't an obscure rumour or fable, but a part of everyday life in Middenheim. The white wolf, the sacred animal of Ulric.

The wolf dashed off among the trees, vanishing in the shadows. Mandred tried to catch some sign of it, standing up in his stirrups, craning his neck as he attempted to see through the thick cluster of trunks. Throughout the chase, he'd always caught sight of the wolf again after it had disappeared. This time, however, no trace of that lupine form rewarded his efforts.

'Stop,' Mandred called out, tugging at his reins. The command was quickly echoed by Beck, and soon the entire patrol was gathered about the prince. He could feel the sullen annoyance of the rangers as they stared at him with questioning eyes. None of them had seen the white wolf, so none of them understood the purpose behind this mad chase through the forest.

Mandred opened his mouth to explain when a strange smell struck his nose. It was the odour of smoke, and beneath it a loathsome stench he'd become horribly intimate with during the worst of the plague, when the refugees of Warrenburg had burned their dead. The stench was that of burning flesh.

Albrecht made a sound like the croak of a raven, a warning signal for the rest to remain silent. Dropping down from his saddle, the trapper gave his reins to one of the rangers and scrambled off into the forest gloom, his steps as silent as any beast of the wild. Beck drew his sword, one of the rangers unlimbered the bow strapped to his saddle. An expectant tension filled the air. These men were veterans of many patrols. This close to the Ulricsberg, they knew what the stink of cooking human flesh meant.

The Kineater was back in its old haunts.

Carroburg
Ertezeit, 1114

Carroburg had been the jewel in the crown of Drakwald. Less cramped and confined than Altdorf, more accessible than Middenheim, spared the foetid atmosphere of Marienburg, the city had been growing in prominence for the better part of a century. It had become a serious rival to Marienburg for trade on the River Reik, once even going so far as to blockade the river and exact a toll from all ships wishing to proceed northwards into Westerland. That practice had ended only after the elector of Westerland agreed to support the bid by a Hohenbach to become emperor.

The line of Drakwald emperors had continued to foster the growth of Carroburg, grooming the city to become a cosmopolitan jewel to rival Altdorf, Mordheim and even Nuln itself. Indeed, there had been many who thought the Imperial court would move to Carroburg when Nuln was abandoned by the Emperor. An old grudge between Count Vilner and the Emperor was rumoured to be the reason for Altdorf's restoration as the capital.

War had brought the first blemish to the glories of Carroburg. When northmen attacked Westerland and occupied Marienburg, a veritable tide of trade was ended, decimating the coffers of Carroburg's burghers and merchants. Worse was to come when the beastmen rampaged through the province, laying waste to the land. The brutes were never so bold as to lay siege to the city itself, but their depredations were felt almost as keenly. The agriculture of Drakwald was virtually annihilated, forcing the rich burghers to spend their hoarded wealth on the extra expense of importing food and wool. Waves of refugees flocked to the city, seeking protection behind its stone walls, further taxing the resources of the burghers.

Then the Black Plague struck. Already on the edge of disaster, the plague was the final push Carroburg needed to descend into the pit. The stream of food reaching the city from downriver slowed to a mere trickle while the waves of refugees increased tenfold. A vast squalor of shacks engulfed the fields beyond the walls, thousands of displaced peasants with nowhere else to turn. In these conditions, starvation ran rampant, disease flourished and the embers of despair grew into the fires of anarchy. Riots broke out across the city and shantytown, exploding into a conflagration of disorder and violence. For ten days the inferno raged, and before it exhausted itself a third of Carroburg was in ruins, a quarter of its people were dead. The shantytown was put to the torch, the land beyond the walls becoming a blackened desolation.

One tiny spark had pushed the dejected and the desperate to cast aside generations of obedience, adherence to the ancient distinctions between peasant and noble. They died by the hundreds in their futile revolt against a system that had enslaved and abused them, giving their lives to tear down the thrones of their callous masters. In the end, the revolt failed, crushed by the knights and soldiers of the Hohenbachs. The rebel dead were cast into an open pit beyond the walls, left exposed to feed worm and crow. Left as a lesson to those who survived that they should be thankful for what little they were allowed to have.

One tiny spark, a new tax upon a people already reduced to nothing, a fee upon each ear on each head. The penalty for non-payment was mutilation. No coin, no ear.

The tax was a penalty exacted upon the people of Drakwald for the role their last count had played in the conspiracy against the Imperial throne. The execution of Duke Konrad had done little to placate the ire of Emperor Boris. Others had to suffer for his cousin's treachery, even if they'd had no part in it.

Emperor Boris drew back the velvet curtain covering the coach window. He sighed as he looked upon the blackened desolation ringing Carroburg. It seemed such a waste. After more than a year, he would have expected von Metzgernstein to have done something to reclaim the land, put it to some manner of usefulness. There was nothing that upset him more than seeing something that was unproductive, something that wasn't being employed to the utmost to feed the Imperial treasury.

Boris looked away, a scowl on his face. 'Remind us to reprimand von Metzgernstein,' he told the wizened little man sitting next to him. The little man uttered a squeak of surprise and hurriedly drew quill and parchment from the bag he carried. The Emperor waited while his scribe started to write. 'We find his management of the province to be lacking. Perhaps Count Vilner tolerated such laxity, but We will not.' Boris tapped his chin as an idea occurred to him. 'When we arrive at the castle, have his son arrested. Or his daughter,' he reflected, uncertain what manner of relations the seneschal possessed. A lewd twinkle crept into his eye as he gazed across the carriage and stared at the young woman seated across from him. 'Especially if she is pretty,' he added.

Princess Erna's skin crawled as she felt the Emperor's eyes slither across her body. She struggled to keep the disgust from showing. Not from any sense of propriety or courtly decorum, but because she knew Boris enjoyed provoking her.

The effort was wasted. Boris laughed gustily at her expense. 'Is it a crime that We desire to be surrounded by beautiful things?' He laughed again as another thought occurred to him. 'If it is, then as Emperor We will simply have to change the laws!'

'As Your Imperial Majesty wishes,' Erna answered, her voice demure. Years of suffering under Adolf Kreyssig's hate had beaten the spirit from her.

'That goes without saying,' Boris chuckled. He pulled the curtain wide so that all within the carriage could see the burned desolation. 'Everything exists only as long as it pleases Us. The moment it forsakes that sacred obligation to the Imperial crown...' He snapped his fingers as though snuffing a rushlight.

'A wise policy, Your Imperial Majesty,' the rotund Doktor Wolfius Moschner agreed, his voice less that of a wolf and more like a yipping lapdog. 'Noble and peasant alike must remember to whom they owe their loyalty.'

After so many years serving as the Emperor's personal physician, Moschner knew exactly the right things to say to evoke his patron's pleasure. Boris leaned back against the leather cushions lining his seat, smiling as he digested the doktor's flattery. An impish smile teased the corners of his mouth as he considered the other occupants of the carriage.

'What do you think, Pieter?' Boris asked the man seated in the opposite corner. 'Do you agree? Are the nobles as beholden to Us as the peasants?'

The man the Emperor addressed was Baron Pieter von Kirchof, a swordsman of such renown that his fame was known in every corner of the Empire. He had risen to become the Emperor's Champion, defending the virtue of his master in judicial contests and private duels for more than a decade. Few who crossed sword with him had lived to tell the tale. None had ever left the field of honour without feeling the bite of his blade.

Despite the fame of his sword, the formidable reputation he had earned in mortal combat a hundred times over, it was a subdued man who answered his Emperor. Von Kirchof kept his eyes lowered, his tone deferential as he spoke. 'All men are beholden to their Emperor,' he said.

Boris laughed at his champion. 'You more than most, eh? What sort of lands did your family possess before you entered Our service? A miserable demesne in the middle of a swamp with a few hundred inbred peasants to serve you!' The Emperor's eyes left von Kirchof, lingering for a moment on the young woman seated beside him. 'Yes, Pieter, you owe much to Us.'

Von Kirchof's niece looked away as the Emperor scrutinised her, unable to repress the shudder that swept through her.

'We all owe you much, Your Imperial Majesty,' Doktor Moschner said, trying to ease the tense atmosphere. Boris ignored the physician, turning to gaze out the window once more.

'When you have advice about Our health, you may speak,' he told Moschner. 'Otherwise, if We want your opinion, We'll tell you what it is.'

The Imperial procession was passing the gates of Carroburg now, but the scene beyond the window was hardly more cheerful than the blackened desolation outside the walls. The once opulent residences of the burghers were fallen into disrepair, plaster peeling away from timber walls, roofing tiles lying strewn in the streets. Iron lamp posts, an affectation absent even in Altdorf, bore the marks of rust and neglect. The road was pitted with holes, much of the masonry cracked and broken. Heaps of rubbish lay strewn in the gutters, and hordes of rats brazenly prowled the alleyways.

The city that had only a few years before been the great light of the Empire was now a wallow of decay. The handful of people walking the streets were ragged, scrawny apparitions that hid their faces as the Imperial procession rode past, the last dregs of self-respect scourged from them by the Emperor's henchmen and his purges.

Emperor Boris reached to his jewelled belt and removed a few coppers from a leather pouch. Squinting at the coins for a moment, he turned back to the window and threw them into the street. He laughed as he watched the ragged scarecrows rush to retrieve their bounty, hobbling along on withered legs, groping in the gutter with skeletal hands. Still laughing, he took another clutch of coins and threw them in the direction of an old char woman leaning against a lamp post. Caught by surprise, the woman staggered back as the coins struck her. A mob of more observant beggars came running down the street, trampling the old woman underfoot in their hurry to gather up the money.

Boris clapped his hands together, his face glowing in a cherubic smile. He noted the revulsion on the face of the woman across from him. Reaching into his belt, he removed a few more coins. 'Great sport,' he told Erna. 'Would you care to try?' The woman shook her head, but Boris persisted.

Reaching out, he took her hand and forced the coins into her palm. 'Just once,' he told her.

'Perhaps I might try,' Moschner offered.

Emperor Boris directed a withering look at his physician. 'Pay for your own amusements,' he said, then turned his attention back to Erna. 'Go ahead,' he prodded her. 'They're just peasants. They won't bite. They wouldn't dare!' The levity drained from the monarch's features; his voice became a low snarl, his hand tightened around Erna's. 'Do as you are told.'

Her cheeks flushing with shame, turning her head from the window, Erna cast the coins into the street. Emperor Boris leaned his head from the window, laughing at the bedlam as the beggars scrambled for the discarded coins.

'A poor cast,' he chuckled, then grinned as a thin shriek rose from somewhere behind them. 'We're afraid your coins landed in the street. One of the wretches has gotten himself crushed by the Count of Stirland's coach.' He leaned back inside and patted Erna's hand.

'We thank you for an amusing diversion,' the Emperor told her, smiling as he felt the shudder that passed through Erna's body.

Soon the urban mire of decayed Carroburg was behind them. They passed through the western gate, following the long causeway that reached out across the Reik, rising in a spiral of brick and mortar to the crest of a tall hill. Here, upon the natural spire, a succession of fortresses had been built by the old Thuringian kings, culminating in the great stone walls of the Schloss Hohenbach.

The mighty castle dominated the landscape, looming over the sprawl of Carroburg, commanding the approaches along the Reik. It was the situation of the Otwinsstein that had dictated the construction of the original timber tower and the first mud-hut village to shelter in its shadow. It was the existence of the castle that allowed Carroburg its command of the river trade and had many times earned its burghers the epithet of 'pirate barons'.

Now, the Schloss Hohenbach opened its monstrous iron gates to admit a plunderer who made the grasping dealings of Carroburg's worst burgher seem petty. Emperor Boris breathed deeply as he watched the imposing gatehouse with its bronze gargoyles and megalithic statuary draw close.

'The ancestral seat,' the Emperor commented with a smile. 'It is good to be home again.'

'I understood you had never visited this place before,' Erna said. It was the first time she had spoken since the incident with the beggars.

Emperor Boris frowned at the woman's insolence, but after a moment of consideration decided to overlook it. 'One is never a stranger to one's legacy,' he pronounced. A moment of reflection and he motioned for his scribe to record the statement for posterity.

The carriage was soon within the walled courtyard. Emperor Boris waited until von Kirchof left the carriage before making any move to leave his seat. The attempt to usurp his throne had taught him to be cautious. To always let one of his subjects precede him. After a moment, von Kirchof appeared at the door. Bowing low, he waited while his sovereign disembarked. The rest of the occupants followed close behind.

The towers of the Schloss Hohenbach glowered down at them like primordial titans. They were cold and severe, devoid of the artistry and elegance that characterised the Imperial Palace. The castle had been built as a fortress, and ten generations of Hohenbachs had been unable to endow it with warmth or cheer.

Emperor Boris paced across the courtyard, shaking his head as he gazed up at the hoary battlements and ancient towers.

Forcing a smile onto his face, he looked back at Princess Erna and Sasha, von Kirchof's young niece. 'Now, perhaps you ladies understand why it was necessary to bring some pretty things to this place.' He turned away as the rest of the Imperial procession started to enter the gates. Twenty carriages conveying the highest echelons of Imperial society, the most affluent potentates in the whole Empire. The men and women hand-picked by Emperor Boris to be preserved from the plague, to share this refuge from the blight ravaging the land.

'We may be here quite some time,' the Emperor continued. 'Long enough, I think, for all of us to become well acquainted.'

—◄ CHAPTER III ►—

Altdorf
Sigmarzeit, 1114

'A peasant appointed Protector of the Empire!' The outburst was punctuated by the slamming of a mailed fist against the polished mahogany desk. The pink-faced man seated behind the desk winced as he saw the wood scarred by the blow. Almost immediately there was a cloth in his hand and he was rubbing at the injured surface.

'You must curb your temper, Vidor,' the man cautioned his guest. 'There is no arguing with an Imperial decree.' He leaned back and swallowed uneasily, darting a glance at the shelf-lined walls of his office. 'It is also unwise to speak in anger. Your "peasant" has ears everywhere.'

Vidor von Tolkesdorf, Duke of Weissbruck and Margrave of the Helmwald, shifted the steel helm he held under his arm, brandishing it like a cudgel at the man seated behind the desk, provoking an uneasy squirm from the pink-faced noble. Duke Vidor sneered. Lord Ratimir was typical of the men who made up the Imperial court, decadent blue-bloods who had grown soft from the ease of luxury. The least display of force, the smallest threat of danger, and they capitulated to any outrage. Even that of taking orders from a low-born peasant.

'I don't care how many serfs that dung-scraping low-born has in his vaunted Kaiserjaeger,' Duke Vidor growled. 'The Emperor knows my loyalty. He knows there is no more staunch a supporter of his crown than myself!'

Lord Ratimir shook his head, making soft tutting sounds. 'Things are quite different than when you left Altdorf to hunt the errant Reiksmarshal,' he warned. 'His Imperial Majesty has had two years to reflect upon the conspiracy that nearly took that crown away from him. Need I say that it has been Adolf Kreyssig and his Kaiserjaeger who have been investigating that conspiracy and dragging more traitors into the light? It would be unwise… and unhealthy… to make an enemy of the man. Whatever the quality of his blood.'

Duke Vidor turned away from the desk, pacing across the office of the Imperial Minister of Finance. 'He knows my loyalty,' he stated, conviction in his tone. 'I chased that scoundrel Boeckenfoerde across the eastern provinces for eighteen months. Drove that rabble of *Dienstleute* clear into the Ungol wastes!'

Ratimir's sickly countenance was made more grotesque by the smug expression he wore. 'All true, Vidor, but what have you done lately for His Imperial Majesty?' He leaned back in his chair, savouring the look of dawning awareness in his visitor's eyes. 'Yes, you've eliminated the threat of Boeckenfoerde marching his scum on Altdorf. That very accomplishment makes you dangerous. It means you are a strong strategist and a capable leader of men – both qualities that have proven treacherous towards the Emperor in the recent past.'

Frowning, the duke leaned across the desk. 'What will the Emperor do?' he scoffed. 'Surround himself with incompetents simply because they are too stupid to be dangerous to him?'

'No,' Ratimir conceded. 'He will surround himself with men who he himself has created. Creatures like Kreyssig who owe their status and position solely to the beneficence of His Imperial Majesty. Blood and breeding are becoming questionable assets, Vidor. The Emperor doesn't trust men who feel they are entitled to wealth and station.'

Duke Vidor stood back, aghast at the implication. It was already well known that Emperor Boris had ordered the confiscation of all property owned by Prince Sigdan and his fellow conspirators, their titles abolished and their possessions forfeit to the crown. What Ratimir was suggesting went even further: outright suppression of the nobility!

'He knows my loyalty,' Vidor protested, rejecting the fears Ratimir had stirred up.

Ratimir laughed softly, the effort almost choking him. With a trembling hand, he removed a pomander from his frilled sleeve and drew deeply upon its fragrant vapours. 'It is not the Emperor you must convince of your loyalty,' he said when the fit had passed. 'It is the Protector he leaves behind in his stead.'

'I bow to no peasant,' Vidor snarled. 'No noble-born man will!'

Again, Ratimir shook his head. 'After the example of Prince Sigdan, I think you will find that the nobles will put up with a great deal if it keeps them from the wrong side of an axe.'

The light streaming through the *Kaiseraugen* was like the glimmer of a thousand jewels, a dazzling display that caught the breath and captivated the soul. The stained glass was the handiwork of the finest glaziers in Karak Norn, produced and transported at enormous expense. A lesser monarch might have shuddered at the cost, but Emperor Boris wasn't some petty border baron or country count. He was supreme leader of the mightiest realm of man in the known world and such insignificance was beneath his concern. If there were anything troublesome, it was the added expenditure to hurry the project along. It was never cheap to hurry a dwarf.

As he watched the diminutive craftsmen bustling about the half-restored window overlooking the Reik and the sprawl of Altdorf, Boris felt strength course through him. Only he could afford to exert such authority, to take an act of vandalous destruction and turn it into a thing more magnificent than before. The traitors who had smashed the original picture window were to be thanked for their mindless atrocity. The new *Kaiseraugen* would be even greater, a wonder of human achievement and artistry! The stained glass and silver panes would lend it an unparalleled glamour, like a rainbow bound and imprisoned against the face of the Imperial Palace. When it was complete, this hall would sparkle like a treasure vault.

Watching the dwarfs work, Boris's gaze strayed to the open, incomplete section of the window. For a moment, he felt his attention drawn to the ugly blemish of the city below, the dilapidated structures and deserted streets, the sprawl of refugee camps beyond the walls and the hideous spectre of funeral pyres. Quickly he turned away. He would be happy when all the stained glass was in place and blotted out the noxious vision.

Composing himself, Boris marched across the hall and into the gallery beyond. It was unseemly to let something disturb his Imperial poise. When he returned from Carroburg, such things would be in the past. The plague would run its course soon and then things could get back to normal. And if not... Well, the dwarfs would certainly be finished with their work by then.

In the gallery, Boris was joined by a bodyguard of picked men from the Kaiserknecht and the menacing figure of Baron

Pieter von Kirchof, the Emperor's Champion. It was von Kirchof who had stood by Boris during the insurrection of Prince Sigdan. More than his unmatched prowess with the sword, it was this unwavering loyalty that had earned him the indulgence of his Emperor. Boris had heaped riches on his champion, allocating several of the confiscated lands to the von Kirchof family. Now, he was prepared to grant his favoured vassal another boon.

But first he wanted to hear von Kirchof beg.

'The construction goes well, Your Imperial Majesty?' the baron asked as the monarch and his retinue marched down the hall.

Boris took his time before acknowledging that he'd heard his minion speak. Von Kirchof was too well bred to dare decorum by addressing the Emperor again without some response. It was a useful thing, courtly breeding. It conditioned proud men to submit without question.

The Emperor halted before a long mural depicting one of the expansionist campaigns waged by his long-dead predecessor Frederick in the Ungol-infested oblast of the north. His guards immediately formed a circle around him, hands falling to the hilts of swords. Silently they waited for whatever fancy had made their sovereign pause to pass. Boris smiled at their impatience. They would never give it voice, never admit it even to themselves, but it was there and it was held hostage by nothing save his own authority.

'Tell Us again of this girl, von Kirchof,' Boris said at last, his eyes still studying the tapestry. He didn't need to turn to know the desperate hope that shone in the eyes of his champion.

'She is my niece, Your Imperial Majesty,' the baron explained, an explanation he had made many times before. 'There is plague in my sister's fief. It has been most rapacious in her lands and I… She fears for the girl's safety. I would bring her to Altdorf, but the plague is worse here and…'

'And we are leaving for Carroburg,' the Emperor finished for him.

Baron von Kirchof stiffened and made an embarrassed bow. 'I was hoping that you would condescend to allow my niece to join the procession to Carroburg.'

Boris turned away from the tapestry, directing a hard look into his champion's eyes, holding him in the grip of that stare until the baron was compelled to look away. 'The plague is getting worse,' he stated. 'That is why We are leaving Altdorf and seeking the safety of seclusion in the Schloss Hohenbach in the Drakwald. With us We are taking the most powerful personages in the Empire. Grand dukes, arch-counts and great princes.'

Baron von Kirchof kept his eyes downcast. 'I know it is…'

'How old is the child?' Boris asked suddenly, interrupting the apology.

Von Kirchof brightened at the inquiry. 'She has just passed her nineteenth winter,' he said.

'Hardly a "girl" then,' Boris scoffed, toying with the ermine fringe of his imperial robes. 'If she is pretty, you may bring her along,' he said, making the declaration sound as weighty as any affair of state. 'The castle is quite gloomy, as We recall. We shall need a few pretty things to brighten it up while We are there.' He raised a warning finger before the baron could thank him. 'We warn you, the maiden had best be as fair as you attest her to be.'

Boris left the consequences of his disappointment unsaid. As Emperor, there were a great many things he could do to someone who displeased him. He had always found that it was more effective to leave his subjects wondering which of those things was to be their punishment.

No fear was greater than the terror born in a man's own imagination.

Blinded by the flickering glow of a rushlight, it was some time before Princess Erna von Thornig realised she was no longer alone in her dingy cell. As the red blur that had flooded across her light-starved eyes gradually faded, she found two men standing beside the iron-banded door. The chill of her dungeon apartment was nothing beside the chill that gripped her heart as she recognised her visitors.

The stocky, overweight one with the frilled shirt and sombre livery was Fuerst. The other man, his sickly pallor and scarred face rendered still more grotesque by the shadows cast by the rushlight, was Fuerst's master, Adolf Kreyssig, Commander of the Kaiserjaeger and now Protector of the Empire. The villain who had murdered her father and cast her into this prison.

The fiend who was her husband.

An ophidian smile stretched across Kreyssig's face as he watched Erna cringe away from him, her trembling hands clutching the heavy length of chain that connected her to an iron ring set into the wall. He slapped a leather riding crop against his leg, savouring the fear he saw in his wife's eyes. It had taken much time and effort to put that fear there, to beat the boldness out of her. Breaking Erna's spirit had become something of a hobby for him. One that he had enjoyed immensely.

'Don't get up,' Kreyssig hissed at her. 'I am afraid that I don't have much time to squander with you today. His Imperial Majesty is going to officially proclaim me Protector of the Empire in the Great Cathedral of Sigmar.' For just an instant, he saw hate burn its way through the fear in her eyes. He slashed the riding crop at her, being sure to strike low enough that the brand wouldn't be visible in public. The strip of sackcloth draped about Erna's body did nothing to retard the blow. Still, his words had awakened some residue of noble pride and she bit her lip to keep from crying out. Kreyssig drew his arm back to whip her again.

'Your lordship!' Fuerst protested, grabbing Kreyssig's arm. 'His Imperial Majesty has ordered the baroness to attend him when he travels. He will be displeased if…'

Kreyssig rounded on his servant, turning the crop against him and slashing it down his back. He turned and glared at Erna, then returned his attention to Fuerst. 'Get the bitch presentable,' he snarled before storming from the cell.

Fuerst bowed until the door closed behind Kreyssig, then he turned back to the captive baroness. 'I am sorry, your ladyship, but you know better than to bait him.'

'The worst he can do is kill me,' Erna stated, her awakened pride sinking back beneath a torrent of despair. She looked up at Fuerst, managing a weak smile for his benefit. 'He would have killed me already if not for you.'

Fuerst glanced away, colour rising in his cheeks. 'No, your ladyship, you pay me too much favour. The commander does nothing without reason. Even after you tried to… Even then he made no move to execute you, even petitioned the Emperor for clemency.' Fuerst's voice dropped to an embarrassed whisper. 'With your father dead, you are now baroness. It is only through his connection to you that the commander may make any pretension of moving among the aristocracy. Without you, he is just a peasant.'

Erna leaned against the stone wall, her chains rattling against the floor. 'He is a monster,' she said, her voice hollow and bitter. 'I thought I knew what he was when I agreed to kill him, but I didn't. The barbarians who sacked Marienburg are more human than that beast!' She held her hands across her face, shuddering as a new horror impressed itself on her mind. 'Now this animal is going to be Protector of the Empire.'

Fuerst drew closer, excitement in his tone. 'That is where you have a chance!' he exclaimed. 'Emperor Boris might trust the commander more than the nobles, but he doesn't trust anyone fully. That is why he has decreed that you are to accompany him to Carroburg.' Wearing a broad smile, Fuerst unfolded the clothes he carried across his arm, displaying for Erna one of her finest gowns. 'The Emperor knows that it is through you that the commander is able to claim the status of a noble. He feels that by keeping you with him, it will give him a hold over the commander.'

Reaching forwards, Erna let her fingers slide down the soft smoothness of her gown. 'So I trade one captor for another,' she mused.

Fuerst shrugged and pointed at the dank walls of the cramped cell, at the straw pallet and sackcloth shift. 'It can't be worse than this,' he said.

Erna took the gown from Fuerst, hugging it to her breast. 'No, it can't,' she answered before her voice collapsed into an inarticulate sob. Years of torture and isolation – could they finally be at an end? Even as Fuerst unlocked the shackle from her wrist, Erna expected her husband and a gang of Kaiserjaeger to come bursting through the door. It was just the sort of cruelty that would appeal to Kreyssig's humour, to build up hope and then smash it in the most brutal manner possible.

Only when she was dressed and unchained, being led by Fuerst out into the corridor beyond her cell, did Erna accept that her release was real. She had been traded, given into the keeping of Emperor Boris as hostage for her husband's loyalty. Her life against that of every man, woman and child in the Empire.

Ulric have mercy, but to escape the clutches of Kreyssig, Erna was willing to make such a monstrous bargain.

Mordheim
Ulriczeit, 1112

Across the curtain of night, the ponderous notes of temple bells reminded the denizens of the city that even in the darkest hour, when the powers of Old Night waxed strong, the gods were still watching. It was a sound that had once brought comfort and solace to the simple, superstitious folk. The thought that the gods remained vigilant when the creatures of darkness were abroad, when ghouls stalked graveyards, when witches flew through the blackened sky and skin-wolves prowled under shadowed trees.

Of late, however, the voice of the temple bells had taken on a bitter, mocking quality. The Black Plague was abroad, slaughtering old and young, pious and impious, peasant and noble with equal rapacity. If the gods were still watching over mankind, not the wisest of priests could explain their indifference to its suffering.

Ensconced within the cold stone-walled fastness of his chambers, one of those suffering masses looked up from the documents spread across the table before him. He closed his eyes and listened to the bells tolling away the hour. There was another sound, softer yet nearer, a low wailing that filtered through the ancient halls. It was a haunting, melancholy sound, the animate voice of anguish and loss and regret.

Regret? That word brought a cynical curl to the man's pale, pinched face. He swept a jewelled hand through a mane of luxuriant black hair and leaned back in his gilded chair.

There was a suggestion of sardonic amusement in his eyes as he stared down at the scrolls and parchment sheaves piled before him. Like a dragon perched atop its hoard, he hovered above the heap. It would take the treasure of a dragon to rival the wealth laid out on the table, for it was a tangible representation of the lands and holdings that went with the title Baron von Diehl.

A title that had finally passed from Hjalmar von Diehl to his son Lothar.

That transition of wealth and authority had been a long time taking shape. The old baron had been a long time about dying. Towards the last, it had become something of a race to see whether the father would exhaust the legacy of the von Diehls on alchemists and physicians and generous tithes to the temples in a desperate bid to bribe the gods to intercede.

Many times, Lothar had despaired, wondered if he shouldn't employ cudgel or dagger to effect his father's speedy demise. Such impatient temptations were fought back only by the fiercest exertion of will. The spells were doing their work. Slowly but surely his father's vitality had been ebbing, leeched away by phantom parasites neither priest nor physician could discover. When the old baron died, there were none who thought of murder. To even the most suspicious, there was never a notion that the baron was anything but another victim of the Black Plague.

Lothar set a covetous hand against the stack of deeds that represented ownership of three-quarters of Mordheim's riverfront. He smiled as he saw a promissory note from Count Steinhardt himself peeking out from beneath the pile. Great and small, many were those who must credit the Baron von Diehl for their prosperity.

Rising from behind the table, Lothar paced across the cheerless confines of his study. Prosperity had become a bitter word to the people of Mordheim, a mocking echo of better times. With over half the city carried off by the plague, the fields beyond the walls invaded by starving refugees, the violence in Talabecland choking off what river trade still flowed into Ostermark, Mordheim was in the throes of her own slow death.

It was the natural order of things, Lothar mused. People and places were fated to grow, thrive and prosper for a season, but then must come that time when they would wither, decay and die. Not the gods themselves could defy the laws of fate.

A cold smile formed across Lothar's face. The only way a man could ensure his accomplishments was to set himself outside the tyrannical dictates of fate. His grandfather had awakened to that revelation, but had lacked the fortitude to pursue his studies fully. His father, with pious horror, had rejected the researches of the elder von Diehl, burning his books and papers when the barony came into his possession. Hjalmar had been thorough in his fiery purge, but not perfect. A few tomes slipped his notice, and eventually those volumes of forbidden lore had found their way into Lothar's hands. The seeds of the grandfather's work found fertile soil in the grandson's mind.

Staring up at a portrait of his father, Lothar sighed as he recalled all the years he had been compelled to secrecy, labouring away in the disused cellars and crypts beneath the castle, embezzling money from the von Diehl estates to fund his experiments, to procure the obscure books necessary to his research. With the support and understanding of his father, Lothar should have progressed in his studies with cosmic momentum. Lacking such assistance, he'd been forced to trudge away, content himself with the most restrained and insignificant advances. In those long hours, shivering in the clammy gloom of the castle vaults, he realised that if he were to succeed, he must become baron. When rumours drifted into Mordheim of a mighty sorcerer who had arisen in Sylvania and brought the von Draks to heel, a terrible envy took hold of Lothar's heart. No longer would he wait for the power that must one day belong to him!

Turning away from the portrait, Lothar shook his head and tried to blot out the faint wail of professional mourners that wafted through the castle halls. What had been done was done. The bridge had been crossed, the decision made. It would, he vowed to himself, be worth it.

All at once, Lothar's attention was drawn to a tall shelf sunk into the wall at the far corner of the room. The bronze figure of a wolf stood upon one of the shelves, a hammer and bell clenched in its rampant paws. While he watched, the statue revolved from side to side, causing hammer to strike bell and send a tinkling note through the chamber. Lothar watched the gyrations of the figure as he stalked over to a bell-pull beside the hearth. One sharp tug would set an alarm that would see a dozen men-at-arms swarm into the room.

Lothar bided his time, hand poised about the bell-pull, eyes fixed on the bronze wolf and the shelf it rested upon. While he watched, the shelf began to move, rotating away from the wall and exposing a dark passageway with stairs descending into the black depths beneath the Schloss von Diehl.

Lothar relaxed and walked back to his table when he recognised the figure who emerged from the darkness. He was a stocky, fat-faced man with ruddy complexion and bulbous nose. His raiment was simple, lacking the costly dyes and embroidery of the noble classes, yet of immaculate condition and quality. The overall impression was that of a man of means if not social position.

'Marko,' Lothar greeted the man in a cold, somewhat

irritated fashion. When he'd heard the bell sound, he'd half expected his father's ghost to come tromping up those steps, such was the morbid turn of his mind.

'Baron von Diehl now, I believe,' Marko addressed Lothar. He glanced about for a moment and, without awaiting an invitation, sank into a heavy chair opposite the table. His host scowled at the man's temerity but kept his tongue. In their long association, he had been forced to a grudging acceptance of Marko's discourteous habits.

'Your sense of propriety leaves much to be desired,' Lothar upbraided the man. 'My father lies cold in his chambers and you choose tonight to visit.' He made a pretence of examining the documents on the table, directing a dismissive wave at Marko. 'Get out. Leave me to my mourning. Come again in a fortnight.'

Marko leaned forwards in his chair, an oily smile across his face. 'Is that any way to speak to an old friend who has come to offer his sympathy?'

A caustic laugh was Lothar's answer. Marko's smile collapsed into a sullen frown.

'Perhaps the word "friend" offends you?' Marko asked. 'There is another word I might use, but "accomplice" is such an ugly word that noble ears should be spared its utterance.'

Lothar set down the deed he had been feigning interest in and glared at his visitor. 'You dare threaten me? Are you forgetting that I am now *Baron* von Diehl?'

The smile was back on Marko's face. 'Indeed I am not,' he said. 'It is because you are the baron that I have brought you something.' Reaching into his coat, digging into the deep poacher pockets sewn into its lining, he withdrew a thick bundle wrapped in sheepskin.

Whatever annoyance Lothar felt was instantly supplanted by curiosity. Marko had been wrong to refer to himself as an accomplice. He was a facilitator, a provider of the magical treatises and implements needed for Lothar's researches. The peasant had proven himself most capable in his illicit trade, braving the vengeance of both secular and religious law to secure the forbidden tomes Lothar required.

Tonight, however, Lothar could sense that the trader had brought him something special. Cynically, he wondered how long it had been in Marko's possession, if the peasant hadn't been biding his time, waiting until the title and wealth of Baron von Diehl passed into Lothar's hands.

The new baron set dignity aside as he hurriedly unwrapped the package. Within he discovered a large book bound in some strange scaly hide. A golden skull was embossed upon the cover, and it was with a thrill of excitement that he recognised the hieroglyphics beneath it as belonging to the vanished civilisation of Mourkain.

'You will appreciate it,' Marko declared, 'when I tell you that what you hold in your hands is the only known copy of *De Arcanis Kadon*.'

Lothar's knees went weak, dropping him ungracefully back into his chair. There was a tremor on his lips, a shiver in his hands. Shocked by the artefact in his fingers, the baron's heart pounded to the beat of both horror and exuberance.

'You know the story, of course,' Marko said, savouring the emotions warring for control of his patron's mind. 'Kadon was a shaman of the primitive tribes along the Blind River. Sometime before the birth of Sigmar, he built a great city in the Badlands, a place he named Mourkain.' The peasant chuckled grimly. 'In the Strigany tongue, it means "the Dead City". Employing the black arts, he raised an army of the dead to make war in his name. With Mourkain at its centre, Kadon built the kingdom of Strygos. Those who submitted to his power became his slaves. Those who defied him were slaughtered… and became his slaves just the same.'

Marko paused, examining an old sword hanging on the wall, running one of his hands along the blade. 'It is said that Kadon was the greatest sorcerer of his day, and that he used his magic to empower many strange and terrible relics. None, however, could equal the malignity of *De Arcanis Kadon*. Written upon skin flayed from the bodies of his children, scribed in the heart's blood of his own wives, Kadon consigned onto these pages all of his arcane knowledge.'

Marko stared up at the portrait of Hjalmar von Diehl, watching as the flickering glow from the hearth cast strange shadows across the dead baron's face. 'There were nine copies of *De Arcanis Kadon*, patterned after the ancient *Books of Nagash*. Each copy was couched in its own cipher and entrusted to one of Kadon's disciples. The disciples scattered when Strygos was overrun by a mighty orc invasion. Kadon himself perished when the city of Mourkain fell to the greenskins, but through his disciples and *De Arcanis Kadon*, his knowledge endured.'

Lothar ran his thumb along the book's spine, feeling an icy sensation flow down his arm. 'I understood that *De Arcanis Kadon* was lost when the Great Cathedral of Sigmar burned in Nuln,' he said, his voice nothing more than an awed whisper.

'One copy was reputed to be held by the Sigmarites in their vaults,' Marko agreed, returning to the table and lowering himself into his chair. 'Another was burned in Remas by the fanatics of Solkan. A warlock in the town of Mirkhof was reputed to be in possession of a copy when that community vanished from the face of the earth.' Marko laughed. 'The work of elves, some claim.

'There was another copy somewhere in Bretonnia, but much like Mirkhof, the community harbouring it vanished in a night. Undoubtedly the work of the Great Enchanter. If so, then it will never leave the Grey Mountains.'

'Where did this copy come from?' Lothar asked.

'It wasn't easy to get,' Marko assured him. 'It is supposed to have been in the possession of a man titling himself "King of the Strigany" and was, perhaps, handed down from father to son since the destruction of Strygos. It is doubtful the man understood what he possessed, otherwise his caravan wouldn't have been massacred when they tried to camp near an Ostland village. It seems there was talk that the Strigany were spreading the plague, so the men of the village rose up and massacred the entire caravan. Their fear of the plague didn't keep them from looting the dead, however. Among the plunder, the villagers found *De Arcanis Kadon*. The miraculous thing is that they didn't destroy it to steal its gold adornments.' Marko laughed again, but it was an uneasy sort of laugh. 'Maybe it was the book exerting its magic on their simple minds, protecting itself from their ignorance and fear.

'Eventually the book found its way to Wolfenburg and into the hands of one of my... associates.' Marko stood up, setting his hands on the table and leaning towards Lothar. His voice dropped into a warning hiss. 'You will never be closer to such power, herr baron! The few who have truly understood that book have learned secrets that have been forbidden to men for a thousand years. They accomplished great things, feats of magic that have been immortalised in myth and legend.'

Lothar looked up from the ancient tome. His voice quaked as he questioned Marko. 'What of those who couldn't understand, who couldn't unlock Kadon's secrets?'

'They were driven mad,' Marko admitted with a shrug. He smiled and stood away from the table. 'That is why, when I ask you for two thousand gold crowns, you will oblige me by paying before you begin your researches.'

Lothar's expression became indignant. At the same time, he

wrapped his arms protectively about *De Arcanis Kadon*. 'Two thousand gold crowns! That is robbery. I will not pay it!'

'You will pay it,' Marko assured him. 'I have never sold you false merchandise, never lied to you. Two thousand crowns is cheap for the knowledge that book can bestow on you.' He looked down at the table, littered with deeds and promissory notes. He waved his hand over the heap of documents. 'What is wealth except a means to power?' he asked. 'And what power is greater than knowledge?'

Lothar raised his head, listening to the faint wail of the mourners. It was true, what the peasant said. In trying to secure temporal wealth, he had stumbled upon true power – the power of magic and the arcane. What did lands and titles matter beside the ability to invoke death with a touch, the power to raise the dead from their tombs?

'You will have your money,' Baron von Diehl promised. 'But let us wait a little.

'I have a father I must bury first.'

Sylvania
Vorhexen, 1112

The smell of burning thatch and timber boiled across the air, the tang of man-thing blood laced with man-thing fear was borne upon the breeze, the stink of rat-fur and skaven musk rolled down the muddy lanes. They were exciting, invigorating smells that filled Seerlord Skrittar's nose and teased his olfactory organs, but none of them were so enthralling as the burning scent of warpstone.

The seerlord's grey paw closed tighter about the black nugget it held, a little wisp of smoke rising from his clenched fist as the warpstone singed his fur. He was oblivious to the caustic emanations of his prize, too absorbed in the enormity of what it represented. That nugget was the first, the first of a treasure so vast it would reshape the whole of skavendom!

A blood-chilling scream scratched across Skrittar's hearing, causing him to turn and watch as a lone man-thing tried to fend off a pack of clanrats. The sword-rats of Clan Fester weren't the mighty killers of Clan Rictus or Clan Mors, but they were more than equal to the hapless peasant they menaced. Warily, the skaven circled around the man, making little mock attacks that drove him steadily backwards. Each step he took allowed the ratmen to spread out, the skaven at either extremity fanning out to nip at the peasant's flanks.

There was nowhere the man-thing could retreat to. The wattle-and-daub wall behind him was smoking away, cinders dribbling from its burning face. The building beyond it was fully engulfed, its roof a fiery pyre that blazed into the night sky. There were a few man-things inside the building – their screams made that clear – but bullets from Fester's slingers were keeping the Sylvanians penned up inside the burning structure. No hope for the doomed peasant there.

Moved by some caprice, Skrittar stretched forth his horned staff, channelling magical energies into the warpstone talisman set between the curled horns. He chittered an invocation, drawing down the malignity of the Horned Rat. Despite the fires blazing away in the village, a chill crept into the air as he worked his sorcery. A green glow leapt from the talisman, flashing down the lane. One of the sword-rats squeaked in agony as the light slashed through him, boring a smouldering crater in his shoulder. Undiminished by its incidental victim, Skrittar's spell struck onwards, slamming into the embattled peasant's head and popping it like an engorged tick.

Skrittar chittered maliciously as the surviving clanrats

scattered, terrified by the grey seer's display of magic, leaving their stricken comrade to writhe and bleed in the mud. The seerlord savoured their fear. It was good to remind the vermin of Clan Fester who was in charge, who held the real reins of power in their little alliance.

The seerlord whipped his tail through the mud in annoyance. Left to his own devices, he would have preferred to avoid the inconvenience of an alliance altogether. But that ten-flea tyrant Vecteek had made decrees limiting the number of grey seers the Order could maintain and had further placed prohibitions on the Order possessing any warriors of its own. He had seen to it that the Order would never be self-sufficient, claiming that the grey seers must serve the needs of all skaven rather than their own selfish interests. Of course, the despot hadn't made similar conditions to control the upstart heretics of Clan Pestilens! The plague monks were more powerful now than ever, with two seats on the Council and the entire Under-Empire squeaking their praises because of the Black Plague!

They would soon squeak a different tune. With the rat-power of Clan Fester's teeming masses to provide him with the brute force he needed, Skrittar would fill the halls of the Shattered Tower with warpstone. He would curb the dictatorship of Vecteek and Clan Rictus, usher in a new age of balance and cooperation among the clans where no one voice was supreme among the skaven. All would hearken to the Voice of the Horned One through His chosen instrument, Seerlord Skrittar. The clans would be led by the wisdom of their god, and any that wouldn't hearken to Skrittar's words would be exterminated.

Casting his gaze across the burning village, Skrittar watched as Clan Fester's slaves scurried about the fields and meadows, pawing at the dirt as they retrieved nuggets of raw warpstone from the ground. His spell had performed even more magnif-icently than he had dared dream. The land was littered with warpstone ripped from the moon, so much that he could see a green glow on the horizon when he squinted his eyes. It might take years to gather it all!

Not that Skrittar intended to be so patient. He'd contact Warlord Manglrr Baneburrow and demand he send more labourers. He didn't care exactly where Manglrr got them. There were plenty of weaker clans Fester could conquer and enslave to deliver the workers he needed.

Manglrr would obey, too. There was no question of that. Sylvania was ripe for the picking, helpless at Skrittar's feet. Half the province was dead because of the plague, and the other half had been poisoned by the warpstone.

Who was there left with the strength to oppose the skaven?

⎯⟨ CHAPTER IV ⟩⎯

Middenheim
Sigmarzeit, 1118

There were many stories about the Kineater, but the most popular held that the thing had been born to the family of a prosperous raugraf. The rural lord was desperate for an heir, and after giving birth to daughters for twelve years, his weary wife had prayed to the Ruinous Powers for a son. In their malice, the Dark Gods had answered her, but the son she bore was far less than human. For many years, the raugraf had kept the mutant child locked inside a hidden room in his castle, but with the coming of the Black Plague, his lands had become too desolate to feed the horrible monster. One night, wracked by hunger, the mutant had escaped, butchering its own family to sate its appetite. Since that time, the Kineater had prowled the Drakwald, preying upon any human it could catch.

It was only a few minutes before Albrecht returned, his face as pale as snow. Before he even acknowledged his prince, the trapper went to his horse and removed a clay bottle from the saddle bag. Taking a deep draw from the bottle to fortify himself, he related what he had seen. 'There's a small clearing ahead,' Albrecht said. 'Around a dozen beastmen. They're cooking a couple of travellers.'

'The Kineater?' Mandred asked. Beastmen were primitive brutes, creatures that normally preferred their meat raw. It was the Kineater who was accustomed to cooking its fare.

Albrecht answered with a nod. 'We're downwind. I don't think they're aware we're here.'

'We can slip back to the trail then,' Beck decided, an uneasy look on his face.

'They'd be gone before we could come back with more men,' Mandred cursed. Ending the depredations of the Kineater wouldn't make the Drakwald safe, but it would avenge many a slaughtered traveller.

Albrecht took another draw from his bottle. He hesitated before speaking, knowing how the prince would react to the rest of his report. 'They have two more travellers,' he said. 'Live captives.'

Mandred cast his gaze across the face of each of his followers. They knew what Albrecht's words meant. Prisoners taken by the Kineater wouldn't stay alive very long. If they went back for help, they would only find gnawed bones upon their return. Without a word, Mandred lowered himself from his saddle. The horses would be awkward to manoeuvre through the trees, even if the sound of hooves didn't betray them to the beastmen.

'Dismount,' Beck called out, putting actions to words. Grimly, the rangers followed suit. They were brave, valiant men. They didn't demur. Though the odds against them were high, they knew that if they didn't try then none of them would be able to call himself a man ever again.

'Stay downwind,' Albrecht hissed, removing his bow from his saddle. 'We've one chance to surprise them.'

'Strike fast and strike hard,' Mandred echoed the trapper.

He frowned at the whalebone bow his aunt had given him. He'd been so impressed with the finery of the weapon he'd never stopped to consider its practicality. He hoped it wouldn't fail him.

Emulating the ghostly silence of Albrecht, the men crept through the trees. It wasn't long before the crackle of flames and the rough grunts of inhuman voices reached their ears. Soon, they were within sight of the clearing.

Mandred quickly looked away from the horrible vision of the campfire and what smouldered among the embers. He gazed instead at the monstrous creatures ranged about the clearing. They were a motley confusion of fur and horns, hooves and claws. Some of the brutes stood a full head taller than a man while others were short, hunched things. A few of the beastmen affected the rudiments of armour, strips of chain and plate plundered from those they had killed. Others had branded their fur with primitive glyphs and crude symbols, brazenly sporting the marks of their savage gods.

The prince gave a start when he spied a scrawny, slinking shape among the herd. While the other beastmen favoured goats and bulls and beasts of the field, this one had a verminous cast to it. He was reminded of the disgusting mutant he had fought on the walls of Middenheim so many years ago. The horror he looked upon now was very much made in the same loathsome image.

Memories of ratmen faded as Mandred's gaze fell upon the prisoners Albrecht had seen. There were two of them, a slightly flabby middle-aged man and a rather comely woman. Both had been stripped and bound to the trunk of a tree at the edge of the clearing. As he watched, a gigantic beastman stalked towards the captives, a butcher's cleaver clenched in an almost human fist.

Mandred knew this must be the Kineater. While a few of its

herd affected strips of armour or simple loincloths, this brute draped itself in a primitive parody of a nobleman's cloak, stitched together from a horse's tabard and with a collar of human scalps. The thing's hooves were polished to a bright sheen and the massive horns that spread from its forehead were decorated with a litter of silver chains, jewelled necklaces and other gaudy plunder. Below the horns, the monster's face was horribly human, a maddeningly handsome visage, the countenance of some ancient forest god.

The Kineater's lips pulled back in a grisly smile as it reached towards the woman. Mandred saw her flinch as the cold metal of the cleaver touched her bare back. The monster's fingers pawed at her long hair. She struggled to avoid the brute's touch, provoking a bray of laughter that had nothing human in it.

The whistle of a thrush reached Mandred's ears, the sign Albrecht had positioned the last of the men around the clearing. The prince didn't linger. In one smooth motion, he raised his bow and loosed a shaft into the Kineater.

The beast chief cried out in pain as Mandred's arrow caught it in the small of the back. It reared back, throwing aside its cloak and exposing a left arm that was swollen into the clawed limb of a sea creature. The Kineater barked and howled, its fury throwing the rest of its herd into a frenzy.

More shafts came flying from the trees. The rangers struck true with their aim, every arrow hitting its mark. Several of the monsters collapsed, twitching in the dirt. Others whined in pain, struggling to pluck the shafts from their hairy hides. Albrecht had positioned the men well, catching their foe in a murderous crossfire. A second volley sent the beasts into a panic.

The luxury of picking off the monsters with archery, however, was one that the captives couldn't afford. With three arrows sticking from its body, the Kineater turned once more towards the woman, its man-like face twisted into a mask of vindictive hate.

Before the beastlord could raise its cleaver, Mandred burst from the trees. Shouting at the top of his voice, he loosed one last arrow into the monster and drew his sword. The Kineater swung around, eyes glaring at the man who had dared attack it. The last arrow had hurt it, to be certain, but not enough harm to slow it down. Stamping its hooves, the beast charged straight at Mandred.

'Aid the prince!' Beck called out. From the trees, men were leaping into the clearing with drawn swords. Several of the beastmen that might otherwise have rallied to their chieftain turned about and leapt upon these new foes.

The Kineater wasn't distracted. Straight as one of Albrecht's arrows, the beastman came for Mandred, horns lowered and cleaver upraised. The prince awaited the brute's charge, diving away as those jagged horns came at him. Lashing out with his blade, he caught the Kineater just inside the pit of its arm. Steel slashed tendon and muscle in a welter of gore. The beastman screamed in pain as its arm fell limp at its side, and the cleaver tumbled from nerveless fingers.

Mandred followed up the crippling blow with a vicious slash across the Kineater's back, slicing a great flap of hide from its flesh. Before he could attack again, the brute's claw came whipping around. The enormous pincer closed tight around him, only the mail beneath his coat preventing him from being cut in half by the jagged mass of chitin. His sword arm, however, was pinned to his side, locked within the pincer's embrace. He could feel the bones grind together as the Kineater increased the pressure and dragged him to the ground.

Mandred glared up at the monster's handsome face as it

leered down at him. His fist slammed into the Kineater's nose, splashing its visage in its own blood. The brute reared back, wailing in pain, but didn't release the pressure of its claw. Savagely, it drove its hoof down upon Mandred's free arm, pinning it to the earth. Bloodied lips pulled back in a malicious smile.

Slowly, the Kineater bent over Mandred, bringing its sharp fangs towards his throat.

Before the brute could strike, a white blur swept between it and its foe. Mandred turned his face as hot blood sprayed over him. He felt the claw's pressure vanish, the imprisoning hoof lift away. Quickly he rolled onto his feet, raising his sword to fend off a renewed attack. What he saw made him marvel. The Kineater was staggering about the clearing, its claw clamped about its own neck trying to staunch the torrent of blood streaming from its torn throat. The brute stumbled about for a moment, then collapsed, its beauteous face slamming into the embers of the fire.

Mandred could only shake his head in wonder at his strange rescue. He didn't have long to ponder it, however. The clamour of battle yet rang within the clearing. The Kineater was dead, but the fiend's herd was still in the fight.

Ignoring the hurt of his battered body, Mandred rushed to help his embattled patrol.

'Voller and Gustav,' Mandred said, his voice sombre as he stared down at the dead rangers. Victory over the beastmen hadn't come without a cost. Not one man of the patrol was without his wounds, but Voller and Gustav had made the ultimate sacrifice. 'They will be remembered,' he vowed.

Leaving the surviving ranger and Albrecht to prepare the bodies for transport back to Middenheim, Mandred walked across the bloodied battlefield. A few of the beastmen had escaped the destruction of the Kineater. He looked in vain for the carcass of the rat-like monster, so he knew at least that obscenity had gone free. It was just as well. The survivors would seek places in other warherds and take with them the story of this fight. It might make some of the chiefs think twice before straying so close to the Ulricsberg.

'How are they?' Mandred asked Beck as he approached the tree where the captives had been bound. The knight had already cut them from their bonds and the two prisoners were sitting huddled together on the ground. The middle-aged man was draped in Beck's cloak and doing his best to share the warmth of the garment with the shivering woman beside him. Mandred noted with some interest the Kineater's cloak lying in a heap a short distance away.

'Cold and scared,' Beck answered. He sighed and pointed at the woman. 'She refused to wrap herself in the chief's cloak.'

The woman looked up at Mandred. Despite her ordeal and the less than dignified condition she was in, there was a firmness, a pride in that gaze that impressed the prince. 'Can you blame her?' Mandred asked, unfastening the brooch that pinned his own cloak. With a courteous bow, he offered it to the woman.

Beck shook his head. 'Damn foolishness,' he grumbled. 'Preferring to freeze.'

The woman shot him a scowling look. 'You… didn't have… the experience of… knowing your hair was going to end up adorning that… filth.'

The knight's face flushed and he was unable to hold the woman's glare. 'I'll… I'll see about the horses, your grace.' Almost unconsciously, he glanced back at the woman, then hurried away when she tightened Mandred's cloak about herself with an angry tug.

The man paid no attention to the knight's withdrawal,

more interested in the address Beck had used. 'Pardon my insolence,' he begged in a voice that was at once cultured and deferential, 'but that man called you "your grace". Would I be correct in believing we owe our deliverance to Prince Mandred von Zelt?'

'You have me at a disadvantage,' Mandred answered. He smiled benignly at the two wayfarers. 'I don't know how my name is regarded in your land. I would be right in detecting the accent of Reikland in your words?'

The traveller chuckled and bowed. 'There are some who are envious of Middenheim and would like to see her rulers strung up like a Sigmarsfest goose,' he admitted. 'But, that sort tends to stay in Altdorf.' Mustering what dignity his state of undress allowed, he presented himself with such formality as circumstances would afford. 'You see before you Friar Richter, a humble priest of Holy Sigmar and confessor to her ladyship, Mirella von Wittmar.'

Mandred nodded to the priest. 'Brother Richter,' he said. Turning to the woman, he found his eyes lingering on her proud face. 'Lady Mirella,' he said, bowing to kiss her hand.

'I thank you for your gallantry,' Mirella returned. She hadn't blushed under Beck's scrutiny, but colour rushed to her cheeks as the prince released her hand. Mandred pretended not to notice and quickly looked away.

'Would I be correct in the belief that you are seeking refuge in Middenheim?' he asked. It was a foolish question. There wasn't any other reason for a Reikland noblewoman and her confessor to be traipsing about in the Drakwald.

'We beg asylum from your father,' Brother Richter answered. He sighed and seemed to shrink visibly as a great sorrow depressed him. 'Circumstances make it imperative we surrender ourselves to the consideration of Graf Gunthar.'

Mandred stared hard at the priest, puzzled by his manner of

speech. Perhaps it was an affectation of the Sigmarite temple, but for a mere confessor, Brother Richter spoke as though he were the social equal of Lady Mirella. His surprise must have shown on his face, for the noblewoman gave the priest a warning glance.

'There is a price on my head,' Mirella stated, trying to give Mandred something else to think about. 'I was implicated in Prince Sigdan's plot against Emperor Boris.'

Mandred smiled at her frankness. 'Then you are doubly welcome in Middenheim,' he said. He turned as he heard Beck coming back with the horses. A thought occurred to him. 'I fear we'll need one of the horses to carry our dead,' he admitted with a touch of awkwardness. 'I'm afraid you'll have to ride double.'

Brother Richter's face curled in a sly grin. 'I fear I'm a poor horseman,' he confessed.

'You can ride with me then,' Mandred decided.

The flustered priest sputtered a protest. 'Oh, I'll be quite all right on my own,' he said. 'I just… Well… riding double might… be inconvenient.' Rolling his eyes he nodded his head towards Mirella. Mandred smiled when he caught Brother Richter's meaning.

'Lady Mirella, may I offer you my saddle?' the prince asked. Lowering her eyes, the noblewoman sketched the slightest nod of her head.

As they prepared to quit the grisly clearing, Mandred gave one last look at the carcasses of the Kineater and its herd. In accordance with custom, the head of each monster had been cut from its body and staked to the branch of a tree, a warning to others of their breed. Only the Kineater's head had been kept, lashed to Albrecht's saddle, a trophy that would bring a ray of cheer to the people of Middenheim when it was set upon the walls.

'What's wrong?' Lady Mirella asked Mandred. Seated behind

him in the saddle, she had felt the prince start. She followed
the direction of his gaze, but saw only an old log lying just at
the edge of the clearing.

Mandred, however, found himself staring into the frosty
eyes of a great white wolf. A wolf with blood on its muzzle.

'Those with a destiny are watched over by the gods.' Seated
upon Voller's horse, Brother Richter was also staring in the
direction of the log. Mandred glanced at the priest, but when
he looked back, the wolf was gone.

'It guided me here,' Mandred told the priest, feeling a chill
run through him. Even at its most benign, there was an unsettling wrongness about magic. 'What does it mean?'

'Only time may tell,' Richter admitted. 'But is it not reassuring to know that the good gods have not abandoned us?' He
nudged the flanks of his horse with his bare feet, urging the
steed through the trees with a display of expert horsemanship. Mandred smiled and shook his head.

'What was that all about?' Mirella asked, confused by the
exchange between prince and priest, and even more at its cause.

'Your confessor claims I am meant for great things,'
Mandred said. Without any warning, he spurred his horse
forwards, drawing a gasp of surprise from the woman. Mirella
wrapped her arms around him, holding him tight.

Somehow, Mandred was sure the trip back was going to feel
much shorter than the journey out.

Carroburg
Brauzeit, 1114

The appointments within Schloss Hohenbach had no part of
the grim, imposing exterior of the castle. Inside, the halls were

panelled in cherrywood and teak, the floors lined with expensive furs and exotic rugs, the ceilings bristling with chandeliers of silver and crystal. Lavish tapestries, exuberant sculptures and vibrant paintings were displayed in profusion wherever the eye was turned. Rich perfumes rewarded the nose, the melodies of master musicians delighted the ear, silks and satins caressed the skin. The plunder of an Empire had been poured into Boris's palatial hermitage, exhibited in obscene splendour to astound and awe the chosen elite.

While a nation starved, while entire communities perished from want and disease, those within the castle were subjected to every delight they could imagine. Fine foods from every corner of the known world, dancers and performers, liquors and stimulants of every stripe and provenance. Each of the Emperor's noble guests was nightly presented with a chalice of gold filled with elven wine looted from prehuman ruins by the most daring of adventurers. To enhance the richness of the flavour, a pearl of matchless colour and size was dropped into the cup, dissolved in the eldritch inebriant.

For most of his guests, the delights of the Emperor's retreat were exhilarating, allowing them to abandon themselves in the pleasures of the moment and forget the horrors that raged beyond the castle. The Black Plague might reign in Stirland and Sylvania, in Averheim and Altdorf, but it had no place here. Here, the plague could not touch them.

Princess Erna could not share in such wanton indulgence. Each extravagance only increased her contempt for the Emperor and all that he represented. Only a monster could surround himself with such luxury while his subjects were decimated by famine and pestilence, while his realm was wracked by war and disease.

There were others, to be certain, who shared Erna's loathing, but they were too afraid not to hide their disapproval.

The castle offered sanctuary. If they displeased the Emperor, he might eject them from their refuge, cast them once more into the horrors of a world on the brink of apocalypse.

Erna knew she wasn't alone. She saw the way Markgraf Luther von Metzgernstein glowered whenever the Emperor wasn't looking, fuming over the imprisonment of his six-year-old son in the castle dungeons. She watched Baron von Kirchof's alarm when the Emperor's eyes lingered on the shapely figure of his niece. She saw the pious shock in the kindly eyes of Matriarch Katrina Ochs, the Empire's supreme priestess of Shallya, when the Emperor cast aside decency in order to placate one of his jaded whims.

Unlike her, however, these dissidents hid their true feelings. Day by day, she saw their convictions slink deeper and deeper inside them, shrinking a little more with each outrage the Emperor presented. Whether it was making crippled halflings dance a waltz or forcing a stuttering buffoon to recite the line of emperors, Boris's perverse amusements went unchallenged by the sycophants he had gathered to him.

It was strange that while the convictions of others should wither under the influence of Boris, her own courage should be awakened. Kreyssig had failed to beat the heart from her and the daily offences perpetrated by the Emperor and his court caused Erna to rediscover her idealism. From shuddering fear, she began to treat the Emperor with disdain, even insolence. She knew there would be punishment for her openness, her refusal to condone the Emperor's wickedness.

What she didn't know was the shape that punishment would take.

One day, after an opulent luncheon of roast pheasant and minced truffles, the Emperor led his guests out onto the parapet overlooking the approach to the castle. Servants waited upon the dignitaries, presenting the Grand Prince of Stirland with a goblet of Bretonnian wine, offering the High Duchess of Nordland a trencher of pickled sturgeon eyes, enticing the Arch-Count of Averland with a platter of smoked swan. Boris waited while his guests sampled the extravagant fare, then, with a smile that Erna knew was directed solely towards her, he strode to the battlements and beckoned his guests to join him.

'A diversion to feast your eyes as you've just feasted your bellies,' the Emperor announced. He brought his hands together in a loud clap when some of his noble guests were peering down from the parapet, ensuring that Erna was among them. 'There are some of you who disapprove of frivolity,' he announced, waving aside the protests from his more voluble sycophants. 'There are some of you who think that all this pleasure is indecent and wasteful.'

Boris paused, looking straight into Erna's eyes. Down below, a group of soldiers had appeared, escorting a mob of tatterdemalion starvelings that had been culled from the streets of Carroburg.

'Oh, what means this?' Palatine Istvan Dohnanyi, the dapper pretender to the Talabecland peerage, asked, leaning between the crenellations for a better look.

'I think His Imperial Majesty has some clever amusement planned,' the rotund Count Artur of Nuln laughed.

Gustav van Meers, a Westerland peasant who'd earned his place among the inmates of Schloss Hohenbach by dint of his immense fortune – a fortune looted from Marienburg during the Norscan invasion – waved a perfumed handkerchief at the wretches below. 'Not the most appealing specimens,' he observed, hoping to illustrate to his noble peers that he was far above such common beggars.

'What are you going to do with them?' von Kirchof asked. Knowing the Emperor's distaste for the unsightly, he was at a loss to understand why Boris would have such a ragged mob assembled outside the castle. Because he found it disturbing, it was easy for him to forget the sadistic humour that his sovereign sometimes indulged.

Emperor Boris smiled at his champion, and again made a point of locking eyes with Erna. 'Why, we are going to feed these poor creatures,' he said. 'Just as the Thuringian kings of old used to throw table scraps to their dogs.' He waved his hand to the guards below. At his sign, they shoved some of the peasants forwards, allowing them to come close to the wall. Almost at once, the rabble sent whining entreaties to the nobles staring down at them.

Von Kirchof was the first to react to the pleas, reaching to one of the trenchers and tossing a cut of smoked eel to one of the ragged men. Von Metzgernstein followed his example with a slice of pheasant. A few of the noble guests started to likewise throw scraps of food to the beggars. Erna, however, made no move to the wall. She was watching Emperor Boris, watching as his face contorted again into that cherubic grin, as the imp of perversity once more asserted itself.

'Friends! Friends!' the Emperor shouted, motioning his guests away from the wall. 'This is hardly a fitting spectacle! It lacks a sense of theatre. It is not a true representation of the Thuringian lords.' His face still lit by his ghastly humour, he looked down at the hungry peasants. 'It is not fit that such aristocratic sensibilities should be subjected to the presence of wretched beggars. That would be offensive. But if we were to feed a few stray dogs... Well, what man does not show compassion to a dog?'

The Emperor raised his hand, displaying a cut of venison. He waved it to and fro before the hungry eyes of the peasants. Back and forth he teased them until one of the wretches understood what was expected. Dropping to all fours, the man barked and panted and whined. Laughing, Boris dropped the venison to the ground near the peasant. 'No hands,' he warned when the man started to stand. 'Be a good dog.'

The peasant froze, a despondent sob rising from him. Then, obediently, he crawled to the meat and retrieved it from the dirt with his teeth. Emperor Boris laughed and applauded. He turned to his guests. 'Now you see how the game should be played. If they expect to be fed like dogs, then they should act like dogs.'

The Emperor's injunction had the most jaded of his court dashing to the servants and retrieving handfuls of food to throw at the peasants after teasing a humiliating performance out of them. A few of the courtiers hesitated, but were too concerned about drawing Boris's disfavour to restrain themselves. Some made a better show of enjoying the cruel performance than others, but they threw food down to the 'dogs' just the same.

Doktor Moschner mounted the only kind of protest. 'Your Imperial Majesty, I think it is unwise to bring these people here,' he confided to the monarch. 'These are low-born peasants. They may be carrying the plague.'

The cherubic smile dropped from the Emperor's face, the humour fading into glowering severity. 'There is no plague in Carroburg,' Boris declared. 'That is why We removed Our court here, why We left that peasant rascal Kreyssig in charge of Altdorf.'

The physician flinched at the ire in his master's voice. 'Forgive me... I only thought...'

Emperor Boris was already moving away, turning his attention to Princess Erna. Like the doktor, she hadn't taken part in his cruel jest. He stopped a few paces from the woman, a cold smile back on his face.

'Be careful, my dear,' the Emperor advised, staring at her expression of undisguised disapproval. 'If you become too much a boor, then We might decide you don't like Our company.'

The Emperor nodded his head towards the battlements where his sycophants laughed and joked as they tossed scraps to the begging peasants. 'If We tire of you, We might have to throw you to the dogs.'

→ CHAPTER V →

Altdorf
Sommerzeit, 1114

The uproar within the council chamber was almost deafening. From his position at the head of the table, Adolf Kreyssig was afforded a good look at the bedlam. For all their outrage, he knew the fury of the councillors was all bluster. The presence of thirty armed Kaiserjaeger would make the nobles remember their place.

Lord Ratimir rose from his seat, smashing his lead drinking goblet on the table, trying to force some measure of order. 'The Protector has spoken!' he shouted, punctuating each word with a blow against the table. 'He has made an Imperial diktat! His word is law!'

Count Holgwer von Haag shook his fist at Ratimir, then spun around to gesticulate at Kreyssig himself. 'The Emperor will hear of this, you jumped up peasant scum! You have no right to–'

Kreyssig picked up the crystal ewer of wine resting before him and with a violent heave dashed it against the top of the table. Shards of glass exploded among the councillors, causing even the grizzled Duke Vidor to flinch back in alarm. A tense silence descended on the council chamber.

'I have every right,' Kreyssig growled at von Haag. He pointed over his shoulder with his thumb, indicating the empty Imperial throne standing upon its marble dais. 'You were there, all of you, when His Imperial Majesty appointed me Protector of the Empire. Have you asked yourself why he chose me, not a count or a baron or a duke?' He let the question linger, watching little flickers of anxiety play across the faces of his audience. It didn't take an enchanter to know that these blue-bloods had been asking themselves that question every hour of every day since the ceremony at the Great Cathedral of Sigmar.

Kreyssig extended his hand, directing an accusing finger at the men seated around the table. 'His Imperial Majesty chose me because he feels he cannot trust you nobles. The Prince of Altdorf was the ringleader of the conspiracy to depose him. The noble representatives of Stirland and Westerland and Drakwald were party to that treachery. The Graf of Middenheim bestowed his endorsement and support. The noble-born Reiksmarshal turned three-quarters of the Imperial army to treason and brigandry!' Kreyssig's lip curled back in a vicious sneer. 'No, I think the Emperor will sanction my decision to reconstitute this council with men of my choosing.' He leaned back in his chair. 'You are welcome to protest, but know that I will take any such move as seditious and the instigators of such action will be investigated. Do you feel your loyalty is equal to such scrutiny?'

'Mine is,' growled Duke Vidor. He wore the black and gold of the Imperial army's highest echelon, a green griffon rampant embroidered across the breast and a jewelled pectoral hanging from his neck. Except for the Imperial signet, Vidor already bore the paraphernalia of Reiksmarshal. Kreyssig knew how keenly the nobleman desired to wear the signet on his finger.

Kreyssig also knew that there was no man he could less afford to place in that position. Duke Vidor was of the old families, the old blood, boasting a pedigree that went clear back to the age of Sigmar. He was an embodiment of the aristocratic mentality, the arrogance of class and breeding that regarded those of commoner origins as less than animals. No amount of accomplishment or ability could ever overcome the failing of parentage in the eyes of men like Vidor.

There was no warmth in the smile Kreyssig directed at the Duke. 'Your loyalty is beyond question?' he asked, his words dripping with mockery.

'I pursued that traitor Boeckenfoerde across four provinces and routed his rabble into the Ungol wastes!' Vidor roared.

Like a spider drawing in its web, Kreyssig seized his prey. 'Your orders were to bring the traitor's head back and set it at the foot of Our Glorious Emperor's throne!' Savagely, Kreyssig threw back his chair and sent it crashing to the floor. A few steps brought him to the base of the marble dais. His hand pointing at the three steps beneath the Imperial seat, he turned and glared at Vidor. 'Where is Boeckenfoerde's head?'

Duke Vidor glared back at Kreyssig. 'Oh no… You'll not bait me! I did all that was reasonable, chased the cur beyond our borders…'

'Beyond the reach of Imperial justice,' Kreyssig snarled back. 'Some affectation of noblesse oblige, taking it upon yourself to give Boeckenfoerde the choice of exile over execution?'

Vidor was on his feet now, hands clenched at his sides. 'You peasant dog! You dare accuse me!'

'I have been appointed Protector of the Empire,' Kreyssig replied, a menacing calm in his voice. 'It is my duty to accuse those whose service to the Emperor has been… questionable.'

He stalked back to the table, waiting while two of his Kaiser-jaeger righted the upset chair. Seating himself again, Kreyssig glanced around the table, then fixed his gaze on Vidor. 'Your services will not be required,' he told the nobleman. 'I will be appointing Astrid Soehnlein as new Reiksmarshal. If you do not wish to take orders from a peasant, I suggest you retire to your estates. While you still have them.'

Duke Vidor glowered at Kreyssig, his hands closing into fists, his teeth grinding as he clenched his jaw. Without a word, he tore the pectoral from his neck and dropped it on the table.

Kreyssig watched the fuming noble depart. As the door closed behind Vidor, he turned his cold gaze back upon the other councillors. 'I trust the rest of you who are being relieved of your duties will accept my decision with the grace befitting your station.'

The reptilian smile flashed over the Protector's face. 'Otherwise people might develop strange ideas about your loyalty to Emperor Boris.'

Ragged, emaciated, unkempt and unwashed, the denizens of Albrecht's Close emerged from their hovels, drawn from behind locked doors by the commotion in the street. Many had taken refuge in their half-timber homes and earthen grubenhäuser months ago, trying to hide from the plague running rampant through the city. As they stirred from their seclusion and hobbled out into the street, they shaded their eyes against the sting of sunlight and coughed at the forgotten sensation of open air.

The plague had wrought havoc in Albrecht's Close, once the domain of prosperous merchants and their peasant tenants. Many of the buildings were derelict, the white cross of disease daubed upon their doors. Many others had been allowed to fall into horrendous disrepair, their inhabitants not daring to summon craftsmen to effect repairs lest they bring the plague into their homes. One arm of the close was a blackened ruin, the residue of a winter fire that had consumed a dozen homes before its wrath was spent.

It was towards this swathe of charred timbers and soot-stained rock that the ragged crowd was drawn. Gaunt with hunger, feverish with fear, finery reduced to the rags of poverty, they were a typical sampling of what pernicious disease and malignant taxation had done to the common folk of Altdorf. They were a people who felt abandoned by gods and Emperor, cast into the unforgiving darkness of Old Night itself.

They were a people desperate to seize upon any hope. And for their sins, hope had descended upon the inhabitants of Albrecht's Close.

He marched down the street, his powerful build swathed in a cloak of black, a heavy hood framing his sharp, birdlike face. About his neck hung an ornament of shining gold, the icon of a clenched fist. In one hand he bore a heavy book bound in leopard skin and banded in steel. In the other hand, raised high that its light might shine into the shadows of footpath and alleyway, he held a blazing torch. In a stern, booming voice, he compelled the people of the close to stir.

'Altdorfers!' the black spectre shouted. 'The judgement of the gods is upon you! Too long have you wallowed in the sins of wantonness and luxury. Too long have you forsaken the virtue of humility, forgotten your obligations to the divine court! The weight of your inequities has visited pestilence and famine on this city. The gods have turned their faces from you. They have become deaf to shallow prayers issuing from shallow hearts. You beg their grace, but you do so without faith. Without conviction!'

The orator stopped, turning to stare accusingly at the throng filing into the street. He shook the torch, sending embers dancing into the shadows. He brandished the book, letting its pages rustle. 'You implore the gods for solace, ask them to spare your petty lives. Yet you do not spare a thought for the quality of your souls! When the gods remain silent, you lend yourselves to confusion and blasphemy. You seek succour from those who do not believe in the authority of the gods. You despair and would give yourselves over into the deceit of those who cavort with the Ruinous Powers!'

On uttering his last condemnation of the crowd, the speaker turned, shaking his torch at a miserable-looking woman bound in chains and being dragged through the street by a pair of shaven-headed acolytes in the brown robes of flagellants. 'This creature sought to lead you down the path of damnation. Sought to trap you in her profane lies. To cure your flesh by defiling your soul!'

'You have chained Mutti Angela,' a horrified onlooker exclaimed. 'She is a healer...'

'She is a pawn of daemons!' the black spectre roared, his booming voice drowning out the peasant's protest. 'She is a corruption polluting the virtue of this community, a poisonous viper spitting her venom into the hearts of all she touches.' He waved the torch overhead, letting embers shower down onto his hood, drawing the attention of the crowd away from the man who had spoken for Mutti Angela.

'I am called Auernheimer,' he declared. 'I serve the great god Solkan, the divine fist of retribution. I am a witch-taker.' He looked back at the chained woman. 'This creature, this abomination that professes to protect you against the plague, is a witch.'

The statement brought gasps of alarm from the crowd.

Several voices rose in objection, incredulous cries against Auernheimer's claims.

'Your deception is so great that even now you cling to this creature's lies,' the witch-taker declared. His fiery gaze swept across the crowd. 'How long has this obscenity practised her witchery among you? Has it stopped the plague? Has it saved any of you? No! There is only one way to salvation. Submit to the authority of the gods. Bow to the judgement of Great Solkan!'

Auernheimer paused, studying the crowd. Slowly, he lowered the holy book, hooking it to a ring on his belt. Reaching beneath his cloak, he withdrew a long iron needle. 'Still you doubt, but I shall prove to you the veracity of my words!' In a single vicious motion, he thrust the needle into his own cheek. Blood bubbled from the wound as he worried the needle back and forth. The peasants watched in morbid fascination as he pulled the needle free.

'A man will bleed,' Auernheimer declaimed, shaking the bloody needle. 'Should I prick any one of you, you too would bleed. But a witch,' he turned and strode towards the chained woman, 'a witch has no blood in her veins, only the filth of Chaos!'

Before anyone knew what he was about, Auernheimer stabbed the needle into the woman's arm. The captive cried out in fright and pain, but her scream was drowned out by the horrified shrieks of the crowd. Where the needle had drawn blood from the witch-taker, the substance bubbling from the woman's wound was a stinking brown sludge.

'Witch!' a horrified peasant exclaimed. The cry was soon taken up by others. Soon the shout was taken up by the entire crowd.

Auernheimer withdrew the needle, wiping it clean on his cloak before returning it to his pocket. 'Purge the corruption of

the witch!' he roared. 'Cleanse its blight from your community!
Purify this fleshy vestment of evil!' He waved his torch overhead
once more, sending embers dancing through the street.

'Cast out the daughters of Chaos by burning them!'

The witch-taker's invective aroused the terrified mob.
Peasants rushed upon the nearest of the derelict structures,
ripping out shutters and pulling down doors. Furniture was
smashed and broken, shingles wrenched from the edges of
overhangs. Soon, a great mound of wood was growing amid
the burned-out ruins. When it had risen high enough, the
accused witch was thrust forwards, sent crashing into the pile.

Auernheimer waved his torch overhead one last time before
sending the brand flying from his hand to sail into the piled
wood. The debris quickly caught flame. Angela shrieked, scrambling to escape the fire. As she tried to crawl away from the
pile, peasants thrust her back with pitchforks and spades. The
woman's efforts became more frantic as the fire kissed her flesh,
but the more horrendous her injuries, the more determined the
peasants were to keep her from escaping the conflagration.

When Angela's strength failed and she at last collapsed
amid the flames, Auernheimer unhooked the tome from his
belt and led the peasants in a solemn psalm praising the grim
beneficence of Solkan, Father of Vengeance.

For their sins, the people of Albrecht's Close rallied to a new
and terrible redeemer.

Middenheim,
Sommerzeit, 1118

Ar-Ulric cast an appraising eye over Brother Richter as the
priest seated himself at the right hand of Prince Mandred. The

High Priest of Ulric teased his snowy moustache with a wrinkled hand as he walked around the Fauschlagstein, the great stone council table carved from a single block of mountain granite, and took his seat near that of Graf Gunthar. Even when he was seated, the old cleric couldn't keep his eyes from straying towards the Sigmarite or an amused expression from tugging at his face.

Mandred found Ar-Ulric's demeanour puzzling and consequently annoying. The priest was getting on in his years, far older than any wolf-priest before him. Age had lent him a taciturnity that made a dwarf seem chipper by comparison.

Thoughts of dwarfs made him look over at Thane Hardin Gunarsson, chief of Middenheim's dwarf population. More properly, the dwarfs lived beneath the city, deep inside the Ulricsberg – the mountain they called Grungni's Tower – itself. The halls of Karak Grazhyakh ran through the whole of the mountain and, it was said, its mines delved deep into the bedrock below. Thane Hardin was a stoic, studious representative for his people, speaking rarely and then only with cautious deliberation.

Others gathered about the table represented the noble families of Middenheim, such as Duke Schneidereit and Margraf von Ulmann. The graf's chamberlain, the pessimistic Viscount von Vogelthal, was also in attendance, wearing his usual cynical scowl. Grand Master Vitholf of the White Wolves, successor of Grand Master Arno, sat beside the chamberlain, trying to ignore Mandred's presence. The knight blamed Mandred for Arno's death, a grudge that hurt the prince all the more because he himself felt it to be justified.

All those seated around the Fauschlagstein stood as Graf Gunthar entered the room, dressed in the rich blue raiment he always affected at such meetings. The graf nodded respectfully to Lady Mirella and Brother Richter, then circled around to the wolf-armed seat at the head of the table. As he lowered himself into the high-backed chair, his councillors resumed their seats.

For the better part of an hour, the graf and his council listened attentively as Mirella and Richter described the situation in the south, the political climate in Altdorf and the status of the Imperial court. Rumours of much that they had to relate had reached Middenheim already, carried by the trickle of refugees who managed the dangerous journey, but to have the facts related to them by persons who had actually been there was accorded far greater import. Graf Gunthar was particularly struck by the theft of Ghal Maraz, the Hammer of Sigmar and one of the holy regalia that lent the Emperor the authority to rule.

'Stolen by a young knight?' the graf marvelled. 'Right from under the nose of old Boris!'

'Prince Sigdan's intention, I believe, was to bring the hammer here, your highness,' Lady Mirella said. 'Baron Thornig was to conduct the thief, a captain of the Reiksknecht, to your court. Sadly, the baron was killed by the Kaiserjaeger.'

'And this captain? You say that he escaped?' Graf Gunthar asked.

'He did, your highness,' Brother Richter stated. 'Adolf Kreyssig, the so-called Protector of the Empire, has posted a three thousand crown bounty on the head of Erich von Kranzbeuhler.'

The amount of the reward brought appreciative whistles from some of the councillors. Viscount von Vogelthal turned towards the graf. 'With such a large bounty, it is obvious this von Kranzbeuhler still has the hammer.' The chamberlain frowned and shook his head. 'Or at least Kreyssig thinks he does. Just because he didn't reach Middenheim is no reason to think he might not have sought asylum in the court of another count.'

Brother Richter shook his head. 'He didn't,' he declared.

'You seem rather certain of that,' Mandred observed.

'I am,' Richter agreed. 'Because not six months ago I encountered von Kranzbeuhler in a small village south of the Reikwald.'

'Quite a risk, merely to consult a simple friar,' Ar-Ulric commented, a knowing gleam in his eye. He smiled when Richter gave him a worried look.

'Did he still have Ghal Maraz?' Grand Master Vitholf wondered.

The priest nodded. 'You see, I didn't seek him out. He sought me. He wanted my advice on what to do, where to take the hammer.'

'What did you tell him?' Graf Gunthar asked, leaning forwards in his chair, his face anxious.

'I told him to hide it,' Brother Richter said. 'I told him to keep it safe. That Sigmar would reveal to him when the time was right for Ghal Maraz to return.'

'Outrageous!' exclaimed Duke Schneidereit. 'If you had access to the hammer, why not keep to the plan and bring it here? This entire story is preposterous!'

Graf Gunthar fixed Brother Richter with his gaze. 'You understand that with Ghal Maraz I could have made a claim upon the throne? I could have cast this peasant tyrant from the Imperial Palace. I could have restored order to the Empire.' His voice became a bitter growl. 'But a Sigmarite wouldn't stomach an Ulrican on the throne.'

Thane Hardin snorted derisively at the graf's statement. From anyone else on the council, Gunthar would have taken it as a grave insult. Instead, he turned to hear what the dwarf had to say.

'You really think holding Ghal Maraz would make all the other kings bow to you?' Thane Hardin scoffed. 'All you'd get would be a bunch of scoundrels yapping for your blood and calling you a thief. Few men have the honour to set aside their own interests to do what's right. Even fewer when they wear crowns and titles. To be blunt,' he added, as though his speech had been restrained, 'I'm amazed your Empire has held together as long as it has.'

'Thane Hardin makes a good observation,' Margraf von Ulmann said. 'There are many who would refuse to acknowledge any claim on the throne. With the example of Boris Goldgather, they might justifiably fear the domination of another tyrant of his ilk. Then there are men like this peasant Kreyssig, who won't relinquish power unless it is pried from his dead fingers.'

'Men must wallow in the depths of darkness before they will strive towards the light,' Ar-Ulric said, quoting an ancient Teutogen parable. The wolf-priest's wrinkled hands slowly came together, fingers entwined. 'The strength of the pack is tenfold against the lone wolf,' he told the other councillors. 'But until that strength is needed, how much will the lone wolf struggle to keep his freedom?'

Graf Gunthar sat back, sober contemplation knotting his brow. 'That is why you hid the hammer?' he asked Brother Richter.

'It is, your highness,' the Sigmarite answered. 'By itself, Ghal Maraz cannot bring unity. What it can do is bring legitimacy to that unity.' He swept his gaze across the council. 'The Empire is beset on all sides. The Northmen have razed Westerland and are encamped in the rubble of Marienburg. Drakwald is a depopulated shambles. This you know, but things are even more dire in the south. Sylvania is in the grip of the walking dead, stirred from their graves by a terrible necromancer. Averland is beset by orcs from the south. The city of Pfeildorf...'

Richter hesitated, wondering if he dared continue, if any about the table would believe him if he related the fate of Solland's capital, a fate that had also descended upon Wissenburg and nearly claimed Altdorf itself. Would they believe him if he said the Underfolk had scurried straight from the pages of legend to become loathsome, hideous reality? Would he have believed it himself had Kranzbeuhler not shown him the severed paw of one of the monsters?

'Pfeildorf has been lost to inhuman creatures,' the priest stated. 'Beastkin of the most abominable cast in numbers such as even the Drakwald has never seen. Entire villages and towns have been enslaved by the fiends, forced to toil for their monstrous masters.'

Mandred gave a start as he heard Richter speak. He was thinking of that ratty beastman in the Kineater's herd, of the similar creature he had thrown from the walls of Middenheim years ago. A shiver passed through him, those old legends scratching at his mind. He started to speak, but decided better of it. He didn't want to look foolish before his father and the council.

Beastmen came in all shapes and sizes. The ratmen had been nothing but especially degenerate examples.

After all, everyone knew there was no such thing as the Underfolk.

Far below the halls of the Middenpalaz and the streets of Middenheim, the subterranean darkness echoed with the crack of pick and hammer. The low grumble of an old miner's chant whispered down rocky tunnels, catching in fissures and crevices to become a chorus of echoes. The glow of candles and coal-lamps cast a flickering island of light amid the black pits of Grungni's Tower.

The dwarfs smelt of beer and sweat, leather and steel. The

reek of the goat fat used to starch their beards was especially pungent, an odour that announced their presence even more loudly than the glow of their candles and the stink of their lamps. Under concealment of the Khazalid work song and the din of tools, dark shapes crept furtively through the tunnels.

Intent upon the little ribbon of gold they had pursued through the mountain for decades, the dwarfs were oblivious to the foe that stalked them through the tunnels. The vein had been entrusted to their clan by the powerful Engineer's Guild, becoming not simply a source of wealth to them but a matter of pride and honour as well. The work itself was as important as the rewards to be reaped from the golden nuggets they chipped from the walls. A dwarf who didn't put himself fully into his work wasn't fit to wear his beard.

Such was the devoted concentration they put into their labour that the miners didn't notice when one of the picks fell silent. They didn't hear the soft gasp as a sharp dagger was thrust through dwarfish back to pierce dwarfish lung. They didn't notice the change in their song as one of its voices was silenced. They didn't see the shape cloaked in black that carefully lowered a limp corpse to the floor of the shaft.

One by one, the miners were dispatched. Sinister shapes stole upon them from the shadows, striking in deathly silence with the expertise of accomplished killers.

It was the rats that finally alerted the miners to their danger. The vermin were a constant presence in the shafts, an annoyance that the dwarfs endured for the pragmatic fact that the rodents had an eerie ability to sense vibrations in the rock. Even before a dwarf's keen senses could warn him of a cave-in, the rats would be scurrying for safety. An experienced miner would even encourage a few rats to linger in any shaft he was working with scraps of food. Always he would keep half an eye on the animals, wary of any change in their habits.

A grizzled old dwarf rested his pick on his shoulder as he noticed the rats on the floor near where he was working. He'd never seen the creatures so agitated before. It wasn't the mad scramble for safety a collapse would cause. No, the creatures were crawling about, low to the floor, looking for all the world like whipped dogs. Sometimes they would lift their heads and sniff at the air, only to chirp a frightened little squeak.

The old miner raised his gaze from the floor, and his eyes grew wide with alarm as he saw one of the candles further down the shaft snuffed out. The entire length of the tunnel behind him was in darkness, though he knew there should be half a dozen dwarfs between himself and the main shaft. Grimly, he shifted the pick from his shoulder, hands closing about it as they would around the grip of a battleaxe.

Before he could move, a mass of darkness swept towards the miner. His eyes picked out the hunched figure, the lean body of a bestial shape draped in the folds of a long black cloak. He saw beady red eyes gleaming from a furry face, the long muzzle twisted in a toothy snarl. He saw the hand-like paw lick towards him, a crooked blade clenched in its fingers. For an instant, he felt the sizzle of the poisonous blade as it slashed his throat.

The dwarf's killer caught his body before it could collapse to the floor. Carefully, the assassin lowered the corpse to the ground, scattering the frightened rats. The murderer stared down at the ghastly slash he had inflicted, watching as the traces of warpstone from his dagger continued to burn and bubble at the edges of the wound.

Then the skaven reared back, turning his eyes away from the miner. In a single hop, he was at the little niche the dwarf had been working. The assassin's paw flashed over the candle yet burning there, snuffing it out. As darkness enveloped the ratman once more, he cast his gaze further down the shaft, where the sounds and smells of dwarf yet prevailed.

Deathmaster Silke twitched his whiskers in amusement.

There was nothing quite like killing helpless prey to make a skaven feel pleased with himself.

⤙ CHAPTER VI ⤚

Altdorf
Vorgeheim, 1114

Cold fire seared through Kreyssig's arm, an agony that seemed to stab down into the very core of his being. When he thought he could take no more, the pain intensified, forcing him to endure.

'Pain heals,' the witch's soft tones whispered through the desecrated chapel. 'Pain is life. It is through pain that we find our strength.'

From the corner of his vision, Kreyssig could see the Baroness von den Linden pace around the room, her delicate fingers gliding across the ruined masonry and smashed statuary on the walls. As always, there was a fearful fascination about the witch. Her every step had a grace beyond mere woman. She was like some great feline on the prowl as she circled the stone altar.

'How strong do you want to be, commander?' the baroness mused. 'What are your limits?'

Through clenched teeth, Kreyssig hissed an answer. 'There… are… no… limits.' He squeezed his eyes shut, clenched his jaw as spasms of suffering pulsed through his flesh.

An almost coy smile teased the corners of the witch's mouth as she watched her patron's ordeal. If the decision were left to him, she did believe he would allow the pain to mount until the aethyric harmonies caused his heart to burst. It was an impressive display of determination, and the baroness wasn't one to impress easily.

'The will may be a thing of iron, but the body is still mere flesh,' the witch declared. She waved her hand, the obsidian gargoyle circling her forefinger blazing with an eerie light as she siphoned off the magical emanations surrounding the altar. Before they could build again, she stepped forwards and brushed away the herbs and offal surrounding Kreyssig. The Protector rose, grimacing as pain shot through his body.

'I could have taken more,' he complained, flexing his arm, the arm he had been told would never mend.

'All things in their season,' the baroness cautioned him, extending her hand and helping Kreyssig down from the altar. 'Power must be marshalled slowly and with care.'

Kreyssig gave a pensive nod, deferring to the witch's knowledge of the black arts. 'These dalliances, pleasant though they are, have become somewhat dangerous.' He marched across the chapel, retrieving his clothes from the dusty floor. 'Just today, my Kaiserjaeger captured a man who was following me here. It didn't take long to make him admit he was a spy in the service of Duke Vidor.'

'You pulled the duke's fangs when you made Soehnlein the new Reiksmarshal,' the witch pointed out. 'Surely there is nothing he can do to you now?'

Kreyssig paused as he buttoned his tunic, frowning as he noticed he was employing only his right hand. It was a habit he was going to break, a legacy of his former weakness he would purge.

'Ordinarily, I would squash Vidor like a bug,' Kreyssig said, enjoying the twinge of anxiety mention of insects provoked in his benefactress. 'But it is too soon to act out of hand. The nobles need time to understand the new status quo, to appreciate the authority Emperor Boris has bestowed on me. As you have said, all things in their season. Vidor will attend the Scharfrichter. But until then he can make trouble.'

The baroness swept forwards, assisting Kreyssig as he dressed. She leaned close to his ear, her voice lowering to an alluring purr. 'You are the Protector of the Empire, surrogate of His Imperial Majesty. What man would dare challenge you?'

'Even an Emperor must beware the gods,' Kreyssig said, recalling a bit of wisdom the departing sovereign had given him. It wasn't a warning about impiety, however, but rather an admonition to pay close attention to the clergy. The Emperor was master of the bodies of his subjects, but their souls were claimed by the priests and their gods. The power of faith and superstition was one any ruler ignored at his peril.

'The ravages of the plague have aroused strange ideas in the heads of the peasants,' Kreyssig explained. 'With every new outbreak, the people descend a little further into their morass of superstitions. They turn to plague doktors, bonesetters and leeches to preserve them from the disease. And when these measures fail them, they flee into the shadows of superstition. They cling to faith in the gods, hearken to the words of zealots and fanatics, in their despair.'

Kreyssig pulled away from the witch's arms, turning around so that he could stare into her eyes. 'Witch-takers stalk the streets of Altdorf, burning old midwives and herb-mongers, alchemists and astrologers. They have stirred the fears of the rabble and from that fear they have claimed their own brand of power.'

'Your power is greater,' the baroness said, a slight trace of fear creeping into her voice. 'You could exile these murderers or hang them from the city walls.'

Kreyssig shook his head. 'It is not so simple. These madmen have preyed upon the faith of the commoners, given them a new hope, however irrational. Hope dies hard, and never with more tenacity than among people with nothing left to lose.'

'What will you do then?' the baroness asked. The witch had good reason to worry. Rumours about her unnatural talents had long been a subject of gossip among the intimates of the Imperial court.

'First, I must know how much longer I must attend these treatments,' Kreyssig said. 'Vidor's next spy may prove more capable than his last one. I can't have him using my connection with you to foment unrest among the rabble.' A caustic laugh hissed through his teeth. 'I'll have to redirect the hopes of the peasants. Channel their superstitious fears away from the witch-takers and to a more respectable institution.'

The baroness reached out, stroking her hand along Kreyssig's cheek. 'And how will you accomplish such a feat?'

'The Temple of Sigmar has been leaderless since the death of Grand Theogonist Thorgrad,' Kreyssig stated. 'The Sigmarite hierarchs have dallied over electing a replacement, citing the confusion wrought by the plague and the unrest among the southern provinces. That lack of leadership has fostered doubt in the hearts of their congregations, made their belief stray in strange places. A new Grand Theogonist could set things right, restore confidence in the Temple.'

'Who will this new leader be?' the witch purred, raking her fingers through Kreyssig's hair.

'Someone useful to me,' he said. 'Someone I can mould and control. Someone obligated to me.

'Someone who will bow to the Protector of the Empire even before his own god.'

Slime glistened in the rushlight, dripping down from the sub-terranean walls. In the streets above the swelter of summer gripped Altdorf, but here there was only dank, clammy cold. Hacked from the limestone beneath the foundations of the Courts of Justice, there were many sub-levels and annexes to the dungeons of Altdorf, but none so infamous as those black vaults spoken of in hushed whispers as the Catacombs.

The Catacombs were the preserve of Kreyssig's Kaiser-jaeger, a private hell of their own creation. Torture theatres, execution chambers, isolation cells and dark oubliettes, interrogation rooms and mortuaries, the Catacombs piled horror upon horror. Even those who were released back into the world above never really escaped these crypts of terror. Within them there would always be the memory of this place, a black cloud to smother every happy moment they had ever known.

Moans and screams echoed through the black tunnels, a chorus of torment that was never silent. Since the attempt to usurp Emperor Boris, there had been no dearth of victims for the Kaiserjaeger to drag down into these depths. One and all were traitors, either by fact or by confession. Kreyssig's men never failed to extract a confession when it was needed.

The commander emerged into the infernal glow of his pri-vate torture chamber, the room which he called the Dragon's Hole. Its main feature was a great bronze dragonhead, its jaws agape, little iron rings dangling from its horns. The statue's jaws were a cunningly designed oven, the iron rings clever shackles of exacting craftsmanship. A priest of Ranald couldn't slip through those shackles. Kreyssig knew because he'd tested it several times.

Today, however, it was the servant of a different god who had attracted Kreyssig's attention. Lector Stefan Schoppe was one of the scions of the Sigmarite faith in the Reikland, a man respected by his peers, almost deified by his congregation in the diocese of Helmgart. He was a cleric venerated by the faithful throughout the Empire, a priest above reproach. Exactly the sort of man to suit Kreyssig's needs.

Kreyssig turned away from the dragonhead and the liveried torturers raking the smouldering coals in its oven. He cast an appraising gaze at the assortment of hooks and tongs, chisels and mallets displayed on the oak worktable which rested against one wall. Almost absently, he lifted one of the tongs, a vicious thing of spiked barbs and serrated edges. For a moment, he toyed with the mechanism, opening the jaws.

'This looks uncomfortable,' he said, setting the instrument down. He turned and, for the first time since entering the room, looked at his prisoner. 'Do you not think so, your eminence?'

Lector Stefan was shackled hand and foot to the wall, an iron collar about his neck. Dirt and blood stained his priestly robes, the legacy of his abduction from Helmgart. The cleric's eyes were wide with fear, roving between the torture instruments on the table and the bronze dragonhead.

'You have been implicated in the plot against His Imperial Majesty,' Kreyssig stated, glancing at the little desk set in one corner of the chamber. The wizened clerk sitting behind the table produced a scroll and began reading the indictment.

'Lies! All lies!' Lector Stefan shouted.

Kreyssig grinned at him, slowly crossing the room until he was only a few feet from his captive. 'I know,' he confessed in a whisper. 'Down here, though, people will say what they are told to say. Even if it is sacrilege.'

Fresh horror gripped the priest. That fragile hope that his

arrest had been a mistake deserted him in an agonised groan. Kreyssig feigned surprise at Lector Stefan's reaction.

'Be at ease, your eminence,' he said. 'These… barbarities aren't for you.' Kreyssig pointed to the table and the dragon-head. 'What is the sense in torturing a priest? If they are truly sincere in their belief, then they would rather die than betray that belief.'

Kreyssig brought his hands crashing together in a loud clap that echoed through the chamber. In response, a pair of burly Kaiserjaeger came marching into the room. Between them they half dragged, half carried a sobbing shape dressed in a sapphire gown. Lector Stefan recognised that gown and the long blonde hair that fell about the woman's face.

'Gudrun!' the priest shouted in a horrified wail.

'I thought you might appreciate a familiar face,' Kreyssig said. 'When my men removed you from Helmgart, I arranged to bring your daughter as well.' Snapping his fingers, Kreyssig motioned the Kaiserjaeger to take the woman to the bronze dragonhead.

'You wouldn't dare,' Lector Stefan cried. 'Whatever you think I have done, she is innocent. Touch her and you will bear the curse of our lord Sigmar!'

Kreyssig scowled at the bound priest. 'His Imperial Majesty once told me that the gods have only as much power over us as we permit them to have.' He looked at the grim stone walls around him. 'I have heard many prayers uttered in this room. None of them did any good.'

Lector Stefan watched in mounting agony as the Kaiser-jaeger shackled Gudrun to the horns of the dragon. An inarticulate moan escaped the gagged woman as she recoiled from the heat of the coals. 'Curse your black soul! Let my daughter go!'

'That,' Kreyssig hissed, 'is entirely the wrong attitude.'

Snapping his fingers again, he set the two Kaiserjaeger turning the wheels mounted at the base of the dragonhead. In response, the horns began to tilt, pulling the captive down towards the heated surface of the bronze head.

'Stop this, Kreyssig!' Lector Stefan thrashed in his chains. 'Mercy of Sigmar! Don't do this thing!'

'I've gone to a lot of trouble to bring you here,' Kreyssig said. 'Far too much to stop now. At its highest degree, torture is an art unto itself. Did you know that, your eminence?'

'Whatever you want! Whatever lies you want me to confess to! Just stop this!' the priest pleaded.

'Later, your eminence,' Kreyssig told him. 'There will be time enough to explain what I want from you later. For now, just enjoy the show.'

The ghastly demonstration continued for hours. Throughout the ordeal, Kreyssig was deaf to Lector Stefan's desperate entreaties. Even the reason for inflicting this horror wasn't explained. Between cries for mercy, appeals to Kreyssig's humanity, anguished offers to be tortured in his daughter's place, the priest called upon his god. If any prayer reached Sigmar's ears, no miracle manifested to spare the priest.

Kreyssig smiled at the sobbing Lector Stefan, listening to the agony of a shattered heart and a broken faith. Again he snapped his fingers. One of the torturers crouched beside the mutilated body, lifting the head by its blood-spattered hair.

Lector Stefan gasped in incredulous wonder. For the first time he gazed upon the countenance of Kreyssig's victim and it wasn't the face of his daughter! The build, the hair, even the gown had been similar enough to deceive him.

In the midst of Lector Stefan's exhilarated relief, Kreyssig clapped his hands together. While the first pair of Kaiserjaeger dragged the dead woman away, two more soldiers marched into the torture chamber. This time, there was no mistaking the identity of their captive.

'Now you know what will happen,' Kreyssig told Lector Stefan. 'You know every stroke, every cut, every stripe that your daughter will suffer.' He smiled coldly at the priest, seeing the abject defeat in his eyes. 'I will give you a moment to ask yourself what you would do to spare her such a fate.

'Then, I will tell you how you are going to serve your Emperor.'

Mordheim
Hexentag, 1113

The sound you hear is dripping blood. That thought brought a cruel twist to Baron Lothar von Diehl's face.

This is the start of Hexentag.

The necromancer's black cape billowed about his lanky body as he swept down the marble-floored aisle, his eyes darting from one wall to the other, assuring himself that the sacred icons flanking the hall had been properly defiled. Bound to a pillar, her body inverted so that the blood might flow more freely from her slashed throat, the last of the priestesses shuddered and died. Her once pristine robes were soaked crimson, the silver dove icon torn from her throat and in its stead the dead carcass of a carrion crow. Even in death, there was a look of shock in the woman's expression. She shouldn't have been surprised. In this age of plague and ruin, what place was more accustomed to death than the Temple of Shallya, the goddess of mercy and healing?

Lothar could feel those morbid energies, could almost taste them on the air. When he closed his eyes, he could see them as an after-image, a ghostly crackle that throbbed all around him. This was the power he sought, the power *De Arcanis Kadon* had promised him. The place, the hour and the sacrifice. All three had been brought together.

There was a dread potential within a defiled temple, an aethyric reverberation that turned a holy atmosphere back upon itself and could be exploited to magnify the powers of darkness. Lothar was disappointed that he'd never taken vows himself, for if the potential of a profaned temple was magnificent, it was nothing beside that of a heretical priest. Kadon had been a holy man, in his way, before he'd discovered the true path to power and domination. Before him, there had been Black Nagash, priest-king of Khemri until he created the forbidden art of necromancy.

Yes, it was a pity he'd never taken vows, but Lothar would overcome that impediment with determination and ruthlessness. Nothing would stand in his way, not convention, not tradition, not mercy. And not familial affections.

Stalking down the aisle, Lothar could feel the eyes of his men on him, fear in their gaze. Rogues and murderers, one and all, the scum of Mordheim recruited for him by Marko that he might seize the temple. These were the sort of villains who hadn't balked at slitting the throats of old priestesses or clubbing the brains from helpless plague victims lying on the pews. Yet even these men were offended by the outrage their employer now intended.

Even Lothar had balked at first, shying away from the ritual he had uncovered. Some timid element within himself had cringed away from this crime. It had taken weeks to silence that last foolish vestige of morality. Morality was the refuge of cowards, something to excuse their weakness. A part of him had tried to cling to such idiocy to the very last, but his determination, his need to *know* had prevailed at last. He had progressed as far as he could with *De Arcanis Kadon*; now he must be far more daring if he would unlock the rest of its secrets.

The sacrifice was bound to the altar, tied hand and foot in hair cut from corpses, clothed only in a shroud stripped from a suicide's grave. The alabaster statue of Shallya that stood behind the altar was draped in black, the head knocked from the stone shoulders to be replaced with a grinning skull. There was a symbol daubed upon the skull's forehead, but it was a thing so terrible even Lothar couldn't stare at it directly, only snatch the briefest of glimpses from the corner of his eye.

The killers were muttering nervously among themselves, shocked by what they had been told to do, frightened of what their master might do next. Standing at the foot of the altar, Marko alone understood the purpose behind it all. Perhaps that was why he looked even more anxious than the others.

Peasants! As though their thoughts and fears were of the slightest interest to a baron. Theirs were small minds and even smaller ambitions. To steal and drink and rut, perhaps at the very end try to make some atonement to the gods and redeem their pathetic souls. Such miserable desires placed them where they belonged – with the beasts!

Lothar would achieve far greater things. He had been born to a superior breed of man, endowed with a mentality that strove for something beyond crude urges and base lusts. Through his veins flowed the blood of thirty generations of von Diehls and the legacy of their great deeds. He had inherited the desire for knowledge, not as some abstract understanding or a means to some materialistic end, but as something precious in itself. If he could unlock the great secrets the gods had jealously kept from mankind, the nature of eternity, for example, then he would consider himself vindicated of all his failings. In that hour, he would be the greatest of the von Diehls.

Nothing would keep him from that achievement. Nothing.

The necromancer mounted the short flight of steps, holding a thin hand towards Marko as he passed the peasant. Marko hesitated for an instant, then with an uneasy expression, placed within Lothar's grasp the ancient bronze knife. Clutching the arthame in his bony hands, the baron approached the altar.

The sacrifice looked up at him, eyes wide with desperate entreaty. Perhaps, once, Lothar would have been weak enough to submit to that appeal, to allow the petty affiliations of family to stay his hand. But that time was long gone. There was only one thing he wanted from his mother now. One swift strike sent the arthame plunging into her breast. Lothar could feel her agony flow up the dagger. Savagely, he twisted the blade. He was already a patricide, after all. Why should he hesitate now?

It was the work of a few minutes before Lothar rose from the gore-splattered altar and lifted his prize to the grinning skull. The empty sockets seemed to stare down into the shivering heart, watching as the last drops of blood oozed from its veins.

The necromancer could feel the power gathering about him. When he closed his eyes, his vision was ablaze with the glow of aethyric vibrations. His skin crackled as magic pulsed around his body. Lothar's mind churned with weird images and phantom landscapes, ghostly voices hissed in his ears. It was an effort to subdue the force coursing through him, an effort only a spirit as focused and determined as his own could achieve.

When he closed his eyes, he could send his spirit hurtling down the long eternities, riding the deathly emanations through the ageless cycles of dissolution and decay. He could see the rise of kingdoms, the ebb and flow of empires. He saw the great necropolis of the desert, watched as megalithic pyramids rose from the sand of aeons, heard the intonations of priests more than half dead themselves as they made obeisance to the mummies of kings. He was there as the Black Pyramid reared up into the sky, a colossus spun from midnight and redolent with emanations of foulest sorcery and obscenity. He was witness to the Great Ritual, the apocalypse that heralded the eternal night and blotted out a mighty people in a single breath.

He smelt the rot of thousands, watched as a simulacrum of life crept back into withered flesh and ancient bone. In his vision, he saw the dead heaped in the streets, piled in palace and temple. He saw them stir, saw them stumble up onto fleshless feet, saw them stagger towards the pyramids and necropoli. An entire race, annihilated and resurrected in a single night. A people slaughtered and restored by a single dominating will and the magic discovered by that great and terrible intelligence.

The same magic that was the source of the necromancer's art.

As Lothar stirred from his dark epiphany, he was aware of fresh vibrations, new stirrings of the death energy in the temple. Shouts and the clash of swords pierced the chorus of ghosts in his ears. Turning from the altar, he saw the doors of the temple had been flung open. A mob of ragged peasants and a mixture of armoured men in the livery of the watch had forced their way into the building and were fighting with Marko's thugs in an effort to reach the sanctuary.

The necromancer inhaled the invigorating smell of spilled blood, then extended his hand. Flush with the power of his matricidal sacrifice, Lothar von Diehl fixed his mind upon a single purpose. Dropping his mother's heart to the floor, he withdrew *De Arcanis Kadon* from beneath his robes. Almost with a volition of its own, the book fell open at the spell he intended to evoke.

'We must flee, your lordship,' Marko was pleading. 'The mob will show no mercy, even to one of your rank!'

Lothar looked down at the little rogue. Marko had been very useful to him in the past, but that usefulness was at an end. Turning his gaze again to the aisle, he watched as the thugs were dragged down one by one, butchered beneath the avenging hands of the mob. Marko was right, they would do the same to him for what he had done here. That is, if they were given the chance.

Raising his voice in a cry that was almost reptilian in its slithering tone, Lothar intoned the dread names of ancient Nehekhara, drawing upon those primordial powers the liche-priests of Khemri had bound behind those names. The infernal energies that had been gathered about him were now loosed, transformed and harnessed into a conjuration far beyond what even Kadon might have achieved. The skull set atop the shoulders of Shallya's decapitated statue burst apart in fragments as the necromantic energies were channelled through it, leaving only the bloody symbol suspended in the air. The levitating symbol was ablaze with a fell light, like some charnel star. Eldritch rays shot forth from the hieroglyph, streaking through the temple with snaky, sinuous motions.

The mob at the doors fell silent as the atmosphere within the temple became frigid and dark magic streamed down from the altar. The surviving thugs cried out in abject horror as they saw those bolts of sorcery seep into the dead plague victims strewn about the pews. Where before there had been only dead clay, now there came a stirring, a hideous awakening. Emaciated hands clutched at the benches, smashed heads rose from pools of gore.

Screams filled the temple as both invaders and defenders watched the dead lurch into ghastly life. Dressed in foul rags, their bodies shrivelled from malnutrition, their skin blotched with the black sores of the plague, the zombies shambled out into the aisles. Upon the pillars, the bound corpses of the priestesses flopped and flailed, trying to slip their ropes to assault the living flesh so near at hand.

The obscene intonation of Lothar's spell intensified, the rays of pallid light emanating from the altar burst into a fresh frenzy, speeding through the temple, burning paths through walls and ceiling. The mob at the doors was in full flight now, Marko's thugs fleeing alongside them. The wounded were abandoned, left to shriek as the zombies converged upon them with clawed hands and clacking jaws. Deep within the sanctuary, Marko attacked one of the stained-glass windows in a frantic effort to escape. He had just brought a heavy chair smashing through a glazed panel when the first zombie reached him, bearing him down with its dead weight. The rogue flailed and struggled as the thing tore at him with its teeth. Before he could free himself, a dozen other zombies were crouched over him, pawing at him with dead fingers, relenting only when the man was reduced to a shapeless pile of meat.

Lothar was oblivious to his erstwhile accomplice's fate, focused entirely upon the mighty magic he had unleashed. All across Mordheim, tendrils of sorcery were snaking through the streets, seeking out the morbid harmonies of grave and tomb. Into the mausoleums of the Steinhardts and the crypts of the nobility and the unmarked plots of the destitute, the rays seeped. Coffins burst, sepulchres groaned open, marble doors gaped wide. From cemetery and plague pit, the dead of Mordheim were called forth, shuffling out into the streets on rotten feet and skeletal claws.

Not a living soul was abroad when Lothar von Diehl marched out from the defiled temple. The only things moving on the streets of the great city were undead – the cadaverous legion his sorcery had brought from their graves. He felt triumph swell inside him as he watched fleshless skeletons and decayed zombies troop past the steps of the temple. Centuries of Mordheim's dead, all enslaved to the will of one man!

He could feel the living inhabitants of the city cowering behind locked doors and peering out from closed shutters. Their terror was an almost palpable thing. It would be so easy to crush them, to kill them all. A single thought and he could turn his undead loose against them and make himself master of Mordheim!

Lothar shook his head, letting the childish impulse fade. What need had he to rule a city, to carve a kingdom from the rubble of plague-ridden Ostermark? Such desires were simply a temporal delusion, a simulacrum of true power. Clenching his hand tighter about the scaly binding of *De Arcanis Kadon*, he knew that real power was at his very fingertips, if he could but unlock its secrets.

Though it stung his noble pride, Lothar was forced to concede his own limitations. Even the powerful magic the sacrifice of his mother had unleashed was puny beside the knowledge yet locked within the unholy tome.

There was one, however, whose ability in the black arts might be great enough to decipher *De Arcanis Kadon*. Raising the dead of Mordheim had been no arrogant display of power, there had been purpose behind Lothar's feat. With an army of the undead at his command, he would march into Sylvania and confront Vanhal. The peasant necromancer would unlock the secrets for him. If he proved capable, Lothar might even deign to allow him to act as his apprentice afterwards.

Dreaming of the knowledge that would soon belong to him, Lothar von Diehl stepped out into the street, joining the walking dead as they began their long march south.

⭠ CHAPTER VII ⭢

Middenheim
Nachgeheim, 1118

Prince Mandred directed a desperate look in Beck's direction, but for once his bodyguard was proving inattentive. The phrase 'dereliction of duty' ran through his mind as he watched the knight ponderously scrutinising an old bit of Unberogen pottery that had been standing in the hallway. He promised there would be an accounting for Beck's desertion.

Though he doubted it would be nearly so onerous as the one he was enduring. Finding no help from Beck, Mandred turned back to listen as Sofia lashed at him with words that he was surprised a lady of her breeding even knew.

'Spending more time with that Reikland slattern!' Sofia raged. Mandred cringed at the tone, silently whispering a prayer to Ranald that she wasn't–

The prince ducked as a bronze candlestick went sailing past his ear. Though Ulric was his patron god, he reflected that he really should pay a little more consideration to Ranald, the fickle god of luck and good fortune.

'Flitting all over the city with that vagabond doxy hanging

off your arm!' The mate to the first candlestick came flying across the room. Mandred yelped as it careened off his thigh and went rolling under a wardrobe. Hopping on one leg, he tried to muster an ingratiating smile. So long as Sofia didn't employ formal address, he knew he could calm her down…

'What charms has that whore favoured you with? The same perversions she used to seduce Prince Sigdan? And you, marching along to join her collection of princes!' Venom crept into her tone as she added with a spiteful hiss, 'Your grace.'

Mandred hobbled forwards as quickly as he could manage, hurrying to keep the enraged woman from reaching a heavy looking crystal decanter. 'It isn't like that…' he protested.

Burggraefin Sofia von Degenfeld spun around with the speed of a viper, her dark tresses hanging across her face, her slender hands splayed into claws, each painted talon poised to wreak havoc. The breast of her gown trembled with the sharp, short breaths sneaking past her fury. With an angry shake of her head, she threw her long hair away from her face, exposing a pretty vision of forest-green eyes and delicately upturned nose. Even in her anger, Sofia's skin possessed a soft, milky colour, like polished alabaster on a crisp winter morning.

'Don't you dare lie to me, Mandred,' Sofia snarled at him. She flung her arms out in an exasperated flourish. 'The entire court is talking about it!' Her eyes narrowed to malicious pinpricks. 'Though I can understand, stumbling on her in such a condition. She must have kept herself very trim, a hag of her age!'

'Lady Mirella isn't that old…' Mandred started to say. He heard a snort of laughter from the hallway behind him. Even Beck knew it was absolutely the worst thing that could have rolled off his tongue. Yes, Mandred was certainly going to have a few words with his errant bodyguard. If he survived that long.

Sofia glanced over at the decanter, then turned a withering glare on the prince. 'So the dashing young knight is going to sample the favours of his damsel in distress?' she snapped. 'Oh, I understand quite well her point of view! Coming to Middenheim without a stitch to her name, the son of Graf Gunthar must present quite a catch. After she seduces you she must remember to light a candle for the Kineater!'

Mandred could feel his temper rising. 'Yes, I'm sure getting herself scalped and eaten by beastmen was all part of a grand plan to put herself in the Middenpalaz!'

'Well, it worked, didn't it!' Sofia accused.

The prince glared back at her. It was three years ago that he'd first become infatuated with the beautiful burggraefin. If not for the difference in their social class, they would have been married by now. Of course, as the son of the graf, such a decision was beyond his control. When he wed it would be a matter of politics, not mutual affection, one of the sacrifices a ruler made for his subjects. It was an understanding between them, the knowledge that whatever love and happiness they shared could never last. Perhaps it was that knowledge that had inflamed their passion and their devotion.

Except when she got like this, Mandred thought, listening to another harangue from his lover. When Sofia fell into one of these jealous fits, she was deaf to all reason. She couldn't be talked to, only endured until her temper cooled. Today, he decided, he didn't have the patience for such theatrics.

'I'm going,' the prince told her, turning on his heel and marching towards the hall.

'Where?' Sofia demanded. 'Back to your slut?'

'That's none of your concern,' Mandred answered without turning around. He reached the doorway just as the decanter came hurtling towards him. Nimbly, he swung the door to block the heavy missile, suppressing a slight shudder when he felt the crystal shatter against the panel. He stood behind the door for a moment, letting his own anger drain out of him. It wouldn't do for the Prince of Middenheim to go stalking through the streets of his city looking like he wanted to murder every person he saw.

Faintly, from behind the door, Mandred could hear Sofia crying. A twinge of remorse had his hand reaching for the handle, but the magnitude of her unreasoning rage stayed him. Let her sob, he decided. Maybe it would teach her to curb her temper in the future.

'Everything all right?' Beck asked, finally stepping away from that pot he'd found so interesting. Mandred shot his bodyguard a black look.

'For me,' the prince said, snatching his hat from Beck's fingers. 'I can think of an inattentive guard who won't be able to say the same.'

Sheepishly, Beck followed his master as Mandred stormed from the von Degenfeld manse. 'Where are we going, your grace?'

'To the Middenpalaz,' Mandred told him. He glanced back down the hall at the room he had so recently quit. 'I think I'll pay a call on Lady Mirella and inquire if she would like me to show her the rest of the city.'

'You should have seen it before the plague,' Mandred declared, waving his hand as he gestured towards the wide expanse of farmland that stretched away to the west. The tall stalks of wheat swayed in the mountain breeze. They were of a hardy strain that thrived in colder altitudes and possessed a magnificent coppery colour. Under the right conditions and with the right amount of sunlight shining down on them, the effect was like gazing upon a sea of gold. Indeed, the dwarfs who had first cultivated the strain had bestowed upon it a name that evoked gold somehow. Mandred's familiarity with Khazalid and dwarf customs was sketchy at best, so he couldn't remember the particulars of the name.

Beside him, one of her slender arms closed around his own, Lady Mirella gasped in admiration as a stronger gust of wind set the entire crop dancing. 'It is beautiful,' she declared.

Mandred shook his head. 'In a few weeks the crop will be harvested, then there'll only be empty black earth clear to the wall.' He sighed, regret catching in his voice. 'This used to be the Sudgarten and it was filled with trees and shrubs. Songbirds used to flock here and there would be rabbits and squirrels capering about in the brush. We even kept herds of deer and only hunted them on Ulric's holy days.'

The grip on Mandred's arm tightened in an expression of sympathy. 'Nothing lasts forever,' she said.

'Some things should,' Mandred answered, still seeing in his mind's eye the forest that had stood where only crops now grew. 'Those trees had been there since before the first Teutogen crawled up out of the tunnels and reached the top of the Ulricsberg. Losing them felt... felt like betraying a trust.'

'You kept your people alive through the winter,' Mirella reminded him. 'How strong would Middenheim be today if you didn't have the resources to provide for yourself?'

Mandred turned away from the Sudgarten, and led Mirella back into the narrow confines of the Westgate, the densely populated district at the extreme edge of the city. Many of the refugees who had been permitted to settle atop the Ulricsberg had built their homes here, simple buildings of timber and thatch. The Middenheimers had struggled to impose some degree of order on the confusion of shacks and huts, but had eventually abandoned the effort as causing more trouble than

it was worth. The resentment engendered by the programme
had left a lingering mark in the hearts of the settlers. Indeed,
it was considered inadvisable for any of the Middenheim
nobility to wander about the Westgate without an adequate
guard.

The prince, however, was the one exception to that rule. The
people here might resent the high-handed authority imposed
by Chamberlain von Vogelthal, but they also remembered
Prince Mandred's bold ride to save Warrenburg from the
beastmen. It was ironic that an event that had brought him
such severity from his father, an act that had cost the lives
of many brave men, a thing which he himself regarded with
guilt and regret, should have earned him a hero's welcome
among the settlers.

'Yes,' Mandred said as he and Mirella walked back along the
edge of the Westgate, 'we are strong. But what has been the
price for that strength?'

Mirella frowned at the dour note in her escort's voice. Tugging at his arm, she tried to divert his thoughts in another
direction. 'You said you would show me the dwarfs today,'
she reminded him. 'I am eager to see their temple. Do you
think they would allow us inside?'

The question gave Mandred pause. 'Don't they have dwarfs
in Altdorf?' he asked.

'Oh, certainly,' Mirella said, 'but not like here. Altdorf
doesn't have an entire city of them under its streets.'

Mandred smiled at the statement. 'Karak Grazhyakh isn't
exactly a city,' he corrected her. 'It's more of an outpost, one
of their strongholds.' He became pensive for a moment. 'To
be honest, I'm not really sure how many of them are down
there. Thane Hardin isn't one of my father's subjects, more
like a friendly neighbour.' He paused, picturing the dwarf's
perpetually grim visage. 'Well, a neighbour anyway. The

dwarfs pretty much keep to themselves and so long as they abide by my father's laws when their business brings them into Middenheim proper, we are content to leave them alone.'

'They do have some presence in the city, though?' Mirella asked.

'Oh, certainly,' Mandred replied. 'A few craftsmen who have set up shop here, though apparently they are either apprentices at their trade or dwarfs who couldn't match the standards of their guilds. Either way, no dwarf would have anything to do with the goods they turn out, though they're very impressive if you ask anyone else. Then there is the Dwarf Engineer's Guild. They have a big stone building down in the Wynd with a big walled-off yard attached to it. They do a lot of testing with some foul-smelling black dirt that explodes when exposed to fire. Probably too scary to play with down below, so they moved operations upstairs.'

'And the temple?' Mirella persisted.

'That's down in the Wynd too, if anything even bigger and more imposing than the Guildhall.' Mandred turned and stared in the direction of the building, though it was hidden behind the sprawl of the Southgate district which lay between the Westgate and the Wynd. 'The dwarfs call the Ulricsberg "Grungni's Tower", and even before the first stones were set down to build the Middenpalaz, they were at work building a temple to their god. I've never been inside it. I don't think any man ever has. The dwarfs are more tight-lipped about their religion than they are about anything else. But I can say that the exterior is absolutely magnificent. The entire face is marble, the stones set so close together that you'd think it was carved from a single block. Two immense statues stand guard before the entrance, one holding a chisel and the other an axe. I've seen dwarfs bow to them, so I think they must be connected to Grungni somehow. A giant door of ironwood banded in gold opens into the temple, and there's always a smell of oil and coal wafting out every time it is opened.'

'But you've never been inside?' Mirella's voice was soft, her mind caught up in the picture Mandred's words conjured.

The prince shook his head. 'No human has,' he repeated. 'I don't know if anyone has ever had the temerity to ask. I do know now isn't the time to start. The dwarfs have been even more touchy of late. They've become almost reclusive. Withdrawn. Something's bothering them, though I'm sure a human will be the last to know what it is,' he reflected.

For a moment, Mandred's troubled mood infected Mirella, her eyes taking on a pained expression. The prince found himself caught in those eyes, sensed the empathy between himself and this aristocrat from the south. He shifted uneasily as he thought of Sofia and the row they had had.

'Come along,' Mandred said, deliberately misinterpreting Mirella's attitude for one of disappointment. 'Perhaps I can't show you the temple of Grungni, but I can show you the temple of Ulric.' Before she could say anything, he was marching her towards the north.

'We're going to Ulricsmund,' Mandred called back to their tiny entourage. Beck and Brother Richter had kept their distance during the stroll past the Sudgarten, trying to remain discreetly unobtrusive yet near enough to be at hand if they were needed. At the prince's call, Beck went dashing up to join the two nobles. Richter hesitated, a tinge of worry pulling at the corners of his mouth. It was almost with reluctance that he followed after them.

A reluctance born of much more than simple religious differences.

* * *

Carroburg
Hexentag, 1115

The guests of Emperor Boris gathered around the immense ring of black drakwood. Legend held that the round table dated from the time of King Otwin and had been gifted to the Thuringian chief by the druids of Rhya. The chiefs of the tribe had held council around the great table, planning their wars against enemies human and inhuman. After the coming of Sigmar and the absorption of the Thuringians into his Empire, Otwin's table had been removed to the ancient fortalice over-looking the River Reik. Many towers and forts had been built and razed since that time, but the relic had endured, a valuable prize for whichever noble was given dominion over the Drakwald.

Sometimes the round table had been drawn out from storage for some state feast or in observance of some celebration, but by and large it had been left to the seclusion of its own vault deep within the castle. Wondrously carved, magnificently fashioned, there was nevertheless a blemish about the round table, a nameless sensation that provoked uneasiness in those who remained in its presence for too long. It was the residue of eldritch magic, the taint of druidic sacrifice and ceremony that had soaked into the drakwood.

For Boris's purposes, Otwin's table was perfect. The Emperor couldn't have asked for a better prop to adorn the festivities he had planned for Hexennacht. Hoary with age, steeped in legend and saturated with mysterious magics, the table would set the proper atmosphere. He was so pleased, in fact, that after von Metzgernstein told him about the table, he agreed to release the seneschal's son from the dungeons. The gesture, however, proved a bit empty. The boy, it seemed, had taken ill and expired the month before.

Thinking of this, Boris glanced along the table until he found the dejected-looking seneschal. The fellow was being quite irrational over the loss of the stripling. Von Metzgernstein was still young, he could certainly sire another one. Perhaps the Emperor would offer to have his marriage annulled. A saucy new wife might help the man put things in better perspective.

Smirking, the Emperor patted the hand of the young woman seated next to him. As always, Princess Erna trembled at his touch. He could imagine her skin crawling under his fingers, feeling a thrill of power that he could command such fear in the headstrong wench. His arrogance wouldn't consider the possibility that the reaction was one of disgust rather than fear.

'We think this should prove very entertaining,' Boris told her, wagging a finger at the uneasy dignitaries assembled around Otwin's table. The matriarch of one of the Empire's major temples, seven electors, dozens of landholders who between them controlled a third of all the agriculture in the Empire, even a few generals and the grand masters of several knightly orders were in attendance. Some of them had even brought along their wives; many more had the good sense to bring along their mistresses. Boris chuckled as he considered the power these men claimed to possess. For all their pretensions, when he'd invited them to seek safety behind the walls of Schloss Hohenbach, they'd come running.

Which of the wives should he seek to conquer next, Boris wondered? The months of isolation were becoming a bit tedious, even the performers he'd engaged were struggling to justify their continued presence with new entertainments. For all her charms, there were times when he tired of Erna's defiant streak. Toying with an ambitious baroness or a wanton countess made for a nice break in routine and never failed to bring a frown of disapproval from the papess Katrina Ochs.

Still, the high priestess wasn't the only member of their company with a set of strict, prudish morals. The Emperor gave Erna's hand a tight squeeze and leaned close to her. 'What do you think of von Kirchof's niece?' he asked, nodding his chin towards the dainty young lady seated opposite them. 'Pure as new snow, We understand,' Boris continued. 'Her uncle has been keeping a careful eye on her for Us. Can't have any of these blue-blooded degenerates plucking the rose.' He chuckled as he felt Erna's nails dig into his palm as her body became tense.

'Please,' she whispered. 'Leave her alone. Don't befoul her.'

Boris leaned back in his chair. 'What a treasonous thing to say,' he observed with feigned shock. 'As though she could aspire to any greater purpose in her miserable life than a dalliance with her Emperor.' He turned one of his mischievous grins on Erna. 'They can't all marry a dashing young peasant, after all.'

The Emperor relished the pain his remark inflicted, then sighed and released Erna's hand. It was too easy to provoke her on that subject, stripping it of any degree of satisfaction. Rising from his chair, Boris swept his Imperial gaze across the great hall. The usual furnishings had all been pushed to the walls to make room for Otwin's table, but a path had been left clear to the connecting passage leading to the tiny chapel of Sigmar. He glared impatiently at the doorway.

'What's keeping that conjurer?' Boris hissed. He turned his head, nodding to the two Kaiserknecht who attended him. The knights stalked away, their hands closed about the hilts of their swords. The Emperor watched as they walked down the passage. A few minutes later, the knights reappeared, dragging a tall, gaunt man between them. With a final shove, they deposited the man on the floor near Boris's seat.

'We are waiting,' the Emperor stated in a tone as cold as steel.

The man on the floor looked up at his sovereign with panic in his eyes. He was of indeterminate age, his long beard yet displaying streaks of black among its white, his face devoid of wrinkles beyond the crow's feet attending the corners of his eyes. He wore a long blue robe, its folds adorned with stars and moons and yet more obscure esoteric symbols. In his arms he held a battered teakwood casket.

'Forgive me, Your Imperial Majesty, I was readying my para-phernalia for the experiment,' the bearded man apologised. 'Under ideal conditions, it takes a month to prepare for…'

Emperor Boris waved away his warlock's excuses. 'We are already becoming bored with your magic. If We are expected to wait a month for your conjurations, We may reconsider your usefulness to the court.'

Karl-Maria Fleischauer shivered at the Emperor's threat. His studies of the black arts were well known, and only the protection of the Emperor kept the Inquisition of Verena and the witch-takers from burning him at the stake. To lose the Emperor's favour would be a death sentence for the warlock.

'Of course, of course,' Fleischauer whined. 'I shall make everything ready at once.' He stared at the teakwood casket, doubt flickering across his face. Quickly he composed himself and scrambled to the high-backed seat that had been reserved for him.

Boris watched with undisguised impatience as the warlock took his place and opened the casket after a few muttered incantations and passes of his hands. Fleischauer removed an orb of polished crystal from the box, winding a strip of gauzy cloth around it before setting it on the table before him. The cloth gave off an offensive odour, and Boris realised it had been cut from a funeral shroud. Again he sighed. It was so like a warlock to collect such noxious trappings.

Holding a séance had seemed like such a novel idea when it occurred to Boris two days before. It would be just the sort of scandalous entertainment that would appeal to sensibilities that had become jaded to more mundane diversions. Now, however, he was becoming annoyed by the warlock's foolish theatrics. He knew the peasant could work magic. It was time he stopped dawdling and got down to it.

After a few minutes, Fleischauer asked that the doors to the hall be closed and all the lights extinguished save two candles, one set to either side of the crystal ball. A murmur of anxiety passed through the guests assembled about Otwin's table as the room was plunged into darkness.

'All must link hands,' Fleischauer said. 'Those who would call upon the spirits of the dead must form an unbroken circle. Whatever you see, whatever you hear, do not break the circle!' His warning given, the warlock began to chant in a sibilant, slithery language. His body went rigid, his eyes rolling back until only the whites were visible.

A clammy cold filled the hall. The crystal ball began to glow with a spectral blue luminance.

Boris couldn't decide if the moan preceded the wispy, vaporous spectre or if the apparition formed before the sound. Certainly one impressed itself upon him before the other. The moan was a ragged, grisly noise, like a corpse being dragged across gravel. The ethereal image was no less uncomfortable, reminding the Emperor of the grave cloth Fleischauer had wrapped about his crystal ball.

Gradually, both the moaning sound and the apparition began to change, becoming somehow more distinct. Even with this impression of change, when the final resolution came, it was shockingly abrupt. The moan became the dry, brittle voice of a woman. The nebulous spectre became the semblance of a plump rural duchess.

'Artur! Artur, you murderous cur!' the ghost wailed, spinning around where she hovered a few inches above the table until she faced the trembling ruler of Nuln. The apparition raised a phantom finger and jabbed it at Count Artur. 'I wait for you in the gardens of Morr, assassin! Adulterer!'

Boris chuckled as he listened to the ghost's harangue. It seemed Count Artur had removed his domineering first wife through the expedient of poison, disguising it to look as though she'd succumbed to the plague. A delicious bit of scandal that the woman's wealthy relations would be interested to learn. The Emperor was annoyed that he hadn't had the foresight to have his scribe attend the séance.

After a time, Count Artur's wife faded away, her voice evaporating back into the speechless moan, her form melting into the formless wisp. Soon another spirit manifested itself through the medium, another voice rising from the moan, another figure emerging from the wisp. Brothers, sisters, sons and daughters, friends and servants, many were the ghosts evoked by Fleischauer's magic. Many were the dark secrets the wraiths related. Boris chuckled at each embarrassing revelation, promising himself he would make good use of all he learned when he was back in Altdorf. Indeed, he'd never imagined magic could be so useful. If Kreyssig wasn't such a capable and dangerous man, he might suggest he add sorcery to his intelligence network. Handing such a tool to such a man wouldn't be wise, however. Perhaps if he were removed and a more pliable commander put in his place...

Distracted by his plotting, Boris didn't see the wisp form itself into the barbarous figure of Baron Thornig, Erna's father. He didn't hear much of what the ghost had to say to his daughter. What little he did hear made him curse his distraction.

'Endure,' Thornig moaned. 'The night will end. The dawn will come. Wickedness and corruption will be purged from the Empire. He who loves you best will return. He will return what was stolen. Together you will have justice. Endure, and know you suffer so that Light may shine once more.'

The Emperor tightened his hold on Erna's hand as the spectre of her father started to fade. Viciously, he twisted her arm, provoking a gasp of pain. 'What did he say?' Boris growled. 'What did that hell-damned traitor say!'

Lost in his anger, Boris was again inattentive of the spirits. He didn't see the wisp reform. Only when a familiar voice called to him did the Emperor turn away from Erna. He quivered as he found himself staring into the mournful countenance of his own father, the man who had been Emperor Ludwig II.

'Woe, my son,' the shade wailed. 'You bring ruin to the House of Hohenbach.'

Emperor Boris cringed away from the apparition. Frantically, he broke the hold of those seated to either side of him and leaped away from his chair. Almost at once, the ghostly image winked out and the hall was plunged into darkness as the candles sputtered. Screams of alarm filled the darkness until servants threw open the doors and brought more candles.

'I think we've had enough amusement for one night,' Boris declared, sounding anything but amused. His sardonic composure rattled, he hastened from the hall without so much as a glance at the prostrate form of his warlock. The abrupt disruption of the séance had sent the aethyric energies snapping back into Fleischauer's body, breaking his trance and leaving him more dead than alive.

Princess Erna glanced from the stunned warlock to the fleeing Emperor, unsettled by her own ordeal. Against her will, she felt sympathy for Boris. Where her own father had returned to bestow words of hope, his had offered only condemnation.

━━◄ CHAPTER VIII ►━━

Altdorf
Nachgeheim, 1114

The chambers of the Holy Synod of Sigmar had been unused since the completion of the Great Cathedral some hundred years ago. It had only been the death of Grand Theogonist Uthorsson and the transplantation of the Holy Seat from Nuln to Altdorf that brought the vast hall of marble and alabaster into prominence. For years, the chambers had been made ready, prepared for the ecumenical council of theologians, priests and augurs who would debate the election of a new Grand Theogonist.

Plague had kept the Holy Synod empty, the fear of the strange death that was laying waste to the Empire. To gather the leadership of the Temple in one place, to expose them all to the threat of dissolution, was something the Sigmarite elders would not countenance. Since the founding of the man-god's cult by Johann Helsturm over a thousand years ago, never had the prospect of annihilation been more pronounced. An orc invasion, religious warfare with one of the other temples, natural and arcane catastrophe, these were things that might wipe out a city or devastate a province, but never were they so widespread as to threaten the whole of the Empire. The Black Plague had spread its pestilential grip into every corner of the land. Nowhere was safe. Like the locust, it might seem to recede only to bide its time and explode afresh with renewed vigour. This plague had neither pattern nor rhyme. It was unpredictable. It was a thing of Chaos.

Seeing the hand of the First Enemy in the Black Plague, the Sigmarite elders had deferred the election of a leader until such time as it was considered safe to convene in sacred council. To do otherwise, they felt certain, would be to tempt the profane Ruinous Powers into exerting their hideous strength and wiping out the very foundation of the Temple. They must wait, wait until the plague began to abate and the power of Chaos waned once more.

Waiting, however, was an option that was no longer available to them.

It was a small group that was gathered in the Holy Synod, a feeble echo of the great congregation for which the vast hall had been built. The rows of cherrywood pews, rising in tiers and surrounding the central nave, were empty. The stained-glass windows depicting Sigmar's victories over beast, monster and man stared down upon only a tiny clutch of robed figures gathered before the jade altar in the sanctuary at the front of the chamber. Their voices echoed through the deserted room.

'What you ask is impossible.' The words were spoken in a carefully measured tone, a voice struggling to smother the intense emotion stirring in the heart of the speaker. Arch-Lector von Reisarch was the Consultator of the Sacred Rites, successor to Arch-Lector Hartwich and, with the death of Grand Theogonist Thorgrad, the highest-ranking priest in the whole of Altdorf. Known as a jovial father of the faith, he was held with almost paternal fondness by the Sigmarites of Altdorf, a warm and friendly face to a religion that could at times be cold and distant.

It was a very different expression von Reisarch wore now from that jocular visage known to his diocese. The priest's face was severe, his jaw set in defiance, his eyes smouldering with unspoken rage. The exuberant old man who wasn't above slipping a jest about the foibles of priesthood into a sermon was gone, subsumed beneath the angered patriarch who glared at the Imperial personage who had intruded upon the sanctity of the Holy Synod.

Adolf Kreyssig's expression was no less severe. 'I ask nothing,' he said. 'I am the Protector of the Empire, invested with the authority of the Emperor... Authority bestowed upon him by immortal Sigmar himself.'

'Secular authority,' von Reisarch countered. 'The power of the Emperor is secular, not spiritual. You have no jurisdiction over the politics of the Temple.'

Kreyssig glanced across at the vicar-general and the other priests attending von Reisarch. 'You must be very important now, your beatitude. The Arch-Lector of Altdorf, once the hierophant of all Sigmarites in the Imperial capital, at least until Grand Theogonist Thorgrad relocated the Holy Seat. Then you were simply reduced to another functionary, a number-two man. How you must have missed the taste of power! The second son of an old and privileged estate. No inheritance from his family, so he must seek his fortune by taking up holy vestments.'

'You dare,' von Reisarch gasped. 'You dare utter such blasphemies in this sacred place!'

'I would dare anything to preserve the Empire,' Kreyssig retorted. He pointed to the great stone hammer suspended above the shrine. The symbol was more than simply that of

Sigmar as god, but of Sigmar as uniter of mankind.

'I am versed in the symbolism of faith,' von Reisarch growled, his voice like acid.

'But do you understand it?' Kreyssig challenged. 'Your refusal to convene the Holy Synod and elect a new Grand Theogonist threatens the unity of the Empire. The people look to the Temple of Sigmar for hope and guidance, to assure them that despite the plague and unrest there is stability. Faith in Sigmar is the bedrock of the Empire, the rope which binds the people together and endows them with a sense of unity. When the Temple is seen to be strong, the spirit of the people is strong. When the Temple is seen to be weak, the people lose faith. Their hearts stray into strange places.'

'You are a fine one to speak of faith,' von Reisarch accused. 'It was on your orders that Arch-Lector Hartwich was arrested and would have been executed had he not fallen victim to the plague. It was through your scheming that the Bread Massacre brought bloodshed overflowing in the streets. It was your barbarous murder of Grand Master von Schomberg that pushed men like Prince Sigdan into revolt. Tell me, who has done more to break the spirit of Altdorf?'

'I can tell you who will restore that spirit, and how,' Kreyssig said. He removed a folded proclamation from his tunic, setting it down on the altar. 'You will convene the ecumenical council. You will elect Lector Stefan Schoppe as Grand Theogonist.'

Von Reisarch's eyes blazed. 'You not only demand the impossible, but you add the sacrilege of dictating the decision of Holy Sigmar!' The other priests with the arch-lector began to whisper angrily among themselves, horrified by Kreyssig's arrogant blasphemy.

'I demand what is necessary to keep the Empire intact,'

Kreyssig stated. 'As Protector, that is my duty. The people need a strong Temple to unite them. The Temple needs a Grand Theogonist to make it strong.'

The arch-lector removed the scroll from the altar, casting it to the floor with a contemptuous gesture. 'This Temple is answerable to the will of Sigmar, not the machinations of a power-mad peasant. There will be no ecumenical council!'

Kreyssig's eyes blazed as he stared down at the discarded scroll. 'There will be an ecumenical council,' he said, his voice dropping to a venomous, threatening tone. 'Do not make the mistake of dismissing the "machinations of a power-mad peasant". I have been most thorough. My Kaiserjaeger have pursued inquiries in many places. I am quite aware of the Temple's dirty little secrets, of what happened that night Grand Theogonist Uthorsson burned with the cathedral in Nuln. Tell me, how do you think the people would react if they learned Uthorsson was a servant of the Ruinous Powers, or that Thorgrad was a murderer?'

Von Reisarch's face turned as pale as his white robes. The priest wavered, his attendants rushing forwards to support him before he could fall.

'They might think the Sigmarite clergy was responsible for bringing the Black Plague upon us,' Kreyssig continued. 'They might rise up, tear this place down with their bare hands. Betrayal can make even the most loyal dog turn on its master. Then there are the other temples to consider. The wolf-priests of Ulric would be quite happy to see the Sigmarite faith abolished and, of course, the inquisitors of Verena are most zealous in their persecution of Chaos.'

The arch-lector leaned against the altar, vitality seeming to visibly drain from his body. 'It will take time to bring the other arch-lectors to Altdorf,' he said. 'Three have already been claimed by the plague. It will take months for the others to make the journey.'

'Then you will do without them,' Kreyssig said. 'Issue a decree reducing their authority, subsuming them to the Altdorf temple. If you present it as divine will necessitated by the crisis threatening the faith, I think you can make them understand. A little power is better than no power, after all.'

Kreyssig nodded his head at the scroll lying on the floor. 'You seem to have dropped my proclamation, your eminence.' He darted a withering glare at the vicar-general as the cleric bent to retrieve the scroll. 'I want that pious blue-blood to get it,' he growled.

Chastened by the threat hanging over his head, the archlector knelt on the floor and picked up the proclamation. 'Sigmar will not forgive this,' he warned.

'The gods are only as powerful as the Emperor allows them to be,' Kreyssig sneered. 'You would do well to remember that, von Reisarch.'

'Is that a lesson you have already taught Lector Schoppe?'

Kreyssig smiled. 'He understands something you have yet to learn. You will either be my ally, or you will be my victim. It took some persuasion, but his holiness made the right choice in the end.'

The distant tolling of temple bells sounded faintly in the distance as Adolf Kreyssig marched through the empty halls of the Imperial Palace. At such a late hour, there were few functionaries about; even the overworked clerks under Lord Ratimir had slipped away to steal a few hours of rest before poring over the records of tax revenue from the eastern provinces. Emperor Boris had imposed a fine against the Grand Duke of Stirland for the reduction in grain and timber tariffs being collected in the province. Excuses about some necromancer running amok in Sylvania had only made the Emperor more determined to see the fees collected. Allow

Stirland an indulgence and every warherd raid or goblin mischief would have the other counts begging for a reduction in their Imperial tithe.

A pair of armoured Kaiserjaeger flanked the doorway leading into Kreyssig's chambers. Regarded as peasant rabble, *Dienstleute* by the nobles of the court, the Protector of the Empire preferred them to the more prestigious and esteemed Kaiserknecht and other knights at his disposal. It wasn't so long ago that the Reiksknecht had been disbanded and outlawed. There was no knowing how many friends the outlaws might still have among the knights of the other orders. No, it was far safer to look to his own men to safeguard him.

Kreyssig gave a brief nod by way of acknowledging the stiff military salute his guards gave him as he approached. Arguing with that pious ass von Reisarch had worn him out. As satisfying as it had been to sink the cleric's superiority, it had tested Kreyssig's restraint to the utmost. He'd dearly have liked to kill the priest then and there, but without the archlector's subjugation, he knew he could never proceed with his plans.

'Commander!' Fuerst beamed as Kreyssig stepped into the lavishly appointed anteroom that separated his bedchamber from the hall. The servant rushed forwards to relieve his master of hat and gloves. Kreyssig shrugged out of his cloak as Fuerst ministered to him.

'It has been a trying day,' he told Fuerst. His face contorted in an expression of disgust as he considered how even with the threat of ruinous scandal hanging over his cult, von Reisarch had imposed conditions and terms upon his capitulation. The end result would be the same, but von Reisarch wanted these concessions so that he and his god might save face. It was a contemptible display of hypocrisy.

'I am going to retire early,' Kreyssig said, waving his servant

away. Fuerst bowed out, retreating to the little door concealed in the side panelling that led to his own quarters. All
of the Imperial apartments were similarly appointed, doors
disguised in the panelling to provide ingress for wardrooms,
servants' quarters and other such unseemly places whose
presence was convenient but whose existence was best unob-
served and unobtrusive.

Kreyssig withdrew into his chamber, sinking into sleep
almost as soon as he lay down in the enormous bed.

It was still dark when he was awakened. Groggily, Kreyssig
stared up at the velvet canopy, a dim blur in the shadowy
murk of the room. The temptation to retreat back into slumber was almost irresistible, but even in his semi-coherent state
his mind was vexed. What was it that had disturbed him?

The smell. There was a foul, animal stink in the room. That
was what had disturbed him.

It was a smell that wasn't unknown to Kreyssig. Furtively,
he slipped his hand beneath his pillow, reaching for the dagger he kept there. Careful as he was, his action still evoked a
warning hiss from the darkness.

Turning over in the bed, Kreyssig could make out a set of
beady red eyes glistening in the darkness. The creature those
eyes belonged to was only a dark outline, a black shadow
behind the murk. He wasn't sure which was worse, seeing the
mutant or not seeing it.

'I did not send for you,' Kreyssig snarled at the shadow.
'This is the Imperial Palace. You don't belong here.'

The creature chittered, a sound that was unsettlingly like
laughter. 'Kreyssig-man want-need talk-talk,' the mutant
hissed. 'Friends of Kreyssig-man listen when he talk-talk with
god-man. Friends not like-like.'

Kreyssig snorted with contempt at the creature's expression of displeasure. Was this sewer-crawling vermin actually

trying to dictate terms to him? Angrily and without care for the mutant's warning, he fished the dagger out from under his pillow.

'I don't care what you like and what you don't,' Kreyssig declared. 'You should feel fortunate I tolerate you mutants to exist at all. My dealings with the Temple of Sigmar are my own affair. I employ you to spy for me, not on me!'

The mutant growled at him from the darkness, Kreyssig had the impression of fangs gnashing angrily. 'Kreyssig-man promise much-much,' the creature said. 'Gift-give grain. Want-need more.'

Kreyssig fingered the hilt of his dagger, his skin crawling at the close proximity of the ratman in his chambers. He would never have given the slinking little beasts credit for such audacity as to violate the Imperial Palace itself. Now the loathsome mutants were compounding audacity with impudence. 'You've already been given grain for your people,' Kreyssig said. 'Two storehouses. Enough to feed all of Altdorf for the winter.'

'Want-need more,' the mutant repeated its demand.

A horrible thought came to Kreyssig as he listened to that monstrous, insolent hiss. Enough grain to feed Altdorf for three months, yet these mutants already needed more. If their numbers were as few as he'd been led to believe... But could he believe? How many of the verminous things were actually down there?

Kreyssig shifted to the far side of the bed, setting his feet on the floor and taking a firm grip on one of his pillows with an idea to exploit it as a makeshift shield. 'Why do you need more grain?' he demanded.

The rat-mutant chittered again. When it spoke, its voice was more measured, each word unhurried and distinct. 'Need more grain. If Kreyssig-man will not give, then we will take.

Need god-priest to stay dead. If Kreyssig-man makes new god-priest, then we will kill.'

'Will you?' Kreyssig cried, lunging forwards, his dagger flashing at the darkness. The blade slashed only shadows. The red eyes were gone, vanished as though they had been no more than a phantom. Before Kreyssig could consider where the mutant had retreated, light was streaming into the room from the open doorway. He spun around, but nothing more menacing than Fuerst greeted his gaze.

'I heard you cry out, commander,' Fuerst said, a cudgel clutched in one hand, a candle in the other.

Kreyssig waved Fuerst inside, motioning for him to raise the candle high and illuminate as much of the room as he could. The two of them made a thorough search, but there was nothing to find. Kreyssig's visitor had evaporated into the night.

'You can go to sleep,' Kreyssig told Fuerst. When his concerned servant lingered, he made the suggestion an order.

Despite the disturbing visitation, Kreyssig wanted to be alone. He wanted time to think, to consider his dealings with the mutants, to balance his experiences with them against the dim fables of childhood. He wasn't so sure now if his subhuman spies really were mutants. At least human mutants. The old legends spoke of other things, other things shaped like rats that could walk and talk and think like men.

The cold clutch of fear closed around Kreyssig's heart, that organ that so many of his victims had described as black and immovable. Now it was a sick, frightened thing, a thing plagued with doubt and foreboding.

What if they truly were what Kreyssig now feared they might be? Not mere mutants or monsters, but the ghastly Underfolk themselves!

Again he thought of those storehouses. He would have the Kaiserjaeger open them tomorrow, check to see how much the mutants had already taken. It was one way to estimate their numbers.

Because Kreyssig was afraid that there might be more ratmen under Altdorf than he would find in his darkest nightmares.

Sylvania
Nachexen, 1113

The satisfying stink of fear filled Seerlord Skrittar's nose as he strode down the muddy lane. There was a panoply of other delectable scents in the air. The smell of grain and dried meat, cheese and bread. The man-things of this village had been quite industrious. The formidable palisade they'd erected around their village was a clear indication of how much they intended to keep the fruits of that industry. They'd been better armed than most Sylvanian settlements too, and better prepared to fight.

None of which had, of course, availed them in the end. It never ceased to amuse Skrittar how much faith humans put into walls to protect them. It was only a matter of hours for Clan Fester's skavenslaves to burrow under those walls and bring them crashing down. Before the man-things were fully aware of what was happening to them, the ratmen were upon them, cutting down those who tried to defy them. With the humans' enemies already inside their defences, the struggle was exactly the way Skrittar preferred – brief and one-sided.

Those man-things that had displayed the good sense to cower before the skaven had been spared, at least for a time. It wasn't just the satisfying smell of their fear, but simply a matter of good policy. Man-thing slaves were generally stronger than their skaven counterparts, and when they eventually did wear out they made for much better eating.

A little trickle of drool fell from Skrittar's fangs as he considered the various ways man-meat could be prepared. He'd have Manglrr's sword-rats fetch him a nice young human for dinner. The young ones were so much more tender, and their flesh seemed to absorb spices much more readily than that of older specimens.

Turning his attention to the clanrats swarming through the streets, Skrittar lashed his tail in annoyance. Miserable tick-sucking wretches! If they could think past their bellies, then they might be worth something! These constant diversions to gather provisions were becoming intolerable. They were distracting them from their real purpose: collecting the warpstone. He hadn't expended so much magic, arranged the martyrdom of twenty-four of his most powerful grey seers, simply so Clan Fester could traipse about Sylvania glutting their insatiable appetite!

Irritably, Skrittar struck a passing clanrat with his staff, knocking the ratman into the mud. Before he could rise, the seerlord was snatching the radishes from the skaven's paws. Spinning about, the clanrat stopped short of baring his fangs when he saw who had assaulted him. Squeaking with fright, he scurried off, leaving Skrittar to gnaw at the purloined food.

As he digested the radishes, Skrittar became aware of a change in the air. There was a new tang to it, a rotten stink of spoiled meat and crawling worms. It was not unlike the reek the skaven had found clinging to those humans who died from the Black Plague, but this was much stronger. The grey seer was just starting to wonder if some of Manglrr's over-eager vermin had excavated a man-thing bury-hole when a new smell crept into the air.

It was the smell of fear, but far thicker and pungent than that exuded by humans. Skrittar knew that smell quite well, might even have admitted to producing it himself if such an admission wouldn't be a sign of weakness. The reek was that of skaven musk, spurted from their glands in times of agitation. Why Manglrr's mangy minions were frightened now, when the village was already subdued, was an absurdity the grey seer couldn't understand.

'Mighty-great seerlord!' a shivering voice yelped. Skrittar caught the scent of Manglrr Baneburrow long before he saw the warlord. To smell one of the Council of Thirteen in such agitation brought a contemptuous flicker to his whiskers. Truly it could never have been the Horned One's intention that such weak-livered mice should have a share in ruling the Under-Empire! Such conniving cowards were fit only for exploitation by their more intelligent peers. It was the main reason Skrittar had chosen Clan Fester to assist him in recovering the warpstone.

Manglrr's posture was hunched and cowed when he came scurrying up to Skrittar, the burly stormvermin accompanying him displaying a similarly meek and abased attitude. The seerlord was wary of accepting such appearances, but a whiff of their scent was good indication that their despair might be genuine. There was no question that the frightened attitude of their warlord had sent a thrill of panic sweeping through the ratmen ransacking the village.

'Honoured mage-rat, Supreme Prophet of the Horned One!' Manglrr whined, almost touching his nose to the dirt as he bowed before Skrittar. Such grovelling from one of the Grey Lords filled Skrittar with disgust... and not a little anxiety.

'Speak-squeak!' Skrittar demanded, wondering what catastrophe the warlord was about to relate. If Warmonger Vecteek had discovered this expedition, the whole of Clan Rictus might even now be marching after them! If that was the case, Skrittar would have to start thinking about how he could place all the blame on Manglrr's tail.

'Man-things!' Manglrr shuddered, licking a carved toe-bone he wore about his neck as he gave voice to his fear. 'Many-many man-things marching to village-nest! Kill-slay all-all try to stop!'

In his terror, Manglrr was slurring his words, letting them trip over each other like any common ratman. Skrittar forced his own voice to be more controlled. 'Man-things?' he sneered. 'You squeak like a runt dragged from its mother's teat! Get your craven sword-rats over there and kill-slay! Must Mighty Skrittar do everything for you?'

Manglrr's fangs clattered and he directed a look over his shoulder. The panic that had set in was definitely spreading now, augmented by the ragged, bloodied skaven streaming back into the village from the outlying fields. It didn't matter to the ratmen that they hadn't seen for themselves what had caused their warlord's fright. The musk of fear alone was enough to drive them into unreasoning flight.

'Man-things,' Manglrr repeated, one claw clinging desperately to the hem of Skrittar's robe. 'Won't die-dead when sword-rats attack! Won't stop-die! Slash-stab much-much, but man-things stand-live!'

Skrittar glared at his fellow Grey Lord. It was so tempting to stretch forth his hand, conjure up a spell and burn the idiot's head from his shoulders. What sort of insipid babble was he spewing? Man-things that his sword-rats wouldn't fight because when they did fight, the humans just shrugged off their blows? It was too absurd to be believed. Even an orc respected a decent stab to the gut or a nasty slash to the back of the head, and there were few things tougher to convince to stay dead than an orc.

'Fool-meat!' Skrittar snarled, snatching his robe from Manglrr's paws. 'There are no dead-things! It is a human trick.

They want to take back village-nest!' A kick from the seer-lord's foot sent Manglrr stumbling back. Skrittar directed a warning look at the warlord, but he just sat on his haunches staring at the grey seer with frightened eyes. The seerlord gnashed his fangs in annoyance. 'I'll see-scent for myself,' he growled, motioning with his claws for two of Manglrr's stormvermin to lift him onto the roof of a nearby hut. Fortunately, they weren't so subdued by fear that they forgot the advisability of obeying a grey seer.

As his paws found purchase on the thatch roof, Skrittar cast his gaze down into the streets. The panic Manglrr had incited was everywhere – he could even see skaven discarding their plunder as they fled! The seerlord cast a sideways look at the warlord below, wondering who would replace Manglrr should he suffer an accident. Certainly it couldn't be a bigger fool!

A twinge of alarm crept into Skrittar's mind as he turned towards the north, the direction the bedraggled war-rats had been streaming from. From his position, he had a good view of the fields beyond the village. The tall stalks of wheat were swaying violently, and it soon became apparent that what was disturbing them wasn't foraging skaven. Through gaps in the crop, Skrittar could see human shapes, shapes that moved in a disturbing, awkward fashion.

Squeals of terror from the opposite end of the village set Skrittar's heart pounding even faster. Reluctantly, he cast his enhanced senses to the south, dreading what he might find. His projected gaze raced above streets teeming with fright-ened ratmen, swept out into the pastures and fallow fields to the south. There, ranked across the landscape, was an unbro-ken line of rotting humans. Silently, they marched towards the village; together with the fiends in the fields they moved to close a ring that would see the skaven trapped at its centre!

Skrittar thumbed a nugget of warpstone into his paw, feeling the reassuring burn of its energies sizzle against his fur. His mind raced, pondering the possibilities. He didn't like the idea of pitting his magic against so many foes, and he wasn't keen to trust his safety to the dubious valour of Clan Fester. They didn't seem aware of his importance and their own expendability. If it wasn't for the warpstone, he'd use his magic to get away and leave the vermin to fare as they would. The loss of the warpstone, however, was too awful to countenance. Somehow, Skrittar had to salvage the situation.

The clash of steel diverted Skrittar's attention back to the north. He focused his gaze on the road beyond the fields, surprised to see a great host of humans marching down the path. At first he suspected they were simply reinforcements for the ones already ringing the village, but then he noticed that the newcomers were assaulting the creatures forming the cordon. Immediately Skrittar likened the action to that of his own factious race: two rival clans of man-things were struggling for dominance! In the resultant confusion, there would be opportunity for escape!

Taking a moment to preen his whiskers and assure himself that his scent was relaxed, Skrittar dropped back into the street. With an imperious bark, he ordered Manglrr to his feet. 'Fetch-gather Fester-rats,' Skrittar snarled. 'Through me, the Horned One has set my enemies against one another! My magic has made the dead-things fight. While they kill, we will return to the tunnels with my warpstone!'

Manglrr looked dubiously at Skrittar, but some of his suspicion fled when he heard excited squeaks passing back down the street. The cordon was breaking apart. The man-things were fighting each other!

'Back-back to tunnels!' Manglrr chittered, drawing his

sword and waving it overhead to emphasise his command. 'Back-back to Rotten-Hole!'

Skrittar caught Manglrr by the scruff of the neck before the warlord could make any more bold commands. 'We're not going back to your burrow!' the seerlord snarled, baring his fangs. 'You've barely gathered any warpstone! There's too much still out there. I'm not leaving it behind!'

The rasp of blades being drawn reminded Skrittar that he was threatening the warlord of a clan he happened to be surrounded by. A clan so frightened that they might even forget all the curses they'd acquire if they killed a grey seer. Carefully, he released Manglrr, giving the warlord's neck an affectionate pat for good measure.

'I'll get more help,' Skrittar promised. 'More sword-rats to kill-slay man-things!'

Manglrr brought his sword flashing down, letting the blade slice the space between himself and the seerlord. 'Bring-fetch plague monks!' he demanded. 'Use Black Plague to kill-slay stink-things!'

The seerlord felt his fangs grind as he heard the demand. Involve Clan Pestilens? Let those heretics take a share in the treasure that rightfully belonged to him? It was obscene! Profane! He wouldn't do it!

Of course, without Clan Fester, he'd need to get another clan to help him. The more clans who learned about the warpstone, the more likely the secret was to get out. Once the story spread, half the Under-Empire would be swarming over Sylvania stealing his treasure. No, he had to keep Clan Fester, whatever it took to appease them and allay their fears.

'Yes-yes,' Skrittar hissed through clenched fangs. It was unspeakable that this ten-flea warlord would have more faith in the heretical concoctions of Clan Pestilens than the divine protection of the Horned Rat. 'We will use the Black Plague to make stink-things die. I will get-fetch plague monks to help us.'

Manglrr bobbed his head happily. Snarling orders to his stormvermin, he joined the general exodus of skaven streaming from the village. Seerlord Skrittar stalked after him, already wondering how he would keep his promise while at the same time turning it to his advantage.

From atop his palanquin, Vanhal supervised the tightening of the noose around the village of Bistra. At his command, the skeletons and zombies began their slow march towards the settlement, cutting down the strange creatures foraging in the fields. They were vile, abominable things, upright, man-sized rats that wore crude armour in outrageous mockery of humanity. Never had he imagined such unclean things could walk the land. Exterminating them was more than simply expedient; it felt almost ordained, as though some ancient wrong were being set right with each of the vermin his undead slew.

Of all the terrors he had seen besetting the people of Sylvania, from plague to tyranny to starvation, this was the most loathsome. To be preyed upon by disease and famine or even the soldiers of the von Draks was awful enough, but to be preyed upon by humanoid rats was a perverse abomination. Vanhal's magic would spare the Sylvanians such horror and humiliation. Human prey and verminous scavenger alike would be struck down by the cleansing blades of his army.

While his undead troops converged upon Bistra, a new disturbance drew Vanhal's attention. Through his witchsight, he could see the black cloud of sorcery drawing down from the north. Before the first skeleton marched into sight, he knew the nature of what was coming. Even as mortal kings must struggle over their domains, so his arcane power had drawn a rival to contest his might.

Dourly, Vanhal waited while the rival force marched ever closer. The other necromancer possessed some skill; the spells that had cloaked his army's advance for so long proved that even more than the immense size of that army. There were tens of thousands of zombies and skeletons in that host, far beyond the capability of a mere dabbler in the black arts.

In eerie silence, the undead troops struck Vanhal's battle line. Rusted swords chopped down into desiccated flesh, corroded bludgeons smashed rotten skulls. The intruders stormed across the outer ring of Vanhal's army. It was a weird, ghostly fight, devoid of blood and screams. No cries for mercy or shouts of triumph, only the march of bony feet and the cleaving of decayed flesh. Deathless, fearless, the two undead hosts collided.

With reluctance, Vanhal drew his forces away from Bistra to confront this new foe. He watched as the intruders continued their violent advance, biding his time as he studied the tactics of his enemy and attempted to judge the extent of his magic. There was a callousness and arrogance in what he saw, an almost sneering contempt that bespoke either supreme ability or colossal over-confidence.

At last, as the intruders were storming across the fields, Vanhal found what he had been waiting for. In the midst of the horde was a great black coach drawn by skeletal steeds. Seated within the coach, wrapped within the folds of a black cape, was his rival. Vanhal could see the streams of power coursing through the other necromancer, could sense the enormity of the aethyric energies he had harnessed. Strangely, the very magnitude of that power emboldened Vanhal. The sorcerer was an amateur after all, despite his pretensions. No truly knowledgeable practitioner would dare invest such a magnitude of power within his own body. Simply looking at the man, Vanhal could see his own power eating him, withering his flesh and thinning his hair. Every breath he took leeched his essence of an hour. Simply by withdrawing from the field, Vanhal could overcome his enemy.

Pride refused such action. It had been pride that drove him into exile as a boy, set him on the path that would bring him to Sylvania and ultimately to embrace the black arts. Pride did not relinquish its hold now. Exerting his will, Vanhal set the multitudinous legs of his palanquin scuttling across the fields towards the decayed ranks of the enemy. At the same time, he stretched forth his hand and focused his will upon the carcasses lying strewn behind that advancing horde. Drawing upon his magic, Vanhal concentrated upon the little wisps of spirit energy escaping from the twice-slain corpses, gathering them together, knitting their disparate energies into a single whole. Bit by bit, he drew the wisps into a monstrous energy, a phantom juggernaut of howling spectres. Ghastly faces gibbered and screamed from the ectoplasmic colossus, skeletal arms clawed and groped from the swirling mass. Like the surge of some ghostly hurricane, the spectral host crashed through the ranks of skeletons, scattering them like leaves before a storm. The black coach was pulverised, its deathly chargers shattered into bony shards, its passenger flung through the air.

Vanhal saw his rival crash amidst the splintered wreck of his conveyance, sensed the expenditure of energy that preserved him from more serious harm. Closing the fingers of his hand, Vanhal drew the raging spirit-storm back upon the necromancer, directing its full fury against him. Ghoul-fires and ghost-lights flashed from the embattled necromancer as he strove to defend himself against the phantom tempest. In his panic, he neglected the great army he had summoned.

Vanhal did not forget them. Maintaining the spirit host, he was still able to direct his own undead legion. Steadily they cut a path through the intruders, each wisp of essence speeding away from the destroyed husks to replenish the energies of the spectral storm raging around the necromancer.

Bit by bit, Vanhal could see his rival's great power waning. Before the sorcerer's energies could falter entirely, the spirit host was dispersed by an unspoken command from the former priest. By now, Vanhal's legion had cut completely through the intruding army. As the swirling apparitions faded into nothingness, a vanquished foe found himself staring up at a palanquin fashioned from animated bone, and a masked man clad in the habit of a Morrite priest.

'When you die,' Vanhal told the defeated necromancer, 'your flesh belongs to me.'

Raw terror filled the man's eyes. 'Spare me, great master!' he pleaded. Frantically, he dug beneath his robes to produce *De Arcanis Kadon*, holding the book towards his vanquisher.

Vanhal's eyes narrowed behind the skeletal mask, his lips moving as he silently read the hieroglyphs on the cover. 'What is to prevent me from simply taking the book from you?' he asked.

'This book contains all the secrets of Kadon,' the man announced. 'I came to seek your help unlocking its secrets. Much… much of it is beyond my comprehension,' he admitted. 'It may even be beyond your skill,' he added, then hurried to continue. 'Together, perhaps, with our combined knowledge…'

Vanhal raised his hand, and a bony arm emerged from the face of his palanquin to snatch the tome from the man's grasp. Shifting through the mass of the palanquin, the arm finally thrust itself from the skeletal floor beside the necromancer, holding the book for him as he perused it.

'I will allow you to live,' Vanhal decided, still studying the bloody pages. 'Not because of your gift, or because I am impressed by your mastery of the black arts.'

The other necromancer stared in frank astonishment at Vanhal, disbelief in his face. 'Why then do you spare me?' he asked.

Vanhal looked away from the tome, fixing his new apprentice with a weary gaze. 'I need someone to talk to,' he confessed.

'Someone I didn't conjure from the grave.'

⊰ CHAPTER IX ⊱

Middenheim
Ertezeit, 1118

There was deception about Kurgaz Smallhammer's name. The weapon clenched in the dwarf's brawny hands was taller than he was and nearly equal to his own weight. Gromril runes were etched into its massive head, flowing across it in an intricate spiral of heritage, tradition and magic. Drakdrazh, it had been named in the long ago, crafted by the ancient rune-smiths for the War of Vengeance. Wyrms had died beneath that hammer, their reptilian skulls shattered by the force of runemagic and dwarfish determination.

After the War of Vengeance, Drakdrazh had never again been inflicted upon such tremendous foes, a circumstance that provoked endless grumbling around the hearths of the Smallhammers. For generations, the family had been forced to settle for lesser enemies, adversaries unworthy of facing them in battle, unfit to stand before the might of Drakdrazh.

As Kurgaz brought his hammer swinging around, the gromril runes burned with eldritch fire. The effect when the weapon connected with his foe was an apocalyptic spectacle.

The creature didn't crumple, didn't collapse. Instead, its carcass was splashed across the wall in a welter of black blood and furry meat.

The magnitude of the skaven's destruction brought shocked silence to the subterranean gallery. Dwarf and ratman alike paused in their battle, their attention riveted by the thunderous clap as Drakdrazh slammed into its victim. The obliteration of the unfortunate ratkin sent a thrill through all who witnessed it. For the embattled dwarfs, it was a fiery rush of exhilaration. For the skaven, it was the stuff of raw terror.

The dwarfs had descended into the lower workings after it became clear that something was preying upon their miners. No survivors had reached the halls of Karak Grazhyakh, leaving the exact nature of the predator unclear. Loremasters and greybeards had speculated on everything from night goblins to a basilisk. It was surprising that none of them had considered skaven as the culprits. Perhaps if they had, the punitive expedition they sent into the mines would have been larger.

Leaping across the residue of his splattered foe, Kurgaz was thankful for the elders' lack of foresight. Skaven were a cringing, cowardly enemy. They never revealed themselves unless they felt certain of easy prey and a quick kill. Much larger an expedition and the foul vermin might never have stirred from their hidey-holes.

That was something no dwarf worth his beard would have liked.

Drakdrazh ploughed into a second ratman, a bulky brute in scraps of plate and chain. To its squeal of horror was added the shriek of shorn metal as its body was obliterated. Steam now rose from the runes carved into the hammer, black blood boiling as it splashed across the letters.

'The Hammer of Doom is upon you!' Kurgaz roared. There would be at least a few of the scuttling vermin who understood what he was saying. They could take his war-cry back to their burrows, a horror story to tell their pups in the dead of night.

The dwarf's bellow and the utter havoc visited by his hammer cured the skaven of their desire for battle. When they had swarmed out of the mine shafts and tunnels in their hundreds, they had smelt easy prey. Just a few dozen dwarfs in a lonely gallery, a place they could easily surround and isolate. Honourless vermin, they had no compunctions about engineering a massacre.

Now, however, it seemed they were the ones courting a massacre. Glands clenched, spilling the musk of fear into the air. Frightened squeaks dripped past shivering fangs. Those ratmen closest to the tunnels and shafts quickly deserted the gallery. As the first fled, the rest quickly followed. Rodent shrieks echoed through the mine as some of the vermin threw themselves down open shafts in their mindless terror, hurling themselves and those climbing below them to an ignominious doom.

Growling their own battle-cries, the other dwarfs charged the retreating skaven. Scores of the beasts were cut down before they could desert the gallery, hacked to pieces by dwarfish axes and battered to paste by dwarfish hammers.

Kurgaz stepped away from the mess of pulp that had been the last enemy to fall before him. He glanced around, but there were no ratkin within his reach. He spat at the fleeing vermin in contempt. Lower than greenskins, these filthy skaven. At least an orc had the spine to stand and fight. There was no glory in a battle like this, victory against such an easily routed foe rang as hollow as an elven promise.

The dwarf swung Drakdrazh onto his shoulder, grunting as its weight pressed down on him. He wondered if the weapon shared his disappointment, his frustration that the fight was over before it was properly begun. A runeweapon had a spirit all its own, a divine spark pounded into it by the runesmiths who forged it. How the hammer must lament the fall from ancient glories to the culling of slinking ratkin!

'Victory, Kurgaz!' a sallow-bearded dwarf warrior shouted, sprinting towards the champion. Blood dripped from the warrior's torn ear and there was a gash in his forearm where a skaven spear had pierced him, yet he seemed to give small consideration to his hurts, gripped by the jubilation of victory. 'The skaven will think twice before they defile Grungni's Tower again!'

Kurgaz scowled at the younger dwarf's enthusiasm. 'They turned and ran before the fight could even start,' he cursed, kicking the rodent mush at his feet.

'The honour is yours, Kurgaz,' the warrior told him. 'If not for you, the ratkin might have overwhelmed us. Broken out into the upper workings.'

'What honour in slaughtering vermin?' Kurgaz shook his head and patted the haft of his hammer. 'They were unworthy of Drakdrazh.'

At that instant, a loud report echoed through the gallery. Kurgaz staggered as he was struck from behind, the shot slamming into him with such force that his mail was shredded by the impact. Acrid smoke and a torrent of blood rose from the wound. The dwarf took a stumbling step, then slammed face forwards onto the floor.

The dwarf warriors clearing out the last knots of lingering ratmen looked up, stunned to see a lone skaven dangling from one of the ventilation shafts. The creature was suspended by ropes, hanging upside down above the gallery. Clutched in its paws was the lethal bulk of a jezzail, smoke rising from its muzzle. Before any of the dwarfs could react, the verminous sniper slung its gun across its back and scampered back up the ropes, a chitter of sadistic amusement drifting down as it made its retreat.

'The filth has shot Kurgaz Smallhammer!' The shout echoed through the gallery almost as loudly as the shot had. In a matter of heartbeats, a ring of grave-faced dwarfs surrounded the prostrate form of their hero. They stared at the horrible wound in Kurgaz's back, at the smouldering hole that had burned its way through layers of chain and leather to strike the flesh within.

One of the dwarfs, an old veteran with flecks of silver in his crimson beard, lifted Kurgaz onto his side and pressed his ear to the hero's chest. 'Take him to the stronghold!' he called out. 'Take him to his father while there is still breath in him!'

Solemnly, the dwarf warriors lifted their champion from the cold floor. Many of them had never seen a skaven jezzail before, but all of them recognised the corrupt nature of Kurgaz's wound. The triumph of only a moment before was gone, stolen by this cowardly act that condemned a bold hero to an inglorious death.

The fortress-like façade of the temple of Ulric dominated the Ulricsmund, the flanking watchtowers and central spires rising far above the cluster of chapels, archives and rectories that crouched in the shadow of the main sanctuary and the Great Tower. The temple had been constructed in the earliest days of Middenheim's founding, built by Wulcan, first to bear the title of Ar-Ulric. Dwarf architects had lent their expertise to the construction, affording it a brooding solidity not seen in human designs. In those bygone days, when the summit of the Ulricsberg was yet dominated by unexplored forest, when the Teutogens were but a primitive tribe of hunters, the temple had acted as refuge as well as sanctuary, it walls built to defy the assaults of beastmen, goblins and giants.

There was still a martial feel to the temple complex, something that was only natural given that Ulric wasn't simply a
god of winter and wolves, but of warfare as well. Knights of
the Teutogen Guard stood duty before the great oak doors of
the temple and patrolled the parapets of its walls. Many of
the wolf-priests wore breastplates of steel or bronze as part of
their clerical regalia. Upon the walls of the sanctuary, inter-
spersed with the pelts of wolves and the skulls of giants, a
wild profusion of swords, hammers and axes were displayed
in places of honour, wooden placards announcing the deeds
of each weapon. Where the image of Ulric was represented in
human rather than lupine form, he was always depicted with
his great axe, Blitzbeil.

As a Sigmarite, Brother Richter found the overall effect disturbing. Sigmar too was a god of war, but for his followers
warfare was a sombre, brutal affair. It was grim necessity. The
Temple of Ulric gloried in war, revelled in it, extolled it as a
virtue in and of itself. For the Sigmarite, war was a means to
defend civilisation. For the Ulrican, war needed no excuse. It
was an elemental force as powerful as the sea and the forest,
as vital and omnipresent as life and death, luck and fate.

The Ulrican faith had been the bedrock of the Empire.
Sigmar had worshipped Ulric, had used the god of war to
build his Empire and drive the enemies of man beyond its
borders. Yet that had been long ago. Civilisation had grown
from the barbarism of those days. Sigmar had ascended to
take a place among the gods, and through his wisdom he
had bestowed upon mankind a better way than the violent
path of Ulric.

Brother Richter was sensitive to the nature of his thoughts.
His personal misgivings about Ulric would certainly be considered blasphemous by the wolf-priests, just as their own
misgivings about Sigmar's divinity would be anathema to

himself. It was, he supposed, a doctrinal impasse that could never be bridged.

Having no desire to intrude upon the Ulricans in their own temple, Brother Richter lingered at the entrance to the sanctuary while Prince Mandred, Lady Mirella and the knight Beck walked towards the altar, a great slab of alabaster that resembled a block of arctic ice. Richter could hear their footfalls echoing down from the vaulted ceiling. Dwarfcraft, that was the only explanation for such incredible architecture. The ceiling was over a hundred feet above the floor, and designed in such a fashion as to magnify and project the sounds coming from the fore of the temple. A speaker standing in the pulpit might send his slightest whisper rebounding to every corner of the sanctuary.

The Sigmarite didn't contemplate the ceiling for long. Almost against his will, he felt his eyes drawn to the area beyond the altar, the spot of bare stone which was, in truth, the heart of both the temple and the city of Middenheim. Richter was uncomfortable gazing at it, feeling as though its very existence was a challenge to his own beliefs.

The cause of his discomfort was a great pillar of flame, a cold, white fire that blazed from the bare rock. It was one of the divine proofs the Ulricans espoused as evidence of their god's dominance. The fire was called the Sacred Flame and was said to have been started by a spark from Ulric's axe when the god cleaved the top from the Fauschlag and left the plateau upon which Middenheim was built. The fire had burned for thousands of years, without any visible source. It was claimed that so long as it burned, Ulric would protect Middenheim. The most aggressive of the wolf-priests challenged the clerics of other gods to present such evidence of their own deity's presence.

'The pure of heart may step within the Sacred Flame and

suffer no hurt,' a quiet voice spoke almost in Brother Richter's ear. The Sigmarite gave a start, turning to find Ar-Ulric
standing at his elbow. There was a curious, almost mischievous twinkle in his eye. 'Would you care to test your virtue,
brother? Or do you hold too many secrets to tempt the fire?'

Brother Richter smiled uneasily. 'Only a proud man believes
himself virtuous,' he said. 'And pride is the handmaiden of
the Ruinous Powers.' Boldly, he met the high priest's gaze.
'Have you made the test yourself, holiness?'

Ar-Ulric laughed and stroked his beard. 'No,' he admitted.
'Like you, I believe testing a god is the best way to show that
you are unworthy of him.' His smile again became cunning.
'I would be interested to discuss questions of dogma with you
some time.'

'I fear I am unworthy of such consideration,' Brother Richter answered with a bow. 'As a simple friar, how could I fairly
debate with the High Priest of Ulric?'

'And if you were Arch-Lector Wolfgang Hartwich?' Ar-Ulric
asked. 'Might you debate me then?' He raised his hand to
silence whatever protest was on the Sigmarite's lips. 'I may be
old, but my memory is keen as a razor. Better than your own,
it seems. You forget that we met when that monster Boris was
elected Emperor.' He chuckled again as he added, 'I was one
of those who didn't condone his ascension.'

Hartwich felt the barb as though it were a dagger thrust. It
was true, the Temple of Sigmar had voted in favour of Boris
Hohenbach. Another of the many crimes inflicted upon
the Temple's dignity by the late Grand Theogonist. In his
own way, he'd done his best to atone for such ecclesiastical
misdeeds.

'Remember my invitation,' Ar-Ulric said, proceeding down
the central nave towards the altar and the Sacred Flame.
'I stand ready to receive Brother Richter or Arch-Lector

Hartwich whenever they might call upon me. And there's no need for worry. *I* don't have any friends in Altdorf interested in hearing of your miraculous resurrection.'

The high priest laughed again. 'Now *that* should be a most illuminating topic for discussion, don't you think?'

The atmosphere within the cavern was stifling, rife with the stink of thousands of furry bodies, hot with the breath of swarming skaven. The might of Clan Rictus, most powerful of the warrior clans, was gathering faster than new burrows could be excavated to contain them. The excess had started to spill over into the dwarf mines, threatening to expose the magnitude of the skaven presence.

Upon a throne crafted from the pelts of vanquished rivals, Grey Lord Vecteek, self-appointed High Tyrant of Skaven-dom, watched the multitude sweep past his perch. These were his chattel, his slaves. The greatest army in the whole Under-Empire, the hordes of Clan Rictus! Until now, he had been content to conserve the power of his clan, to allow others on the Council to weaken the man-things, to carve their petty victories from the carcass of the man-thing Empire.

The time for such intrigues was over. Now Clan Rictus would bare its fangs, show its despised rivals the only meas-ure that mattered: power! Raw, merciless, brutal power! The other Lords of Decay would learn their place – laprats to their master, Vecteek the Vanquisher! Vecteek the Victorious!

The black-furred skaven scowled down from the rocky out-cropping, drumming his claws against the spiked breastplate he wore. How many spies were down there, he wondered? How many ears had the other Grey Lords turned against him?

'Dread tyrant, Plague Lord Puskab Foulfur kneel-bow before you.'

Warmonger Vecteek turned about in his throne, directing

his scowl at the bloated apparition that genuflected before him. His nose wrinkled in revulsion at the necrotic stink wafting from the plague priest's foul robes and diseased antlers. He resisted the temptation to have his Verminguard butcher the filth out of hand. Clan Pestilens still had a role in his plans and killing one of their Grey Lords was a good way to incite the whole of the clan against him. Far better to bide his time until they no longer had any value.

'Speak-squeak,' Vecteek demanded, lashing his tail against the rock. 'When will man-nest fall to Black Plague?'

'Soon-soon,' Puskab promised. The plague priest had earned his place on the Council by creating the Black Plague, after the small detail of defeating a disgraced Grey Lord in ritual combat. There was no one else in the Under-Empire more familiar with the disease and its spread. Still, Vecteek was growing tired of the plaguelord's assurances. For thirty food-cycles, the skaven had been sneaking into Middenheim, trying to spread the plague without any noticeable results. 'Need-want direct passage to city. Must-must,' Puskab twitched his ears nervously. 'Dwarf-things in way,' he confessed.

Vecteek bristled at the excuse. 'Kill-kill all dwarf-things!' he raged, tearing his sword from its sheath as he reared up from his throne.

Puskab's rheumy eyes glittered in the illumination of a worm-oil lamp. 'Mighty-wise Vecteek,' he said. 'You lose-die many clanrats fighting dwarf-things. Hurt-harm attack on man-things.'

The Warmonger's fangs peeled back in an expression of savage challenge. 'Think-think Clan Rictus weak?'

'No-no!' Puskab whined, bowing still lower, trying to placate the enraged tyrant. 'But why waste-use Rictus-rats fighting dwarf-things?' His tail twitched as he made a suggestion, one he knew would appeal to the paranoid despot. 'Use-waste Mors-mice!' he said.

Vecteek settled down in his throne, his sword across his lap. Use Clan Mors to attack the dwarf-things? Clan Mors, the most despised of Rictus's rivals! He could order Warlord Vrrmik to bring his warriors to the Wolfrock, use them in the wasteful fight with the dwarfs. Meanwhile, the strength of Clan Rictus would be unleashed in its full fury upon the weak, plague-stricken humans. Clan Rictus would claim the victory and Clan Mors would be bled dry by the dwarfs!

A wonderful plan, Vecteek reflected, dismissing Puskab with a wave of his claw. He was happy he had thought of it. But, then, that was simply another reason why he was superior to the rest of the Grey Lords.

Carroburg
Nachexen, 1115

There were fewer of his guests on the battlements when it came time to distribute food to the peasants of Carroburg. Where only a few weeks before none of his subjects would have dared offend him by staying away, now only the most weak-willed of his sycophants stood upon the walls. The weak-willed and those who genuinely shared the Emperor's vicious humour.

Boris blamed the séance and the spectre of his father. The ghost's words had diminished him in the eyes of his subjects, made them doubt the power and authority of the living Emperor. It was tempting to thrust the ingrates from the castle, but that would only spread the discontent when they returned to their own provinces. No, he had to reinforce to them that he was in control, that he wasn't going to be ruined by some phantom's words of doom.

Down below, the soldiers herded a group of peasants towards the walls. By now, the beggars were accustomed to the humiliating ordeal. They didn't need to be goaded into dropping onto all fours and acting like dogs in order to retrieve the scraps the nobles threw down to them. Their acceptance provoked the Emperor, cheating him of his enjoyment of the scene.

'Stop!' Boris growled at his guests, arresting several of them in the very act of throwing food to the peasants. The Emperor smiled at their quick obedience. Still smiling, he leaned out between the crenellations. His gaze swept across the ragged mob, finally picking out one of them to persecute. 'You! Woman! Stand up!'

Hesitantly, the peasant woman gazed up at him. She was either too frightened or too stupid to obey him at once, so Boris snapped his fingers and brought one of the soldiers hurrying forwards. Roughly, the dienstmann jerked the peasant to her feet.

'Let's have a look at you,' Boris declared. There were a few titters of amusement from his hangers-on. Again, he had to motion for the soldier to take a hand. The hood was pulled away from the woman's head, exposing a dull, plain face.

One of the other peasants stood suddenly and approached the wall. 'Please, Majesty,' the man said in a tremulous voice. 'She's my wife.'

Boris grinned at the statement. 'That is pitiable,' he said. He glanced aside at the nobles around him. 'You must be poor beyond words if you are reduced to bedding such a creature. Look at that cow! She must have been sired by an orc! A blind one if her mother looks half as bad as she!'

The cruel jest brought raucous laughs from the nobles on

the wall. The peasant man lowered his face, hiding the tears of shame and impotent rage streaming down his face.

Boris smirked and shouted down to his soldiers. 'We desire to know if the rest of that thing is as revolting as what We've seen.' He laughed when the woman tried to pull away from the dienstmann's grasping fingers. The solider tore her shawl as she twisted from his grip, sending her tumbling to the ground.

The peasant man took a step towards his wife, hesitated as he saw more of the soldiers coming towards her. Desperately he looked to the beggars around him, but one and all they turned their heads. Helplessly, he appealed to the gloating Emperor above.

'Have mercy, Majesty!' the peasant cried.

A sadistic chuckle was the man's answer. 'We just want a peek at that curious specimen you brought to Us,' Boris called down. 'If she's interesting enough, there might be a piece of silver waiting for you. The Imperial menagerie has been a bit anaemic of late.' The Emperor's jeering brought cruel mirth raining down on the man. Sobbing, the peasant fell to his knees and began pounding the dirt with his fists.

The soldiers had caught the woman and waited for the Emperor's command. When he favoured them with a curt nod, one dienstmann started to rip away the peasant's dress. Almost at once, the soldier jumped back, gasping. The other men released their prisoner, likewise drawing back in horror.

Boris frowned, his view obscured by the first soldier. 'What's wrong? Is that half-orc even more vile underneath those rags?' The sneer left his face when the soldier moved and he had a look at the woman's partially clothed body. Ugly black boils marred her flesh, the buboes of the Black Plague!

'Plague! Gods preserve us, it is the plague!' Count Artur

shuddered. The cry was taken up by others, threatening to become a panic.

The Emperor glared down at the soldiers. 'What do you mean bringing... bringing that...' He spun around, snarling orders to the troops inside the castle. 'Guards! Seal the gates! Archers... To the walls!'

Before the soldiers or peasants below could react, bowmen replaced nobles on the battlements. Arrows pelted the wretches, sparing none. On the Emperor's command, the archers sent volley upon volley stabbing down until the bodies lying strewn before the wall resembled pincushions.

'Merciful Shallya,' Palatine Dohnanyi cried. 'The plague is in Carroburg!'

'We are doomed!' wailed Gustav van Meers.

Emperor Boris waved the archers away from the walls and confronted his guests. 'The plague might be in Carroburg,' he conceded, 'but it isn't here. We have provisions enough. The gates are closed and shall remain so. No one can come in and if they can't come in, they can't bring the plague with them.'

Palatine Dohnanyi shook his head. 'The spiders!' he cried. 'The plague is carried by hordes of black spiders! One bite! How can you keep out spiders?'

'No! It is ravens, harbingers of Old Night!' argued Count Artur. 'They piss in your drinking water and give you the plague! What do castle walls mean to birds?'

Emperor Boris rounded on the terrified men, turning his own doubt and fear into a show of contemptuous anger. 'We promised you protection,' he reminded them. 'This refuge was prepared against the plague! Priestess, doktor and warlock, we have defences against whatever would bring disease here.' His lip curled in a sneer. 'Or would you prefer to take your chances down there?' He jabbed his thumb downwards, indicating the arrow-riddled corpses below.

'Gods! Doktors! We've tried them all before,' Gustav van Meers objected.

'Then we will try the warlock's magic,' Boris growled back. He saw the terror in the Westerlander's eyes, saw it mirrored in those of the others. If he were to maintain control of them, he had to do more than offer them hope. He had to remind them that there were other things beside the plague they had to fear.

'Gustav is leaving us,' the Emperor declared, waving his soldiers forwards. The merchant knew what was coming. Uttering a frightened yelp, he tried to flee back into the castle. The guards caught him before he could reach the door. Savagely they dragged the man to the battlements and threw him over the edge. Gustav's scream ended in a sickening crunch. Groans drifted up to the parapet. The fall might not have killed him, but he wouldn't be going anywhere with his broken bones.

Count Artur gawked at the callous incident. 'He was a wealthy man...'

'He was a peasant,' Emperor Boris sneered. 'No loss to anyone. There's no shortage of scum just like him, even with the plague.' He stared hard into the count's face. 'Did you want to argue about Our ability to keep the plague away from this castle?'

The rotund noble blanched at the threat in Boris's tone. 'No, I have every confidence in Your Imperial Majesty.'

'Good,' Boris said as he made his way back into the castle. 'Ease your minds, friends. We mean what We say. The plague will never touch us here.'

The dungeons of Schloss Hohenbach had been neglected for some time. Pushed to the limit by the depredations of the beastmen and the plague that followed, the lords of Drakwald had been unable to maintain the luxury of prisoners. Mutilation, exile and execution had become the punishments of choice. Until the confinement of von Metzgernstein's son, the vaults had been without human occupant for two years.

If humans no longer inhabited the dungeons, there were things that did. Rats and spiders, beetles and slugs. And sometimes larger vermin. Vermin that padded through the cellars on two feet, that cloaked their crook-backed bodies in raiment of black and grey. Creatures that chittered to one another in a language of squeaks and hisses.

The skaven would have been amused to hear Emperor Boris's assurances to his guests. There was always something funny about prey that deluded themselves that they were safe.

As though anywhere in the Empire was safe from the rat-men and the plague they had engineered.

The Horned Rat had promised His children that they would one day inherit the surface world.

The time of the Great Ascendancy would soon be at hand.

⤙ CHAPTER X ⤚

Middenheim
Brauzeit, 1118

Mandred paced angrily outside the von Degenfeld manse. He'd had everything plotted out so carefully in his mind that he was having a hard time accepting that his plan wasn't working the way he had imagined. After that day escorting Lady Mirella around the city, he'd realised that perhaps Sofia's concerns weren't so unfounded as he'd initially thought them to be. Mirella von Wittmar was a charming, intelligent and exceedingly brave woman, just the sort that would turn any nobleman's fancy.

To be certain, he'd had dalliances before, but never with anyone he could be serious about. There had never been any real threat to Sofia… until now. Perhaps she had seen it first, some sixth sense of the female that warned her of a rival. Lady Mirella was of the upper strata of the Altdorf aristocracy. Maybe not of the breeding that a prince could marry, especially not with things as confused as they were in Altdorf, but Sofia might not be aware of that. What was it she'd said? 'Add

him to her collection of princes?' It was only now, with the
stirring of emotions in his heart, that Mandred appreciated
the import of those words, the undercurrent of fear behind
them. Sofia wasn't as resigned to losing him as he'd believed,
as they both had professed over the years. Lady Mirella might
have been only a consort to the Prince of Altdorf, but in her
fear Sofia had imagined she might do much better with the
Prince of Middenheim.

'Are you sure you want to do this?' Mirella asked him.

Mandred hesitated before answering, his resolve wavering
when she asked the question. They'd discussed it, of course.
Been quite blunt, actually, in their discussion of their mutual
regard for one another. At the same time, he still held Sofia in
his heart. Decorum and simple decency demanded he make
a choice between the two women. It had hurt him deeply to
make that choice, but he felt chivalry called for him to stay
true to Sofia. As he'd explained to Mirella, there was every
chance that her regard towards him was simply gratitude for
saving her from the Kineater. He felt it wasn't fair to exploit
an affection built upon such traumatic soil.

No, the thing to do, he'd decided, was to bring Mirella to
see Sofia, to tell her that there was nothing between them. It
was a dangerous ploy, but they had Brother Richter to act as
chaperon. Mandred was hoping that the presence of a priest,
even a Sigmarite one, would at least restrain Sofia's temper.

'I am sorry, your grace, but Burggraefin Sofia is indisposed.'
It was the second time the major domo of the burggraefin's
manse had come back with that answer. Mandred directed
a glowering gaze upon the servant. He wasn't about to be
balked at this stage by some peasant.

'You can move aside,' Mandred told him, 'or I can have
you moved aside.' He nodded towards Beck. The bodyguard
dropped a hand around the hilt of his sword when the servant

looked in his direction. 'I'll let you make the decision.'

Swallowing a knot that had suddenly formed in his throat, the major domo stepped aside and bowed the prince in. 'Please forgive me, your grace. I was simply obeying the orders given me by my mistress.'

Mandred waved aside the servant's apology. 'Where is she?' he inquired as he stepped into the hall.

The servant demurred for a moment, even at this stage trying to figure out some way to preserve the burggraefin's privacy. Beck noticed the man glance towards the broad oaken stairway at the left. Brushing past the major domo, he marched to the stairs. 'This way, your grace,' the knight said.

Mandred glowered at the servant one last time and followed Beck. The major domo was close behind, his tongue still stumbling over an assortment of appeals that did nothing to dissuade the prince. If anything they only made him more determined to see Sofia.

The von Degenfeld manse was an old haunt of the prince's, and Beck knew the way to Sofia's chambers almost as well as Mandred himself. Many had been the cold night the bodyguard had spent outside that room. Now, however, he strode boldly to the engraved panel of dark Drakwald timber. Beck knocked once, waited a moment, then looked to his master.

'I told you, the burggraefin is indisposed,' the servant declared. Mandred frowned and nodded at Beck. The bodyguard stepped away from the door and brought his boot smashing into it. The first impact merely rattled it on its hinges. The second kick sent the door slamming inwards. His hand falling instinctually to the hilt of his sword, Beck stormed into Sofia's bedchamber.

An instant later, the knight was back in the hall, a hand clasped around his nose and mouth. His eyes were wide with fright. Mandred felt his pulse quicken as the fear in his guard's eyes infected him. Hurriedly, ignoring the protests of the major domo and the puzzlement of Mirella, he rushed to the room. Beck caught at him, trying to keep him in the hall, but he pulled free of the knight's clutch.

The room, luxuriously appointed in the best Middenland style, seemed indistinct to Mandred's gaze. It was as if his vision were blurred by the foul, sick-house stink in the chamber. Like Beck, his first action was to cover his face. Unlike his guard, however, he didn't retreat into the hall but swept towards the canopied bed. Dreading what he would find, he reached for the embroidered curtain and drew it back.

A pale, wizened figure stared up at him, and somewhere beneath that nest of black boils a face squirmed into the semblance of a smile. 'I'm afraid I'm not receiving... today... my prince.'

'She has the plague, your grace,' Beck called from the doorway. The knight had failed to keep Mandred from the room, but he was more successful in keeping Lady Mirella from the chamber.

Mandred didn't need Beck to tell him what hideous affliction had descended upon Sofia. He'd seen the Black Plague at work in Warrenburg. He knew its stink, he knew the marks it left upon its victims. He knew even breathing the same air as the afflicted was to tempt Grandfather Pox.

A hundred thoughts stampeded through his mind, but only one roared so loudly as to command his body. Clenching his jaw tight, Mandred reached down and bundled the pathetic scarecrow-figure in a heavy blanket. Ignoring Beck's frantic warnings, the prince rose from the bed, Sofia in his arms. 'How long has she been like this?' he snarled at the major domo.

'Three... No... Four days, your grace,' the servant answered.

'Then there's not much time,' Mandred growled back, marching from the room with Sofia.

'Ulric's sake, your grace,' Beck cried. 'The woman's going to die anyway. You can't jeopardise yourself like this!'

Mandred stared at his guard, at the frightened cast of Mirella's features. 'This time mine will be the only life I risk,' he said, thinking back to that fateful ride when he'd led brave men into the plague's domain. 'Take Lady Mirella back to the Middenpalaz.'

'Where will you go?' Mirella demanded, tears forming in her eyes.

The prince looked down at Sofia's wasted frame. 'There's an alchemist who has taken over the old hospice of Shallya. He's reputed to be something of a wonder worker. I'll take her there.'

Beck stepped forwards, blocking the prince's way. 'I can't let you risk yourself. Give me the girl. I'll take her.'

Mandred shook his head. 'This is my burden,' he said. 'You've always been a loyal knight. Do as you are ordered.'

Reluctantly, Beck stepped aside. Along with Mirella and the major domo, he watched Mandred walk away, eighty pounds of plague swaddled in his royal arms.

Mandred could think only of the draconian quarantine measures his father had undertaken the last time plague had threatened Middenheim. Great and small, Graf Gunthar had spared none who bore the marks of the Black Plague on their skin. He'd banished all those who'd even come in contact with the disease from the Ulricsberg, condemning them to the squalor of Warrenburg. Virtually the whole of the Shallyan sect had perished because of that edict. They'd refused to abandon the plague-stricken refugees and so had decamped en masse for the shanty town at the foot of the mountain. Most had died there, victims of the plague or marauding beastmen. The few survivors had remained in their little wooden chapel down below, resolute in their determination to stay where they felt most needed.

Graf Gunthar's cruelty had been the salvation of Middenheim, Mandred knew that. An ugly truth was a truth all the same. Because it was truth, he knew how his father would react if he were to learn the plague had returned. There was nothing he wouldn't do to spare the city, to honour what he felt to be a sacred trust between ruler and ruled.

No, Mandred corrected himself, guilt gnawing at his belly. There was one thing that would make his father forsake that trust. The graf wouldn't sacrifice his own son, no matter who was at risk.

The stone walls of the hospice seemed to exert a preternatural chill, an atmosphere of desolation. The humble folk of Middenheim shunned the place: nobles complaining that it was in disrepair, peasants claiming that when her priestesses deserted the hospice, Shallya's beneficence departed with them.

Mandred prayed that such wasn't the case. Forgetting the dignity of his position, he bent on one knee and begged the goddess to intercede on Sofia's behalf. The alchemist, a silver-haired Nordlander named Neist, ignored the prince's lack of decorum as he examined the sick woman. It wasn't long before he rose from beside the pallet and replaced his tools in the little leather bag he carried. Mandred sprang to his feet as the alchemist started to leave the tiny cell.

'Where are you going?' Mandred demanded, his fist tightening about the capelet fringing the alchemist's cloak. 'You have to make her well!'

Neist favoured the prince with a tired, indulgent smile. 'It's the Black Plague,' he explained, not quite managing to keep his tone from possessing a patronising quality.

'I know what it is,' Mandred retorted, tightening his hold. 'Make her better.'

The alchemist laughed, a bitter and cheerless sound. 'If I knew how to do that I'd be the richest man in the Empire!' He held his hands out for the prince to inspect. Mandred automatically released the man, recoiling when he saw the pox-scars all along Neist's skin.

'It caught me six years ago in Wolfenburg,' Neist said. 'I don't know how I survived when so many didn't, but I know it wasn't anything of my doing.'

'How can you be sure?' Mandred asked, despair almost choking his voice. The alchemist beckoned to the prince, motioning him to withdraw into the corridor. Glancing one last time at Sofia's bed, staring into her wide, fearful eyes, Mandred forced himself to follow Neist.

The alchemist closed the door when the prince had withdrawn. Sighing, Neist removed a piece of chalk and scratched a crude cross on the panel. 'I'm sure,' he said, gesturing with his arm to the rest of the long hallway. Both sides were lined with similar doors. Once this place had acted as a dormitory for the priestesses and their servants. Now it provided a refuge for Neist's patients. As the alchemist pointed, Mandred found his attention riveted by a detail he'd been too distraught to notice when he was bringing Sofia here. Dozens of the doors were marked with the white crosses that indicated plague.

'I've had ample opportunity,' the alchemist declared. 'First in Wolfenburg, then in Talabheim, then in Nuln.' He wiped his scarred hand across his brow. 'It seems if you somehow live through it, the plague can't touch you again. A horrible feeling, to watch a city dying around you, knowing you'll be the only one left.'

Horror was coursing through Mandred's veins. 'When?' he managed to ask.

'Three weeks ago, the first ones came. Two little boys.' The alchemist shook his fist. 'They died. Then there were more.

They died too. I had to burn them in the old garden. Couldn't risk dumping them over the Cliff of Sighs, Morr forgive me.'

'How many?' Mandred pressed, feeling his fear swell with each heartbeat.

Neist scratched at his beard. 'Nearly a hundred now. I'm not surprised they haven't noticed in the Middenpalaz, though.' He jabbed a thumb at the door to Sofia's cell. 'She's the first Von to catch it. The rest have just been peasants.'

Almost at once, Neist regretted his choice of words. More than most nobles, he knew Prince Mandred's reputation for helping his people regardless of class. 'I apologise, your grace,' he said. 'That was an unjust thing for me to say. I saw the city of Carroburg put to the torch by nobles afraid of the plague. That isn't an easy memory to forget.'

'Manling quack!' a gruff voice bellowed through the hall. 'A beardless grave for all your clan!'

The alchemist flinched when he heard the cry. Mandred followed Neist as he hurried down the corridor. 'That was a dwarf? I understood they couldn't catch the plague.'

Neist didn't look at the prince as he answered, too busy rummaging in his bag for a slim bottle of blue glass. 'Kurgaz Smallhammer's affliction is quite different, I assure you.' Another bitter laugh as he hurried on. 'It is quite an honour for a human to be allowed to treat a dwarf. Though in hindsight I think a seasick troll would have made a more pleasant patient.'

Altdorf
Brauzeit, 1114

A brisk autumn breeze wafted through the narrow streets of Altdorf, bearing upon it the infamous stink from the riverfront slums that had caused Emperor Siegfried to curse the city as 'the Great Reek' and remove his throne to Nuln. Emperor Boris had returned the throne to Altdorf, but that hadn't changed the odour that crawled up from the river, slinking into the manses and palaces of the Empire's great and good.

Walking along the cobblestone lanes winding between the half-timbered residences of the nobility that clustered around the Imperial Palace, Adolf Kreyssig dipped his hand beneath the folds of the heavy cloak he wore, fishing the silver pomander from his pocket and inhaling its perfumed vapours. It was more than a concession to discomfort – one of the prevailing theories about the origins of the Black Plague had it emerging from noxious odours. A pomander stuffed with cinnamon was, supposedly, a sure-fire preventative. Kreyssig scowled at the pomander as he tucked it back into his pocket. The fact that only the wealthy could afford cinnamon might have had more to do with the prescription than any medicinal value. Physicians were a special kind of thief, stealing more with a gloomy word than any cutpurse could with a knife.

These were the same men who had told him he would be crippled, Kreyssig reflected. He flexed his arm, feeling the powerful muscles ripple beneath his doublet. Ignorant charlatans! Fortunately he had found a better way to heal his wounds. If the Black Plague should try to take him, he would know how to beat it back.

Kreyssig stopped in the street, alarmed by the turn his thoughts had taken. All of his life he had learned never to rely on anyone. The beneficence of a master, the loyalty of a friend, the fidelity of a servant, none of these could be trusted. Yet he was becoming dependent on the magic of a witch, an ambitious noblewoman at that. He was too clever to be taken in by her intrigues, or deceived by her amorous attentions. She was using him, exploiting him to get closer to the Imperial throne. Even knowing this, however, he couldn't escape the fascination she held over him. At times he felt like a fly caught in a spider's web, every effort to escape only drawing the trap tighter about him.

He cast a wary glance at the street around him. At this hour, the lane was nearly deserted. The days of early-morning productivity were long past, casualties of a rumour that held the plague was most active during the threshold hours of twilight and dawn, those moments midway between night and day. Only the harshest stewards were able to rouse their households at such times and even then to little effect. Those shops that still had wares to peddle wouldn't be open until well past the dangerous time.

What companions Kreyssig had as he ventured through the streets were those too dejected or desperate to cling to shelter. Beggars rummaging in the gutters, muck-rakers shovelling night-dirt, rat-catchers clearing out their traps before hungry cats or even hungrier peasants did the job for them. By rights, such rabble should be restricted from the districts of the rich and powerful, kept to their shanties and hovels beyond the walls and across the river. But, like so much since the plague had struck, the diligence of the Altdorf city guard, the Schuetzenverein, had diminished. The Schueters were suffering the same shortages as the rest of the city, losing men to plague, murder and outright desertion. Most of their best had been drawn away by conscription into the army Duke Vidor had used to chase the traitor Boeckenfoerde, the confused horde Altdorfers alternately called the 'replacement army' or 'Vidor's Graues Haufen'. What was left were the old, the young and a thuggish rabble too undisciplined for soldiering. Given the choice between beggars and patrols of the Schueters, most of the nobles had brains enough to risk catching disease from a tramp over a knife from a guard.

Even in such lowly company, Kreyssig was careful. The shabby cloak he wore enveloped him from head to foot, making him seem just another peasant scavenging in the streets. No armed escort, no panoply of attendants, nothing that would make anyone suspect that the Protector of the Empire was abroad. A few Kaiserjaeger in the nearby streets watching for spies was the only entourage he needed. The best defence, he had always felt, was to be inconspicuous.

With a last look around, Kreyssig shifted direction, darting into the cramped alleyway between two houses. He had passed this spot several times already in his circuitous ramble through the neighbourhood, allowing his Kaiserjaeger ample opportunity to catch any tails he had acquired. Now he would delay no longer.

Reaching an iron-banded door set into the wall bordering the alley, Kreyssig fished a key from his pocket. The portal groaned as he opened it and slipped into the shadowy environs of a small wood room. Piles of logs, heaps of kindling littered the floor – and something more that came to his attention only as he locked the door and started to walk towards the opposite entrance. It was a curious object to find, a single leather shoe sitting in the middle of the room. It was enough for Kreyssig to puzzle over, but not enough to alarm him.

In the kitchen beyond the wood room, Kreyssig found the other shoe. It was still attached to the foot of a liveried servant, the steward of Baroness von den Linden's household. The man was lying sprawled before the brick oven, his head mashed into a red paste. From the way the rug he was sprawled upon was curled, it looked as though the man had been struck down in the wood room and dragged here.

Kreyssig's fist closed about the dagger he wore beneath his cloak, dragging the blade from its sheath. He spun around, intending to retreat back through the wood room, but even as he started to move, the route was cut off. The door of the pantry exploded outwards, disgorging a trio of tatterdemalion figures with drawn, starveling faces and a vicious gleam in their eyes. Each of the men held a cudgel in his hand.

The men from the pantry blocked the entrance to the wood room. As Kreyssig turned towards the other doorways leading out from the kitchen, he found more antagonists rushing towards him. Some were less ragged than the three from the pantry, some weren't quite so haggard and sickly in condition, but there was the same rage smouldering in each eye.

The mob descended upon Kreyssig in a mass. The first to reach him howled as his dagger slashed out, a forearm cut to the bone. A second foeman pitched to the floor, clutching at a stabbed belly. Then they were on him, smashing him down with wooden clubs and the iron hilts of knives.

'Don't kill him!' a commanding voice boomed. From beneath the confusion of kicking boots and flailing clubs, Kreyssig saw a hulking shape in a black cloak descend the half a dozen steps between dining hall and kitchen. 'This creature must burn with the witch!'

The witch-taker's words brought fresh savagery to the mob. Brutally, they dragged Kreyssig to his feet, ripping away the concealing cloak in the process. One of the rabble, his tones more cultured than the rest, gasped in horror as he recognised the face of their captive.

'Commander Kreyssig!' the man wailed, drawing back in fear. His fright spread to the rest of the mob, who relented in their violence, cringing away from their terrible foe.

It needed but a moment more and the mob should have fractured and fled. But that moment was denied Kreyssig. From the doorway, Auernheimer berated his followers for their fear. 'Seize this spawn of Chaos!' he roared. 'Do you fear a man more than you fear the gods?'

Kreyssig tried to break away as Auernheimer's oratory poured courage back into his mob. He was too slow. With an angry growl, the rabble was on him again, catching him and pinning his arms behind his back.

'This is treason!' Kreyssig raged. 'Your heads will rot on the palace walls for this!'

Auernheimer sneered from the shadows of his hood. 'What matter a man's head when his soul belongs to the gods?' He pointed at his prisoner. 'Solkan has guided us here, set us to where we might fight the canker that rots the Empire. You, the so-called Protector! You, the pawn of daemons and witches! The corruption that makes the gods turn their faces! The wickedness that would damn us all to plague and famine!'

The witch-taker swept his hand, waving the mob into the dining hall. 'Bring this heretic,' he snarled. 'Solkan has given us the honour of purging this blight from our Empire. This creature burns with his mistress!'

Struggling against his captors, Kreyssig was dragged up from the kitchen and marched across the dining hall. The great table that had once dominated the room was gone, smashed into kindling and piled along with other pieces of furniture at the centre of the room. The bodies of several servants lay draped about the base of the pile. More servants, bound and gagged, lay higher up on the heap. At the very top, her body fairly smothered in rope and chain, her mouth banded about with choking straps of leather, Baroness von den Linden fixed a despairing gaze upon Kreyssig.

'There is purity in fire!' Auernheimer declaimed as the mob began to tie Kreyssig's arms behind him and lash his legs together. 'By fire did Great Solkan cleanse the fog-devils from Westerland, by fire were the heathen Kurgan driven into the

Wastes!' The witch-taker brandished a steel mace adorned with razor-edged flanges. 'By fire will we purge this place.' He glared into Kreyssig's eyes. 'The flames will consume your evil, your pain will cry out to Great Solkan and draw His eye upon our suffering! He will know the justice of our cause when we deliver to him the souls of an arch-traitor and his witch!'

Thrashing against the rough hands that bore him, Kreyssig was carried over to the pyre, dumped with all the ceremony of a sack of rubbish next to the trussed figure of the baroness. Auernheimer gestured with his flanged mace again, motioning several of his mob towards the fire blazing away in the hearth. The witch-taker's eyes reflected the flames, shining with the chilling fanaticism of the true zealot. He cocked his head to one side, his brow knitting as a sudden thought occurred to him. Swinging his mace around, he waved a few of his peasant followers back into the kitchen. 'Remove the last of the witch's minions,' he commanded. 'All must be consumed in the holy flame.'

Kreyssig watched the men shuffle away, dread pounding in his heart. Once they recovered the body, added it to the base of the pile, the witch-taker would order the pyre put to the torch. He rolled his eyes, managing to meet the panicked gaze of the baroness. For all her vaunted mastery of charms and enchantments, her magic hadn't preserved her against her enemies. She was trussed like a Sigmarsfest goose and just as helpless. There was no help to be had from that quarter, and he cursed himself for thinking there could be. His relations with the witch were the root of his destruction, not the source of deliverance. He had come here in secret, even his Kaiser-jaeger didn't know his destination. There was no prospect of rescue, no one to deliver him.

Only a miracle would prevent the Protector of the Empire from the mob justice of the rabble.

Sometimes, however, miracles did manifest. It was a dark miracle that delivered Adolf Kreyssig from his doom.

Soon after the peasants Auernheimer had sent to retrieve the steward withdrew into the kitchen, there arose chilling screams. The men tried to flee up the steps and back into the dining hall, but not one of them managed the attempt. They were struck down from behind, pierced by jagged spears and slashed by rusted swords. The mangled peasants pitched and fell, their shrieking bodies dragged back into the darkness of the kitchen.

A moment of horrified silence followed, a silence that was broken by an explosion of inhuman chitters and growls. From the blackness, a grotesque swarm of verminous shapes flooded into the dining hall. The muck of sewer and cellar clung to the ragged strips of cloth they wore and the mangy brown fur that covered their lean, hungry bodies. Their hand-like paws clutched a motley confusion of swords and axes, spears and knives. Long scaly tails whipped behind them as they charged, and froth bubbled from the fangs of their rat-like heads.

The mob stood stricken with a paralysis of superstitious terror as the bestial swarm descended upon them. Only Auernheimer was unfazed, unperturbed in his stalwart zealotry. Swinging his mace overhead, snatching a brand from the nearest of his followers, the witch-taker roared his defiance of the monstrous horde. 'Daemons of the witch! Rejoice, brethren, in this test of our sacred conviction!' He added deeds to words, bringing his mace smashing down into the snout of the first ratman to draw near him. The monster squeaked in agony, collapsing in a shivering mess at his feet.

The witch-taker's rabble rallied, charging at the oncoming monsters, meeting them at the middle of the hall. Swords clashed, knives slashed and screams human and inhuman echoed through the house. Some of the combatants broke away, fleeing down passages, hotly pursued by vengeful foes. In the space of only a few heartbeats, a dozen bodies littered the floor.

Auernheimer seared the eyes of another ratman, blinding it before bashing its skull with his mace. The witch-taker looked beyond his collapsing foe, watching with grim fatalism as more of the monstrous vermin swarmed up from the kitchen. 'Ernst! Andreas!' he shouted. 'Light the pyre! These daemons shall not save their mistress!'

The peasants Auernheimer called out to broke away from their enemies. Alone among his rabble, these two had been soldiers, *Dienstleute* that had survived the massacre of Engel's Bread Marchers. They had the skill at arms and the martial discipline to carry out the witch-taker's command. What they didn't have was the opportunity.

Ernst and Andreas snatched glowing brands from the hearth, but as the men rushed towards the pyre, their destruction climbed the kitchen steps. A tall, wizened ratman dressed in black robes, its visage a confusion of scars and metal, tubes and wires dangling from its face and jaw. The monster's eyes were enormous rubies that bulged from its sockets. The fangs in its mouth were metal, and blue sparks crackled from them as the strange creature snarled at its minions.

The robed ratman raised one of its withered paws, displaying a brilliant green jewel embedded in its palm. The creature pointed the jewel in the direction of Ernst and Andreas. More sparks crackled about its fangs as it squeaked an incantation.

A bolt of coruscating energy burst from the ratman's jewel, searing a path through the hall. Vermin and human alike were caught in the path of that beam, burning fur, charring skin and boiling blood. The robed ratman cared not for these incidental casualties, and upon Ernst and Andreas it directed the full malignity of its magic.

The two *Dienstleute* weren't burned, weren't charred or singed. Their bodies seemed to simply evaporate within that beam of unholy power. In that searing flash, their chests turned to vapour, leaving the extremities to crash to the floor. The brands they carried fell from dead fingers to smoulder on the bloody rugs.

The obscene sorcery shattered the fragile courage of Auernheimer's mob, their zealotry unequal to this display of magic. The ratmen fell upon the terrified peasants, dragging them down and butchering them where they fell.

Only the witch-taker himself maintained some measure of composure. Smashing down three ratmen as they lunged at him, Auernheimer turned and threw himself straight into the stained-glass window that fronted the hall and offered a prospect of the street outside. The fanatic's plunge brought him through the window in a shower of shattered glass and fractured lead. For an instant, he lay crumpled in the street, but then he was on his feet and fleeing down the lane.

Some of the ratmen rushed to the broken window, eager to cut down their wounded prey, but a sharp bark from their robed leader brought them slinking away from the window.

Kreyssig could only marvel at this incredible escape. He had berated these mutants for keeping tabs on him, but now he was almost prepared to forgive them their audacity. Almost, for his relief was mitigated by a new, fearful appreciation for the abilities of his verminous agents. The display of magic executed by their leader was more intimidating than anything he had seen from Baroness von den Linden or even old Fleischauer, the Emperor's pet warlock.

Some of the mutants began to turn away from their butchery of the zealots. With hungry squeaks, they approached the pyre, dragging away the bodies of dead servants. One of the ratmen scrambled nimbly up the pile and crouched over Kreyssig. Deftly, the creature brought its knife slashing across the ropes binding him.

'Kreyssig-man free-safe!' the vermin squeaked, its muzzle flecked with blood from some peasant it had killed.

Painfully, Kreyssig reached one of his numbed arms to his mouth and removed the gag. In his joy at being rescued, he was almost prepared to feel gratitude to these ghastly mutants. They had proven themselves far more capable than he had imagined.

Then, he noticed that the ratmen weren't freeing any of the servants. The creatures were leaving them bound as they carried them down from the pyre. Even Kreyssig's calloused heart was moved to pity when he beheld the raw horror in their eyes as the ratmen bore them off into the darkness of the kitchen. The partially devoured bodies of Auernheimer's men left little doubt as to their eventual fate.

'Those people are not my enemies,' Kreyssig told his rescuer, pointing at the bound servants.

The ratman's ears wiggled and its body shivered with an amused chitter. 'See-know much-much,' the creature explained with a wave of its paw. 'Never say-tell what they see-know!'

Kreyssig spun around as more of the ratmen swarmed up towards him, his heart going cold as he considered that they might bear him away to their lair along with the doomed servants. Instead, the creatures reached out with their paws for Baroness von den Linden.

Kreyssig saw the witch's eyes go wide with raw terror, compelling him to action. Heedless of their numbers, he dived at the ratmen, pushing them away. The mutants leapt back, their tails lashing and their fangs bared.

'You will not have her!' he shouted at the vermin, the leg of a broken chair clenched in his fist.

The ratmen glared back at him, their whiskers twitching, fangs glistening. The ratman who had cut his bonds circled him, waiting until it was behind him before pouncing. Kreyssig felt the rusty edge of the knife press against his throat.

The ratmen surged upwards once more, closing about the helpless baroness. One of them, a crook-backed thing with sores across its muzzle, leaned over her, snuffling loudly as it nuzzled her body with its nose. A moment of this loathsome action and the ratman reared back, chittering in a bestial approximation of laughter. It squeaked something in what might have been a language of sorts, bringing similar snickers from the rest of the verminous throng.

'This is your breeder?' the mutant holding a knife to him asked. Kreyssig was struck by the calm directness of the question, devoid of the fawning excitement with which the creatures usually treated him. He wondered how much of their ignorant subservience was merely pretext.

'She is my woman,' he told the mutant. Again the ratman laughed.

'Kreyssig-man take new breeder,' the ratman declared. The baroness screamed into her gag as the vermin began to lift her from the pyre. Kreyssig tensed, mustering himself for a desperate rush against the ratmen.

'Leave breeder-meat,' a raspy voice snarled from below. The ratmen carrying the witch dropped her instantly with a frightened squeak and scampered back down the pile. The mutant with the knife withdrew with similar haste.

Kreyssig rushed to the baroness's side, fumbling at the knots that bound her. He paused when that grisly voice called out again. Turning his gaze downwards, he wasn't surprised to find that the speaker was the ghastly rat-sorcerer.

'Kreyssig-man may keep his breeder,' the monster said. 'He will remember-know his friends. He will do when he is told what to do.'

It didn't take a flash of the creature's sparking fangs to drive home the threat in its words. Kreyssig kept his eyes on the grotesque monster until it shuffled off into the kitchen, withdrawing back into the cellars and sewers and whatever black burrows the vermin made their lairs. The rest of the ratmen did not linger after their leader, slinking after him in a bestial procession.

Only when the monsters were gone did Kreyssig think to remove the baroness's gag. When he did, the witch's dry mouth could cough only a single word, a word she invested with every ounce of horror her voice could command.

'Skaven!'

⤙ CHAPTER XI ⤚

Middenheim
Brauzeit, 1118

The alchemist stopped at a doorway far down the hall, very near the temple sanctuary itself. Unlike the other doors, this one bore no cross. Muttering prayers to both Verena and Shallya, Neist opened the door and walked right into a stream of Dwarfish invective.

Mandred followed Neist into the room, surprised to see a brawny dwarf lashed down to a stone bench. His torso was wound about in thick strips of bandages, and big black candles were arrayed all around his makeshift bed. Sticks of incense smouldered nearby, filling the room with a pungent scent.

'Time for more of that snake-spit you call medicine?' Kurgaz yelled at Neist. The dwarf thrashed against the straps holding him down.

'Does it still itch?' the alchemist asked. 'You know you can't scratch at it or any poison still in there will spread.'

Kurgaz glared murder at the alchemist. 'If you were anything like a real healer...' he started.

201

'Your father seemed to be of the impression that a dwarf doktor would have fussed and studied so long that you'd be dead now,' Neist told him in a placating tone. He had only a small idea of what it must have cost Kurgaz's father to entrust his son to a human healer. The degree of despair that must have gripped the older dwarf would have been immense to force him into such a breach of tradition and propriety. It was humbling to be the recipient of such a trust, even if he was the option of last resort. Despite the sombre thoughts in his head, he kept his tone towards his patient jocular. 'Maybe your own doktors were leery of incurring a grudge when they failed to help you.'

Kurgaz struggled against the bindings, the leather straps creaking ominously. 'What does a manling know of grudges and honour!'

'Nothing,' Neist admitted. Stepping to the bench, he unstoppered the bottle and allowed Kurgaz to take a long pull from it. 'That's why I'm trying to help you... Even if I end up in a beardless grave with squirms gnawing my bones.'

The dwarf coughed and spluttered as he swallowed the medicine. When he found his voice again, it was perhaps slightly less hostile, though far from apologetic. 'Squigs,' he said. 'It's squigs that'll be chewing on your bones.' The dwarf twisted his head around, fixing his irate eyes on Mandred. 'And I'm not some pickled abortion to be showing off to bored gawkers for a few coppers a peep!'

'I thought dwarfs knew better than to cuss out royalty,' the alchemist scolded Kurgaz. The dwarf's eyes went wide with alarm for a moment, then he quickly subsided into a surly silence.

'What's wrong with him?' Mandred asked. 'Is he insane?'

Neist shook his head. 'No, though I think the pain of what he's endured would have driven any man insane.' He wiped his hand on the hem of his cloak and reached into the pocket on the breast of his doublet. Carefully, he extracted an ugly looking blob of blackish green stuff. Mandred couldn't decide if the thing were more like stone or metal. What he did know was that it had an evil look about it. 'I took that out of him,' Neist explained. 'Seems there was a fight down in the Crack and Kurgaz was shot with this.' He chuckled and shook his head again. 'He claims it was fired at him by something called a skaven, though I think he's just too proud to admit it was some lucky goblin that got him.'

'Grimnir take all fool manlings,' Kurgaz cursed from his bed. 'Won't believe anything unless they see it. Count your blessings you've never seen a skaven!'

Neist was laughing again, but Mandred looked at the dwarf with renewed interest. Underfolk, ratmen who lived beneath the world. Why wouldn't the dwarfs be more familiar with such things, dwelling in the same places the monsters haunted?

'Kurgaz, what do these "skaven" look like?' Mandred asked, approaching the bench.

Before the dwarf could answer, Neist cried out in horror. The alchemist sprang away from the door as a hideous creature lunged at him. It was clad in a filthy brown robe, a heavy hood drawn close across its face, but there was no concealing the long naked tail that dragged behind it or the furry paws that gripped the rusty daggers it held. The thing was another of the verminous mutations Mandred had seen twice before!

The prince started to draw his sword to confront the first ratman when a second leapt into the cell, its daggers slashing at him. The filthy blades raked across the front of his coat, ripping it open and narrowly missing the man beneath it. Hissing and snapping, the monster pressed its attack, driving Mandred towards the corner of the cell with a flurry of attacks. The prince's forearm was gashed and cut as he tried to protect his face from the monster.

The ratman's speed was hideous, something Mandred remembered from his previous encounter. Recalling that fight, he also remembered that its strength was less formidable. Gritting his teeth, he prayed the same held true for this example of the breed.

The brute had him nearly to the wall now. Mandred could see a third monster slinking into the room, a heavy bludgeon in its paws. The thing uttered a happy squeak when it spotted the helpless dwarf lashed to the bench. The sight decided the prince. When his own foe slashed at him again, he pressed his body forwards, leaning into its attack. He felt the dagger cut deep into his arm, but at the same time he was able to catch the thing's wrist. With a brutal twist, he felt he ratman's bones snap. The vermin howled, springing away.

Mandred ignored the beast and whipped out his sword with his free hand. In one flash of steel, he raked the blade across the length of the bench, slashing through the leather straps. He heard the dwarf roar, the ratman with the club squeak in fright. Then he was too busy to worry about Kurgaz. His first adversary was back on the attack.

Holding its injured arm against its breast, the ratman sprang at Mandred, hoping to disembowel him with a rake of its blade. Years of fencing had driven home the proper response to such an assault, yet even as he darted backwards the monster's great speed allowed its dagger to stab his thigh.

Despite the agony of the wound, Mandred was grateful. For an instant, the weapon caught in his flesh. For a moment, the ratman was defenceless and within reach of his sword. It was all the time he needed. With a backhanded riposte, he opened the ratman's throat and sent it thrashing to the floor, coughing on its own blood.

Mandred spun about to confront the ratman attacking Kurgaz, but the dwarf already had the creature sprawled across the bench, its brains dashed in with its own club. Turning, he found the first ratkin, the one that had charged Neist. The brute was leaning over Neist's body, its paws frisking the alchemist's clothes. When it saw Mandred limping towards it, it bared its teeth and sprinted for the corridor.

The fiend never reached the hall. Before it could clear the doorway, a blade was thrust into its side. The ratman writhed on the impaling sword for an instant, then crumpled to the floor. Mandred noted that one of its paws was clenched, but as death claimed it the paw fell open and the strange bullet rolled from its fingers.

'Ulric's Axe!' Beck cursed, stepping into the cell. The knight's clothes were covered in blood. With an effort he tore his eyes away from the creature and looked to his prince. 'Your grace, you are hurt!'

Mandred waved away his guard's concern, tried to limp towards the corridor. Beck moved to help him despite the admonition. 'Forgive me, but I couldn't obey you. My first duty is to protect Prince Mandred von Zelt, even when it conflicts with your own orders.'

'We have to help Sofia... Make sure...'

Beck frowned at the desperation in his prince's voice. 'You can't help her now. These... things... were already there.'

All the vigour seemed to evaporate from Mandred's body. If not for Beck's support, he would have fallen to the floor. His mind whirled at the news, his heart cracked at the thought that Sofia had perished under the blades of such filth.

Why? Why had they killed her? His despairing gaze fell upon the weird bullet. Had the beasts been following that? Tracking it through the hospice, killing wherever it had been?

A gruff laugh thundered above the prince's sorrow. Shuffling out from behind the bench, his hands still clenched tight about the club that had nearly killed him, Kurgaz Smallhammer regarded the mourning Mandred. 'Aye,' the dwarf said, spitting on the verminous corpse. 'Now you know what skaven look like.'

Puskab Foulfur looked up from the mouldy tome he had been consulting. A flick of his claw sent the scabby slave holding his reading lamp slinking off into a darkened nook. The plague priest folded his paws across the ratbone lectern and regarded his visitors with pestiferous scrutiny. It was seldom that any but the plague monks dared the noxious caves Puskab had made his lair, and they only with the gravest business.

The skaven who stood before him was a black-furred killer, draped in a cloak that might have been skinned off a shadow, an array of exotic weaponry fixed to his belt. Puskab knew the weaponry to be mere adornment. The assassins of Clan Eshin never displayed the real tools of their trade.

'Speak-squeak,' Puskab ordered, a malicious gleam in his eye. One of the apprentices of Deathmaster Silke, Nartik Blackblade had fallen out of favour with his terrifying master and been given the hazardous duty of spying on the plague monks. Fortunately for him, Nartik had enough sense to turn the potential death sentence into a boon. Instead of spying *on* Puskab, Nartik was spying *for* Puskab.

'Gutter runners failed to get the jezzail bullet,' the assassin reported. 'Warmonger Vecteek mad-hate! Ordered Silke to kill-slay all gutter runners that escape!' Nartik chittered with amusement. 'I listened to one of them before...' He made a ripping motion with his claw across his throat. 'Say-tell that man-thing king-pup knows about us now.'

Puskab's tattered ears twitched in pleasure at the report. Things were going even better than he had planned. With

Clan Mors on its way, he'd decided there was no good reason to delay infecting the humans with the Black Plague. Exploiting Nartik and the gutter runners, they'd been able to spread the disease without waiting for the direct route Vecteek thought necessary. The extra weeks would make the humans much weaker when the attack finally came.

Now, however, there was a new wrinkle to consider. The dwarfs were embattled below, but they'd be too stubborn to ask for help from the humans above. But if the humans were to offer that help without the dwarfs asking, would they refuse it?

Too proud to ask for help, but not too proud to take it.

Puskab chittered as he pictured the scene. Hundreds of humans marching off to help the dwarfs, leaving their own city as a helpless morsel to be devoured by Grey Lord Vecteek.

Yes, everything was certainly going much better than he'd imagined.

Carroburg
Jahrdrung, 1115

'Don't permit this.' The plea was voiced by Princess Erna, spoken with a frantic vehemence. 'You can't do this. Even if the warlock's magic works, how can you accept your life at such a price?'

Emperor Boris glared at the woman. He started to raise his hand to strike her, but desisted. It was for low creatures like Kreyssig to hit a lady. He had more dignity than that. Still, he wished she would stop nagging at him. He wasn't without his misgivings. The girl wasn't some peasant, she was of good breeding and background. He mourned the waste of a young woman of such attractiveness. It was tragic, but how much more tragic would it be if the Empire were to be deprived of its Emperor because of the plague?

He paced across the thick bearskin rug sprawled before the hearth in his bed chamber. Sometimes Boris would glance over at Erna seated at the edge of the bed. It wasn't lost on him that for once she'd come to his room without an armed escort. It was clear what she was offering if he would indulge her entreaty.

Part of him wanted to. Part of him was sickened by what Fleischauer's magic demanded. But that part of him wasn't strong enough to overcome his fear. Not simply fear of the plague, but fear of losing control. The great and noble guests he'd assembled here formed the core of his power. Without their confidence he knew he wouldn't be able to wield his authority in their domains. Enough provinces were already rife with open defiance; he couldn't afford to lose any more.

Boris stopped pacing and scowled at the goblet of wine in his hand. 'This is vile stuff,' he declared. 'It needs some honey to sweeten it.' The cherubic amusement was back on his face as he turned towards Erna. 'Did you know the Imperial Palace has an indoor apiary? Dwarfcraft, of course. Cost a small fortune to build, but it allows Us to have fresh honey even in the dead of winter.'

'There has to be another way,' Erna insisted, ignoring his talk of bees and honey.

The Emperor dashed his goblet to the floor. 'The divine protection of Shallya?' he scoffed. 'Matriarch Katrina is as terrified as any of us! If she doesn't have faith in the goddess, why should anyone? Or maybe We should trust Moschner and his peasant medicine?'

'He's kept you healthy this long,' Erna said.

'If medicine were the answer, the plague wouldn't be killing three-quarters of Our subjects!' He turned away and gazed into the fire blazing away in the hearth. 'No, Fleischauer's magic is the only answer. The Black Plague stinks of sorcery and Chaos, it only makes sense that similar means would counteract it.'

Erna rose from the bed, came close to the Emperor. 'Then you know this is evil,' she told him.

Boris rounded on her, his eyes blazing as fiercely as the fire. 'Then you don't have to partake!' he raged. 'Exclude yourself! Go ahead and catch the plague!'

'Better that than the alternative,' Erna stated.

'If you catch the plague, We'll have you thrown over the wall,' Boris threatened. 'Don't think for a moment We won't!'

Erna turned from him, retreating across the room and into the hall. 'I'm certain your fear will spare no one,' she said as she left him.

Otwin's table no longer dominated the great hall, but the room was once again denuded of furnishings. The only object that reposed in the hall was a marble plinth in the very centre of the room. The statue that had once rested upon it had been removed, consigned to some distant corner of the castle. In its place stood an object of obscene horror.

In his desperation, this time Emperor Boris had allowed Fleischauer all the time he needed to prepare for his ritual. It had taken the warlock a fortnight to finish his conjurations and their attendant atrocities. Day and night the closed great hall had resounded with horrific screams and sinister incantations. Strange smells had seeped into the passageways, eerie lights had shone from under the doors. The icy emanations of sorcery had throbbed and pulsed and undulated. A foulness beyond the merely physical had emanated from the hall, warning people away far better than any diktat issued by the Emperor.

The end result of Fleischauer's labours was propped up on the top of the pedestal, a cushion supporting its ghastly mass. There was some resemblance to von Kirchof's niece Sasha, but the familiarity increased the horror rather than lessening it.

The woman's flesh had taken on a chalky tone and texture. All the hair had been shorn from her scalp. Across her body, strange runes had been inked with a needle of daemonbone, the symbols encompassing even her face and scalp. Situated in the gaps between the runes, their slimy black bodies seeming to be extensions of the horrible tattoos, were blood-leeches. The parasites could be seen gorging themselves on something far weightier than merely the blood of their victim, drawing into their foul bodies slivers of her innocence, of her very soul.

Sasha herself looked like a leech. Through some unholy magic, her body had been altered in unspeakable ways. Her arms and legs had atrophied, withering into stick-like stubs that were folded in upon her torso. Her teeth had fallen out, leaving behind only blackened gums and a tongue so shrivelled that it could utter only a flat, croaking susurration.

It was an abominable, unspeakable fate, a misery no sane mind could endure.

As they filed into the great hall and saw the horrifying husk of the woman, many of the Emperor's jaded followers sickened and excused themselves. Boris allowed them their moment of weakness. He knew they would be back. The magic Fleischauer offered them was too important to turn away. What man could say no to life, whatever the price?

'Everything is in readiness, Your Imperial Majesty,' Fleischauer declared with a bow. He waited for a nod from his patron, then crept across the hall to the pedestal. 'Observe,' he said. Reaching to his victim, he plucked a leech from her neck and popped it into his own mouth. More of the nobles fled as their stomachs revolted with this new horror.

'The leeches draw the magic from her essence,' Fleischauer explained when he had finished chewing the parasite. 'When they are removed, the magic is passed on to whatever eats them.'

Emperor Boris took a wary step towards the pedestal. 'This will prevent the plague?' Almost he hoped his warlock would tell him it wouldn't.

Instead, Fleischauer nodded his head in affirmation. 'For a time,' he said. 'It will be necessary to replace the leeches with new ones. They act as a preventative, but not an immunisation, to employ the secular words of dear Doktor Moschner.' The warlock paused for a moment, looking about to see if the physician was in attendance so he could gloat. He sighed when he didn't see the man. 'One leech each week should be enough. If it isn't, I can create another host.'

Boris suppressed a shudder at the suggestion. 'This is horror enough,' he said. He turned and called von Kirchof to him. The swordsman's stride lacked his usual confidence and his face was nearly as bloodless as that of his niece. Guilt, shame, self-loathing, all of these were etched upon his features and his eyes were as empty as those of a doll. When the Emperor ordered his champion to remove one of the leeches, he did so without looking at the thing Fleischauer had dismissed as their 'host'.

One by one, the others came to follow von Kirchof's example. Despite the horror of the situation, Boris felt a twinge of satisfaction when he saw Matriarch Katrina pluck one of the parasites from Sasha's body. If the High Priestess of Shallya could be driven to such despair, Princess Erna would soon recant her lofty morals.

* * *

The tiny chapel of Sigmar within the Schloss Hohenbach displayed the signs of neglect everywhere. It had been generations since Sigmar had been venerated with much zeal in Drakwald. Older gods like Ulric, Taal and Rhya were of more prominence to the Drakwalders. Count Vilner and his son Konrad had had little reason to be kindly disposed towards a deity who enabled a man like Boris to wield supreme power over them. Dust lay thick upon the floor and altar, cobwebs clung to the granite comet and bronze hammer hanging upon the wall. Woodworms had bored holes in the pews and mice had gnawed at the rugs.

Despite the dilapidation of the chapel, Erna felt a sense of peace as she knelt before the altar. As a Middenlander, she too had been raised in the faiths of older gods; however, she had also seen too much to discount Sigmar's power. She had need of that divine strength to endow her with the will to persevere. To endure as the shade of her father had told her she must.

Whatever the consequences, she wouldn't partake of the obscenity fostered by Fleischauer. Sigmar was a god who decried witchcraft and sorcery. Perhaps He would respect her determination to shun the progeny of such unholy arts.

The creak of groaning wood turned her away from the altar. Erna was surprised to see Doktor Moschner seated on one of the wormy benches. The physician's face was drawn, haunted.

'I didn't think anyone was here,' he apologised. 'Do you mind? I'd rather not be alone.' He pointed towards the hammer above the altar. 'Strength through unity. That is what Sigmar taught us. If only He had explained the lesson better.'

Erna studied the doktor as he sat in the pew, his body shaking like a leaf. 'You've seen what the sorcerer did?' she asked.

'Do not ask,' Moschner answered. 'By all the gods, do not ask and do not look.' He turned his head away from the altar and regarded Erna. 'I know I am a mere peasant, but you must believe me. Spare yourself.' He shuddered again and his body heaved as his empty stomach clenched. When the spasm passed, he again apologised.

'His Imperial Majesty has feted his guests,' Moschner hissed. 'He's fed and pampered them well!'

'Did none refuse?' Erna pressed him.

Moschner gave her a disgusted look. 'Two,' he said.

'We must pray for them,' Erna said.

'It's too late for that,' Moschner said. 'There's no help for us. The gods will have nothing to do with us now.

'We are the living damned.'

⫷ CHAPTER XII ⫸

Altdorf
Brauzeit, 1114

Under cover of night, Kreyssig's Kaiserjaeger removed the Baroness von den Linden and her paraphernalia to the abandoned residence of Lady Mirella von Wittmar. Mistress of the traitor Prince Sigdan, the noblewoman had fled Altdorf in the aftermath of the disastrous coup against Emperor Boris. Her townhouse had stood vacant and desolate since then, not even the most desperate peasant willing to seek shelter beneath such an ill-regarded roof.

The witch was far from her usual composure. Her appearance betrayed no sign of her recent ordeal. To the eye she was as ravishing and seductive as when Kreyssig had first met her. He wasn't sure if it was cosmetics or magic that covered her bruises, but whatever the cause, the baroness's vanity was intact.

No, it was a more subtle air of tension and unease that clung to the woman as she stalked through the dusty chambers of her refuge. She snapped curt commands to the men carrying her effects, alternately urging them to greater care or greater haste.

When the last of her things had been brought in, she drew near Kreyssig, gripping his arm in a clutch that was almost as cold as ice. 'Get rid of them,' she whispered into his ear.

Kreyssig bristled at the assumed authority in her tone, but his defiance wilted as he met her intense gaze. Clapping his hands together, he dismissed his troops, ordering them out into the street. When the last of them marched away, he motioned for Fuerst to close the great oaken doors and seal off the entry hall.

The baroness stared at the portly servant, causing a flush to creep into his face. Fuerst couldn't hold her gaze, turning his eyes to the floor and shuffling his feet anxiously.

'Fuerst is dependable,' Kreyssig reassured the witch. 'You can trust to his discretion.'

'It is not *I* who must fear his tongue,' the baroness retorted.

Fuerst bowed in his master's direction. 'I can wait outside...' he started to offer.

'Stand where you are,' Kreyssig snapped. It was a small, even petty thing, but he wasn't inclined to submit to the baroness's demand. He had to prove, even if only to himself, that he could defy the witch.

Her jaw clenched, the baroness spun around and stalked upstairs. Kreyssig smiled and followed her.

The witch led him into what had been the master bedchamber. Now it was littered with boxes of books – the hastily removed contents of her library. She glanced at the boxes for a moment, then descended upon one of them like a hawk swooping down on a dove. Without hesitation, she removed the topmost volumes and retrieved a heavy tome banded in black leather. Watching the proceeding, Kreyssig felt his hair stand on end, discomfited by the uncanny way the witch was drawn straight to the book she wanted.

A piebald cat came creeping out from some corner as the

baroness settled onto the musty bed sheets. The brute sat beside her feet, becoming as still as a statue. 'He will warn us,' the witch said, 'if there are rats in the walls.' She extended her hand, beckoning Kreyssig to join her.

Careful to keep his distance from the feline sentinel, Kreyssig positioned himself at the head of the bed. He glanced at the cobwebbed walls, unsettled by the woman's mention of rats. Better than anyone, he knew the efficiency of verminous spies.

He was soon to learn how little he really knew.

The baroness laid the book in her lap, folding her hands across its cover. 'You have heard of the Underfolk?'

There was an absurd quality in such a ridiculous question being asked with such grim severity. Despite his feeling of unease, Kreyssig laughed at the witch. 'What child hasn't been threatened with fables about the Underfolk!'

The baroness did not share his humour. 'A truth too awful to accept is quickly dismissed as a fable,' she warned. 'The Underfolk are real, Adolf. They are what the dwarfs have called "skaven" and fought many wars against in their long history. They are the fiends that lurk and slink in the darkness, watching and waiting to usurp the realms of men.'

Again, Kreyssig laughed, but this time it was forced laughter. 'Conquer the realms of men? Those disgusting mutants?' he scoffed.

'It has happened before,' the baroness cautioned. She opened the tome in her lap, displaying pages of illuminated text. The words were written in a cramped, spidery script, the drawings crude and horrible. A glance at the frontispiece was enough to make Kreyssig's stomach churn. 'This is an ancient Tilean text, written before the time of Sigmar. In Reikspiel, its title would be *The Tower Falls*. It describes an ancient city of men, the most powerful in the world, a kingdom that shone like the sun. For all its might, for all its magic, the city was brought to ruin by the skaven, razed so completely that even its name has been lost to legend.'

'More fables,' Kreyssig declared.

The baroness shook her head. 'Not fables – a warning. The book describes how the ancient kingdom was destroyed. The skaven didn't assault the walls with armies. Instead they burrowed beneath those walls, ferreted out men whose ambition they could exploit. Meek and fawning, they offered their services to those who would betray humanity for power. Through their proxies, they set brother against brother, fragmented society until it festered with enmity and hate. Then, when the kingdom was sufficiently weakened from within, they rose up from their hidden burrows.'

Kreyssig scowled at the baroness. The fable she was relating drove too close to his own dealings with the mutants – the skaven as she named them. He couldn't forget their demands for more and more food, food far beyond even the most gluttonous demands of the small handful of ratmen he had been led to believe dwelled beneath Altdorf. No, even without the evidence of his own eyes when the vermin had rescued them from the witch-taker, Kreyssig knew the creatures were duplicitous, pretending to be something they weren't. It was all too easy to believe the baroness when she said their ultimate ambition was to visit ruin upon mankind.

'If these creatures are what your book tells you they are,' Kreyssig said, 'then what does it say about stopping them?'

He could tell from the hollow look in the witch's eyes that whatever knowledge was inside her book, how to overcome the ratmen wasn't one of its secrets.

Kreyssig was silent for a moment, mulling over everything the ratmen had done for him. Had done for themselves. For the first time, he appreciated how the vermin had used him to their own ends. Exposing Prince Sigdan's conspiracy, the treason of Reiksmarshal Boeckenfoerde, this information hadn't been given to benefit himself or the Emperor. The skaven had done it to weaken the Empire. They had used him as their pawn.

Kreyssig had a peasant's resentment at being used. He would pay his duplicitous allies back, and in their own coin. It would need bold, immediate action to salvage the situation.

'Tell me all you can about these skaven,' Kreyssig told the baroness. He glanced out the room's window, watching the faint glow of dawn shining through the shutters. 'Then I must arrange a meeting with the new Grand Theogonist. We will need the support of the Sigmarites in the coming battle.' He favoured the witch with a cold smile. 'It is never wise to underestimate the ability of faith to motivate men.'

'In my time of need, my faith faltered.' The thunder of Auernheimer's voice was muted to a contrite rumble. The witch-taker's head was lowered, his eyes staring at the lavishly embroidered rug under his feet. His arms were folded across his breast as he sketched a half-bow towards the man he addressed.

That man leaned back in an enormous chair carved from a single piece of Drakwald timber. His jewelled fingers drummed against the clawed arm rests. When he spoke, Duke Vidor's voice was anything but low or humble.

'You worthless peasant scum!' Vidor roared. He leaned forwards, clenching his fist and shaking it at Auernheimer. 'I arranged everything for you. I practically gave them to you as a Sigmarsfest present. All you had to do was kill them. You admit they were in your hands!' Vidor snatched the dagger he wore on his belt and angrily dashed the weapon to the floor.

'Draw a blade and slash their throats. Nothing elaborate. Just kill them and be done!'

'Death would not purge the evil,' Auernheimer said, his voice still subdued. 'The corruption must be cleansed, burned away by fire. Only that will appease Great Solkan.'

'Old Night rot Solkan and all heathen gods!' Vidor raged, rising from his chair. He stalked across the hunting hall, glaring balefully at the witch-taker. He pointed at the stuffed heads of boars and wolves that adorned the walls. 'Dead!' he snapped. 'Dead! Dead! Dead! That was all you had to do. Dead, this scum Kreyssig would no longer be able to defile the Empire. He wouldn't be able to profane the halls of the Imperial Palace with his peasant's feet!' Vidor sneered at Auernheimer. 'He wouldn't be able to transgress upon the sacred traditions handed down to us by most holy Sigmar.'

Auernheimer kept his eyes on the floor. 'I have failed and I shall atone for my mistake.'

'How?' Vidor scoffed. 'It was merest luck that my spies discovered that Kreyssig was meeting with the witch to begin with. Now he will have her hidden someplace we'll never find her.' He stared carefully at Auernheimer, a suspicion growing. 'Don't think you can attack the Protector without evidence,' he warned. 'If there is no evidence linking him to the black arts, you will be denounced as an assassin. The Emperor will have you drawn and quartered – when the Kaiserjaeger tire of torturing you.'

Auernheimer raised his head, turning a pair of cold eyes upon Vidor. 'I am prepared to die for my god,' he said. 'I will not fail Solkan again.' With a flourish, the witch-taker drew back his hood, exposing a bald head that was a patchwork of grey scars. Slashing across the scars, blood streamed from fresh cuts.

Vidor stared aghast at the fanatic's display, finally tearing his gaze away. 'Cover yourself,' he hissed in a trembling tone before he remembered his noble bearing. Forcing himself to glare back at Auernheimer he added, 'You are dripping all over my floor.'

The witch-taker replaced his hood. 'The heretic must burn,' he stated simply.

Duke Vidor grimaced at the remark. When he had conceived the idea of employing Auernheimer as his cat's paw, he hadn't realised the twisted mentality at work inside the man. He had assumed he was simply some charlatan, some opportunistic sadist playing on peasant fears to aggrandise himself. Auernheimer and his rabble had seemed the perfect instrument to destroy Kreyssig, able to act where Vidor dared not. If Kreyssig's death were laid at Vidor's door, there would be scandal at the very least. Disgrace and banishment should the Emperor decide to make an example of him.

Now, for the first time, Vidor was realising the mistake he had made. Auernheimer was no charlatan. He was that most dangerous of men – the true believer. His fanatical devotion to Solkan was no pretence, it was horrible, hideous reality. There was no outrage such a man would not commit if he believed it were the will of his god, and he would do so without a moment's thought of his own life. That the witch-taker had failed once would only make him that much more determined to become a martyr and make amends before his god.

The witch-taker's death wouldn't bother Vidor, but if he should murder Kreyssig without the evidence to make even the Emperor incapable of punishing the Protector's killers…

Vidor sat back in his chair, taking a firm grip on the rests as he spoke in soft tones to the bleeding fanatic. 'Auernheimer,' he said. 'It does no good to kill Kreyssig. We must get the witch too. If we leave her alive, then she will simply bewitch someone else and use them to corrupt the Imperial court.' He smiled as he watched the witch-taker's expression fade from one of fatalistic determinacy to uncertainty. 'We must leave Kreyssig alive for the moment, wait for him to draw her back out. Only when we can get them both can we act.'

Auernheimer looked undecided. 'What of her daemons? The witch summoned a horde of daemons to rescue her. She may set such monsters loose upon the city if we don't stop her.'

'We have to find her first,' Vidor said, his words slow, patient and patronising. Reasoning with the fanatic was like reasoning with a stubborn child. He didn't believe a word of Auernheimer's story about being thwarted by a horde of rat-faced daemons. More likely, Kreyssig's Kaiserjaeger had burst in while the witch-taker was lingering over his superstitious rituals. Unable to admit that he had fled from mere men, Auernheimer had decided it was a host of daemons that had made him forsake his duty.

'Leave things to me,' Duke Vidor said. He reached again to his belt, but this time it was a sack of coins he tossed at Auernheimer's feet. 'Take that and find yourself a place to keep out of sight. When the time is right to act, I will send for you.' He saw the doubt on the witch-taker's face. 'My spies found the witch once, they will do so again.'

As he watched Auernheimer walk from the hall, Vidor wondered about his own words. Kreyssig would be doubly careful now, and after his dismissal he had few friends in the Imperial Palace. The only one of any importance was Lord Ratimir, who had retained his position as Minister of Finance.

That a weakling like Ratimir could offer any help, however, was doubtful.

Lord Ratimir cringed against the wall behind his desk, his eyes clenched tight, every muscle in his body trembling in terror. He was like a frightened child, hiding his head under the blankets to blot out some nightmarish bogey in the innocent supposition that if something went unseen then it wasn't really there.

Ratimir didn't need to see the thing to know it was still there. He could hear its paws slapping against the floor, the scrape of its tail against the cold stones. He could hear its short, wheezing breaths and the guttural coughs it uttered. He could smell the rank, mangy stink of its fur. He could feel its abhorrent presence tainting the air, turning it to foul slime that dripped against his skin.

'Rati-man,' a monstrous, scratchy voice squeaked in debased Reikspiel. The words ended on a note of chittering laughter.

'Go away!' Ratimir pleaded. He could hear the thing creeping closer. He tried to blot out the memory of its appearance, of that verminous shape slinking out from the passageway hidden behind the wall. Desperately he tried to wish away those fangs and claws, the wicked inhuman understanding shining from those beady red eyes.

Unseen, the thing crept closer. Ratimir could feel its foetid breath against his neck.

'Not leave, Rati-man,' the thing squeaked. 'Want-need speak-squeak with Rati-man. Can-will help Rati-man,' the monster promised. 'Rati-man can-will help,' the thing added with a threatening growl.

'No… No…' Ratimir sobbed. He raised his hands to cover his ears, to block the sound of that verminous voice. He wailed in disgust as furry paws seized his wrists and pulled his hands away.

'Rati-man listen-learn,' the skaven growled. 'Make Rati-man rich-strong!' A chitter of malevolent humour rippled from the monster's throat. 'Or make Rati-man Rati-meat!'

* * *

Sylvania
Sigmarzeit, 1113

Here I shall build my tabernacle.

The words still sent a shiver rushing down Lothar von
Diehl's spine. After only a few hours consulting *De Arcanis
Kadon*, Vanhal had instilled a new purpose in the vast horde
of undead. They had turned away from the northern reaches
of Sylvania, marching back into the interior, circling down
along the banks of the Eschenstir, past the battlements of Fort
Tempelhof and into the verdant plain between the vastness of
Grim Wood and the Grey Forest. For weeks the walking dead,
now including the reanimated bodies of Lothar's own army,
prowled through abandoned fields and pastures, passing
desolated villages whose sickly inhabitants cowered behind
locked doors and prayed to unheeding gods.

Lothar had felt something akin to panic growing inside him
as he observed the increasing desolation. The noxious star-
stones that had rained down on Sylvania were more prevalent
here, turning the land foul with magical emanations. He
could almost see the vegetation withering, watch the magic
seeping into its roots to twist and destroy. It was a blight that
would never be erased, a corruption that would befoul these
lands for all time. Even if the Black Plague passed, Sylvania
would never recover from this poison from the sky.

Yet it was here, deep within this corruption, that the senior
necromancer led his new pupil. Lothar knew better than to
question Vanhal's actions, even as he knew he must swallow
his pride and accept the humiliation of a noble being apprentice to a peasant. The fallen priest's power was too great, his
sorcerous knowledge too vast to challenge. His only choice

was obedience or death... And even death wouldn't free him from Vanhal's domination.

As he stared out across the plain, he could see the ancient ring of dolmens rising from the yellowed weeds and blackened grass. The weathered stones were a relic of elder ages, perhaps reared by prehuman hands. Even in such eldritch epochs, there must have been power here, a force that even inhuman minds had recognised and paid homage to. The Starfall had visited an inordinate amount of its fury upon this ancient site, fairly plastering the landscape with glowing black rocks, altering the very terrain with the magnitude of its celestial violence.

Now that terrain was being altered still further. Lothar watched as thousands of zombies and skeletons laboured around the dolmens, heaping great blocks of stone about them, transforming the standing circle into a solid ring. The blocks were quarried from hills deep within the Grim Wood, dragged by the tireless undead miles through the forest to the site of the construction. Before each block was laid into place, a patina of crushed star-stone was placed upon them, the noxious dust sizzling as it seeped into each block.

Lothar had enough magical aptitude to feel the power of this place, and to appreciate why Vanhal had been drawn here. The site of the dolmens was a sorcerous confluence, a wellspring of aethyric energies where the arcane and the mundane crossed and blended. It was what some erudite scholars had called a 'window area', a place where the veil between physical and metaphysical was worn thin. In such an environment, the power of evocations would be amplified, fed by the fountainhead itself. Here, it would be possible to effect conjurations that would make even his matricidal ritual seem insignificant!

But Vanhal intended even more than simply tapping that

wellspring. The construction he had initiated would bind and harness the aethyric power, magnifying its potential a thousandfold. The castle he was building would act as a magical fulcrum, a nexus of arcane energies. With such power to draw upon, he would be able to perform feats of sorcery not seen since Nagash the Black strode the earth.

It was both a frightening and awesome prospect.

Lothar turned away from his observation of the undead labourers and studied the source of the tremendous will that drove them on. Vanhal was seated upon his morbid palanquin, legs folded beneath him, *De Arcanis Kadon* lying open in his lap. The necromancer's eyes were closed, his breathing so shallow that no frost formed in the chilly air. To all appearances, he seemed more lifeless than the zombies building his castle.

Carefully, Lothar stole towards the palanquin, concerned that Vanhal's magic had sent his spirit somewhere that made it impossible to return to his body. For all his injured pride, the possibility alarmed the baron. There was so much he still needed to learn. To be cheated now, when he had gained an inkling of how vast his mentor's abilities and ambitions were, was too awful to contemplate.

He was just climbing onto the palanquin to check for evidence of life when Vanhal's cold voice brought his pulse racing. Startled, Lothar dropped back to the blighted ground.

'Separate a thousand workers from the construction,' Vanhal said, the words coming more as a ghostly vibration than an actual voice. 'Send them to scour the bogs and graveyards. I will need more hands to build my tabernacle. Have them bring me those hands.'

Lothar looked back at the construction, fear once again asserting itself. Vanhal already had more undead under his control than any magician Lothar had heard of outside of legends. Indeed, he was amazed that the necromancer could maintain command of so many. To try to raise and control still more was madness.

'Do as I say,' Vanhal's phantom tones demanded, as though taking note of Lothar's hesitation and reading his mind. 'All must be prepared before Geheimnisnacht.'

Mention of the night of sorcery explained the urgency behind Vanhal's command, but only served to increase Lothar's uneasiness. He expected the castle to be built in only a few months! It would take an army several times greater than the one already under his control to achieve such a feat. Surely Vanhal didn't intend to try and control so many undead?

One of the eyes behind the necromancer's mask opened and directed a baleful look at Lothar. 'All will be in readiness before Geheimnisnacht,' he said, this time in a deep and menacing voice. Lothar's objections withered before that stare and that voice.

'It shall be as you desire, master,' Lothar said, bowing before the sinister necromancer.

Vanhal closed his eye, refocused his mind to manipulating the undead labourers. Lothar shuddered, wondering if his master were mad. There was, of course, another possibility: that he could do everything he believed himself capable of doing. The idea of such power vested within one man's mind and body rekindled Lothar's faltering determination. Bowing again, he hurried from the presence of his master. He would detach some of the undead, send them to steal corpses from graves. He would see how far Vanhal's abilities could stretch.

It would be a good lesson. An indication of how far his own ambitions might rise.

* * *

In normal circumstances, the smell of rotting meat mixed with warpstone would have been a delicious combination to the nose of any skaven. The promise of food and wealth all in the same sniff! Somewhere along the way, however, some insidious fiend had turned the normal state of existence on its tail. Seerlord Skrittar wasn't certain what malefic force was behind this cataclysmic reversal, but he was certain this calamity was directed solely against himself.

His careful plans, his elaborate rituals to break pieces from the moon and seed them in the earth had been so perfectly flawless. The man-things were sick from the plague, the other Grey Lords were busy plundering the nests and warrens abandoned by the humans. Nothing should have interfered!

Then the stinky-things started showing up. Since that first encounter, when the cowards of Clan Fester had tucked their tails between their legs and scurried off in abject terror, the skaven had been unable to range more than a few food-stops before running into the wormy man-things! What was worse, the filth-things had started to gather warpstone. They were stealing Skrittar's treasure out from under his very whiskers!

It was enough to make a less disciplined skaven grind his fangs to stumps. Skrittar, however, wasn't about to concede defeat. Magnanimously setting aside his personal disagreements with their... unique... interpretation of the Horned Rat, he had invited Clan Pestilens to take a hand in gathering the warpstone. Vrask Bilebroth and his disciples weren't quite outcasts, but with Vrask's rival Puskab Foulfur on the Council of Thirteen, they weren't the most popular plague monks. It had been embarrassingly easy to entice the plague priest from hiding by promising to lend him the protection of the grey seers against any retaliation his pestilential enemy might be planning.

Vrask had better be worth the effort Skrittar had expended

on him! Watching the plague priest and his disciples sneak across an open field, the seerlord had to concede that the fanatics had a certain amount of bravado. Mad as bedbugs, but brave. It was a combination he might wish his other lackeys possessed, but Warlord Manglrr was such a craven mouse he wasn't even present to watch Clan Pestilens at work – he'd left that duty to a sub-chief while staying behind in the comfort of the tunnels. It was an outrageous dereliction – especially after his loud demands that the Black Plague be brought to bear against the stink-things!

The stink-things were just beyond the fallow field Vrask and his disciples were crawling across. There was a man-thing bury-plot there. They had been busy for some time excavating the graves, piling the desiccated bodies on carts. It was a mad sort of exercise; there couldn't be more than a few bites of meat on any of the bodies, and what was there would be tough and chewy. Certainly the stink-things weren't very smart if this was their idea of foraging.

Skrittar lashed his tail in frustrated anticipation, waiting for the plague monks to confront the enemy. Vrask had promised a great deal with his new strain of plague, a refinement of the disease concocted by Puskab. The grey seer was anxious to see if Vrask's boasts were justified.

After what seemed an eternity, the enemy appeared to finally notice the plague monks. First a few, then several dozen of the stink-things turned around to stare with glazed eyes at the fallow field. It took the creatures almost a minute to react to the approaching enemy, but when they finally did it was with chilling purposefulness. The stink-things advanced in a shambling mass towards the creeping skaven.

As the foe began to emerge from the graveyard, Vrask rose to his feet and snarled a command to his green-robed fanatics. The plague monks rose from the earth, the foremost of them bearing massive poles of brass and bronze, a metal ball suspended from the tip by a length of chain. Chittering their heretical psalms, the ratmen tore away the thick folds of cloth bundled about the cage-like orbs. With the covering removed, noxious fumes billowed from inside each censer as strips of plague-ridden meat slowly dissolved beneath a coating of acid.

Even from a distance, Skrittar could sense the deadly properties of those pestilential fumes. He could see the exposed arms of the plague monks shedding fur, could smell their naked skin blistering in the caustic clouds. Corrosion dripped down the metal poles and from the spiked frames of the censer balls. Nothing living could withstand such a lethal admixture!

Skrittar's thrill of triumph faded as the plague monks charged into the slowly advancing zombies. Swinging their censers like enormous flails, the skaven fanned the fumes full into the faces of the stink-things. Flesh peeled and blistered, the foul sores and buboes of the Black Plague spread across enemy skin. It was a hideous, magnificent sight! But that magnificence soon transformed into horror. The ghastly damage the censers visited upon the stink-things, the corrosive disease that should have slaughtered an entire city of humans, did little more than slow the creatures down. The odd bit, an arm here, an ear there, dropped away when the flesh binding it to the body became too corroded to restrain it, but the loss scarcely phased the stink-things. With monotonous, steady tread, the undead closed upon Vrask's disciples.

The Black Plague, that much touted super-weapon of Clan Pestilens' had failed! For an instant, Skrittar wondered if the plague priest had tried to trick him, to fob off some fraudulent strain of pox as the infamous Death, but a single sniff of the abject horror in Vrask's scent told him otherwise.

Vrask was genuinely shocked at the plague's ineffectiveness. He stood in the field, watching as the stink-things advanced towards his disciples and began to drag them down one after another, rending them with rotten hands and smashing them down with rusty spades. His shock was such that only when his disciples began to flee past him did Vrask's instinctual self-preservation kick in.

Manglrr's chieftain and the other representatives of Clan Fester were already scurrying back to the tunnels, the plague monks close behind. Skrittar, however, lingered. There were two reasons for such a display of courage. First, it would drive home to the vermin that the seerlord was far above them, so mighty he need not fear the things that brought them terror. Second, he'd already noticed that the stink-things weren't pursuing the plague monks, but instead were shambling back to the graveyard.

A third reason for lingering on the field of battle presented itself as Vrask Bilebroth went scurrying by, his decayed robes fluttering behind him like the tattered wings of a cave bat. Skrittar's eyes narrowed, lips peeled back from his fangs. Extending his staff, he sent a bolt of power smashing into the fleeing plague priest. Vrask was sent tumbling snout over tail with such violence that one of the horns fitted to his cowl snapped off and went spinning into the night. Skrittar scowled at the presumptions of Clan Pestilens. The heretics were required by custom to deliver the horned skaven born to their breeders to the grey seers for indoctrination and train-ing, but they were boldly lax about such obligations. Many of the plague priests and festering chantors within their clan sported horns and antlers in open challenge to the grey seers, some of them natural growths, others affectations of their costume. Vrask, it seemed, was one of the latter, a mundane skaven posing as a mage-rat.

Skrittar covered the ground between himself and the sprawled Vrask in a series of bounding hops, bringing his staff crashing down on the plague priest's head before he could rise. He heard fangs splinter under the blow, smelt skaven blood oozing from Vrask's mouth.

'Mercy-pity!' Vrask whined. 'Not kill-slay loyal-true Vrask!'

Skrittar glared down at the cringing plague priest. 'You lied to me, flea-nibbler!' he spat, raising the staff for another strike. 'Promise-say that the plague will kill all stink-things!' He waved a paw at the graveyard where the creatures were already resuming their excavation. 'Does that look like you killed them? I needed you to reassure those mice of Fester, now I'll be lucky if the whole inbred clan doesn't go scurrying back to Skavenblight!'

Vrask folded his paws over his head, trying to protect himself from the coming blow. 'Yes-yes, I take-take blame-fault! That is why you need-want Vrask!'

The staff froze a hair from Vrask's horned cowl. A cunning gleam crept into Skrittar's eyes. It was true, the fault did lie with Vrask. He'd failed to destroy the stink-things and thereby he had proved that Manglrr's faith in the efficacy of Clan Pestilens was misplaced. More than anything Skrittar could have said or done, Vrask had exposed the limitations of his heretical clan. The rats of Fester would be confused and dispirited by the plague's failure, but if Skrittar struck quickly and boldly, he could turn that to his favour. He could redirect that disillusion into a more zealous adherence to the Horned One's true dogma and His sacred voice on earth – Seerlord Skrittar!

'On your feet, tick-licker!' Skrittar snarled, kicking Vrask until he obeyed. 'You are right, I can use you to show Manglrr where his faith should rest.' The seerlord sucked at his fangs as he glanced back at the graveyard. Disgracing Clan Pestilens was all nice and wonderful, but that still left the problem of what to do about the stink-things.

A hideous thought occurred to Skrittar. Ignoring the whining Vrask, he raised his snout and sniffed again at the air. Yes, there was something wrong about that decayed smell, that tang of dark magic he could detect running beneath the stink of skaven fear musk. It was the smell from the fields, and it was a smell he didn't like. It was a smell that made him think of abhorrent moments from countless generations past, when the Under-Empire made war against the Curse-thing of Cripple Peak.

Just the idea of that horrifying place made Skrittar's glands clench. For generations entire clans had perished trying to seize the warpstone mines under Cripple Peak, vying for control with a terrifying mage-thing and the dead-things at its command. The tale of that conflict had passed into legend, a parable to warn future litters.

The foes they fought now, these decaying thieves who stole his warpstone, they were like the dead-things of Cripple Peak! They were the undead, creatures immune to the plagues of Pestilens because they weren't really alive. Unleash a thousand poxes, and the monsters would keep coming.

As he considered the problem, Skrittar gnashed his fangs. There was a solution, of course, but it would mean letting other paws into the food stash. He didn't like to invite further complications into what had already become an overly complicated scheme, but there was no getting away from the fact that if he didn't then he'd never gather the warpstone before the entire Under-Empire was aware of it.

Clan Fester was afraid to fight the undead. Clan Pestilens was unable to fight them. But there was one clan who had built their very identity around their legacy as killers of the dead. They were the last clan to leave Cripple Peak, the survivors of the long war against the Accursed One.

Yes, Skrittar decided, it was time to form an alliance with Warlord Nekrot and the grave-rats of Clan Mordkin.

⫷ CHAPTER XIII ⫸

Sylvania
Nachgeheim, 1113

They sat within a hall of black stone, the walls climbing higher around them as the indefatigable undead pursued their ceaseless labours. With each layer of stone, Vanhal could feel the energies of the site swelling, magnified, like the current of some invisible river being funnelled into a smaller channel. Idly, he wondered if this place had known such power in the distant age of Kadon, when primitive tribes had congregated here to commune with the spectres of their tribal totems. Were his efforts increasing the energy or simply restoring them to levels they had once enjoyed?

It was a debate for philosophers. The answer to such a question could only be inconsequential to Vanhal's pursuits. What mattered to him wasn't the power this site had once possessed, it was the power with which it might again be endowed. Power to remake the world, to strip away all the misery and confusion and bestow true peace upon all mankind.

Vanhal glanced over at his companion, the noble von

Diehl. The baron was busily studying the plans for the construction, blueprints drawn by a phantom hand during the séance the two necromancers had conducted under the dark of the moon. From Lothar's changing expression, the wonder in his eyes, it was apparent that the intricacies of those designs were not lost upon him. This building would be unlike any other, engineered not as a home or fortress, tomb or temple. It would be devoted to an arcane purpose, its every stone set in such a way as to evoke an aethyric resonance and bolster the magical harmonies.

The séance chamber had been one of the first rooms Vanhal's legion completed, built with seventeen angles to do homage to the gods of Nehekhara, twelve doors to allow passage of netherworld winds, and a single great mirror of obsidian to form a permanent window into that netherworld. Sixteen circles were etched into the floor, each ring demarked by a series of intertwining glyphs, runes, sigils and pictograms – all invocations or proscriptions towards unseen forces. Each ring was broken by a narrow door, a gap that would be sealed with lines of saltpetre and myrrh when *powers* were to be evoked. The least entities would require only the small, inner circles to be sealed. The outer rings, pressing almost to the walls of the chamber, would guard the conjurer against even the mightiest of principalities.

The spirit Vanhal had evoked last night had required the sealing of six of the circles. From the dust of ages, the necromancer had summoned the shade of Hotepk, grand priest and chief architect to Settra the Imperishable, mighty pharaoh of lost Khemri. When he had first manifested, the ancient spectre had affected the appearance of a lion-headed godling, hurling curses and threats down on the heads of the mortals who had dared intrude upon his slumber. Lothar had been cowed by the ghost's malignity and might, but Vanhal was unmoved. Using formulae he had deciphered from *De Arcanis Kadon*, invoking *names* unspoken for two thousand years, he subjugated the apparition, binding it to his will. The lion-headed godling dissipated, leaving behind it a glowering, dusky man in the robes and kirtle of ages past. After another threat, drawing on the fearsome rage of Usekhp, the Dreaming God, the ghost acquiesced into grudging servility and drew up the plans for Vanhal's tower.

Hotepk's brilliance in life hadn't been diminished in death. Under the command of Vanhal, the spirit designed a structure that would at once increase, focus and contain the powerful aethyric energies coursing through the site. This place would become a magical fulcrum like no other, surpassing even the dread potentialities of the Black Pyramid and Castle Drachenfels.

As he studied the designs, Lothar von Diehl was awakening to that scale of power. 'This upper gallery,' he exclaimed in an awed gasp. 'It is like a permanent manifestation of Zahak's Ritual of Sendings! And this... This concentric ring of cells aligned to a central arcade overlooking the core of the tower. With the proper specimens restrained in those niches you would be able to create a soul cage of unprecedented scope. The blackest daemon would be a plaything inside such a trap!'

Vanhal simply nodded and turned his gaze to the zombies shambling about the scaffolding, levering the heavy blocks of stone into place. 'Pride is a wasteful thing,' he said, his voice a cold whisper. 'The braggart is the lowest form of erudite. For those who truly understand, there is no need to boast. Accomplishment is the end in itself.'

Lothar stared at the former priest, an expression of incredulity on his thin face. He ran a hand through his decaying scalp, a clump of greying hair coming away with his fingers.

'Humility is the refuge of those without courage,' he protested. 'I have moved among the nobility, I have watched
those who command and those who obey. It has taught me
one thing: the only thing that matters in this world is power.
Raw, merciless power. The ambition to acquire it. The ruthlessness to use it.' He slapped his hand against the blueprints.
'This is power such as the world has never seen. Vanhaldenschlosse will become the throne of the Empire, all men will
bow down before the threat of this place!'

The baron's words faded in a pained choke. Clutching at
his throat, he dropped to the floor, gasping for breath as
spectral fingers tightened around his neck. Vanhal stared at
his apprentice, observing his struggles with cold indifference.
'Already I can make any man I wish bow down before me.
What does such a thing accomplish? It feeds the ego, dulls
the mind with delusion and attachment. Fear and hate...
love and loyalty, what are these things measured against the
long march of history?' He paused, studying the changing
shades of Lothar's face, watching the pleading hands groping
towards him. 'Your mind is deluded. You still think of this
power as something to exploit and use, to conquer others
and dominate them. Such blindness,' he said, shaking his
head. With a flick of his hand, he dispelled the ghostly coils
about his apprentice's neck. The constriction removed, Lothar
collapsed to the floor, sucking great breaths into his starved
lungs.

For an instant, murder gleamed in the baron's eyes. He
should have suffered no peasant to lay hand on him!
Quickly, Lothar turned his face, forcing himself to be composed. Fighting down his pride, smothering his very identity,
he crawled across the floor on his knees and grovelled at the
foot of Vanhal's skeletal chair. 'Please, master,' he pleaded.
'Help me to see. Help me to understand as you understand!'

A cold, knowing smile crawled across Vanhal's lips. 'First,' he warned his apprentice, 'you must learn to control the spirit inside you if you would aspire to control the spirits *outside*. If you cannot be true to yourself, then you are doomed to ignorance.'

Lothar backed away from the seated necromancer, a feeling of horror pounding through him. Again, he wondered at the limits of the man's power, wondered if Vanhal were able to peer into the mind and soul of his apprentice. Wondered if what was residing within the flesh of his mentor was merely the spirit of a fallen priest or if something else, something from *beyond*, had seeped into that body.

'I will… I will supervise the construction,' Lothar promised. 'Under my direct guidance, the pace will increase. Vanhalden-schlosse will be completed as you command.'

Vanhal nodded, accepting his apprentice's display of rekindled servitude. 'Raise another multitude. Beyond the Grim Wood you will find Hel Fenn. The bogs are heavy with the Fennone dead buried there. Call them up, bring with them their grave goods, the weapons and armour entombed with them.'

'You talk as though you expect an attack,' Lothar said. 'Have your powers given you a premonition? Is Count Malbork moving against us?'

'I have been given warning,' Vanhal said. 'From the first, I have seen that it would be necessary to give battle to the enemy. Not the Sylvanians, but an enemy who is also so blind as to think dominance is the only purpose of power.' Waving his hand, Vanhal dismissed his apprentice.

Staring again at the rising walls of his tower, Vanhal considered the name Lothar had given this place. *Vanhaldenschlosse*, 'Vanhal's Castle'. Somehow, the name managed to send a shiver through the necromancer. He was thinking of another place, another site of power that had become the namesake of its builder.

The doubts lurking in Lothar's mind, the suspicion that there was something *else* within the body of his master – these were questions that brooded within the deepest recesses of Vanhal's soul. Sometimes his own thoughts seemed alien to him, rising from some influence he didn't understand. The pain of his family's destruction was still there, but what of the love that had brought that pain? It was but a distant echo, devoid of intimacy. Try as he might, he couldn't revisit those memories without an inexplicable aloofness.

When he had conjured the ghost of his brother's wife, the woman he himself had loved what seemed a lifetime ago, Vanhal had been warned. Raising Aysha's shade had been his first act of necromancy. In that moment, she had tried to warn him. *Sympathies of spirit and mentality have flung open the gate that can never be closed again.*

Sympathies, but with what was he supposed to be in sympathy?

Dressed in armour made from the bones of their own clan-kin, the skaven host scurried through the sacred grove of ash and yew overlooking the sprawl of Tempelhof's graveyard. The ratmen reeked of death, their scent carrying a carrion stench not unlike that lingering about vultures and jackals. It was a scavenger stink imbued from a diet of rotten meat and bone marrow, a smell generations of grave-rats had cultivated until it oozed from their glands.

Seerlord Skrittar had always found that stench both nauseating and threatening. Clan Mordkin was something of an enigma within the Under-Empire. They had been the last to stand against the Curse-thing in the burrows beneath Cripple Peak. For generations they had warred against the dead-things when the rest of skavendom decided to abandon the mountain to the undead. Mordkin had become isolated and alone, scratching an existence at the very fringes of civilisation. When at last they had conceded defeat and retreated from the pits of Nagashizzar, their return had been a frenzy of carnage. Instead of crawling back with tails between their legs and throats exposed, Mordkin had prowled about the edges of the Under-Empire, attacking weak clans and seizing their burrows. Only when they grew formidable enough to stand on their own had the grave-rats allowed themselves to be properly restored to society.

As a pup, Skrittar had heard the stories of Mordkin. They were the bogey-beasts of skavendom, the dark menace every warlord invoked to intimidate his minions. 'Don't rat on your chief or Mordkin will invade your warren and eat you all!' It was a threat that was well founded. Where other clans would subdue and subjugate those they defeated, absorbing them into their own ranks as slaves, Mordkin took no prisoners. Every ratman they conquered was butchered – left to rot until the meat was putrid enough to satisfy creatures accustomed to the flesh of zombies and ghouls.

Insular and mysterious as they were, Mordkin had one saving grace, at least in the eyes of the grey seers. Generations fighting against the Curse-thing had rendered them devout worshippers of the Horned Rat, hearkening to the words of the grey seers a bit more attentively than clans like Rictus and Mors. If it weren't for their peculiar belief in achieving a greater connection to the Horned Rat by nibbling the bones of His prophets, they might have been a formidable weapon in the seerlord's arsenal. Instead, they simply presented a convenient way of disposing of troublesome grey seers. Even the most wily didn't last more than a few months in a Mordkin burrow.

Even now, surrounded by Warlord Manglrr and the copious bodyguard of stormvermin which accompanied him, Skrittar felt his fur crawl every time the eyes of Bonelord Nekrot glanced his way. Such worshipful piety was horrifying when accompanied by that hungry twitch of Nekrot's whiskers. Skrittar kept one paw tight about the mummified cat's paw in his pocket, a talisman that never failed to bring him good luck. In case the paw decided now was a good time to betray him, the seerlord kept reciting the formula for a particularly potent spell under his breath and hoped Nekrot didn't have a mummy paw in *his* pocket!

Bonelord Nekrot was a grisly sight. It was the tradition of Clan Mordkin that their leaders wore the bones of their predecessors; indeed, it was the first act expected of any warlord after usurping the position. Any too weak after such a fight to strip the bones from their fallen leader would be quickly killed by some ambitious underling of their own. That was how Nekrot had gained his own supremacy, waiting until his chief, Hussk, killed Bonelord Karkus in single combat, then falling upon his injured master.

It was the bones of Hussk that Nekrot wore, tribute to the half-minute the chief had been warlord of Clan Mordkin. The bleached fangs of Hussk's skull framed Nekrot's furless snout and narrow head. The ribs and spine of his betrayed master enclosed Nekrot's torso, and sectioned halves of other bones guarded his limbs. Hussk's tail had been stretched and dried, forming a ghoulish belt. A broad-bladed sword of bronze, a khopesh that had been plundered from one of the Cursething's Dark Lords, hung from Nekrot's belt, sheathed in a scabbard wrapped in the pelt of Karkus.

Everything about Nekrot's scent and appearance screamed death. Not the cold, efficient death promised by the cloaked adepts of Eshin or the slinking stranglers of Skully. It was the hungry, unreasoning threat of a rabid wolf-rat, the predatory gleam of a prowling cat, the scavenging stare of a hovering vulture.

'Watch-see, Holy One,' Nekrot's sepulchral moan wheezed across the fangs of his helm. His black, hungry eyes again turned to Skrittar. 'My grave-rats will kill-kill all dead-things.' He rubbed his pale, almost colourless, paws together and shifted his gaze to Manglrr. 'We show-tell Fester-rats how to fight.' Lips peeled away, exposing yellowed fangs in a threat-display as Nekrot gazed past Manglrr and studied the cloaked figure of Vrask Bilebroth. 'Show-tell why Fester-rats should stay true to Horned One,' he added with a touch of contempt. Vrask glared back at the bonelord, but the plague priest was wise enough to keep his tongue.

'You promise much-much,' Skrittar sneered, gnashing his fangs. 'One third of my warpstone goes to your bone-lickers,' he added, nearly choking on the words. 'But only if they can really protect from the dead-things!'

'Watch-see!' Nekrot repeated, fur bristling. Huddled under the nest of interwoven branches that roofed the little shrine built by the man-things inside the grove, the skaven warlords observed as the ghoulish army emerged from the cover of the trees and descended upon the graveyard beyond. The cemetery was far older and larger than the one in which Vrask's plague monks had failed to subdue the foe. Consequently, the undead defiling the graves were much more numerous. Even so, Clan Mordkin rushed at them with almost un-skavenlike boldness and ferocity. The way they ripped into the zombies was like watching a pack of starving wolf-rats.

Skrittar bruxed his fangs. That, of course, was the trick! Reared on a diet of decaying flesh, the grave-rats of Mordkin associated that smell with food. The odour of the zombies was throwing them into a frenzy born of hunger, driving out even their basest fears! It was an impressive exploitation of his underlings' psychology on Nekrot's part, and staging this display was having the desired effect upon Manglrr and the leaders of Clan Fester. After this slaughter, their confidence would be restored.

They would need it! After weeks drawing upon his store of divination spells and augury rituals, Skrittar had discovered the source of the undead infestation. Destroying that source would be a formidable task, one that would require the full might of both Clan Fester and Clan Mordkin to overcome. Certainly, there would be awful casualties, but afterwards they would have a free hand in Sylvania.

Besides, Skrittar reflected, if anything did go wrong he could blame it all on Vrask.

With that happy thought in mind, the seerlord settled back and enjoyed the spectacle of Nekrot's ravening horde.

Middenheim
Kaldezeit, 1118

'Does anyone want to argue with that?' Kurgaz Smallhammer bellowed, hefting the filthy skaven carcass onto the Fauschlagstein. Fleas hopped from the loathsome carcass as it slammed down. The assembled councillors recoiled in disgust, von Vogelthal jumping from his chair and scrambling to the far side of the room.

Graf Gunthar sighed at the dramatic display. He'd seen the carcass some hours before, when Mandred had returned to the Middenpalaz with both the dwarf and the thing that had tried to kill him. It had certainly done much to impress upon him that a strange and sinister threat was menacing Middenheim.

Even so, he'd hoped to present the evidence in a more diplomatic fashion, to prepare his court for the horror of what they faced. Instead, the council's bickering had grated on Kurgaz's patience. Thane Hardin had warned him about the warrior's volatile temper.

Grand Master Vitholf was the first to recover his poise. Leaning across the table, he poked at the body with his sword. 'It's a ratman,' he conceded, nodding first to Kurgaz, then to Thane Hardin. 'You say your people have been fighting these things for months?'

'The grudge with the ratkin is ancient beyond human reckoning,' Thane Hardin corrected him. 'The present infestation afflicting Grungni's Tower began four moons ago.'

Vitholf digested that information. The dwarfs had discussed much about these skaven, putting flesh to the old human fables about Underfolk. It was a disgusting thing for a man to contemplate. A society of humanoid rodents dwelling under their feet, plotting the downfall of civilization itself. The dwarfs insisted that such was the truth.

The story was borne out by Prince Mandred, who related his earlier encounters with representatives of the breed. Once in company with the Kineater and once lurking about with a cult of plague-worshippers on the walls of Middenheim. The implications of that first incident were almost too horrific to contemplate.

'The outbreak of plague in Middenheim would coincide with the infestation in Karak Grazhyakh,' Mandred said. His wounds had been dressed and bathed in healing unguents, but he was still weak from loss of blood, lending his voice an uncharacteristic air of fatigue. 'The two must be related.'

'I agree, your grace,' Brother Richter pronounced. 'The southern provinces have been beset by entire armies of these things. The brutes that enslaved Averland and Solland, burned Wissenburg and Pfeildorf were kin of this vermin. History tells us that Sigmar once drove this abomination from the Empire, but even His priesthood has ignored the veracity of His deed, finding it more politic to treat the account as mere legend.'

Ar-Ulric scowled at the carcass, knocking its tail away from where he was sitting. 'Men would find it hard to sleep at night knowing things like that were scurrying around in the dark,' the old priest declaimed. 'It is one thing to accept the beastmen, the northmen and greenskins. Those are enemies out in the wild or beyond the borders.' He brought his hand slapping against the table. 'These... These strike at where we live. Even a wolf must feel secure in its den.'

'His holiness is right,' von Vogelthal stated. Slowly the chamberlain returned to the table, a visible shiver coursing through him at every step. 'The peasants would revolt if they found out such things were prowling about under their toes! Why toil for their noble lords if those same lords cannot protect them from walking vermin?'

Thane Hardin nodded sadly. 'That is why my people did not warn you about the fight in the tunnels. We feared you would flee Middenheim, abandon the city out of terror.'

'Your opinion of men must be very low,' Graf Gunthar said, pain in his voice.

'You squabble and bicker among yourselves so much already,' Kurgaz grumbled, 'that any crisis is apt to set you at each other's throats. Is it any wonder we prefer to do our own fighting?'

Brother Richter turned towards Kurgaz. 'That is an injustice,' he stated. 'To be certain, humanity is more fractious and turbulent than dwarfkind, but our differences make us stronger, not weaker. Sigmar united twelve tribes, bound twelve different peoples into a single purpose. Through Him, the divergent traditions and ideas of the tribes were disseminated, spread throughout the Empire. The adversity of war brought men together in a way that peace and tranquillity never would. You fear that a crisis will bring out the worst in men. I reject that idea! I tell you that it is through crisis that you find the best in men.'

Kurgaz looked away from the Sigmarite, staring instead at Mandred, recalling how the prince had exposed himself to attack in order to cut the dwarf's bonds. 'I think I've already seen that,' he admitted.

'Karak Grazhyakh will need the resources Middenheim can provide,' Graf Gunthar said. 'Food, timber, cloth and fur. Soldiers too.'

Thane Hardin shook his head at the last offer. 'My people are accustomed to fighting in the tunnels and understand something of the foe. We will drive the skaven back. It is only a matter of time.'

'With all due respect, thane,' Mandred said, 'time is the one thing we don't have. If these fiends are behind the plague, then every hour they infest the Ulricsberg allows them to spread disease among the people of Middenheim. This battle may be fought in your domain, but this fight doesn't belong to dwarfs alone. Our people are at risk as well. You must allow us to help purge the mountain of these vermin.'

Ar-Ulric took up the call for battle. 'A decisive thrust against the skaven, delivered by men and dwarfs. The reinforcements could be just the edge needed to tip the balance. Moreover, if we wait to fight we risk losing the battle to the plague.'

Thane Hardin and Kurgaz held a brief consultation in Khazalid, their words unintelligible to nearly all of the men around them, only Richter being versed enough in that language to follow some of what they were saying.

'All right,' Thane Hardin declared. 'We will allow human

troops in the tunnels. But we want their commander to be someone we can trust.' He pointed a stubby finger at Mandred.

Graf Gunthar rose from his chair, glowering at the dwarf leader. 'Impossible,' he said. 'My son is still healing from his wounds.'

'He'll get better,' Kurgaz observed. 'We'll bring up some medicinal ale that'll have him spry in no time.' He flexed his stiff arm, wincing as a flash of pain from his wound shot through him. 'Better than anything you have up here,' he added. Without the worry of incurring a grudge, dwarf doktoring could work wonders in a very short time.

'Father, I want to go,' Mandred said. 'The dwarfs helped build Middenheim. Even if we were sure of our own safety, we'd be obligated to help. Honour demands nothing less of us.' He glared at the carcass. 'Besides, I have a personal reckoning with these monsters.'

Reluctantly, Graf Gunthar settled back in his seat, lines of worry wrinkling his brow. Without a word, he nodded at his son.

'Only the soldiers accompanying his grace should be made aware of the kind of enemy we face,' von Vogelthal suggested. 'If the knowledge were to become public it would spread panic just when we can afford it least.' He bowed in apology to Brother Richter. 'Not to contradict your speech about strength in adversity, but it is a wise man who prepares for the worst possibility.'

'Then prepare we shall,' Graf Gunthar declared. 'No public speech, I agree with you there. That would breed panic. What we must do is to be subtle.' He cast his gaze from one councillor to another. 'Each liege lord will take his vassals into confidence. His vassals in turn will disseminate the truth to his subjects. From master to servant, piece by piece, we spread the word. We feed each man's pride with a sacred trust instead of fostering a general panic. Frightened men panic, proud men fight.'

Proud, stubborn, the dwarfs fought to the last warrior to defend the lower workings. It took the hordes of Clan Mors three days and a thousand slaves to overwhelm the thirty dwarfs who made their stand in the gallery. By the time it was over, the floor was caked in black blood and fur.

Warlord Vrrmik gnawed on the severed finger of a dwarf as he surveyed the carnage. It wasn't the loss of life that upset him – there were always more slaves to be had. Clan Mors was renowned for ferreting out weaker clans and enslaving them. The toughness of the enemy didn't bother him either – he'd fought dwarfs often enough to know they were always more trouble than they were worth.

No, the burr in Vrrmik's fur was the indignity of it all! Any victory he achieved was bitter and hollow, as empty as a dried-out flea. Warmonger Vecteek had summoned Clan Mors to Wolfrock under false pretences. Vrrmik had imagined he would share in the victory, that some of the triumph enjoyed by Clan Rictus would rub off on Clan Mors. Now, as Vecteek mobilised Mors, Vrrmik was discovering the depth of the tyrant's duplicity.

Clan Mors was nothing but a diversionary force, meant to distract and draw off the dwarfs while Vecteek was leading the main body of skaven by a circuitous route into the heart of the dwarfhold!

Vrrmik was a horrifying sight as he prowled among the dead, his white fur standing stark against his black armour. Forged by the artisans of Clan Skryre, the steel plates had been steeped in powdered warpstone, lending it a horrendous capacity for damage. Some among the chiefs of Clan Mors had seen a hydra break its fangs on that armour, more than a few had cursed it for deflecting the blades of their hired assassins. Out of his armour, Vrrmik was formidable, huge and powerful even by the standards of a clan known for breeding hulking warriors. In his warp-plate, Vrrmik felt almost invincible.

'Splendid victory, Great Warlord Vrrmik,' Puskab Foulfur's phlegmy voice coughed in the white skaven's ear. The warlord almost choked on the finger he was gnawing. Springing away, he bared his fangs at the plague priest. One of the handicaps of his armour was that so much warpstone close to him had rendered his sense of smell quite feeble.

'Plague-spitter,' Vrrmik hissed at the antlered priest. 'Go back to Vecteek. His paws might need licking. Hurry-scurry!'

Puskab coughed in a diseased semblance of amusement. 'The Horned One favours Vecteek,' he said.

Vrrmik gnashed his fangs. It was another point that disgusted him, the way the grey seers fawned over Vecteek and declared him the Horned Rat's favourite pup! Just thinking about it made him want to kill something. He hoped his scouts would find some more dwarf tunnel fighters soon.

'Clan Rictus steal-take all glory for itself,' Puskab continued. 'Leave nothing for Clan Pestilens. Less for Clan Mors.'

'What do you speak-squeak?' Vrrmik wondered aloud. It occurred to him that the plague monks were dire enemies of the grey seers and had their own brand of heretical religion. To date, they had been supportive of Vecteek and prospered by that alliance. Perhaps, however, Arch-Plaguelord Nurglitch wanted something more than simple wealth for his clan.

'Vecteek has his plan,' Puskab said, creeping closer, his eyes glittering in the torchlight. 'We will have our own plan,' he chittered.

The plague priest's voice dropped to a low whisper as he described what those plans would be.

—< CHAPTER XIV >—

Altdorf
Brauzeit, 1114

Flanked by dour warrior priests, sombre in their black robes
and grey cloaks, Adolf Kreyssig felt distinctly ill at ease as he
strode through the echoing marble halls of the Great Cathedral. Alabaster busts of Sigmarite scions frowned down at him
from niches carved into the forest of stone columns supporting the vaulted ceiling hundreds of feet overhead. Sprawling
tapestries depicting the victories of Sigmar stretched across
the walls, commemorating the triumphs of Sigmar the man.
Stained-glass windows towered above the tapestries, each
scene recalling a different miracle visited upon the Empire by
Sigmar the god. Kreyssig had long ago cast aside his credulity
for gods and miracles, but even he felt small surrounded by
the grandiose iconography of the temple.

The warrior priests conducted their charge down a set of
marble steps and into a wide corridor that led away from
the main sanctuary and past the monastic cells of their own
militant order. The few persons they passed wore the brown
habits of mendicants or the white cassocks of friars. None of

the higher clergy, the temple elders, were in evidence.

The Protector of the Empire shifted uncomfortably as the cat he led on a leash rubbed against his leg. One of the baroness's creatures, of course, intended to warn him if there were skaven about. He hesitated a moment as the feline perked up its head and glanced about the hall. After a moment, it subsided, returning to that lazy indolence that had characterised its attitude since he'd acquired it. He stared uneasily at the animal, then glared at the curious faces of his guides. It wasn't for men of their station to question the habits of their betters.

Mounting a spiral stairway, Kreyssig was led up into the great spire that rose high above the cathedral. Narrow windows cut into the exterior wall overlooked the city, affording an almost breathtaking view of Altdorf. He could see clear to the Reik, watch the few ships stubbornly plying the river trade navigating between the mid-channel islands. He could see the vast sprawl of the Kaisergarten, the scorched wreck where Breadburg had once stood, the ramshackle slumland that had grown up in the shadow of the capital's walls. He could see the Courts of Justice and the Imperial Palace. From this height, even these imperious structures seemed small.

When he thought they could climb no higher, one of the silent priests motioned for Kreyssig to wait. Stepping ahead of the Protector, the priest drew a heavy key from around his neck, thrusting it into a door that blended in so perfectly with the wall that Kreyssig was unaware it was even there until the cleric began to draw it open. With a bow, the priest gestured for Kreyssig to enter.

Kreyssig's breath caught in his throat as he beheld the magnificence of the chamber. Inwardly, he chided himself for ever being awed by the *Kaiseraugen*. Emperor Boris's picture window was a crude, crass thing compared to what he now saw. Except for the floor and a hip-high stripe of wall, the entire chamber seemed composed of glass, only the steel framework spoiling the transparency of the curved ceiling overhead. The effect when he walked into the room was like stepping onto the clouds themselves. He felt his head swim for a moment as a feeling of vertigo tugged at his brain.

It didn't take an architect to recognize that no human hand had built this chamber. There was something esoteric, magical about it. Dwarfcraft, but on a far more magnificent scale than Boris Goldgather's windows and apiary. Those had been constructed with no greater ambition than the gold the Emperor was paying. The dwarfs who had laboured on the Great Cathedral had done so for far more profound reasons, repaying ancient debts of honour and friendship.

'Welcome to the observium,' a dolorous voice pronounced.

By force of will, Kreyssig turned his gaze from the dizzying vista beyond the transparent walls. He stared at the speaker, the cleric in his golden robes, a massive pectoral of jade hanging about his neck. Stefan Schoppe wasn't the same man who had begged and pleaded in the Dragon's Hole. His ascension from mere lector to Grand Theogonist had transformed him into the most powerful cleric in Altdorf. There was fire in his eye as he met Kreyssig's gaze, an almost palpable and entirely understandable animosity.

Kreyssig bowed his head. 'I bring affections from your daughter, your holiness,' he greeted the Grand Theogonist. With all the majesty of his surroundings, all the power he now wielded, it was prudent to remind Stefan that his daughter was still a guest of the Kaiserjaeger.

The fire flickered in the priest's eyes, but did not go out. The Grand Theogonist slowly stepped away from the cherrywood lectern and the vellum star chart he had been perusing. Gripping the long stave that formed part of his regalia, he approached his impious petitioner, sweeping past the ordained astrologers who bustled about the set of parchment-strewn tables that dominated one side of the room. For an instant, he paused, turning his head and glancing at the other side of the room. Here there were no tables, only a number of small stone benches spaced equidistantly along the length of the chamber. Upon each bench there knelt a woman dressed in thick cream-coloured robes. Each of the women was bald as an egg, a thick blindfold wrapped about her face. Rumour claimed that there were no eyes beneath the blindfolds, that in exchange for their divine vision the Sigmarite augurs removed their real eyes as an offering to their god.

'The augurs have told me much about you, Kreyssig,' the priest said as he came closer, unmistakable threat behind his voice.

Kreyssig nodded, appreciating that there were other ways of learning things beyond spies and traitors. The Temple howled for the blood of witches and warlocks, but they had no compunction about exploiting such abilities for themselves. They just called their witches augurs and prophets.

'Perhaps we would be better discussing these things in private, your holiness,' Kreyssig suggested. The Grand Theogonist didn't hesitate, but brought the end of his staff against the marble floor. At the sound, the warrior priests withdrew and the astrologers quit their labours and quietly filed out onto the stairway. The blind augurs, however, remained where they were. If they had truly disclosed his secrets to Stefan, there was small point in demanding they leave.

'Rumours have reached these holy halls,' the Grand Theogonist said. 'The streets of Altdorf whisper that the Protector of the Empire is a heretic, that he consorts with witches and daemons. They say that he has used spells to corrupt the Emperor and force him from his palace. They say it is because of him that the gods shun these lands and plague runs rampant through the city.'

'Lies and fabrications,' Kreyssig snorted derisively. 'Peasant babble that means nothing and threatens less.'

'The common folk are starving,' the Grand Theogonist observed. 'Their families sicken, they count their dead by the bushel. They feel their Emperor has deserted them and that their gods punish them for the wickedness of their noble lords. They seek out a cause for their troubles, something they can understand and fight. At the moment they are too afraid to act upon the rumours they spread. But there comes a moment when fear burns itself out, leaving only hatred and resentment behind.'

The Grand Theogonist's hand clenched tighter about the haft of his staff. 'And, of course, even the most humble man has an obligation to Sigmar. A duty to root out heresy, to destroy those who would call upon the Ruinous Powers, to purge the land of all tainted by the touch of Chaos.' He closed his eyes, reciting a passage from the *Deus Sigmar*. '*Accursed be they who treat with the witch, for they abandon themselves to obscenity. Blessed be they who suffer not the abomination among them, for they shall be known as the pure.*'

'There is a time for dogma and a time to be practical,' Kreyssig hissed at the priest.

Opening his eyes, the Grand Theogonist glared at Kreyssig. 'A mandate from the divine,' he cried. 'A holy duty to overwhelm and destroy heretics like yourself, no matter where they be found!'

Kreyssig scowled at Stefan. Almost absently, he removed a fold of cloth from under the sleeve of his doublet, a strip cut from the dress of Stefan's daughter. He laughed darkly when he saw the irate priest flinch at the sight. 'For all your pious doggerel, there is a man under those robes, the heart of a father beating in that breast. You have invoked the name of your god, I call upon the name of your daughter... and her continued good health.'

The Grand Theogonist seemed to wilt against his staff, despair draining the rage from his eyes. 'I should never have become hierophant of Mighty Sigmar,' he muttered. 'I am too weak to do His work.'

'But not too weak to serve the Empire,' Kreyssig stated. He waved his hand at the silent augurs. 'Haven't your harpies told you? There is a greater threat menacing Altdorf than a lone witch and her spells.' He studied the dispirited Stefan. In choosing the lector as the new Grand Theogonist, he had chosen well. A man who was too weak-willed to oppose him. As Emperor Boris always said, a ruler must never let the gods become more powerful than himself.

'They have told me,' the Grand Theogonist said, his voice low. 'They have told me that the forgotten enemy has returned, the creeping pestilence Mighty Sigmar exterminated from these lands.' The priest's body straightened, a trace of fierceness crept into his voice. 'They have told me you have allied with these horrors, encouraged their vile presence in the city.'

Some of Kreyssig's assurance faltered as he heard the growled accusation, too much truth in the priest's words for him to deny. 'That is why I am the only man who can save Altdorf. I admit, I made a mistake. I treated with these monsters without knowing who and what they really were. That damage is done, but if they had not worked through me they should have found themselves someone else. Perhaps, it was Sigmar's will that it was I they thought to work through.'

'You dare invoke Sigmar's name?' The Grand Theogonist shook his head.

'Call it what you will, then,' Kreyssig snarled back, 'but the fact remains that I have spoken with these vermin. I know something of how they think, how they work.' He tapped the side of his head. 'That knowledge is the only thing that can save this city.'

Again, the Grand Theogonist stiffened. 'The grace of Sigmar is our only salvation.'

Kreyssig smiled at the remark. 'Indeed, I shall need Sigmar to help me. I will need his sanction to prepare this city for the battle that is coming. I will need you to bestow the god's blessing upon my edicts as Protector.'

The Grand Theogonist scowled at Kreyssig. 'That would be blasphemy, a violation of this holy office.'

'If we are to save this city – and your precious temple – you will have Sigmar sanction all that I do,' Kreyssig said. 'Otherwise, we will all be at the mercy of these monsters. In a few hours, I will deliver the first in a series of edicts. My first step will be the seizure of noble property.'

'They will never stand for it,' the Grand Theogonist warned. 'No matter your position or the blessing of the Temple.'

'The Vons will submit,' Kreyssig said. 'They will submit because they don't want to be torn apart by the starving masses of Altdorf's peasantry. They will submit because it is the only way any of them will survive.' He laughed bitterly. 'You see, there is going to be a great scandal, a few traitors in the Imperial court who have been siphoning off food stores and selling them to the nobles in Talabheim. After a little blue blood is shed, the rest of the nobles will stay quiet.'

'I cannot lend my authority to such a murderous falsehood,' the Grand Theogonist stated.

'You will do more than lend your authority to it,' Kreyssig said. 'You will publicly accuse these nobles of heresy! The Temple of Sigmar will rouse the peasants, stir them until their howls for blood echo in the ears of the Vons. While the other temples sit idle, the Sigmarites will rally the people of Altdorf.'

'To what end? How do these lies prepare us for a confrontation with the Underfolk?'

Kreyssig smiled, amused by the priest's lack of vision. It seemed there were things his augurs couldn't tell him. 'We will pursue a new war against Talabheim. I will initiate conscription to rebuild the Imperial army, requisition arms from the guilds and knightly orders. When I am finished, the army of Altdorf will be the strongest force in the Empire. All it will take is a bit of cooperation from the Temple.'

'Blasphemy, you mean,' the priest said.

'A necessary evil,' Kreyssig stated. 'An ill-tasting morsel to digest if we are to save Altdorf.'

The Grand Theogonist glared back at him, a flame of fervour in his eyes. 'I am no longer Stefan Schoppe,' he said in a voice as hard as granite. 'A Grand Theogonist takes on a dwarfish name when he dons the golden robes. You may call me Gazulgrund.'

Kreyssig chuckled at the severity with which the priest intoned his adopted name. Perhaps to a Sigmarite such ceremony was important, but to him it was just so much superstitious nonsense.

'Call yourself whatever you like,' Kreyssig said. 'So long as you do not fail me.' He studied the Grand Theogonist a moment, then turned away. 'I suggest you get yourself a cat,' he called as he strode from the observium. 'They'll warn you if any ratty ears are around.'

Even after Kreyssig was gone, Grand Theogonist Gazulgrund continued to glare where the man had stood, hate burning in his eyes.

Sythar Doom reclined on a mattress stuffed with mouse-down and wrapped himself more tightly in a ratskin rug, a precaution against the clammy chill seeping into the warren from the river. He turned his ensorcelled gaze upon the stalactite ceiling far above, watching as bats flittered about the roof.

His tail lashed from side to side as he watched a clutch of skavenslaves creeping about the ceiling, trying to catch the flying rodents. Batwing soup was a delicious delicacy, but only if the wings weren't torn. For some reason they lost their taste if they weren't intact. Hence the best way to gather the wings was to climb up and snatch the beasts from their roosts.

The Warpmaster of Clan Skryre lashed his tail in amusement as one of the slaves lost his grip and went crashing to the cavern floor. There was no cry; like any good hunting slave his tongue had been cut out long ago. No scream disturbed the bats, only the meaty thump of the ratman as he smacked into the unyielding limestone floor. The twitching corpse was quickly dragged away by a Clan Mors quartermaster. With an army as large as the one Sythar Doom had assembled, every little bit of meat was a blessing.

Sythar ran a paw along the tube fastened to the underside of his jaw, checking it for ticks. The filthy parasites sometimes congregated there, incinerating themselves as soon as they bit into the warpstone-infused lining. The shrivelled husks were a tasty titbit with a delicious crunch to them. Sadly, none of the insects rewarded Sythar's preening. They'd become noticeably scarce in Skavenblight since the collapse of Clan Verms. It was almost enough to make him regret the Wormlord's demise. Almost.

Metal fangs gleamed as Sythar shifted himself around to face the massive warp-lantern that towered beside his pillowed bed. The Luminator scrambled about the many dials and flywheels, making certain the sliver of warpstone providing the eerie green light didn't exude too much energy. Early experiments with the warplight had resulted in some unfortunate accidents, but those incidents had become noticeably less frequent over time. Since the Luminator was chained to his machine, Sythar was very confident the skaven would do his utmost to ensure the warplight's stability.

'Report-talk from Rati-man.' The whining voice of a Clan Skully rodent drew Sythar's attention away from the warp-light. The jewelled eyes gleamed balefully in the green luminance as he stared down at the spy.

'Speak-squeak,' Sythar declared, a note of annoyance in his posture.

'Abin-gnaw Hakk,' the skaven said, affecting a loathsomely human bow. Sythar glared at the piebald creature, his body draped in the scarlet cloak of Raksheed Deathclaw's elite cult of murder-rats. Whatever expression there was on Abin-gnaw's face was hidden behind the crimson cloth wrapped across his muzzle. From the arrogance of the spy's posture and the boldness with which he announced his identity, it was obvious he was trying to draw attention to himself.

Sythar chittered happily. Any messenger who declared himself to his superiors could only be the bearer of good news. Most likely, the original message had started much lower on Clan Skully's food chain before Abin-gnaw snatched it for himself.

The Warpmaster sprawled back on his mouse-fur cushions and flicked one of his claws at Abin-gnaw, motioning him to speak.

'Man-things train-teach army,' Abin-gnaw squeaked. 'Take-bring much weapons. Much armour.'

Sythar rose from his cushions, sparks flashing from his fangs. What was this fool-meat babbling about! The humans were raising an army. They were taking up arms. By what mental deficiency did this low-grade mouse-fondling moron think this was good news!

Abin-gnaw wasn't fool enough to ignore Sythar's anger. With an almost boneless motion, he flopped to the floor and twisted about so he could bare his throat to the Warpmaster in the universal skaven gesture of submission. 'Listen-wait!' the spy squeaked. 'Man-things make war on other man-thing nest!'

The Warpmaster stood for a moment, digesting the frantic report. He glanced at the armoured warpguard who flanked his throne, stared up at the slaves slinking about the ceiling, at the confusion of sycophants and underlings who littered the floor of the cavern, waiting to attend the merest twitch of his whisker. Sythar could smell the excitement in their scent, knew the same odours were spilling from his own glands.

The humans were going to fight one another! He would have to take credit for this before one of the grey seers declared it a beneficence from the Horned Rat!

Abin-gnaw slowly rose to his feet, bowing again to Sythar Doom. This time the Warpmaster took no notice of the humanlike gesture. He was thinking instead about the abilities of Clan Skully's murder-rats, their proficiency with the strangler's noose. At the moment, there were three leaders of the expedition to conquer Altdorf. Clan Mors had their General Twych, established by Ratlord Vecteek himself as commander of the mission. Then there was that odious Deacon Blistrr from Clan Pestilens. While he was at it, he might add Grey Seer Pakritt to his wish list. Without those three, Warpmaster Sythar Doom would be supreme commander of the campaign.

With the prospect of a protracted war evaporating, with the humans getting ready to fight among themselves, Sythar no longer saw any reason why he should allow these incompetent underlings to leech off his glory!

'Attend,' Sythar hissed, motioning Abin-gnaw closer. Only when the murder-rat was so close that the sparks from Sythar's fangs singed his fur, did the Warpmaster whisper his plans. To Clan Skryre would belong the prestige of conquering the man-thing nest, and Clan Skully would be paid well to eliminate the few obstacles in their way.

Kazad Migdhal
Kaldezeit, 1113

An uncanny coldness had settled into the great hall of Kazad Migdhal, a chill that refused to be expelled however high Bori Wodinsson stoked the fire roaring within the hearth. Keeper of King Skalf's hearth, it was a terrible disgrace to Bori that this chill had been allowed to infest the hall. He kept his gaze downcast, not daring to meet the eyes of the dwarfs assembled about the king's table.

Bori's apprentices, under his direction, dutifully fed more logs into the blaze. The heat of the flames singed their young beards and sent streams of sweat pouring down their foreheads. Bori had already removed his drenched hat and had stripped away his baldric. He was absolutely at a loss to understand how he could feel so cold yet have his body react as though he'd been dropped into an inferno.

'I can still see my breath!' one of the thanes at the table laughed, punctuating his remark by expelling a great cloud of mist. The display brought raucous laughs from the other dwarfs in the hall.

'Leave Bori be!' quipped another thane, gesticulating with a white-capped mug of beer. 'The cold is good for the brew!'

'But not my beard,' grumbled a silver-haired elder. He brought a gloved hand stroking down the length of his face, and held the fingers up for those seated around him to inspect. 'Look! Frost!'

Bori's face turned crimson beneath his own beard. The shame of this night was going to humiliate his family for three generations. It would take a great deal of valour to extirpate this embarrassment, and over so ridiculous a thing. A room that wouldn't grow warm if an entire forest was fed into its hearth!

He risked turning away from the fire for a moment, directing a covert glance at King Skalf's throne. His sovereign sat in stony silence, jewelled fingers closed tight about the stem of a golden goblet. There was just the slightest trace of discomfort on the king's face, a condemnation Bori felt all the more keenly for its subtlety. Bonds of friendship between himself and the king had earned him his position. It was shameful that those same bonds should restrain King Skalf's rightful displeasure. It was an imposition on Bori's part, one he doubted he could ever make amends for.

'Build it higher!' Bori snarled at his helpers, shoving yet another log into the blaze. A finger of flame reached out, searing his fingers and causing him to jump back. Sucking at the burned skin, he glared vindictively at the blaze. What would it take to warm this cursed hall!

Bori never knew what compelled him to raise his eyes to the marble mantle above the hearth or the trophy bolted to the wall above it. Some primitive instinct, some animalistic foreboding of danger, whatever it was alerted the dwarf to something far more horrible than a stubborn chill.

Skalf had made himself king by stealing into the abandoned halls of Karak Azgal and slaying the mighty dragon Graug the Terrible. Karak Migdhal had been established in one of the abandoned stronghold's gatehouses, a dwarf outpost in lands long lost to their kind. The outpost was rich, however, made wealthy by the treasure reclaimed from the dragon's hoard. Skalf had earned not only the title of king, but also that of

Dragonslayer, and far more than his crown, he valued the gigantic reptilian head displayed in his great hall.

The head of Graug had been bolted to the wall, hung there as a mark of Skalf's strength and courage. It was something to awe visitors and impress dignitaries. To the dwarfs who had cast aside old allegiances to make their fortune in Karak Migdhal, it was a symbol of dwarf perseverance against all foes.

Now, however, it was a thing of terror. Before Bori's horrified gaze, leathery lids pulled back from the glass eyes taxidermists had set into the dragon's skull. Scaly lips retreated from sword-sized fangs. The withered stump of a forked tongue flicked out, shivering in the air.

Bori cried out once, then the reanimated head lurched down from its fastenings, tearing the bolts free as it crashed to the floor. The Keeper of the Hearth vanished in the dragon's maw, caught by those immense, snapping jaws.

Dumbstruck thanes and guildmasters looked up from their drinks, staring in disbelief at the revived head. Oaths and curses spilled from their mouths as they watched the huge head flop about on the floor with ghastly life, trying to propel itself towards fresh prey.

'Fetch my axe,' King Skalf snarled, casting aside his goblet and unfastening the royal cloak pinned to his shoulders. He glared at the monstrous head, feeling rage as he watched Bori's blood drip down its fangs.

'I don't know how many times I must slay you, monster!' he roared. 'But by Grimnir, I swear this time I will make a better job of it!'

The captain of Skalf's bodyguard rushed to the king's side, *Wyrmbiter* clutched in his hands. One look at his king told the dwarf it was useless to try and dissuade him from this battle. Reluctantly, he pressed the weapon into Skalf's hand.

The instant *Wyrmbiter* was in his hands, King Skalf was no more. The stoic dignity demanded of a ruler fell away, succumbing to the reckless determination of the adventurer and fortune-seeker. Again, he was simply Skalf Hraddisson, determined to earn the name of Dragonslayer.

Graug's head flailed about on the floor, turning to fix its glass gaze on the advancing dwarf. A loathsome, dry cough rasped up from the stump of neck remaining to the reptile, spraying bits of Bori across the floor.

This final indignity inflicted upon his friend sent icy rage coursing through Skalf's veins. Roaring an inarticulate cry of vengeance, the dwarf flung himself at the dragon. In a great leap, Skalf brought his gromril axe flashing down. The blade crunched through scaly flesh and draconic bone, hewing through Graug's forehead, cleaving down along its snout. When he ripped his blade free, the dragon's skull had been nearly cut in half, bisected down the middle.

Skalf glared down at the mutilated head, watching in disgust as its wreckage continued to wriggle with obscene life. 'Burn it,' he growled at his awestruck subjects, setting *Wyrmbiter* across his shoulder as he stalked from the hall.

Sylvania
Kaldezeit, 1113

Baron Lothar von Diehl ran his hand across the bare expanse of his scalp, finding even the last trace of his black mane had deserted him. The powers of a necromancer did not come without a price, he reflected, and the greater the power the more taxing that price became. He could feel dark magic flowing through his body, inundating every speck of his being

with sorcery. The sensation had only increased as Vanhaldenschlosse came nearer to completion. How much greater might
his power become once the tower was finished?

Could mere flesh endure long enough? It was a question he
feared to ask himself. The toll such magic was taking upon
him was tremendous. Since submitting to Vanhal's tutelage,
Lothar's body had aged decades, withering from that of a
young noble at the prime of life to a scarecrow semblance of
elderly decrepitude.

It had cost him much to learn what he had, but Lothar
would pry still more secrets from his mentor. Watching the
ancient dead rise from the muck of Hel Fenn, seeing those
legions of bog-men enslaved to his every command – that
was power! It was power that belonged to him, power greater
than any man had wielded before.

Any man, except one. How much greater must be the
secrets Vanhal yet kept to himself, that he would bestow so
casually such spells into the keeping of his apprentice? Lothar
had always doubted the wisdom of gods, but to allow such
knowledge to be possessed by a mere peasant was proof that
whatever gods there were, they must be idiots. By his own
words, Vanhal had proven he was an unfit vessel for such
powers. He spoke of ability as its own achievement, but of
what use was a blade if it were never drawn? What did it matter if one could do a thing if there were no purpose behind it?

As he stalked through the gates of the half-formed castle, his legion of bog-men shambling after him, Lothar felt
uneasy. Something was wrong. He could feel a tremendous
energy in the air, a force so powerful that it seemed to pluck
at his own spirit, as though eager to drag it from his flesh. It
was a frightful, abominable sensation, a sickening violation
of his innermost being. For all the revulsion it evoked, the
experience was even more horrible because Lothar knew it

wasn't even directed against him, he simply happened to be within its reach. He was inconsequential to it, nothing more than a hapless bystander.

Anger flared inside the necromancer. Evoking spells of protection, girding his soul in spectral armour, Lothar dashed inside the unfinished fortress, racing down the length of the vast assembly hall. With every step, he could feel the aethyric vibrations growing, a dull hum of energy that caused his ears to ring and a trickle of blood to stream down his nose. A wave of nausea swept through him, threatening to flatten him as he mounted the spiral staircase and began to climb to the séance room. Lothar dabbed his finger in the blood draining down his nose, using the sanguine medium to strengthen his spells of protection. Refortified, he rushed up the steps.

The séance room was a howling tempest of sorcerous energies, gales of spectral power whipping about the chamber. The circles on the floor were struggling to contain that force; Lothar could see the discordant harmonies whirling about inside each ring, his witchsight giving him a glimpse at formless things struggling to possess shape.

This, however, was the least manifestation of the power being drawn into this place. Arrayed about the séance chamber were the tops of the pre-human menhirs. The ancient stones were ablaze with eldritch emanations, tendrils of light that crackled and danced as they ascended through the half-formed tower. Lothar craned his head, following their gyrations until they were lost in the night sky. For an instant, each stream would flicker, divert itself inwards. With a feeling of dread, he realised that there was a rhythm to those diversions, a horrible suggestiveness. It was like watching the pulsations of a beating heart.

'Vanhal!' Lothar cried out. The peasant necromancer had been cagey, dispatching his disciple on a meaningless errand before beginning some forbidden rite he wished to keep secret! Bitterly, the baron reflected on his foolish appreciation of the power he had evoked at Hel Fenn. Beside this, such magic was nothing.

'Vanhal!' he shouted once more, making no effort to hide the anger in his tone. The fallen priest had played him for a fool with his talk of enemies and armies. As though any foe would be so mad as to challenge the necromancer in his citadel.

'Vanhal!' Lothar roared a third time. There was hesitancy in his voice now. With a full appreciation for the power of this site, he wondered if even Vanhal could manipulate such energies. Perhaps his master had been too ambitious, had initiated an invocation he couldn't control? The pleasure of seeing Vanhal brought low was tempered by the realisation that if he expired, his secrets would pass with him. Having had a taste of such power, to lose all chance of making it his own was a horror too ghastly to contemplate.

Panicked, Lothar mounted the scaffolding and ascended the rickety framework. For the first time he realised that none of the workers were around. The absence of Vanhal's undead gave the baron pause. Where had they gone? Had they slipped past the necromancer's control and simply wandered off, or had they been consumed by the magic he had unleashed? It was a terrifying prospect, to be annihilated by a surge of undirected vibration, consumed so completely that not even dust should remain.

Hundreds of feet above, Lothar could see the pulsing streams of light bowing inwards. Again, he could not shake the impression of a beating heart. There was only one heart that could have provoked such resonance. Whether he was still in control or not, Vanhal was alive.

How long he could remain that way was something Lothar

didn't know. No man could tap into such forces, channel them through mere flesh and spirit for long. Whatever his purpose, Vanhal had to be restrained before the power he had unleashed consumed him.

The altar of bones rotated upon a nimbus of wailing emanations far above the framework of Vanhaldenschlosse's highest tower. The stone roof below was rendered almost transparent by the phantom harmonies, its substance taking upon itself something of the spectral essence of the forces rushing through it.

Lothar could feel his own flesh fading, evaporating into an ethereal shadow. Only by fierce exertion of his will was he able to maintain his grip on corporeal substance. As he climbed onto the half-circle of the roof, he stared up at Vanhal's levitating altar above him, at the grotesquery of the necromancer himself, his black robes whipping about him as daemon winds clawed at his spirit. He stood in a nimbus of ghostly fog that blazed with fearful fires. Green ghoul-lights blazed from Vanhal's eyes, ghostly flashes of energy rippled from his outstretched arms. With each pulsation of the energies rising from the menhirs, the necromancer appeared to flicker, to phase out of reality only to reappear before he could entirely fade away.

Vanhal was doing more than simply harnessing the magic rushing up through his tower – he was *becoming* one with that power! As impossible as such a thing might seem, when Lothar lifted his gaze to stare at the sky above the skeletal altar, he received an even bigger shock. The stars were aligned differently than they had been when he entered the tower. Somehow, Vanhal had caused the castle to slip through time, to fall into the vacuity between seconds and emerge in another. In the rest of the world, the stars sat in the month of

Vorhexen. But the tower had leaped ahead. It existed in the dark hours of Hexentag!

The baron nearly lost his concentration, that fragile link that kept his flesh from fading into a ghostly vapour. The enormity of such a feat was beyond anything he had believed possible. Yet there must be some motive behind Vanhal's act, some dire need that had pushed him to such a supreme and dangerous evocation.

Hexentag! That was the answer. The aethyric current flowing through the tower would be even more potent in the haunted hours of that ominous day. Yet the answer itself begged another question: why did Vanhal need all this arcane energy?

Casting his gaze away from the stars and the necromancer's altar, Lothar looked down to the plain far below. At once he saw the massed formations of Vanhal's undead legions, arrayed across the landscape like chessmen on a board. The size of that army would have impressed him had it not been for the still greater host scurrying towards the silent ranks of walking dead. Skaven! The verminous Underfolk of myth turned into hideous reality. This was the enemy Vanhal had tried to prepare for, but the monsters had come too soon. Their multitudes were innumerable. They were a chittering colossus descending upon the puny army arrayed against them.

Lothar could hear the first bestial shrieks as the ratmen struck the front ranks of zombies, hacking and clawing their way through decayed flesh and bleached bone with murderous fury. The undead tried to repel the vermin, but their numbers were too small to hold the foe back.

'The gnawing rat will not befoul the dream,' Vanhal's words slashed across Lothar's ears like a knife. 'Not this time,' the necromancer vowed, his eyes blazing more brightly.

'Nothing can stand against that,' Lothar protested, waving his hand at the swarming vermin below. 'You must use your magic to make the tower disappear!'

'I have used my magic,' Vanhal hissed. 'But it is the skaven who will disappear.' The necromancer raised his hand, ribbons of spectral light rippling along his fingers, making the bones glow beneath his wizened flesh.

Lothar followed the pointing finger of his master. What colour was left in his pale countenance drained away as a gargantuan shape soared down from the heavens, blotting out those incongruous stars. As it descended towards the tower, the luminescent tendrils of power revealed its monstrous form, a scaly leviathan of muscle and sinew, of decayed flesh and exposed bone. Tattered pinions held it aloft, fanning a necrotic stench across the tower. A great tail undulated behind it, the forked tip flashing through the streamers of aethyric vibration. No face, no matter how horrific, could have matched the grisly stump of neck that projected from the gigantic shoulders. The head had been cut clean away long ago, leaving only a gaping wound dark with clotted blood and wriggling worms.

It was a dragon. Vanhal had used his magic to raise the bones of a dragon as one of his undead slaves! This was the weapon the necromancer's sorcery had drawn to destroy the skaven horde.

'The most recently killed of dragonkind,' Vanhal pronounced. 'He will be your warhorse. Strike down the skaven. Leave none alive.'

As he stared up at the zombie dragon, Lothar almost felt sorry for those slinking creatures down below.

◄ CHAPTER XV ►

Altdorf
Brauzeit, 1114

Kreyssig turned away from the empty throne and slowly descended the steps leading up to the dais. He ignored the pair of armoured Kaiserknecht who flanked the throne Boris had left behind when he retreated from the plague-stricken city. For their part, the knights did their best to ignore him too. Their grand master had made no secret of his displeasure over taking orders from a commoner.

Still, whatever his feelings, Grand Master Leiber had too many ideas about honour and duty to refuse Kreyssig's commands. So long as Kreyssig wore the regalia of the Emperor's chosen Protector, he could depend upon the unwavering loyalty of the Kaiserknecht – whatever he asked them to do.

Half a dozen of the armoured warriors came trooping into the Winter Audience Hall, their steel clattering as they filed through the frescoed entry and passed beneath the magnificent lattice of silver and ivory that hovered between the ornamental pillars lining the entry. Between them, looking dishevelled and unruly, the left side of his face purple with a fresh bruise, Duke Vidor loped into the hall, his arms laden down with iron manacles and a great collar locked about his neck.

A thin smile formed on Kreyssig's face as he observed Vidor's humiliation. There was something supremely satisfying about seeing a noble brought low, humbled and humiliated as they humbled and humiliated the thousands of peasants they exploited. Given the chance, he would see all of the blue-bloods in chains, dragged through the streets like cattle before being strung up by their perfumed necks.

Only for a moment did Kreyssig relish that vision of an Empire free from the parasitic nobility, free from the tyranny of breeding and pedigree. An Empire where even a mere peasant might become ruler if he were cautious enough. Ruthless enough.

For the moment, Kreyssig had to balance the two, caution and ruthlessness. The nobles were too entrenched to depose. Nor was it desirous to discard them out of hand. Not when they might still prove useful.

'Leave us,' Kreyssig told the duke's escort. The knights saluted stiffly, then filed from the room. Kreyssig turned his head, repeated the order to the Kaiserknecht beside the throne. Without a word, the armoured warriors withdrew.

Kreyssig waited until the knights were gone before approaching the shackled duke. 'Now we can speak more freely,' he said.

Vidor's face contorted into an expression of withering contempt. 'If you expect me to beg, you may as well just kill me now. I'll not grovel before a peasant.'

'If I wanted to hear you beg, I would never have brought you to the palace,' Kreyssig said. 'You would have gone to the Courts of Justice with all the other profiteering traitors.'

'What happened?' Vidor scoffed. 'Couldn't your Kaiserjaeger

fabricate enough evidence for you? Or did somebody warn you that you have already gone too far? The nobility won't sit idle while you cart them off on trumped up allegations of treason!'

'I have only purged the Imperial court of a few villains who were seeking to aggrandize themselves while their liege lords are away,' Kreyssig said, though he made little effort to put any conviction in his voice. 'I don't think Altdorf will miss a dozen or so grasping counts and barons, do you?'

Before Duke Vidor could answer, Kreyssig was walking back towards the Emperor's throne. Vidor gasped in shock as the Protector sat in the Imperial seat. Kreyssig smiled at the noble's offended dignity. Deftly working his fingers under the throne's armrest, he pulled at a concealed knob.

Vidor's shock was redoubled when the entire throne began to pivot, swinging out from the dais and exposing a flight of stairs concealed beneath the throne. 'The entire palace is a maze of hidden corridors and secret passages. Prince Sigdan was fortunate to catch Emperor Boris in one of the few chambers without a hidden exit.' Kreyssig laughed. 'Actually, the Harmony Salon did have a hollow wall, but the Emperor had it filled in because he felt it was detrimental to the acoustics.'

The commander rose and stepped away from the throne, posting himself at the head of the hidden stair. Vidor watched him with growing nervousness, tempted to bolt and run while Kreyssig was seemingly distracted. The indignity of such a retreat stifled such intentions. He might cower before an Emperor, but he would be damned if he were going to flee from a peasant.

Kreyssig bent over, reaching down into the hidden stairway. A slim hand, gloved in purple, reached up from the passage beneath the throne, accepting the commander's waiting grip. Soon he was escorting the Baroness von den Linden, svelte in a close-fitting gown the colour of ambergris, down the steps of the dais. Behind them, the Imperial throne rotated back to its former position.

'What... what is that... witch...' Vidor gasped, fear for the first time unseating the enforced calmness demanded by his noble bearing.

'Have a care, Vidor,' Kreyssig snarled. 'It is by her ladyship's grace that you are here and not down in the Dragon's Hole.'

The baroness stepped away from Kreyssig as she reached the floor. Stroking the kitten she held in the crook of her arm, she approached the chained Vidor. The aristocrat began to shiver as the witch drew near, Auernheimer's story about summoned daemons rising unbidden in his memory.

'He will be more useful to us here,' the baroness declared. Her gaze was cold as she locked eyes with Vidor. 'Having failed once, he won't be so foolish as to move against us a second time.' She wagged a finger at the shackles and collar. 'I think those are unnecessary. You must speak to your Kaiserknecht about their zeal.'

Kreyssig reached into a pocket, removing a large brass key. He contemplated it for a moment. 'I should scold them for their laxity,' he observed, tossing the key at Vidor's feet. 'It doesn't appear they broke any bones when they collected his grace.'

Vidor stared in confusion from the key to Kreyssig and then to the baroness, wondering what sort of trap they had set for him.

The witch noted his hesitancy. 'There is no trick, your grace,' she said, demonstrating the claim by leaning down and retrieving the key, slipping it between Vidor's fingers. 'Adolf has demonstrated his reach. This little display was arranged to impress upon you that, whatever his parentage, you *are* subject to his authority.'

'My Kaiserjaeger weren't able to find that fanatic you set after us,' Kreyssig grumbled. 'Otherwise you'd have a much more memorable display to impress you.' His voice dipped, losing its element of forced charm. 'When I find him, I'll be sure to send the pieces to you.'

Vidor fumbled at the lock to his shackles, still expecting some kind of trick. When the chains fell from his wrists, there was a look of disbelief in his eyes. Quickly, he repeated the procedure with the heavy collar.

'That should convince you of our sincerity,' the baroness said.

Vidor looked from her to Kreyssig, uncertain which of them was in control. Which of them he needed to placate. 'What about the others?' he asked.

'I told you, they are profiteering traitors,' Kreyssig declared. 'They will be publicly tried and executed. Their titles will be abolished and their holdings forfeit to the crown.' Again, he reached into his pocket, removing a ruby-encrusted signet ring. He scrutinized it for a moment, before returning his gaze to the duke. 'Baron von Forgach's lands in the Oster-mark have been something you've wanted for a long time.' With a last look at the signet, he tossed the ring to Vidor. The duke wasn't surprised when he saw the von Forgach coat of arms emblazoned on the jewel.

'Von Forgach was a traitor,' Kreyssig stated boldly, 'leaving all of his lands to the crown for redisposition.'

'You have proof of this?' Vidor asked.

Kreyssig laughed darkly. 'The best. A signed confession.'

Duke Vidor grimaced at the peasant's lack of candour. Just the same, he drew a merely ornamental ring from one of his fingers and slipped the signet in its place. 'Do not think you can buy my loyalty.'

Kreyssig's grim humour expressed itself in a grotesque

smile. 'If I cannot buy it, then I will compel it,' he warned. 'When you say that there would be an uproar if I were to try and prosecute you, it was something that had occurred to me. I wouldn't presume to try such a thing. Not at all. If it comes to it, you will be dragged before the proctors of the Temple of Sigmar and tried for...' Kreyssig paused, looking at Baroness von den Linden.

'You will be arrested for heresy, your grace,' the witch said. There was a dark gleam in her eyes as she added, 'Anyone can be made to sign anything given the right incentive.'

'And even your staunchest supporters will desert you if it is the Temple of Sigmar, not Protector Kreyssig, who prosecutes you,' Kreyssig stated.

Vidor glared at his enemies, realizing how utterly he had fallen into their clutches. 'What is it you want of me?' he demanded.

Baroness von den Linden smiled slyly. 'One last present for you. The Protector is going to reverse his earlier decision. You will be appointed the new Reiksmarshal and given command of the army we are building.'

'I need to use the veterans of your previous campaign as the core of this new force,' Kreyssig said. 'As soon as my programme began, I realized Soehnlein was out of his league. I don't have time for my soldiers to adapt themselves to a new leader. I need a leader they already know and respect. That makes you necessary.'

It was Vidor's turn to laugh, appreciating now the reason for such gracious treatment from Kreyssig and his witch. 'You must be planning to move against Talabheim soon,' he stated, guessing now the source of all the inflammatory rhetoric that was upsetting the commoners and even ruffling the feathers of some of the nobility.

Again, the duke was due to be surprised. 'The enemy we

prepare for isn't Talabheim,' the baroness said. 'The real enemy is much closer.'

Vidor was puzzled by her statement, and by the nagging familiarity with which she said it. Suddenly he recalled a sermon given by Grand Theogonist Gazulgrund, something about 'the inhuman enemy in our midst'. Indeed, of late the priests had been making quite a point about warning their flock about Old Night and its monstrous progeny.

What sort of enemy, Vidor wondered, was it that these two were afraid of? What threat hovered over them that they needed an entire army to guard against it?

And, more disturbing, how soon did they expect that threat to be realised?

Abin-gnaw bent almost double as he abased himself before Sythar Doom. The Warpmaster's gemstone eyes reflected the green luminance of the warplight as he turned away from the piebald tinkerer, who was filing his metal fangs and cleaning them of rust. The Grey Lord's lips peeled back, exposing those fangs in a threatening snarl.

'Disturb me, murder-rat, and you will feed the burrow-worms,' Sythar hissed. He started to turn back to the tinkerer when his nose twitched, detecting a scent that had been nearly stifled by rat-dung and skaven blood. He peered down at Abin-gnaw, noticing for the first time the trembling cloaked shape huddled beside the ratman. Now that he focused upon the figure, he could tell that here was the source of the scent – the smell of frightened human.

Abin-gnaw had done an expert job of concealing the creature's smell, hiding its presence from the other skaven in the warren. That didn't, however, explain why the murder-rat had brought a man-thing into the presence of a Lord of Decay. Suspicion flared through Sythar's mind. Had one of the other leaders bribed Clan Skully to remove him as he had had Deacon Blistrr eliminated? General Twych wasn't keen enough for such insight, but Grey Seer Pakritt might be! Hurriedly, Sythar swung around, tilting his head so that his groom-mechanic could reconnect the power cable to his jaw. At the same time, he gestured wildly with his paws, waving his warpguard to surround Abin-gnaw and the human.

'Great Sythar! Most Exalted of Tyrants! Most Potent of Calamities! Most Fertile of Sires!' Abin-gnaw had his nose to the floor now, arms extended in an appealing gesture. 'This humble-loyal servant wish-want to squeak-speak!'

Sythar Doom's fangs crackled with sparks as he turned. His electrified bite could burn through any garrotte the slinking murder-rat might carry. Then again, the killer might be clever enough to have something else in mind. Yes, it would be good policy for Clan Skully to use a poisoned throwing star and blame the assassination on Clan Eshin! Before the same idea could occur to his tinker-dentist, Sythar caught the hapless ratkin by the neck and dragged him between himself and Abin-gnaw.

'Woe! Peril, Most Terrible Despot!' Abin-gnaw wailed as the warpguard pointed their halberds at him. The murder-rat flinched away from the sharp blades. The human beside him moaned in terror and tried to bolt. Abin-gnaw must have noticed the motion out of the corner of his eye, for his scaly tail whipped out, tripping the man as he started to run.

'Squeak-speak!' Sythar Doom growled from behind the thrashing body of his living shield. The idea occurred to him that a dead shield would be just as viable as a living one. The tinkerer's fur sizzled as Sythar's metal jaws clamped down around his neck.

'Man-things try to trick-lie!' Abin-gnaw squeaked. 'Kreyssig-man make army to fight-fight skaven!' The murder-rat turned quickly, almost earning himself a jab from the closest halberd. Nimbly, the ratman seized the prostrate human and pulled him to face Sythar Doom. 'Speak-squeak, Rati-man!' he growled, kicking the human with his clawed foot.

Shivering from head to foot, every hair on his body bristling with fear, Lord Ratimir, Imperial Minister of Finance, related to the ghastly Warpmaster what he had discovered. He told of the irregularities in the treasury, the diversion of taxes and tribute not towards the army but to bribes sent to Talabheim's ruler, Grand Duke Cvitan. Even a human wasn't stupid enough to send treasure to an enemy right before attacking him. No, that bribe was to convince the grand duke that for all the antagonistic posturing, Altdorf wasn't going to march against Talabheim.

Why, then, was Kreyssig building up an army? It wasn't paranoid to guess the answer. With a snarl, Sythar Doom pointed his claw at Lord Ratimir. Abin-gnaw chirped in terror and dived away as the Warpmaster sent a bolt of searing energy from his hand into the human spy. Ratimir's body crumbled into a jumble of charred stumps and blackened ash.

'Kill-kill! Slay-slash! Burn-maim!' Sythar Doom roared, glowering at Abin-gnaw. 'Take-fetch all murder-rats!' he ordered. 'Find Kreyssig-meat and kill it!'

Sythar Doom barely noticed Abin-gnaw's genuflection as he scurried off to carry out his orders. The Grey Lord's mind was awhirl with fresh plans, remoulding his carefully conceived intrigues to fit the changing situation. He'd have to cancel the assassinations of Twych and Pakritt. He'd need both of those mouse-sniffers now! The army that had been gathering under Altdorf would have to march at once, strike against the humans before they were ready.

The Grey Lord's fangs crackled as he licked them with his

tongue. At least, he reflected, the warpcaster was finished.
Unleashing the full potential of the invention in something
more than a fratricidal field-test would mark a new level of
achievement for Clan Skryre, would demonstrate to all of
skavendom the enormity of their might and malice. They
might even allow the other clans to buy their own warpcast-
ers, with a few modifications so that regular maintenance by
a warp-engineer would be essential.

Exterminating several thousand humans would make quite
an impressive demonstration. One Sythar Doom would make
certain Vecteek and the rest of the Council didn't soon forget!

Middenheim
Ulriczeit, 1118

In all his life, Mandred had never imagined anything could
be as dark as what he found filling the vaults of Karak
Grazhyakh. It was a blackness that seemed to have mass and
substance, a cloying presence that pressed in all around as the
humans marched into the depths. He could feel the weight of
the mountain above him, on all sides of him. The impression
of walking into a vast tomb was almost impossible to shake.

Entrance had been effected through a tunnel hidden
beneath the temple of Grungni. No more did the prince have
to wonder about what lay behind those massive doors. It was
somehow anticlimactic, really. The dwarf temple had been
brooding, ponderous even, but it fell far short of the megalithic construction Mandred had seen in the dwarf stronghold
itself. Those regions illuminated by oil lamps and sputtering
torches had been beyond magnificent. Great pillars of stone
soaring up to meet arched ceilings in a seamless harmony

that made him wonder if the dwarfs had carved them out of the living rock when they'd first dug the halls. Gigantic statues of ancient ancestors and mighty kings frowned down at them from niches gouged high upon the walls. Great stretches of runescript adorned entire tunnels, prompting Mandred to wonder what the Khazalid script said and what had been so important that the dwarfs had set it into solid rock to withstand the ages.

No marching songs roused the humans into quickening their step as they descended deeper and deeper into the mountain. The same oppression of spirit that gripped Mandred was shared by those he led. Occasionally, the tones of a whispered prayer might be heard, but that was all. Some of them might have wondered about this world beneath the streets of Middenheim, but none of them had ever imagined they would actually probe its depths. To their credit, despite the fear that dogged their steps, not a man of his expedition turned back. Noble or *Dienstleute*, the soldiers kept true to their oaths. Not since that fateful ride to relieve Warrenburg had Mandred felt such pride, such kinship, with those he would someday rule.

Would that pride withstand the real test, he wondered? These men had been told the sort of enemy they would face here in the dark beneath Middenheim, but could any warning really prepare them for the hideous reality? Would they stand before the skaven, or would they break and run?

'A cheerless lot,' Kurgaz Smallhammer opined. Marching beside Mandred, guiding the column into the depths, the dwarf cast a suspicious look over his shoulder. The same thoughts that had bothered the prince had likewise afflicted the dwarf. 'Not a laugh, whistle or fart among them. If they're trying to sneak up on the skaven they needn't bother. The ratkin will smell them even if they don't hear them.' Kurgaz slapped the haft of the hammer he carried, a vicious-looking weapon he'd brought down from the temple. 'Wish I had Drakdrazh with me,' he grumbled for the hundredth time. Mandred rolled his eyes, bracing himself to hear another complaint about how Kurgaz's younger brother Mirko had availed himself of the chance to bear the magic hammer into battle. Even now, he was down in the mines helping fend off the skaven incursion with Kurgaz's preferred weapon.

Fortunately, Mandred was spared the bitter relation of that story. With an abruptness that startled the prince, Kurgaz fell silent. The dwarf lifted his hand, motioning for those behind to stop marching. His normally gruff voice became a hissed whisper. Soon the other dwarfs accompanying the humans came dashing forwards, joining Kurgaz at the head of the column. There was a brief consultation, then the dwarfs fanned out across the tunnel, axes and hammers at the ready. Kurgaz turned back to Mandred.

'Get your soldiers ready,' the dwarf warned.

'Trouble?' Beck asked, the bodyguard as ever keeping close to the prince. The knight's sword was already in his mailed fist.

Kurgaz tilted his head to one side. 'The rock sounds wrong,' he stated. His eyes hardened as he focused on a particular patch of the tunnel. 'Hollow sound. Like something moving behind the walls.'

Belting out orders to the other dwarfs, Kurgaz unlimbered his warhammer and scratched a line in the floor with the iron toe of his boot. 'This far and no further,' he vowed. The fact that the oath was made in Reikspiel rather than Khazalid wasn't lost on Mandred.

'The enemy is coming, men!' he shouted to the soldiers behind him as he drew his sword. 'We hold them here. Steel yourselves. Let the fury of Ulric pour into your hearts. This is where we turn back Old Night and make its children wish they'd kept to the dark!' The prince's voice brought blades rasping from sheaths, jaws clenching in grim resignation. It wasn't the defiant enthusiasm Mandred had hoped to evoke, but at least the men were standing firm. In the ponderous gloom of the Crack, he supposed that was more than he should have expected.

The dwarfs maintained their vigil over the wall, a tense silence gripping the men who watched them. No one knew what to expect, and all were looking to the dwarfs for the first warning.

Hearkening to every scrape and scratch their sharp ears detected behind the wall, Kurgaz and his dwarfs kept the Middenheimers aware of what was happening. When the dwarfs suddenly scrambled away from the wall, scattering a few yards down the tunnel, Mandred knew the attack was imminent.

The wall came crumbling down, big blocks of stone tumbling into the corridor. Gritty dust billowed through the tunnel, stifling the torches and lamps the men carried, making the subterranean darkness still blacker. Through the cover of that blackness, inhuman creatures spilled into the passageway. Mandred could hear their scuttling claws, their bloodthirsty squeaks. He could smell their mangy fur and rotten breath. The skaven were upon them.

In that first flurry of viciousness, the ratmen dragged down a score of soldiers and even a few of the dwarfs. The skaven exploited the confusion of their assault to the full, attacking with such savagery that many of their own kind perished in fratricidal thrusts of spear and blade.

If the vermin had broken their discipline in that moment of horror, Mandred doubted any of his troops would have survived. They would never outrun the skaven and any sign of weakness would only embolden the monsters. Their only hope was to maintain the line, defy the panic that clawed at their hearts.

'Khazuk!' Kurgaz's roar boomed through the tunnel, echoing from every wall and pillar. 'Khazukan Kazakit-Ha!' The war-cry was taken up by the other dwarfs, rolling like the boom of cannon.

'For Ulric!' Mandred added his own shout to the bedlam. 'For graf and wolf!' He lunged through the blackness, slashing at a figure he could only dimly see. There was no mistaking the skaven for anything human or dwarf, even with nothing but a shadowy outline to attack. His sword sang true, hewing through the beast's forearm and eliciting a feral bleat of misery. A second slash of the blade had the thing flopping on the floor.

Soldiers rallied around the prince, taking up his war-cry. Soon the shout of 'wolf and graf' drowned out the bestial snarls and squeaks of the enemy. With spear and axe, sword and mace, the men pressed the vermin back towards the wall. Fresh torches were lit, more lanterns were brought forwards and light streamed down the tunnel.

There were well over a hundred of the skaven, with more of them spilling into the tunnel from a jagged tear in the wall. The ratmen were a motley sight, ranging from armoured brutes with black fur to scrawny, starved wretches with protruding ribs and only the simplest bone knives and wooden spears in their paws. However ragged and foul, the vermin fought with savagery, hurling themselves at the men with desperate ferocity.

In those brief flashes when he wasn't cutting down an enemy or shielding himself from slashing blades and snapping jaws, Mandred thought his force must be overwhelmed. The floor under his feet was slippery with black skaven blood, the bodies of dead vermin littered the floor. Scores, perhaps hundreds of the beasts had been butchered and yet still they came rushing from the hole. It was a vision from the hells of Khaine, the Murder God's infernal legions boiling up from the netherworld.

On, on they fought, until their arms grew weary from the killing, until their lungs sickened at the stink of blood and their ears were deafened by the wailing song of slaughter. Tears of despair rolled down Mandred's cheeks. Pride in the valour of the soldiers beside him turned to bitterness in the knowledge that bravery could never stem such a horde. The skaven would drown them all beneath their swarming hosts.

In the midst of his despair, Mandred's blade flashed out and for once didn't sink itself in furry flesh. Dimly he reconciled the shock with the vision in his eyes, hordes of ratmen scurrying back to the hole. Squeaks of fright replaced screams of battle as the skaven retreated, abandoning their wounded and dead.

Mandred drew upon reserves of strength he didn't know he had. Shaking the weariness from him, he rose and whirled his bloody sword overhead. 'After them!' he shouted, swinging the sword downwards, thrusting its point at the ratmen scrambling into the wall. 'Let none escape!' The soldiers, every bit as weary as their prince, marched forwards, a vengeance on every face.

Before they could reach the hole, their path was blocked by Kurgaz and the other dwarfs. The bearded warriors were caked in gore, their armour foul with the blood of skaven. There was more than mere vengeance in their faces; it was the genocidal hate of millennia, a fury that would be sated by nothing less than total extermination.

Even so, the dwarfs barred the Middenheimers from pursuing the fleeing ratmen. When one incredulous knight tried to shove Kurgaz aside, the dwarf dropped him by driving the haft of his hammer into the man's gut.

'They're escaping!' Mandred roared at the dwarf. Had their allies gone mad?

A dull roar shook the tunnel, not quite drowning out the shrill scream of hundreds of inhuman voices. A column of dust to rival what came before rushed out from the hole as tons of earth and rock slammed down to seal the fissure.

Mandred and his soldiers were thrown to the floor by the tremor, blinded and nearly smothered by the thick cloud of dust. When he regained both vision and feet, Mandred saw Kurgaz still standing between the men and the dirt-choked crack in the wall. The dwarf looked like some horrible wraith, coated from crown to toe in grey dust.

'Never chase a skaven into his burrow,' Kurgaz said, spitting dirt from his mouth. 'Other ratkin always make sure you can't follow.'

Mandred felt a chill run through him as he understood what Kurgaz was saying. The collapse had been engineered, designed to prevent pursuit. He thought of those terrible squeals. How many hundreds of their own had the skaven murdered with that cave-in?

'You'll learn, princeling,' Kurgaz assured Mandred. 'Before we've driven the skaven from Grungni's Tower, you'll be wise to all their tricks.' The dwarf looked across the dirty, tired countenances of the other Middenheimers. 'First thing you'll need to do is work up some stamina. Can't have you burned out after a small fracas.'

Beck stepped forwards, tugging links of mail from the slashed edge of his coif. 'That wasn't their main force?' he asked in a tone of piteous despondency.

Kurgaz threw his head back in a booming laugh. 'Just a skirmish!' He jabbed a thumb at the floor. 'The real fight is down there, in the workings and the deeps. This was just some larcenous ratlord with a sneaky idea to slip upstairs and nab some plunder before anybody got wise to him. If his own lot didn't drop the roof on his head, he'll know better than to try it again.' Kurgaz turned around, swinging his warhammer up onto his shoulder. 'Come along manlings, we've a long way to go. You can rest up on the way.'

Mandred felt the sting of the dwarf's gruff words. No gratitude, no praise. No appreciation. Just a casual dismissal of the entire fight as inconsequential. It grated on his pride as a human, was an offence to his honour as a noble and a slight upon his ability as a leader. He was tempted to turn around and lead his men back into the city, leave the dwarfs to hold the Crack on their own.

Instead, he threw back his shoulders and turned to shout commands to his followers. 'Dispatch the wounded topside! Officers, reform your companies.' He thought about the ferocity of the attack and the suddenness of the skaven ambush. 'Spears to the fore and flanks. Archers behind.' He watched for a moment as the soldiers adjusted to the new formation, then called out in a voice loud enough to carry back to the surface. 'Let's show these beardies how men can really fight!'

When he turned back around to lead his army into the subterranean gloom, Mandred saw Kurgaz looking at him. He wasn't sure if it were his imagination, but he thought he saw Kurgaz smiling before the dwarf turned away.

Dwarfs! He doubted if any human could ever really understand them. Too proud to ask for help, too stubborn to praise it when it was given. Yet help them Middenheim would.

Because in helping the dwarfs, they would be keeping the skaven away from their city.

* * *

Warmonger Vecteek preened his whiskers and squeaked contentedly as the dust-covered messenger made his report. The little force had broken into the dwarf tunnel when the sniffer-moles became agitated. The moles had become accustomed to the smell of dwarfs, so their handlers knew it was something different that upset their keen senses. Breaking into the tunnel, they'd discovered a few dwarfs leading a great company of humans down into the stronghold!

Vecteek didn't care about the details of the ensuing fight. With an angry snarl and a flick of his tail, he set a pair of Verminguard pouncing on the messenger. There was an amusing look of entreaty on the hapless ratkin's face when his head was chopped from his shoulders.

The humans were reacting just as he'd planned. They were rushing down into the tunnels to help the dwarfs. And while they were busy slaughtering Vrrmik's treacherous scum, they'd be leaving their city wide open. Helpless prey for Clan Rictus and the genius of Vecteek!

The Grey Lord's eyes narrowed suspiciously as he leaned over the side of his palanquin. He bared his fangs as he saw Plaguelord Puskab watching him from the shadows. The diseased priest had been arguing for delays, trying to play for more time. He claimed the Black Plague needed a few more weeks to truly spread. Vecteek wasn't fooled by such puerile attempts at deception. Vrrmik and the weaklings of Clan Mors would never hold out that long. The dwarfs would overwhelm them and the humans would return to their city. Vecteek's careful plan to divide and conquer would be undermined!

Or, perhaps Puskab was being truthful. Vecteek licked his fangs as he mulled over that possibility. In that case, the plague would ravage Middenheim, destroy the city without the loss of a single skaven life.

Vecteek's tail lashed out in a fit of fury, slapping one of his

Verminguard. The second possibility was even more abhorrent. No great battle! No chance to display the genius of the Warmonger against a formidable enemy! It was insufferable. If it cost a thousand, ten thousand of his clanrats, he'd have his battle. There was no glory in a bloodless victory. The plague was there to weaken and debilitate, but it couldn't be allowed to claim credit for the final triumph!

'Diggers! Sap-rats!' Vecteek snarled, his voice cracking down the length of the earthen tunnel. Criers scattered through the maze of passages and burrows winding behind the walls of Karak Grazhyakh took up his shout, ensuring it reached the ears of every skaven bearing the brand of Rictus on his pelt. 'Man-things go below to help the dwarf-meat. Now Rictus-rats will strike! Now Rictus will conquer! Now Rictus will reign!'

He leaned around, glaring once more at Puskab, fairly daring the plaguelord to protest his orders. Vecteek considered that the degenerates of Clan Pestilens must have at least a pawful of brains when Puskab wisely kept silent.

'Dig-smash! Break-crush!' Vecteek howled. 'Up! Up into man-thing nest! Up to their streets and their cellars! Up to their granaries and their stockyards! Up to their homes and their temples! All-all belongs to Rictus! All-all belongs to Vecteek!'

Vecteek savoured the clamour of claws on bare rock as his underlings hurried to obey his diktat. The approaches were already prepared; before the next feeding cycle his sappers would be through. The tunnels would break up into the sewers beneath Middenheim. From the sewers, the skaven would filter into every cellar, dungeon and crypt.

The walls of Middenheim were tall and strong, built to keep out any foe. Any foe except the one who chose to ignore them. Now those same walls would imprison the people of Middenheim.

Would ensure that none of Vecteek's prey escaped.

─< CHAPTER XVI >─

Altdorf
Kaldezeit, 1114

'Open in the name of the Emperor!' The command was shouted in a thick voice, punctuated by the hammer-like blows of a mailed fist against old timber. The speaker was a stocky, heavy-set being, shorter than a man but with a stoutness of build that lent him a decidedly powerful appearance. Heavy plates of steel were strapped above the mail he wore, and over his bearded head he wore a close-fitting helm adorned with swirling runes of silver and gold. Rings of gold were threaded through the plaits of his thick beard.

Beset by plague and disease, the collection of revenue had become a logistical nightmare for the Ministry of Finance. Taxmen died by the droves as they succumbed to the illness of their victims, their ranks decimated even more savagely than those of physician and priest. An attempt had been made during the spring of 1112 to employ men already struck by the Black Plague as excise collectors, but the effort had failed miserably. The plague-stricken collectors had spread the disease to every quarter of the city. Worse, with the spectre of Morr already hovering over them, they had proven less than stalwart about turning over the revenue they collected to Imperial coffers, skimming most of the money to squander on such pleasures as they might enjoy before the plague took them.

It was Emperor Boris himself who came up with a solution. Aware that the plague had ignored the halfling population, he had seized upon the theory that the Death was only affecting humankind. Soft-hearted and inoffensive, halflings didn't have the stuff to act as tax collectors. Fortunately, there was another non-human community dwelling in Altdorf that did.

Their own business failing as the plague devastated their customers, many of Altdorf's dwarfish community had responded to the Emperor's summons. Soon an entire cadre of dwarf taxmen were stalking the streets of Altdorf, exacting the Imperial tribute from great and small with the stubborn, harsh tenacity of their dour breed. True, the services of the dwarfs were more expensive than those of human taxmen – for one thing the dwarfs refused to accept Imperial coin after the gold content was reduced, forcing their wage to be drawn in raw nuggets and dust – but their role was essential to maintaining the financial stability of Imperial government.

The dwarfs adopted the grandiose title of 'The Imperial Guild of Excise, Custom, Honour and Fidelity', but to the people of Altdorf they were simply 'Goldgather's Goldgrubbers'. Though they were hated and despised universally, it was still a rare thing for anyone to raise their hand against one of the dwarfs. More than merely the act of defying Imperial law, it was the vindictive nature of the dwarfs themselves that held the abused populace silent. Injure a dwarf and the whole race would persecute the offender's family unto the tenth generation. Dwarfs recorded their grudges in great tomes so that even the slightest insult would never be forgotten.

The few peasants abroad in the streets didn't even turn their heads at the commotion on the doorstep of a once prosperous moneylender. They had become accustomed to shunning the house ever since the warning cross had been chalked across the door. Few even knew if the man or any of his household still lived, nor were any willing to risk the plague to find out. Once a week a corpse-cart would pass down the street and knock at each door. They would find out if anyone were still in there – it was what they were paid to do. The corpse-collectors earned a copper from the Temple of Morr for each nose they brought to the cremation pits outside the city wall.

Grumbling into his beard, the dwarf glanced down at the moneylender's name on the list he carried, noting the balance beside it. It was an appreciable sum, derived from the earnings the man's business had enjoyed before the plague. A small thing like a pandemic would hardly justify a reduction in taxes. Besides, if the man felt the sum was unreasonable, he could protest to his noble lord. Allowing that his liege had survived the plague and hadn't already fled the city.

Either way, the dwarf's job was to collect. He repeated his summons, banging his fist so forcefully against the door that he bruised the wood. He drew back, waiting for any trace of activity. Frowning under his beard, the dwarf tilted his helmet up and pressed an exposed ear against the door. Years of mining in the Grey Mountains had honed the dwarf's hearing to a superhuman degree, enabling him to detect the presence of ore simply by the sound his pick made when striking the wall, warning him of a cave-in by the softest groan from a support beam hundreds of yards up the shaft. By comparison, listening at a keyhole was simplicity itself.

Immediately, the dwarf's ear caught the sounds of furtive shuffling inside the house. He leaned back, adjusting his helmet in place. Pejorative crept into his grumbling. So the cheats thought to hide in there and pretend they weren't home, did they? Well, if they thought a dwarf could be dissuaded from his duty by such a facile deception, they were sorely mistaken.

Stepping away from the door, the dwarf thrust his shoulder towards it and lunged at it. The portal shook in its frame as his armoured weight slammed into the wood. Unfazed by the impact, the dwarf stepped back into the street, allowing himself a better start before charging into the door again.

This time the door collapsed under his impact, flying back on its hinges. The dwarf was propelled into the dingy parlour beyond.

Eyes adapted to the murk of mines and tunnels stared in disbelief at the scene within that parlour. If plague hadn't claimed the moneylender and his household, they would have been better off if it had. The monsters that filled the decrepit building now certainly wouldn't have been merciful to any occupants they found.

The parlour and what he could see of the rooms beyond were swarming with hundreds of skaven.

The dwarf drew his axe, set his feet and roared a prayer to Grungni. Then the vermin rushed at him in a chittering tide of fangs and blades. He cut down ten of them before he was crushed to the floor. After that, despite his heavy armour and his powerful build, it was only a few moments before the dwarf was reduced to an unrecognisable heap of dripping meat.

Dejected and dispirited, the peasants walking the streets had paid only the sketchiest notice to the dwarf's invasion of the house. They paid far more attention to the horde that flooded out through the broken door. A few of them even had time to scream before the ratmen fell upon them.

* * *

It was a scene that was repeated all across Altdorf. From sewers and cellars, from abandoned homes and boarded warehouses, even from the holds of derelict ships, the ratmen came. With sword and fang the seemingly numberless horde rampaged through the streets. Wherever the skaven appeared, death and destruction reigned. The monsters were merciless in their depredations, devoid of any semblance of pity or restraint. Temples filled with the sick and dying became abattoirs in the wake of the chittering horde. Refugee camps erupted in flames as the ratmen surrounded them and put them to the torch, the agonies of those trapped within the ring of fire echoing hideously across the icy waters of the Reik.

Through the *Kaiseraugen*, the men assembled in the council chamber could see the pillars of smoke rising from the burning city. Screams, roars, the bedlam of a city being torn apart wasn't quite muffled by the thick panes of glass. Several Kaiserjaeger stood watch, shouting to the leaders gathered about the table whenever they spotted the enemy in the streets below.

Adolf Kreyssig considered the grim-faced men gathered around him. They were solemn, hardly daring to speak as the magnitude of the attack was borne home to them with each fresh report that made its way to the palace. One of them, the bewigged fop Emperor Boris had installed as burgomeister of Altdorf, sat slumped in his seat, sobbing loudly into a laced handkerchief. Fortunately for the city, the rest of its leaders were made of sterner stuff. Kreyssig had made certain of that when he'd purged the council and made his plans for war.

Duke Vidor shook his head and cast aside the slip of parchment he had been reading, a report from a captain in the Schuetzenverein. 'The area east of the river is cut off,' he declared. 'The ratmen have demolished the bridges. Two-thirds of the army had their billets there.'

Grand Master Leiber pulled at his long moustache, eyes closed as he pondered the dire news. 'At least the heavy horse is stationed on this side of the river,' he stated. 'That leaves us roughly three hundred knights. More if we call upon the templar orders.'

'The Black Guard have been surrounded by the cremation pits outside the walls,' a wizened old count reported. A haunted look crept into his eyes as he considered the full message he had received. 'Thirty knights against hundreds of those things. They won't leave enough for Morr's ravens to find!'

Prelate Arminus nodded in sympathy at the sacrifice of the Black Guard, closing his hand about the whalebone icon he wore around his neck. The priest's voice was apologetic when he addressed the other leaders. 'I fear that the Knights of the Storm are largely absent from the city. With the plague ravaging the river trade, many of them have been serving as marines on those vessels still braving the Reik. Merciful Manann watch over them all.'

Inquisitor Fulk of the Verenan temple drew back the heavy hood he wore, letting his sharp eyes rove across the faces of the men around him. 'My temple stands ready to assist the city, but our strength is sadly diminished. The Black Plague has been most attentive.' The grim priest tapped his fingers on the breast of his robe. 'At best we might rally seventy swords if we left the temple unprotected.' It was clear from his tone that he considered such a move to be sacrilegious.

Kreyssig decided to reject the inquisitor's offer. The Verenans weren't a martial order, their forte was hunting heretics. Torturers and executioners were quite capable of killing in cold blood, but he doubted if many of them were equally capable of hot-blooded killing, of fighting against an armed adversary. No, it was better to leave them in their gloomy temple and let them fare as their god saw best.

'We have almost three thousand foot soldiers this side of the river,' Kreyssig declared. 'At the moment, they are scattered throughout, clumped in their training camps and isolated in their billets.' He raised his eyes, staring out through the window. One of those training camps was built over the wreckage of Breadburg. From here, he could see a great column of smoke billowing up from that vicinity.

Vidor stood up from his chair, addressing the various nobles seated at the table. 'By themselves, the knights will be of little use. The strength of heavy horse lies in the charge and there will be little opportunity for such tactics in the close confines of city streets.' He turned, locking eyes with Kreyssig. 'If we are to have any hope of driving the rat-men from the city, we have to mobilise our scattered foot troops, concentrate them into a single battle group. The rat-kin may outnumber us, but those same close quarters will counter that advantage. Man for monster, even the lowest dienstmann is more than a match for the vermin. If we can concentrate our troops into bodies large enough to resist the numbers of the ratmen...'

Kreyssig nodded. From what he had seen of the skaven, they were a craven breed. They relied upon subterfuge and ambush to fight their battles. They had little stomach for a real fight. So far, the monsters had enjoyed success because they hadn't encountered anyone in a position to seriously oppose them. Upset that tide of success even a little and it might hurl the entire horde into disarray.

'What is your plan, Reiksmarshal?' Kreyssig asked.

'First we will use the Kaiserknecht and as many footmen as are available to penetrate down to the river,' Vidor said. 'Any peasants they find will be drafted as labourers. Once they reach the Reik, they will take every ship, scow and barge and lash them together. The ratmen destroyed the old bridges, so we'll build a new one.'

'It will take time to construct a pontoon bridge,' one of the other generals objected. 'I can appreciate the need to bring the rest of the army across the river, but until they are across the ratmen will have an even freer hand on this side of the Reik.'

The Reiksmarshal shook his head. 'Not so,' he stated. 'Because while they are building the bridge, we will be using the rest of our knights to get messages to the brigades on this side of the river. If we can get all of them to converge upon a single position, concentrate our strength, we can resist the vermin until reinforcements can be brought across the Reik.'

'You said the knights would be useless in city fighting,' Grand Master Leiber pointed out.

'I don't need them to fight,' Vidor returned. 'I need their mobility, their stamina to win clear of the ratmen and reach our scattered troops. A humble task, I grant, but there will be time for valour and glory after we have the strength to mount a credible offensive.'

'Where do you want the troops to go?' Inquisitor Fulk wondered. 'It will need to be somewhere central, well within reach of each brigade.'

'It needs to be a landmark that can be seen from some distance,' one of the barons mused. 'Something visible from wherever the soldiers may be.'

A brief debate ensued, many of the noblemen arguing for the Imperial Palace while others argued that doing so would cause the ratmen to bring their full force to bear against the palace.

It was the heretofore silent Arch-Lector von Reisarch who ended the debate. 'The Great Cathedral,' he said. 'The spire can be seen from anywhere in Altdorf, and it is built at the very heart of Old Reikdorf. Rally the troops to the temple of Holy Sigmar, that they may take courage from His divine beneficence.'

Inquisitor Fulk and Prelate Arminus looked as though they wanted to challenge von Reisarch's suggestion, angered by what they viewed as the Sigmarite's shameless effort to aggrandise his god in the midst of this calamity. At the same time, neither of the priests could ignore the compelling logic behind the arch-lector's argument. The Great Cathedral was ideally located and the peasants would take heart from the idea that they were defending Sigmar Himself by rallying to the temple.

'The Great Cathedral, then,' Kreyssig decided, ending the discussion. He nodded to von Reisarch. 'You may tell Grand Theogonist Gazulgrund to expect me.' It grated on Kreyssig's pride to indulge the Sigmarites in this fashion. Condescending to the Grand Theogonist was to make a public display of the priest's authority – authority that would appear greater than that of the Emperor or his appointed Protector. Still, it would be even more disastrous to allow the priest to fight the coming battle by himself. The people would remember who fought to save them and who stayed safe behind fortress walls.

Kreyssig was just about to dismiss the council when he happened to notice Baroness von den Linden's cat. The brute had been lazing about on top of the table throughout the meeting, indifferent to the momentous events unfolding around it. Now, however, the cat was upright, its back arched and its every hair standing on end. As the animal began to hiss and spit, Kreyssig followed its frightened gaze.

He was just in time to see the dark shapes drop outside the *Kaiseraugen*, swinging on ropes from the roof of the palace. Before even his Kaiserjaeger could shout a warning, the swinging skaven smashed through the window. Kreyssig covered his face as slivers of glass flew through the chamber.

The chittering shrieks of skaven drowned out the shouts of alarm and confusion that rose from the surprised councillors and generals. Moans of agony sounded from the direction of the windows as the fast-moving ratmen attacked the startled Kaiserjaeger. Other skaven rappelled through the shattered glass, hurling tiny orbs into the room. As each orb crashed to the floor, it expelled a billowing mass of choking fumes. The men reeled in the noxious vapour, struggling to escape the debilitating fog. The skaven, their faces wrapped in thick folds of cloth, scampered through the chamber, lashing out with crooked blades.

Kreyssig staggered back, trying to draw his own sword even as his body shuddered in a fit of violent coughing. One of the assaulting vermin uttered a feral growl as it spied him. Leaping to the top of the table, the murder-rat charged at him.

Abin-gnaw stuffed his scimitar back beneath his rat-gut belt and drew the lethal coils of his sacred strangler's cord from beneath his crimson cloak. Squeaking an invocation to the Horned One, a murderous charm taught to him by no less than the Old Rat Under the Mountain himself, the killer cast the noose through the air, looping it about his victim's neck.

Kreyssig gasped as the cord was drawn taut, as the little warpstone talisman sewn into the lining dug into his neck. He could feel his throat constricting, feel the air being squeezed out of him. Nimbly, Abin-gnaw jumped from the table, dropping down behind Kreyssig and forcing the human down into his chair. Pressing one foot against the back of the seat, the skaven used it for extra leverage, extra force to increase that deadly constriction.

Kreyssig struggled to reach the monstrous creature behind

him, tried to twist his body so that he might at least slip free from the chair. Abin-gnaw, however, was too crafty to allow himself to fall within reach of the human's groping hands.

Just as his vision was beginning to darken, as the thunder of his own pulse became a deafening roar in his ears, as his starved lungs began to burn, Kreyssig felt the air around him become cold. It was a cold that had nothing to do with winter. It was the spectral chill of sorcery.

The pressure around his throat suddenly slackened. Kreyssig pulled himself away from the chair, felt the strangling cord drag free from weakened claws. Frantically, he reached to his throat and ripped the noose free, hurling it to the floor in disgust. Drawing his sword, he turned to face his would-be assassin.

Abin-gnaw lay prone, his face-wrappings soaked in blood. Black blood bubbled from the skaven's eyes, the flow increasing with each ragged breath he drew into his dying body. While Kreyssig watched, the murder-rat expired, expelling its last vitality in a grotesque liquid gargle.

Turning away from the dead assassin, Kreyssig looked to intercede in the melee unfolding around him, only to discover that it had largely abated. The top of the table and much of the floor was stained with a greasy, grey film. The room was littered with bodies, both the verminous carcasses of skaven and the corpses of men.

'Commander, are you all right?' The question came from the last man Kreyssig expected to see, his servant Fuerst, a heavy club clenched in his chubby fist. Beyond the peasant, he could see Baroness von den Linden, her silver robes still writhing in the magical energies she had invoked.

'I live,' Kreyssig told Fuerst, brushing aside the servant's concern. The skaven had taken their toll upon the council and the assembled generals, butchering nearly a quarter of them in the brief melee. Many of the survivors continued to cough thick grey phlegm from their throats – the residue of that strange smoke the ratmen had used. The grey filth staining the chamber would account for the rest of that smoke, congealed by the witch's spells.

Kreyssig frowned as he gazed at the baroness. His relief at her timely intervention was tempered by an appreciation that it was no natural force that could have warned her of his peril. Even when it was beneficial, there was something disturbing about witchcraft, something that offended men on an almost primal level.

Studying the faces of the other survivors, he could see the same mix of gratitude and fear. The expressions of Arch-Lector von Reisarch and Inquisitor Fulk were outright malignant.

'On behalf of His Imperial Majesty,' Kreyssig said, loud enough that his tones drowned out any murmurs of misgiving, 'we thank you for your most opportune assistance, your ladyship.'

Baroness von den Linden bowed to Kreyssig. 'It is the duty of every subject of the Empire to defend the realm,' she stated, glancing at the councillors. Kreyssig didn't like the little smile she wore. Most of these men knew he had been visiting her, even if they couldn't guess the nature of those liaisons. In a single act, she had both saved him and condemned him. There would be no more rumours linking the baroness with witchcraft among the council. There would only be simple fact. Kreyssig was now inextricably bound to the witch. He would have to support her in everything, because the same men who would persecute her as a practitioner of the black arts would also damn him as a heretic.

With a predatory, cat-like grace, the baroness stalked through the shambles and joined Kreyssig at the head of the table. 'You must move quickly,' she advised him. Like the

Protector, she ensured her voice was loud enough for all to hear. 'The same divination that warned me of your danger also revealed to me an even greater threat.'

The witch wore a bemused smile as she retrieved the agitated cat from the table and stroked its fur. 'Like yourselves, the skaven are concentrating their forces. They are marshalling for a direct attack against the Great Cathedral.

'In one assault, the ratmen intend to break the spirit of every soul in Altdorf,' the baroness warned. 'When the temple burns, the fire will be seen in every quarter of the city. When that happens, men will know that their dominion is finished.

'When that happens, the vermin shall inherit the earth.'

Sylvania
Kaldezeit, 1113

Seerlord Skrittar drew a deep breath, filling his nose with the smell of victory. The musky scent of aggression dripping from the glands of thousands of skaven warriors; it needed only the appetising aroma of fresh blood to make it properly delicious. That was the downside of fighting these dead-things. Even when they were torn to shreds the walking corpses refused to disgorge anything like proper blood. At best there was syrupy treacle, more often just a pinch of scabby dust.

Clan Mordkin were certainly proving their worth. The grave-rats charged into the ranks of zombies with such feral savagery that even those tick-sniffing mice of Clan Fester were growing bold and mounting their own attacks. Vrask Bilebroth and his surviving plague monks were taking a hand as well, scurrying about the edges of the conflict and supporting Fester wherever it looked like they might be suffering morale problems. As exterminator of the undead, Vrask had proven an abject failure, but as a disciplinarian he was quite useful. Then again, having the decayed snout of a plague monk shoved into your face and snapping orders at you was something most skaven would respond to.

From his position at the back of his army, Skrittar could see the ebb and flow of the battle. It was exactly the kind of conflict that suited him – overwhelming massacre! His warriors outnumbered the undead by ten to one, odds to turn the most spineless mouse vicious. If the dead-things had any sense of self-preservation, they should have been routed at the first sight of the awesome host of ratmen swarming down upon them. Instead, they just maintained their positions and forced the skaven to butcher them where they stood. The outcome would be the same, it was only a delay of the inevitable.

Skrittar bruxed his fangs and uttered a contented hiss. It would only be the matter of a few hours before the skaven broke through their enemy. Then the path would be clear to the jagged tower the dead-things defended. It was a massive structure and exuded a sorcerous taint that sent a thrill through the grey seer's fur. Somehow it reminded him of the Shattered Tower in Skavenblight. There was an auspicious smell about the place, a tantalising odour that went beyond the warpstone sandwiched between the black blocks of stone. He could almost feel the presence of the Horned One, expectant and impatient! It was a humbling, terrifying feeling, yet at the same time filled Skrittar's gut with greedy anticipation. What could be more auspicious an omen for the success of his plans than the attention of his god?

Fixing his gaze on the tower, Skrittar could see the whorls of energy coruscating around it, flickering about the structure like steam from a lava pit. Every wisp of ghostly light was a tendril of magic, a ribbon of sorcery sucked from the void and spewed into the atmosphere. Skrittar felt his pulse quicken as he contemplated the magnitude of what he sensed. If the mage-man was so powerful as to evoke so much magic, then he must prove a fearsome foe! The grey seer's paw tightened about the haft of his staff, feeling the warpstone runes etched into it sizzle against his skin, filling his veins with arcane might. The human knew a trick or two, that was all. If he were truly powerful, his pathetic army wouldn't be demolished so easily! No, the mage-man was just another slab of meat waiting to be cut down by the rightful masters of the world!

Skrittar turned his eyes from the tower, looking instead at the fresh timbers of his conveyance and the massed ranks of stormvermin arrayed about it. The work-rats of Fester had scrambled to build the wooden platform, stealing the iron-banded wheels from dozens of man-thing nests. They were motley and mismatched, causing the platform above to be lopsided in places and requiring an even greater effort from the warriors to move it. Such concerns, however, mattered little to Skrittar. The stormvermin of Manglrr Baneburrow were the strongest skaven in Clan Fester and they would not fail the seerlord. Not if they wanted to live long.

The grey seer preened himself as he stalked across the platform, glaring down at the ranks of brawny stormvermin. He grinned murderously as he drew near the real might of his conveyance. Bound between an arch of stone plundered from an elf-thing temple, a great bronze bell was suspended at the far end of the platform. That bell had been consecrated in the darkest chambers of the Shattered Tower, engraved with runes of ruin and havoc. A piece of pure warpstone, crafted from the biggest chunk they had collected in Sylvania, formed the bell's clapper. The second-largest chunk was the basis of the enormous striker held in the paws of Skrittar's personal slave. The combination of striker, clapper and runes would create an invocation to the Horned One, an appeal that the dreaded god would be certain to answer. A bridge would be formed between mortal supplicants and divinity, a bridge that under the guidance of the seerlord would take shape as spells of unimaginable destruction!

Lashing his tail in amusement, Skrittar stared back at the battle. His army was already halfway through the ranks of the undead. It was time that he put in an appearance and forcibly reminded them that their victory was due solely to his brilliant tactics and selfless leadership.

'Tell your scum to get moving,' Skrittar snapped at Manglrr. Perched at the front of the wheeled altar, the warlord bobbed his head and turned about, ready to crack his whip at his warriors. Even as he did so, the warlord's posture became anxious and his face turned upwards, sniffing at the air nervously.

Soon, the pungent stench of fear musk despoiled the altar. Skrittar rounded on the frightened warlord, smashing him low with the horned head of his staff. 'Fool-meat! Mouse-sniffer!' the grey seer raged.

Manglrr was old by the standards of the skaven, his vigour preserved by a cocktail of alchemy and warpstone transfusions. When he spoke, however, it was in the sort of frightened squeak a litter-pup might make. 'Burn-thing!' the warlord whined. 'Burn-thing!'

Skrittar sighed and brought his staff up to bash the deranged brains from Manglrr's skull. The warlord's senile panic was threatening to upset the stormvermin. More importantly, it was interfering with the seerlord's display of divine favour and tactical acumen! It was a sorry thing to see a Lord of Decay reduced to such a simpering state – he'd have to remember to have everyone who'd seen the spectacle killed.

Before he could deliver the killing blow, however, a loathsome stink swept through Skrittar's nose. It was a rotten, sour smell, decayed meat mixed with reptilian musk. At once, he realised this was the smell that had reduced Manglrr to a cowering flea, but where such a scent could come from, he was at a loss to explain.

Then, with a feeling of dread, Skrittar lifted his head and stared up at the sky. No skaven liked the open sky, that vast emptiness that was so strange and alien beside the cramped comfort of their burrows and tunnels. He was unusual among his race in his tolerance for it, yet in this instant he shared their terror of the heavens more fully than he would have believed possible, primitive instincts racing through his veins and sending a wave of fear through his entire body.

There was something descending from the sky. Something vast and unspeakable! It stank of death and putrefaction, of dried scales and shrivelled flesh. There was no mistaking that awful shape, the powerful pinions and mighty claws, the barbed tail and armoured body of a dragon. No head graced its stumpy neck, however, only a ragged hole and the gleaming tip of exposed spine!

As he watched, the deathly dragon swooped down upon one of the Mordkin formations. From the jagged stump of neck a boiling torrent of rotten meat and writhing maggots showered down upon the massed grave-rats, searing them in their bony armour. Then the dragon's claws were scything into them, tearing skaven apart like some gigantic hell-cat!

Perched upon the dragon's shoulders, looking like some black tick embedded in its decayed hide, a wizened figure stood and gestured with a skeletal staff. Sorcerous energy crackled about the head of the staff, expelling itself in a stream of wailing darkness. The malefic magic gouged into a regiment of Fester's clanrats, withering dozens into mummified husks in the blink of an eye.

Skrittar's lips peeled back from his fangs as he watched the mage-man attack. He would not stand for this. He would not suffer this filthy meat to cheat him of his triumph. Whatever his powers, the creature was still merely human, insignificant beside the austere might of a race crafted by the godliest of gods!

The seerlord popped a small sliver of warpstone into his mouth, feeling its power rush through him as his fangs ground it into dust. Flush with the grandeur of his enhanced prowess, he sent a green bolt of destruction searing down into the stormvermin massed about his altar, cooking one hapless warrior where he stood. 'The Horned Rat will suffer no coward-meat!' Skrittar roared, scurrying across the altar from side to side to ensure the whole regiment was aware of his anger. Certain of their terrified attention, he leaped onto the stone arch and scrambled up to the top of the bell.

'Scurry-hurry!' Skrittar shouted, pointing forwards with his staff. 'I shall kill-slay the mage-meat!' he proclaimed, evoking cheers from the stormvermin. 'You will gloriously slay-kill the dragon!'

In the dead silence that greeted that pronouncement, it was easy for Skrittar to hear the cowards who tried to break ranks. Burning them to a cinder restored the enthusiasm of the survivors.

Verminous flesh shrivelled into dust as Lothar von Diehl stretched forth his hand. He exulted in the power that flowed through him, felt a sense of rapture as he watched ratmen crumble before him. Never before had he imagined such power! All his conjurations, the magic he had learned and practised in secret all those years, they were nothing beside this.

Beneath him, he felt the ancient majesty of Graug the Terrible – a primal force of almost elemental fury revivified as nothing more than a puppet, an extension of some small fragment of the necromancer's will. At his merest whim, the zombified beast would lash out with its claw and extinguish a dozen lives or bring withering death to scores with a blast of corrupt gases and wormy meat. Spears and swords crumpled against the wyrm's armoured hide, and those few that did pierce became lodged in rotten, unfeeling flesh. Hundreds of monstrous creatures swarmed about the dragon, yet they were as helpless and puny as ants.

This, Lothar imagined, must be how Vanhal felt. The raw power of annihilation coursing through his mind and soul, waiting there just beneath the surface, lurking unseen and unguessed until it was called upon. No wonder the necromancer was so contemptuous of conquest and dominance. Truly, what was the power of an Emperor beside that of a living god?

Lothar reached out with his hand, plucking a squirming ratman from the horde arrayed around him. Coldly, he sent tendrils of necromantic energy slashing at the creature, stripping its fur away in ribbons, leaving wet bones glistening in the starlight. He could feel every inch of the creature as death spread through its mangled frame, savouring it as he once might have savoured a Mootland delicacy.

That a low-born peasant such as Vanhal should unlock this miraculous potential within him was something that no longer stung Lothar's pride. It was enough that the potential had been unlocked. Glutted on the power flowing through him, the baron hadn't even felt slighted when Vanhal relinquished control of Graug to him and dispatched him to confront the skaven. Anything that would maintain this power, any impudence or insult was of no consequence. Nothing mattered, nothing except this power!

The baron felt his skin wither against his bones. Flesh, he thought with contempt. Such a poor vessel to clothe the indomitable will of a soul such as his. The flame of mortality was too weak a candle to illuminate the great secret. He could see it now, as he sent phantom energies searing into the rat-men, each death fitting another piece into the cosmic puzzle. All he must do was extend his power a little further, commit those last reserves that sustained him, and he would see it all!

A blast of aethyric malignance slammed into Lothar von Diehl, causing the magical shield he had woven about himself to flicker. The impact sent blood flowing from his ears, nearly pitching him from Graug's mighty shoulders. Dazed, the necromancer shook his head. The reckless, drunken excess of a moment before evaporated as logic subsumed emotion within his mind. Horror flowed through him as he appreciated where his power-crazed desire had nearly led him. Flesh might be a poor vehicle for such power, but it was the only one he had.

Another lash of green lightning smacked into Lothar's defences. He spun around, focusing his attention on draining off the malevolent energies. To his witchsight, the lightning left behind it a glowing ribbon of magic, a trajectory he followed back to its source. What he saw was a blazing bubble of deranged energies, a confusion of aethyric vibrations banded and bound by a crazed medley of strange sigils and bizarre runes. At the centre of that energy was a ramshackle altar mounted on a wheeled platform. A great bell stood above the altar, its clapper shining like a knot of concentrated magic. Above the bell, a horned ratman capered and gestured, energies whipping about it as it snarled and chittered.

Lothar sneered as he saw the skaven sorcerer. He was indebted to the monster for breaking him from his trance. Now he would reward the filthy brute with a quick death. Extending a fraction of his power, he willed Graug into the air, the dragon's tattered pinions smashing low scores of ratmen as it took wing. The dragon's headless bulk soared above the battlefield, hurtling with meteoric fury towards the enemy warlock.

A doleful note rang out as the dragon dived towards the skaven sorcerer. Lothar recoiled as a blast of arcane energy smashed into him, crushing him against the dragon's scaly shoulder. His ears rang, blood streamed from his nose as the sorcerous cacophony from the hellish bell struck. He could feel scaly plates and blobs of meat tear from Graug's rotten hide. The dragon reared back, its wings fanning the air, its claws scraping against an invisible shell of sorcery.

Lothar stared incredulously at the horned ratman, watched in horror as the infernal bell drew back to strike another note. The power of the thing was atrocious, far beyond the aethyric harmonies crackling about the creature. With something approaching fright, he commanded the dragon to lash out with its decayed breath.

The mixture of corpse-gas and maggot-broth spattered across the skaven pushing the bell. Scores of the creatures collapsed, writhing in their death agonies. Yet still the altar and the hideous creature perched atop it remained unscathed. Lothar just had time to digest that fact when the bell tolled again. This time he could see the energy erupt from the clapper and snake its way upwards into the ratman's staff. A lance of searing light crackled from the horned tip, stabbing across the sky.

Even the dragon's mighty frame shook beneath such an assault. The beast's breast exploded in a burst of splintered scales and shattered bone, its left wing nearly sheared from its body. The behemoth plummeted from the sky, slamming into the swarming skaven below, crushing dozens beneath its bulk. The reptilian zombie shuddered and fell still as the eldritch animation motivating it flickered away.

Lothar fared little better. A shattered arm, a broken leg, these were the marks of his own descent. He could feel the shock of the impact in his throbbing bones. Pain pulsed through his body, reverberating through his withered veins. It was an effort to force some manner of coherence into the confusion of thoughts that swirled about inside his skull. His ears still ringing from the dolorous notes of the bell, he couldn't hear his own incantations as he tried to reanimate the dead dragon. A crackle of green lightning scorched the night, driving him to shelter behind Graug's immense claw. The skaven warlock, it seemed, was intent on finishing the job.

Lothar forced a small measure of control back into his senses, driving the distracting buzz from his head. He could hear now the triumphant squeaks of the enemy, rejoicing in the destruction of the dragon. With Graug eliminated, their victory seemed assured.

To Lothar, it was inexplicable. Vanhal had so much power at his command, how could he allow himself to be overwhelmed by these vermin?

Then, into the baron's ears came new sounds. The triumphant chittering was replaced by squeals of panic. An almost arctic chill gripped Lothar, the residue of some mighty sorcery. Raising his eyes skywards, he marvelled at what he saw.

Graug wasn't the focus of Vanhal's conjurations. The undead dragon had simply been a small fragment, a distraction to delay the enemy. The true enormity of Vanhal's power was only now appearing in the sky over Vanhaldenschlosse.

Again, Lothar was humbled by the limitations of his own comprehension. He had thought the summoning and control of a single zombie dragon was a power that should set him amongst the gods.

What words, then, to describe a force that had called scores of the beasts back from the dead?

◄ CHAPTER XVII ►

Middenheim
Ulriczeit, 1118

Lady Mirella stood on the veranda overlooking the marshalling yard within the walls of the Middenpalaz. It was here that Prince Mandred had assembled his expedition into the heart of the Ulricsberg before marching off to the temple of Grungni on the other side of the city.

She had watched them go, every man filled with a grim determination to do his duty, to lay down his life in the name of justice and goodness, to defend civilisation against the monstrous creatures of Old Night. Mirella knew she should have found it an inspiring sight, should have felt pride when she had gazed down into Mandred's face and seen that noble resolve etched across each line and curve. He had saluted her, before turning to lead the soldiers away, a gesture as heavy with meaning as that of a Bretonnian knight seeking a damsel's favour.

Mirella hadn't been able to acknowledge Mandred's show of affection. Quickly she had turned away, unwilling to let him see the dread in her eyes. For she had seen other men, moved by similar motives of justice and goodness. Right had been on their side, their enemy no less monstrous than these fiends from beneath the world. Despite the nobility of their cause, the selfless virtue in their ambitions, they had failed. Death, not victory, had been the price Prince Sigdan and his allies had paid for defying Emperor Boris.

Watching another prince, another man she loved marching off to battle had been more than she could bear. Mirella cursed her weakness, berated herself for the fear that clawed at her heart. Yet try as she might, her courage had deserted her. She thought of that horrible moment, in the sewer beneath Altdorf when they had fled Kreyssig's Kaiserjaeger, that terrifying moment when the rats had swarmed all around them in the dank filth. If she closed her eyes she could still feel their loathsome touch, hear their scurrying, chittering tide rushing through her ears. It was an awful, nightmarish memory, but how pleasant compared to the horror of what Mandred now sought to confront. Hordes of vermin, not mere rats but creatures of malignant intelligence and abominable spirit, things of Chaos spat up by the black pits of the earth!

No, Mirella had been unable to watch as the army moved off. By the same token, she was unable to leave now that they were gone. She lingered upon the veranda, staring out into the empty square, picturing that last sight of Mandred as he waved to her. She had feared he would resent her, would feel she was somehow responsible for Sofia's illness and death. Whatever feelings had developed between her and the prince, she worried that he would deny them in his mourning, reject them afterwards from a sense of guilt. Even so slight a gesture of regard gave her some hope that Mandred's heart was yet tender towards her.

Such a foolish, selfish thing to ponder when the fate of Middenheim itself was in question. Perhaps the whole of the

Empire, for where but in the City of the White Wolf could the strength be found to rebuild the shambles left by Boris Goldgather? The fate of mankind lingered at the edge of darkness, yet she was worried about...

Perspective asserted itself upon Mirella's reflections in the most dramatic and hideous manner she could have imagined. Down in the yard, among the paving stones, a heavy iron grate shuddered in its fastenings, the cover of a drain. The motion drew her attention, but as her eyes focused on the grate, she recoiled in fright. There were fingers clutching at the grate from *beneath* – furry, clawed talons. Something was down in the drain seeking to escape!

Before she could cry out, Mirella saw the cover flung upwards. Even as the grate clattered against the stones, a lean figure lunged up from the drain. She had seen that revolting carcass Kurgaz had thrown before the graf's councillors. She recognized this thing for another of that breed.

Mirella cringed away from the sight, stumbling back against the palace wall as more and more of the beasts boiled up into the yard. Faintly, she could hear shouts and screams echoing from the city beyond the walls of the Middenpalaz. The thought that this scene must be repeating itself all across Middenheim spurred her to action. It wasn't courage that drove her, but terror of the most dire cast.

The woman's scream turned rodent heads upwards, caused beady eyes to narrow. The skaven froze for an instant, like so many rats startled by a sudden candle. The instant passed, the monsters scattered, leaping at the walls where human guards had been alerted by the shriek. Several of the guards were shot down before they could even raise their weapons, picked off by ratkin snipers armed with long jezzails.

A few of the vermin rushed at the palace itself, launching themselves from the yard in an effort to reach the veranda.

Most of the creatures fell short, crashing back to earth with snarls and squeaks. One of the monsters, however, caught the balustrade with its paws. Briefly its legs scrabbled at the edge of the veranda, then it was pulling itself upwards, fangs bared in a vicious snarl.

Mirella found herself unable to move, unable to do anything but gaze in horror at that verminous face. The skaven chittered at her. She could see the muscles under its piebald fur tense as it prepared to spring at her.

Death caught the ratman before it could attack. A ball of spiked steel slammed into its face, splitting its skull and sending a spray of fangs and blood across the veranda. Brother Richter swung the footman's mace he held a second time and sent the corpse tumbling down into the yard. In the next instant, the priest grabbed Mirella and pulled her inside the palace.

Dazed, confused by her astounding escape, Mirella was slow to appreciate the bloodstains on the cleric's robe or the sounds of conflict echoing through the interior of the Middenpalaz. Then it struck her. What she had seen in the yard must be happening everywhere, anywhere there was a grate or drain leading into the sewers. The skaven were bypassing every fortification in the city by attacking from below!

'Graf Gunthar is rallying his warriors,' Richter was telling her as he helped a cluster of servants barricade the door opening onto the veranda. 'They've fought their way down to the cellars and are closing up the entrances!'

Mirella listened to the priest, but his words made little impact on her. Her thoughts were somewhere else. If the skaven were able to reach the city, if they had already prevailed below...

'What about Mandred?' she gasped.

Brother Richter shook his head. 'The graf believes it was

a trap to draw the army below. The skaven must have been waiting.

'Prince Mandred must be dead.'

'Khazuk!' Kurgaz bellowed, staving in the face of a ratman with the head of his hammer. The dwarf laughed boisterously as the carcass went flying backwards, toppling several of the skaven behind it.

Mandred slashed the throat of the monster he fought, nearly decapitating it. 'A fine cast, friend Smallhammer.'

Kurgaz cracked the skull of one of the skaven that had tripped over the corpse of his previous victim. A fierce shout sent several others scurrying away in fright. 'That's naught,' he grumbled. 'You should see me with the real thing!'

It didn't take any explanation for Mandred to know what the dwarf was talking about. It was impossible not to note the fearsome power of Drakdrazh. The temptation to sit back and watch Kurgaz's brother ply the enchanted hammer back and forth among the vermin was almost overwhelming. It was like seeing one of the dwarf ancestor gods in action. Mandred couldn't help but think of Ghal Maraz, the Hammer of Sigmar, and its legendary might. He wondered where the outlaw knight had taken it after it was stolen from Emperor Boris. He wondered if he would ever see it wielded in battle as he now saw Drakdrazh being wielded.

The dwarfs were already locked in pitched battle when the Middenheimers reached the caverns and mines of what the denizens of Karak Grazhyakh called the Fourth Deep. Skaven had swarmed up from the smaller shafts and tunnels radiating out from the Fourth Deep. Fighter for fighter, the ratmen were vastly inferior to the rugged dwarfs, their crude armour and scavenged weapons woefully primitive beside the steel plate and keen axes of their foes. The dwarfs, however, were

unable to match the speed of the ratkin, an advantage that
enabled the skaven to bring their prodigious numbers to bear
upon the foe. The dwarfs presented a solid rock, steady and
impenetrable, but the skaven were like a raging sea, sweeping
in from every quarter to pound at their defences.

How easy it would have been to lose heart when they
reached the battle, when they saw the seemingly endless horde
flooding through the great hall, scurrying across overturned
mine carts and scampering down skeletal gantries. It was one
thing to hear how numerous their foe was, but to see it before
one's eyes was a thing terrible to contemplate. Mandred felt
his own heart buckle when he saw that verminous sea crashing
around the small knots of embattled dwarfs scattered through
the cavern. Yet seeing those doughty warriors, unperturbed
despite being outnumbered and surrounded, combating their
enemy with a stubborn defiance, made an even greater impression. Watching a grizzled old dwarf smoking calmly on his
pipe as he mashed ratmen with his axe, or listening to a young
beardling singing a Khazalid tune as he plied his hammer sent
a fire coursing through their veins. Such courage in such conditions was a magnificence of valour that belonged in legend.
No man could abandon such courage to be overwhelmed and
destroyed. Whatever time he bought by such abject cowardice
wouldn't be life, but merely a hollow existence of shame.

To a man, the Middenheimers had charged into the Fourth
Deep, the fatigue of their long march forgotten as the roar
of battle thundered through them. Shouting 'wolf and graf!'
they had fallen upon the flank of the skaven horde. The ratmen, already locked in combat, were taken by surprise, forced
to give ground before the humans.

If they prevailed, they would be hailed as heroes when they
returned to the surface, paraded through Middenheim as
champions of order and light. If they could turn the skaven

back here, they would break the siege of their homes before it could even start.

The tide of battle was turning against the skaven. Steadily the humans were driving them back, fighting their way across the cavern to relieve the embattled dwarfs one group at a time. Ratmen still swarmed from the shafts and passageways, but now they did so fighting a trickle of skaven seeking to flee the conflict. The sight reassured Mandred. If his army could maintain the momentum, they would make that trickle into a raging torrent that would sweep the verminous horde away.

'We'll soon join your brother!' Mandred called out to Kurgaz, nodding to him.

The dwarf turned away from the mushed remains of an armoured ratman, frowning as he tried to peer over the shoulders of the knights and soldiers around him. 'I'll take your word for it, princeling,' he growled, then hurled himself at another foe.

Beside the prince, Beck was fending off the frenzied assault of a snaggletoothed ratkin draped in a tattered cloak and wielding knives in both its paws. The filthy creature reminded Mandred of the gutter runners that had rampaged through Neist's hospice. He felt no qualms as he drove his sword into the thing's back. Many more would die before Sofia was avenged.

'Thank you, your grace,' Beck huffed, winded by the hard fight. He had barely drawn a breath before he was lunging forwards again, striking down an opportunistic ratkin that was leaping at Mandred's back. The rodent fell in a pool of spilled entrails.

The ebb of battle flowed away from the prince's position. For a moment, he was able to gaze across the cavern, to appreciate the havoc that had been wrought against the skaven. Even as Mandred was feeling the glow of their accomplishment, he saw something that turned him sick inside.

Kurgaz's brother, that great champion with his fabulous warhammer, was beset by a mob of armoured ratmen. Black-furred brutes, they bore great halberds in their paws. While Drakdrazh struck one down, another slashed at Mirko, catching him in the back of the knee. The dwarf's mail blunted the impact, but he staggered just the same. The blazing runes on the haft of his hammer flickered for a moment.

In that moment, a huge white skaven wearing black armour lunged at Mirko, a sword clutched in either paw. The massive ratman brought both blades stabbing down, driving them with such force that they penetrated the mail between neck and shoulder. The monster put his full weight behind the stabbing blades, pushing them down until only the pommels projected from Mirko's shoulders.

The dwarf champion collapsed and Drakdrazh tumbled from his fingers. One of the black-furred skaven grabbed at the hammer, but before he could reach it his white-furred warlord lunged at him, tearing out his throat with gleaming fangs. Mandred's view of the skaven warlord was obscured as the armoured skaven surged forwards to oppose the dwarfs seeking to avenge Mirko.

Another surge of skaven swept towards Mandred's forces, pushing them back and away from Mirko's company. Kurgaz cursed and raged, throwing himself with reckless ferocity against the monsters. He'd heard the great wail set up by Mirko's comrades. He knew his brother was dead.

Mandred redoubled his own efforts, striving for every inch of ground. As the skaven began to give way, as they fell before the swords and spears of the Middenheimers, the prince kept an eye out for the white rat, dreading to see Drakdrazh blazing in the creature's paws.

'Your grace! Your grace!' The cry came from a sweat-drenched man clad only in a linen tunic and woollen breeks.

He pushed his way through the reserves behind the prince. Mandred shook his head at the man's curious raiment. He didn't look like one of his soldiers, which left the question of where he had come from.

'Your grace!' the man shouted again, his cry ringing over the fray. There were more words, but they were garbled in the clamour of battle. Something of their import must have impressed Beck, however. The knight pressed close to Mandred, fending off the prince's foes so that he could disengage.

Mandred fell back, listening with horror as the man's words became clear. He was right, the man wasn't a part of the army. He was a messenger from the surface. From Middenheim.

'We are undone,' the messenger cried. 'Skaven are attacking the surface!'

The report was like a cold knife sinking into the prince's heart. Skaven on the surface! Skaven in Middenheim!

'Your grace, what do we do?' The question came from one of the commanders, a nobleman who had been fighting at the prince's side.

Grimly, Mandred turned back to the battle. 'We fight on,' he said. 'We gave our word to help the dwarfs, we will not forsake them.' He choked back the dread that made his voice falter. 'If we can't turn the enemy back here, we won't be able to save our homes anyway.'

Carroburg
Mitterfruhl, 1115

Plague ravaged Carroburg. Daily, from the towers and parapets, the denizens of Schloss Hohenbach could see the decimation of the city. Corpse-carts prowled the streets, bodies lay stacked in the gutters. White crosses were marked up on the doors of the afflicted, and even from the heights of the Otwinsstein the nobles could pick out the figures of plague doktors, their faces hidden behind their birdlike masks, making the rounds. The trickle of trade still braving the river to reach Carroburg vanished entirely, plunging the stricken populace even deeper into the grip of need and want.

Within the castle, however, a much different world existed. Here the Black Plague held no dominion. Here there was no spectre of starvation, no threat of death and disease. Here there was only indulgence and luxury, the excesses of extravagance. All the vices the plunder of the Empire could buy were brought forth by its Emperor to impress upon his guests once and again the magnificence of his might and his wealth. To make them forget the horror that had become their salvation.

It was a venture doomed to failure. What melody, what dance, what farce, what harmony, what delicacy, what eroticism could make a mind forget what had been done? Never could those who had partaken of the obscene inoculation drive that knowledge from their minds. Not the strongest spirit, not the most potent herb, not the most ardent lover could bring a moment's respite. Yes, Emperor Boris had saved their lives, but their salvation was a tawdry thing, ever haunted by the thing Fleischauer had made.

Emperor Boris brooded upon the problem, watching as the very thing he had hoped to stop was instead accelerated by the warlock's magic. The great men of the Empire were growing to hate their Emperor, not because he couldn't protect them but because he had.

This inverted logic finally placed an idea in Boris's cunning mind. The schemer who had played nobles and provinces against one another, who had ensured that no man was without some potent enemy only the Emperor could protect him from, now set his insidious intellect to this crisis. The answer that came to him was almost an epiphany. If he could not make his guests forget the cause of their good fortune, then he would compel them to embrace it!

The great hall was lavishly adorned, draped with festive garlands and colourful banners. Priceless artworks by the old masters were placed upon the walls, and a band of the most skilled musicians Boris had commanded to the castle assembled at the far end of the chamber. Broad tables displaying poached quail eggs, broiled cormorant and dozens of other items of costly fare lined the other end of the hall. It was the last of the fresh food. After this night, they would have to endure the pickled and preserved stores. This night, however, indulgence was to be the rule.

As the strains of a jaunty waltz rolled through the castle, the noble guests sauntered into the chamber, festooned in an opulence of frill and lace, each face hidden behind a feathered domino mask. Cloaked in the anonymity of their costumes, they entered the hall with a measure of bravado they might otherwise not have shown. Each feared to find accusation and recognition in the face of their peers – even more in the eyes of the thing itself. Wrapped in their disguises, however, they felt no such trepidation.

Boris himself made small attempt to conceal his identity, striding into the hall dressed in a costume that affected the ostentatious regalia of the proscribed godling Vylmar, lord of debauchery and decadence. The small silk mask that covered his eyes did nothing to conceal the impish smile. Even the dullest mind couldn't fail to recognise the griffon-headed walking stick with which he swaggered about the hall, for all had seen that item many times in Boris's possession.

The timid, quiet woman who accompanied Boris made a better effort at concealing her identity, but she was betrayed by the company she kept. It had been several weeks since the Emperor had devoted his attentions to anyone except Princess Erna.

The Emperor made a single circuit of the hall, a gesture that had all the judgemental posturing of an inspection tour; then he turned his back upon his guests and stared directly at the thing that none of them dared acknowledge, the thing they could look at only with shy, quickly averted glances. Boldly, Boris defied the taboo his guests had agreed upon.

The thing's eyes were open, but there was no awareness in its gaze. A line of drool trickled from the corner of its toothless mouth, dripping down its breast to bathe one of the leeches fastened to its pallid flesh. The trunk of the thing was inanimate, only the rise and fall of its chest indicating that it was alive at all.

Brazenly, Boris walked up to the pedestal. From beneath the breast of his brocaded tunic, he brought forth a fold of gaudily coloured cloth adorned with tiny bells. While his shocked guests watched, Boris rose onto his toes, stretching to the utmost to set the fool's cap onto the thing's shaven head.

Music fell silent, conversation died. The atmosphere in the great hall became charged with tension, a dreadful expectancy. All eyes were turned to the Emperor and the grotesque thing resting upon the pedestal.

The shaven head tilted to one side, setting the little bells sewn to the cap jangling. In the silence, the tinkling note sounded like a peal of thunder.

As the thing's head rested against its shoulder and the bells were quiet once more, a boisterous laugh boomed. Emperor Boris pranced about the fearful apparition, genuflecting before it in mocking deference. With his antics, he demonstrated to his guests that the thing they feared was no ill omen, no token of damnation and guilt. It was simply an idiot thing to be made sport of, a mindless buffoon that could accuse no one and nothing of any sin.

The Emperor's laugh spread through the hall, at first half-heartedly echoed by his most spineless sycophants, but soon growing into genuine bursts of amusement. Into that laughter the nobles poured their relief, their last pangs of fleeing guilt. When the musicians again took up their instruments and sent the strains of a waltz flowing through the hall, the celebrants paired off, dancing through the hall, their opulent gowns and coats bustling and swirling around the pedestal and the drooling wreckage perched atop it. With each pass, the dancers jeered at the thing, pointing and laughing, letting their fear become contempt.

Emperor Boris cast his gaze about the revellers, searching for Erna, intent upon joining the celebration. His guests thought they were applauding restored freedom, liberation from the mortal terror that had dominated them since Fleischauer's ritual. In truth, they were enslaved by fetters far more insidious. The Emperor had led them from the shackles of their own conscience, had roused them to embrace the perversity that preserved them from the plague. He had led, and they had followed. So it would always be.

His eyes hardened behind his silk mask as he found Erna near the door leading to the Sigmarite chapel. The princess had distanced herself from the throng, was keeping away from the revelry. Her mask couldn't hide her almost pious disdain for the scene. Here, Boris knew, was one who hadn't followed him, who refused to follow him.

Seated beside Erna was the besotted ruin of Doktor Moschner, dressed in the deerskin of a Thuringian druid, his mask cast aside so that he might partake more liberally from the jar of wine resting beside him. The physician looked up

when he saw his Emperor approaching. He tried to rise, to
bow before his master, but liquor had already weakened his
legs and he instead slumped back in his seat.

'You are a disgrace,' Boris snarled at Moschner. 'We should
have you removed from the castle.'

Moschner blinked up at Boris, a flicker of awful hope passing through his eyes. 'Would you? Can I leave, Your Majesty?'
He waved his hand at the dancers, trying to point a finger
at the thing on the pedestal. 'You don't need me. You don't
need a doktor. You don't need medicine!' He slumped over,
as though his bones had suddenly turned to jelly. 'You have
magic to preserve you...' The last words were drawn from him
in a low sob.

Boris glared down at the physician. He'd come to confront
Erna, but where he might be prepared to indulge her defiance, he would brook none from Moschner. 'You'll be cast
out,' he vowed. 'Dumped over the wall and left to fend with
the rest of the peasant rabble.'

'Please, he is drunk. He doesn't know what he's saying.'
Erna caught at the Emperor's arm. All that pious disdain was
gone now, unseated by raw panic.

'A drunk man speaks the truth in his heart,' Boris told her
in a cold voice, reciting a bit of wisdom disseminated by the
god whose raiment he wore. 'He speaks treason against Us
and will be punished.'

Erna's grip on Boris's arm tightened. She turned him
around so that he again faced the crowd, could see them
dancing and jeering. 'You don't need to. Can't you see that
you've already won?'

The Emperor stared into her eyes and when he spoke, his
words were sombre. 'Have We? We came over here to ask why
you do not dance, why you do not share the cheer We have
demanded from Our subjects.'

The princess withdrew her arm, recoiling from the tone in Boris's voice. 'I cannot…'

'You defy Us openly,' Boris accused. 'You set a poor example for the others. Why We permit this, We do not know, but it ends now. It ends here.'

The colour drained from Erna as she appreciated what it was that the Emperor commanded. 'You won't punish the doktor?' she asked.

Boris reached out, took her hand in his and led her towards the revellers. 'We will spare him. He is a peasant. Nobody cares about peasants,' he added with a cruel chuckle.

The celebrants parted as the Emperor and Erna danced about the hall, watching as their sovereign led his companion in a graceful pirouette. Again and again, they circled the pedestal, drawing near to the idiot thing. At each pass, Erna felt her skin crawl, her soul sicken. Boris saw her revulsion, smiled at the power it implied. He had at last broken her to his will. Even this bulwark had crumbled before his siege.

In the course of one of their passes, with a deft flourish of his hand, Boris plucked a bloated leech from the tattooed thigh and presented the parasite to Erna. 'A pill to preserve the doktor's health,' he whispered to her.

Erna could feel everyone watching her as she took the foulness from Boris's hand. Quickly, before she could think about what she was doing, she put the leech in her mouth.

Laughter rippled through the hall. Emperor Boris had displayed to his guests that no one could resist his authority. Within the castle, he was absolute. Neither men nor women nor the gods themselves could defy him.

Long into the night, the music of the waltz echoed through the castle. Strains of melody drifted down from the Otwinsstein, rolling down from the hill into the desolate streets of Carroburg.

There were few in the plague-blighted ruins to hear the revelry.

Even fewer who listened did so with human ears.

⋖ CHAPTER XVIII ⋗

Altdorf
Kaldezeit, 1114

Sythar Doom gnashed his fangs, sending blue sparks flitting across the massed warpguard surrounding him. A few of the skaven spun around, baring their teeth at whatever had singed their fur. Their ire wilted when they saw it was the Grey Lord himself who had burned them. The hulking warriors cringed, hurriedly returning their attention to the verminous throng surging through the narrow street ahead.

The Warpmaster of Clan Skryre lashed his tail angrily, the hairless appendage whipping across the scarred pelts of the mute, lobotomised slaves who carried his palanquin. The slaves were perfectly matched for size, limbs elongated or cropped when the creatures had been mere whelps. The arms that gripped the runners supporting the palanquin were massive, burly things, swollen to monstrous proportions through injections of warpstone dust. The other arms, superfluous to the only labour demanded of the litter bearers, were absent entirely, amputated in the name of nutritional efficiency.

One day, Sythar Doom vowed, Clan Skryre would remake

all of skavendom as he had remade his slaves. They would cast down the old superstitions and foolishness that had retarded skaven development for thousands of years. Reason, the cold brilliance of intellect and imagination, would become the new foundation of the Under-Empire. Beneath the leadership of the Warpmaster, the old clan systems would be abolished. All skaven would belong to a single nest. The thinkers of Clan Skryre would oversee the breeding pits, use spells and potions to reshape the pups as they were forming in the wombs of their brood-mothers. They would create strains of brilliant, intellectual skaven to further the arcane technology that would make the ratmen masters of the world. They would make strong, fierce skaven to serve as warriors for the new order, being careful to strip them of those mental processes that would lead to ambition or defiance. They would bring into being a pliable underclass of workers, docile and subservient, devoid of even the capability to rebel.

It would be a glorious day, a day when Sythar Doom, Grey Lord and He Who Is Sixth, wasn't scratching his fleas while two packs of miserable clanrats argued over which of them had prevalence at a crossroads!

Treachery! That was the first thought that crept into Sythar Doom's mind. General Twych or Grey Seer Pakritt was behind this, unless of course it was some intrigue set into motion by the late and unlamented Deacon Blistrr. The battle for the man-thing nest-city called for the destruction of their chief temple. Once that was destroyed, the man-things would be a broken rabble utterly at the mercy of their conquerors. The skaven who commanded the attack on the temple would be the victor, acclaimed by the Grey Lords and Arch-Tyrant Vecteek.

That triumphant leader would have to be Sythar Doom. Anything less was an outrage!

'Burn them clear,' Sythar snarled at the captain of his warpguard. The hulking ratman bobbed his head in acknowledgement, and scurried off to growl orders at the rest of the Clan Skryre strike force. In short order, the warpguard were scrambling clear, making way for the fire-throwers. Gigantic casks of worm-oil mixed with warpstone, the wheeled contraptions were dragged forwards by a small army of scrawny slaves. Warp-engineers dressed in oilskins scurried about the arcane controls, throwing levers and pushing buttons, urging the volatile liquid to flow through ratgut pipes and bat-bone tubes. At the fore of each wagon-like barrel-cart, a villainous ratman clothed from snout to tail in wormskin coveralls twisted open the nozzle of a thick hose.

Green fire belched from each nozzle, inundating swathes of bickering clanrats. The skaven shrieked in agony as their fur erupted into flames, as the meat melted from their very bones. The ignited clanrats fled blindly into the packed masses of their own comrades, spreading the flames beyond the murderous streams being vomited from the fire-throwers.

As their first victims burned, slaves pushed the fire-throwers forwards, persecuting the skaven choking the crossroads in a fratricidal holocaust. Burning ratmen leaped onto the walls of buildings, dived through windows and smashed down doors in their desperate efforts to escape. Those not yet within the killing zone turned to flee back up the street, pleading and clawing at the ratkin who blocked their way.

Through it all, the skaven of Clan Skryre continued to advance, pressing their advantage. The fire-throwers continued to take a horrendous toll upon the clanrats, blasting them until even their bones were scorched into cinders. One corner of the crossroads, that facing towards the fire-throwers, had become an inferno, the structures at its periphery blazing like torches as the eerie green flames seared through their walls.

Sythar Doom's entourage hesitated, the bloodthirsty eagerness of the fire-rats curbed by their fear of the very destruction
they had inflicted. There was good reason for their caution
– if the flames from the buildings should be blown back
towards the fuel-carts then the volatile mixture inside might
very well combust! In such a conflagration, there would be
no survivors.

The Warpmaster had little patience to spare, even for caution. 'Fetch-bring the warpcaster!' he raged, slashing the claws
of his feet across a slave's shoulder. When the palanquin
sagged momentarily as the slave winced in pain, Sythar was
tempted to blast the wretch with warp-lightning. Only the
thought that the slaves were a matched set stayed his violent
impulse. Instead, he selected an unfortunate warpguard who
caught his eye, cooking the ratman in his own armour with a
coruscating beam of sizzling light.

The rhythmic hum of machinery, the groan of creaking
wood and the anguished huffs of toiling slaves warned of
the warpcaster's approach. Sythar shifted about in his seat,
whiskers twitching as the arcane weapon came trundling
down the street behind him. It was a gigantic construction, a
wheeled carriage of timber pulled by a hundred slaves. Great
boilers and engines were bolted to that carriage, placed ahead
of an angled crossbeam. A long arm of steel topped with
an immense bowl of cast bronze stretched down the centre
of the carriage. Behind the machine, staggered at intervals,
teams of warp-engineers pushed large wooden carts, sealed
crates to which wheels had been fitted.

As the warpcaster trundled into position, the slaves pulling it sank wearily to the street. A gang of warp-engineers
scurried about the machine, hammering great iron spikes
into the road, chaining the enormous engine to the ground.
When they had driven a dozen spikes into the street, they

gestured frantically at their comrades pushing the carts. One of these came rushing forwards, and in short order the rat-men smashed open the top of the box-like cart and removed pawfuls of curled wood shavings from inside.

For all the haste of their early actions, now the warp-engineers became plodding and methodical in their labour. Gingerly, four of the ratmen used iron hooks to reach into the cart. Slipping the hooks into metal eyes, they lifted a crystal-line sphere from the box. With great care, the skaven bore the globe towards the warpcaster, setting it down in the cold-cast bronze bowl.

Sythar Doom's jewelled eyes gleamed as he stared at the sphere, watching the rampant energies crackling behind the crystal facets. The harnessed fury of raw warpstone, impris-oned in the delicate framework, its ravenous appetite for destruction held in check by the art of Clan Skryre! Biding its time until its masters chose to unleash it upon their foes!

The warp-engineers leapt away from the bronze bowl as soon as the sphere was in place. Cast into the semblance of an outstretched claw, the fingers of the bowl closed around the massive crystal orb. Electricity rippled about the bronze talons as they closed tight. A masked skaven, his body insu-lated by thick layers of cloth and fur, rushed to a mechanism embedded in the side of the carriage. For an instant, the ratman's paws flew across the maze of buttons and levers, adjusting them in a frenzy of activity. The artillerist glanced once at the burning buildings ahead, then threw a final lever.

The warpcaster shuddered as the enormous swing-arm lunged into motion. Propelled by the engines fitted to the carriage, the arm slammed upwards into the arched cross-beam, the impact causing the entire engine to bounce, held in position only by the stakes chaining it to the road. As the arm smashed against the crossbeam, the bronze talons opened and the crystalline sphere was flung from the bucket.

There was an eerie lack of noise when the sphere crashed into the buildings. No explosive detonation, no billowing wall of fire and wreckage. There was simply a flash of eerie green light, a horrendous luminance that washed out the glow of flames. When the light faded, when vision was restored, the conflagration was gone, evaporated by the disintegrating energies inside the crystal globe. A black, charred slime and a few bits of scarred stone were all that remained of a city block, the ground itself gouged and scooped away into a concave depression.

Sythar preened himself as he heard the clanrats squeak in terror and redouble their efforts to flee. The musk of fear rose from the glands of even his own clan-kin. The warpcaster was the most terrifying war machine ever conceived. It would smash the pathetic human resistance and demonstrate to the other Lords of Decay the might of Clan Skryre and its overlord!

'Forwards! Hurry-scurry!' Sythar growled. Obediently, his warpguard marched out into the glowing desolation left behind by the sphere. Behind him, mobs of slaves pulled the stakes from the road and began to drag the ponderous weight of the warpcaster. Sythar watched them for a moment, then slapped his tail against the shoulders of his bearers, urging them into motion.

Victory would belong to Clan Skryre. The warpcaster would guarantee it!

After all, Sythar had ensured there was enough ammunition for the machine to not only demolish the human city, but to exterminate any ratmen who thought to take credit for his triumph.

* * *

Grim-faced, Grand Theogonist Gazulgrund stood upon the broad steps of the Great Cathedral and watched as the verminous horde came flooding into the square. Three sides of the temple were embattled now. It could only be a matter of time before the skaven came swarming down from the north and completed the encirclement. Once they were surrounded, he knew there would be no escape.

That thought brought a bitter smile to the priest's face. For him, escape wasn't an option anyway. Abandoning the temple would be to abandon his faith, and he would do neither. In a long life of fear and confusion, there was only one thing he was certain of, one constant that provided him with strength. That was his faith in Mighty Sigmar. Trust in the man-god had sustained him through his darkest ordeals, had carried him through moments when he felt he could endure no longer. Even in the cruel machinations of Kreyssig, he saw the hand of Sigmar. Because of Kreyssig, he had become Grand Theogonist. He had been entrusted with the leadership of the temple in this, its darkest hour. Another man, a man less secure in his belief, a man less firm in his convictions, such a man might have fled and abandoned the temple.

He was not such a man. His faith had been tested in the horrors of the Dragon's Hole. He had been forced to question everything he held dear, forced to evaluate what was most important in his life. He had come through the anguish of that process a different man. A man who could stand upon the steps of the Great Cathedral and gaze upon his own death without fear. A man could honour his god all his life, but it was in the way in which he embraced death that he paid his final tribute to the divine.

In his hands, clothed in the dragonskin gauntlets worn by the prophet Ungrimvolg during the Third Battle of Black

Fire Pass, the Grand Theogonist held the gem-encrusted haft of Thorgrim, the gigantic mattock crafted for Grand Theogonist Jurgen II by dwarf runesmiths five centuries after the ascension of Sigmar. The mattock was so large that few men could wield it in battle – in life Jurgen had been nicknamed 'Ogreblood' for his prodigious size and strength. The current Grand Theogonist harboured no delusions that his physicality was on a par with that of his ancient predecessor. It wasn't as a weapon he had brought the mattock down from its place of honour on the walls of the Heroes' Hall. Thorgrim was more important as a symbol, a reminder of the awe and might of Holy Sigmar. It was an echo of that great warhammer once wielded by the man-god when he forged his Empire from scattered tribes of savages and brought the light of civilisation to mankind.

Gazulgrund turned his gaze from the swarming horde of monsters to the massed ranks of those who had rallied to the temple to defend it against the ravening fiends. They were a disparate, motley amalgamation of people from all walks of life. He could see simple peasants armed with nothing more than shovels and sickles. There were merchants in the tattered remnants of their finery wielding knives and swords. A great throng of flagellants, whips and flails clutched in their bloodied hands, their monk-like habits tied around their waists to better display their self-inflicted scars. Genuine monks and friars, many of them unversed in the ways of warfare, clinging grimly to staves and clubs.

Mixed among these determined but untrained defenders were small pockets of martial discipline. Bands of Scheuters and former *Dienstleute*, ranks of soldiers who had managed to fight their way to the square. A handful of mounted knights, their warhorses towering above the foot soldiers all around them. Proud in their habits of black and gold, the Templars of Sigmar held themselves at the fore of the battle line, determined to claim the glory of being the first to confront the foe.

Gazulgrund felt his heart swell as he gazed out over the men who had come here, banded together in defence of their faith. Certainly, some were motivated by the refugees who had flocked to the cathedral and even now filled the sanctuary, but many others had come out of devotion to Sigmar. The priest had watched them, watched them approach the immense doors of the temple and prostrate themselves before the ancient statue of Sigmar that rested in a niche above those doors. Certainly, there was a resignation, a fatalism in the pious display, but there was also a steadfastness, a devotion that brought tears to the priest's eyes.

He caught a slight motion near the base of the steps. Staring down, Gazulgrund saw a small boy, no older than his ninth winter, bowing to the statue and making the sign of Sigmar with his left hand. In his right, he held an old wooden sword, stolen no doubt from some training field. Seeing the look of fear in the boy's eyes as he bowed, observing the look of defiance that blazed across his face as he turned back towards the oncoming enemy, Gazulgrund felt warmth flood through his veins.

'Men of Altdorf!' Gazulgrund shouted in a voice that seemed as if it were forged from thunder. 'Men of the Empire! Brothers all! Behold the steel in your hearts! Behold the fire of your faith! Behold the magnitude of your valour! When others flee, when others cower and hide, you stand tall! You stand proud! You stand as free men! You carry the Light of Sigmar within you, and it shall not be quenched by the vermin of Old Night!'

Despite its tremendous weight, Gazulgrund lifted Thorgrim over his head, brandishing it like a standard. 'For Sigmar!' he roared, his voice booming across the plaza, echoing from the spires of the cathedral. He turned to his left, raising the huge mattock a second time. 'For Sigmar!' He turned to the right, repeating the gesture. 'For Sigmar!'

The shout was taken up by the defenders, growing into the clamour of an angry ocean. The verminous host paused, hesitated at the edge of the square, cringing back from the ferocity of that cry. It was only a moment that the monstrous army delayed, then the threats and whips of their leaders drove them on once more. But it was a moment that had broken the spell of terror that had threatened to overwhelm the men. They had glimpsed the craven, slinking nature of their enemy and with that glimpse grew utter contempt for this vile foe. Against such scum, none worthy of the name 'man' would retreat.

'For Sigmar!' Gazulgrund repeated, again raising the enormous bulk of Thorgrim. He did not ponder the impossibility of that action, the uncanny lack of strain that accompanied the feat.

Alone among all those in the square, human and skaven alike, the Grand Theogonist did not see the golden aura that surrounded him or the shining light that gleamed from his robes.

Sylvania
Kaldezeit, 1113

Chittering triumphantly, Seerlord Skrittar drew the screaming vibrations of the holy bell through his body. He could feel the dreadful energies throb through his bones, sense the residue of warpstone in his blood twine about the malignant harmonies as they gathered and swelled. Bending the rampaging power to his own murderous will, he focused the magic into the horned head of his staff.

One exertion of his fierce abilities and it would all be over. He'd destroyed the stupid mage-man's dragon. Now he would do the same to the puny mage-meat. He might keep the fool's bones as a chew toy for his pups back in Skaven-blight. Then again, he didn't believe in playing with his food.

Before Skrittar could extend his staff and unleash his spell, he became aware of a disturbance in the sorcerous harmony. Turning his eyes skywards, he spurted the musk of fear.

The sky was black with dragons! Dozens of undead, decayed bulks, their scaly hides clinging in strips to bleached bones and scabrous flesh, bat-like wings fanning the air in torn tatters. Unlike the first dragon, great reptilian heads snarled from long, serpentine necks, profane fires burning in the pits of their decayed skulls.

Necrotic black vapours spewed from the fanged maws of the dragons as they came hurtling down. Swathes of skaven were annihilated, their bodies crumbling into desiccated husks. Survivors tucked tails between their legs and scurried away in abject terror.

Skrittar shifted his staff and sent the bolt of crackling warp-energy stabbing upwards. He was rewarded by watching the lightning smash through the skull of one dragon, sending the reptile crashing earthwards. For all their hideous power, the beasts weren't invulnerable!

He tried to keep that thought as he watched tendrils of dark magic stream down from the broken tower. Glowing fog engulfed the destroyed dragon, seeping into its rotten bones. Soon, with awkward jerks, the reptile was lurching back onto its feet! Even more horrible, the skaven the behemoth had smashed in its descent were moving, dragging their crushed bodies towards their living comrades!

Eyes wide with horror, Skrittar realised the awful mistake he had made. The mage-meat he'd attacked wasn't the enemy, just a minion sent out to bait the seerlord into committing himself. His true adversary was still in the tower, directing the magic emanations that had summoned a flight of dragons from their graves and which now sustained their obscene semblance of life!

That realisation sent a new determination raging through the seerlord's black heart. To retreat now would be to accept defeat. He'd never get those craven mice of Clan Fester to take the field again, and even Clan Mordkin might lose their appetite for rotten meat after this fiasco. The secret of the warpstone would be out, all of Skrittar's careful planning reduced to nothing as every clan in the Under-Empire came swarming into Sylvania to plunder the wealth that rightfully belonged to him!

No! He wouldn't concede such ruination! He was the Voice of the Horned One, Supreme Prophet of He Who Is Thirteen! He wouldn't allow the ignominy of defeat, not now when the Order of Grey Seers was so vulnerable. He'd spent the lives of twenty-four of his most powerful underlings to make this happen. He owed it to their martyrdom to seize the warpstone and make himself Grand Despot of Skavenblight!

'Ring the bell,' Skrittar snarled down at his slave. The hulking skaven leaned back, driving the warpstone striker against the bell. Another blast of arcane energy swept through Skrittar's body, this time manifesting as a great crevice that snaked its way across the earth. The crushed, crawling skaven zombies vanished in the ruptured earth, the twice-restored dragon toppling into the great pit conjured by the tolling of the bell.

'More bell!' Skrittar shrieked, warp-lightning crackling from his fangs. 'More bell!'

Again, the warpstone striker smashed against the bell,

sending another blast of power through Skrittar's body. A storm of lightning sizzled from his staff, slamming into one of the dragons, tearing its wings to shreds and sending its rotten bulk slamming into the earth. The seerlord paid no notice to the hundred or so Mordkin warriors pulverised beneath the behemoth's bulk. What he did notice was the treacherous way his army was disintegrating, quitting the battlefield in panicked mobs! Such infamy was unbelievable! These flea-fondlers were engaged in the most important work of their miserable lives. They should feel honoured to die for the glory of Skrittar!

'Got-want more bell!' Skrittar hissed. He ignored the protest of the slave with the striker, baring his fangs at the wretch until another burst of power roared up from the grim tolling of the holy bell. Biting down on a nugget of warpstone, the grey seer redoubled the energies, transforming the swirling eddies of power into arching fingers of compulsion that reached out and burned their way into thousands of frightened skaven minds. Viciously, Skrittar probed that facet of their rodent brains devoted to hunger, stirring that lobe until what had been a fleeing mob was transformed into a starving swarm of frenzied monsters.

Froth dribbled from verminous fangs, blood dripped from glazed eyes as the rabid ratmen turned upon the dragons. With savage brutality, the skaven flung themselves at the decayed reptiles, swarming over them in a clawing, biting horde. First one, then a second dragon was dragged down by the sheer weight of its tormentors. Caring nothing for the hundreds smashed by the dragons' claws or obliterated by necrotic breath, the crazed horde continued its rampage, slaughtering its own when there were no enemy near enough to slay.

Skrittar chittered maniacally as he watched the skaven

swarm. He would teach the mice to fight! His lips curled and his tail lashed angrily against the stone arch. There were still too many dragons, and his enemy was keeping them away from the ground and the gnashing fangs of the skaven. To burn them all out of the sky would be impossible, but Skrittar realised that it wouldn't be necessary. The only enemy he had to kill was the mage-man who had conjured up the dead-things to begin with.

Glaring at the tower, ignoring the scattered packs of fleeing skaven who had escaped the death frenzy he had inflicted upon their fellows, Skrittar snarled down at the bell-ringer. 'Need-want more bell!'

The slave cried out in terror, protesting his master's latest command. Skrittar stretched out his paw, crushing the ratman's mind between his claws, reducing him to a fleshy puppet. With clumsy, spastic motion, the slave brought the striker cracking against the bell one final time.

Skrittar's fangs bit down upon another chunk of warpstone, adding still more arcane energy to the reverberations of the spell. The seerlord focused his thoughts, directing the magic into a snaking chasm that would reach out and undermine the tower, send it crashing down. The magical fulcrum and the mage-man who had conjured it would be broken in one stroke of divine fury!

Such was his intention, but as Skrittar tried to focus his spell, he heard something crack inside him. Looking down, he saw his arm bend back upon itself in a fashion he was certain should be physically impossible. An instant later, all the fur on his left side turned into pulpy, twitching feelers, like the legs of a million fat spiders.

Skrittar tried to scream, but by that time it was too late to stop the runaway magic ravaging his body.

* * *

From the top of Vanhaldenschlosse, the metamorphosis of Seerlord Skrittar was like a blazing eruption of volcanic fury. The tower shook from the aethyric vibration and the unleashed Chaotic energies. The whirling current of vibrations faltered for an instant, their harmonies disturbed by the discordant inflection.

Vanhal stirred from his conjuration, his breath coming to him in shallow gasps. Returning his concentration to the three dimensions of mortal space was an ordeal to one who had sent his mentality soaring through vistas beyond the barriers of time and dimension. His consciousness had ridden astral tides, striding at once across powers and principalities to effect his mighty evocation. He had done more than simply form a spell from his will – he had effectually become the spell, channelling his essence into the enchantment.

The zombie dragons drawn from forgotten caves across half the world, the resurrected skaven, the walking dead of Sylvania, these had become more than simply puppets animated by his magic. They had become extensions of himself, extra fingers of his outstretched hand, physical manifestations of his soul. Vanhal had been more than an identity; he had become a multiplicity, an existence that transcended all concepts of mortality and divinity.

What he had discovered was so much more than mundane appreciations of life and death. He had tasted eternity, an eternity of tranquillity devoid of pain and sorrow. He had experienced a world without oppression and fear – a world where all the discord was forced into harmony, all the frayed edges had been mended.

His focus lost, Vanhal could feel the magical vibrations coursing through the tower ebbing. The stars overhead assumed their natural positions as time reasserted its tyranny. Blocks of stone, held in place solely by the aethyric vibrations, fell away, crashing from the walls. The levitating altar dropped to the roof, smashing into bits of bone. Vanhal himself dropped away, landing with a jarring impact on the splintered wreckage.

Beyond the walls of Vanhaldenschlosse, he could hear the frightened squeaks of the fleeing skaven. Briefly, the necromancer sent a little tendril of power into the remaining dragons, enough to sustain their decayed frames while they harried the ratmen back to their burrows. When he had time, he would perform a more complete ritual to reduce the transience of their animation. Alongside the droves of dead the skaven left behind, the dragons would make short work of completing his tower.

A surge of discordant emanations drew Vanhal's attention to the base of his tower. Far below he could see a colossal shape scrabbling up the stones, dragging itself with gravity-defying malignance on a confusion of what seemed at once both legs and tentacles. The thing's shape was that of some insane insect, yet there was also that about it that suggested both crabs and spiders. A motley, piebald fur stretched across most of its grisly body while across its broad back, elongated into an absolute of madness and horror, was the visage of a huge horned rat.

The ghastly residue of Seerlord Skrittar, the foul spawn born of his arcane apotheosis, squirmed up the tower with such swiftness that Vanhal was unable to direct even the most minor of incantations against it before the thing had reached the roof. Whips of aethyric energy crackled about the thing as it clambered up to meet him, the distorted skaven face grinning idiotically as the residue of the grey seer's mentality tried to remember why it was here. One paw, the only portion of the monster that was unchanged, pointed its claw at the necromancer.

'Die-die!' the giant, rat-like head bellowed.

The whips of energy lashed out at Vanhal in a withering discharge of amok magic. The stones beneath the necromancer's feet turned to jelly, the shattered bones of the altar took flight as rainbow-winged insects. Where the energy glanced across his robe, the garment sprouted gritty, coral-like encrustations.

'I have too much to do before that happens,' Vanhal told the insane Skrittar-spawn. The necromancer's eyes blazed with power as he drew the waning energies of the fulcrum into his mind...

Lothar von Diehl stepped around the mess of putrid, steaming fur. No need, then, to ask his master what had become of the monster he had seen climbing the tower. Having sensed the power of the creature, he had worried that Vanhal might not be able to defeat it on his own. Now he felt foolish for having hurried back to render aid.

Turning away from the loathsome puddle, Lothar bowed before his seated master. No sense in wondering how Vanhal had brought his palanquin up from the halls below. Perhaps he'd been inspired by the monster's ascent and simply had the thing climb up the side of Vanhaldenschlosse.

'The enemy is in full retreat, master,' Lothar reported. 'Between the dragons and the destruction of their leader, I think they won't be back.'

Vanhal was silent for a time, eyes closed behind the skeletal contours of his mask. 'Never underestimate the foolishness of mortality,' he said, his voice like an icy whisper. 'The living can only be trusted to do the unpredictable, be they men or rats.'

'What then is the answer?' Lothar asked.

Vanhal opened his eyes, but there was a faraway quality in their gaze. Whatever the necromancer stared at, it was nothing his apprentice could see.

'The answer is to bring them peace,' Vanhal declared.

'The only peace any of them will ever need.'

◄ CHAPTER XIX ►

Middenheim
Ulriczeit, 1118

Vrrmik bared his teeth at the vengeful dwarfs as they struggled to reach him. The stormvermin of Clan Mors were among the strongest and most vicious warriors in the Under-Empire. A fortune in food and armour, weapons and warpstone had been spent to make them an elite force without equal. Entire burrows had been enslaved to cultivate the warpweed that supplemented their carnivorous diet and caused their muscles to swell. They were the terror of a hundred warrens, a thousand burrows. Entire clans of slaves quivered at their very scent.

It was, therefore, quite a shock to the warlord when his super-skaven broke before the vicious assault the dwarfs mounted. The white ratman's eyes went wide with fright when he appreciated that the only thing standing between himself and a throng of enraged dwarfs were a handful of opportunistic clanrats who had thought to loot the corpses left by the stormvermin. As the stormvermin scattered, the clanrats found themselves staring straight into the snarling masks of the dwarfs' helms.

For an instant, the fury of the dwarfs was turned against
the looters. They had the misfortune to be discovered in the
act of cutting rings from the fingers of the dwarf champion
Vrrmik had slain. What the dwarfs did to the scavengers was
horrible enough that the warlord forgot himself and expelled
his glands. Nervously, his claws tightened about the haft of
Drakdrazh.

Scurrying away from the dwarfs, Vrrmik tripped over the
corpse of a ratman who had treacherously died in such a fashion as to make himself an obstacle for his warlord. Angrily,
Vrrmik swung the stolen hammer at the carcass. He was
shocked when the head exploded into a mist of blood and
gristle. A mad titter of awe hissed from his clenched fangs. In
his panic, he'd almost forgotten the reason he'd taken such
risks and involved himself directly in the attack.

Jumping to his feet, Vrrmik met the charging dwarfs. There
were five of them. He swung the warhammer full into the
side of the first dwarf, crumpling his steel shield as though it
were a mouldy leaf, hurling the dwarf across the cavern with
such force that his armoured body left an impact crater inches
deep in the rock wall. The other dwarfs tried to put up a better fight, but the dire combination of Drakdrazh and Vrrmik's
vicious, warpweed-enhanced strength was too great for them
to overcome. One by one, they died.

Vrrmik exulted in the carnage, savouring the smell of blood
as he reduced his enemies to pulp. What need to hide behind
his stormvermin (though those treacherous flea-licking mice
would suffer for abandoning him) when he was a veritable
demigod of battle! An avatar of the Horned One raining
death and destruction upon all those mad enough to oppose
him!

The last dwarf turned and ran, even the stubborn courage
of his kind incapable of enduring Vrrmik's murderous havoc.

The warlord watched him flee, debating whether he should allow the wretch to tell others of what he had seen or whether to smash him into paste as he had the dwarf's comrades. Vrrmik wondered if he could swing Drakdrazh lightly enough to merely maim the dwarf. That would give him the best of both choices.

The scent of human in the air caused Vrrmik to hesitate and allow the dwarf to flee back behind the ranks of his kind. The warlord's whiskers twitched as his cunning restrained his bestial bloodlust. There were far more important things to consider than the slaughter of a few dwarfs. Oh yes, much more important things!

Vrrmik hefted the great weight of Drakdrazh onto his shoulder and scampered back towards one of the mine shafts, watching as more of his monstrous warriors swarmed up into the Fourth Deep. Most of them were mere slaves, axe-fodder to wear down the foe. Vrrmik didn't think twice about spending their lives, yet at the moment there was no purpose to further fighting. This sally against the dwarfs had achieved what Grey Lord Vecteek expected. Now it was time to give the verminous tyrant what he deserved.

Raising a curled horn that had once adorned the head of a grey seer, Vrrmik blew a doleful note, a manic cachinnation that rippled across the cavern. At the sound, the skaven withdrew from their enemies, fleeing down the shafts and passages in a panicked rout of such suddenness that it left the dwarfs and their human allies too stunned to react.

Vrrmik lashed out with Drakdrazh, slaughtering a dozen of his minions as he cleared a place for himself in one of the tunnels. The gory example wasn't one he needed to repeat. The ratmen gave their warlord all the room he needed.

Vrrmik savoured the smell of their fear. Soon all the Under-Empire would fear him the same way. There would

be changes in Skavenblight when Vecteek failed to return.
Changes that Vrrmik – with the support of Clan Pestilens –
would exploit to the full.

Poor Vecteek, Vrrmik thought. With the human army down
in the deeps, he would think himself safe to launch his attack
on Middenheim. What would the despot do when that army
suddenly came rushing up at him, trapping him between the
enemies on the surface and the ones in the dwarfhold?

It was an amusing image, one Vrrmik was almost sorry he
wouldn't see for himself.

Fires raged through parts of Middenheim, thick plumes
of smoke rising into a darkened sky, columns of flame
reaching up to paint the twilight a hellish crimson. Entire
neighbourhoods were burning, put to the torch by attackers
and defenders alike, both sides using fire to constrain and
contain the other. The hovels of the Westgate district were
an inferno, the tortured screams of those trapped within the
maze-like warren echoing across the city.

Graf Gunthar watched the conflagration with fatalistic
resignation. The ratmen had plotted and planned well. They
were inside the city's defences before anyone was even aware
of the peril. Their hordes seemed to be everywhere, making
a feeble mockery of Middenheim's thick walls and numerous defence strategies. What assembly for the militia when
the skaven already controlled the streets, when the vermin
swarmed through the squares? They pillaged across the fields
and gardens, stealing the crops Middenheim had taken such
pains to cultivate in the cold mountain air. They ransacked
homes and shops, plundered inns and temples. Wherever a
man's eye turned, he found the skaven already there.

Now it was Warrenburg's turn; Graf Gunthar's thoughts
turned bitter. Middenheim had watched from the safety

of the mountain while the shanty town at the foot of the Ulricsberg burned, thankful that they had been spared such catastrophe. Now, it was Warrenburg's turn to be thankful, to look up and shudder at the fiery glow high on the mountain.

'Your excellency, what are your commands?'

The graf looked aside, his eyes not seeming to see Grand Master Vitholf seated upon a hulking black destrier. Master horsemen, the Knights of the White Wolf had remained in the city when Mandred led his army into the bowels of Karak Grazhyakh. Now they formed the core of the motley defenders who had rallied around the Middenpalaz. Watchmen, templars, hunters, foresters, rangers and mercenaries, they were a ragged collection from across Middenheim. Every man who could hold a sword or string a bow had, it seemed, converged upon the palace, looking to Graf Gunthar for guidance, trusting in their noble lord to lead them to victory.

Victory? There was a truly bitter thought. What victory could there be for Middenheim against such a horde? What victory for Graf Gunthar when he knew his only son lay dead somewhere in the dark beneath his feet?

A wolf dies on its feet, a dog on its belly. The words of the Ulrican proverb rang through the graf's mind, reverberating through his very soul. Choking back his own despair, he answered Vitholf in a grim voice.

'We ride to our doom,' he told the knight. 'We ride into the flames of vengeance, into the cauldron of slaughter. We ride to reap and slay, to kill and die. We ride to seek an end that will not shame us in the eyes of Ulric.'

Sombrely, the ragged host followed their graf as he led them from the bloodied courtyards of the Middenpalaz and past the burning manors of Teutogen nobility. Across the blasted fields of what had been the Konigsgarten they marched, cavalry at the fore, footmen behind. Sometimes tattered groups of men would stagger out from the rubble to join the grim procession. More often they would find only clumps of pillaging skaven. Seldom did the creatures linger to fight so large a company, but instead turned tail and fled.

All of that changed when the graf and his followers reached the streets of the Eastgate district. Here, among the despoiled homes and savaged shops, the skaven gathered in a great mass, chittering and hissing at the humans in triumphant mockery. Snipers hidden in garrets and clinging to spires picked off victims with impunity, the great range rendering them immune to the archery of Middenheim's defenders. To fight the ratmen, the humans would be forced to take the battle to them.

Graf Gunthar looked back at his army, feeling his heart tighten as he saw the expectant, hopeful light in the eyes of his men. Surely they knew the fight was hopeless, that there would be no victory here? Yet none of them, from the highest noble to the lowest beggar, glared at him in accusation, held him to account for the doom that had come upon them all. Even in this hour, they looked to him as their leader.

It was a realisation that made Graf Gunthar feel unworthy. What was this quality within him that deserved such loyalty? What was this divine ember that invested him with such right? And as he gazed into the faces of his people, he understood that the answer to those questions didn't lie within himself. It was in those he ruled, it was their faith and their trust that ennobled him.

In this last hour, Gunthar vowed he would not betray that trust. Sitting straight in his saddle, throwing back the wolf-skin cloak draped about his shoulders, he drew his sword from its sheath. Like a finger of daylight, the graf's sword burned in the night. Legbiter, one of the famed runefangs forged by the dwarfs for the twelve kings who united under

Sigmar, the blade had ever been the symbol of Middenland's count and Middenheim's graf. As its ancient magic rippled across its surface, even Gunthar felt a sense of awe. It was as though Ulric – or perhaps Sigmar – were reaching down, letting the warriors of Middenheim know that they had not been forsaken.

Swinging his sword overhead, Gunthar shouted his defiance of the scuttling vermin infesting the streets of the Eastgate. 'Death!' he howled. 'Death and ruin! Death and havoc! Death! Death! Death!' Spurring his horse, the enraged graf charged the skaven. The earth shuddered as the knights and horsemen he led urged their own mounts to the attack. The snipers in the rooftops desperately tried to blunt the charge, but their efforts were like casting pebbles into the sea. Nothing would stop the surge of Middenheim's vengeance.

Into the streets Graf Gunthar led his men, hewing ratmen asunder with Legbiter at every turn. The mockery of the skaven collapsed into frightened squeaks as the humans rode them down. Knights drove their horses through shops and homes in pursuit of the ratkin, spearmen ranged through alleyways to skewer hiding skaven, archers loosed arrows into the backs of vermin seeking to escape down side streets.

What started as a desperate fight became a bloody slaughter, slaughter gave way to massacre. The warm thrill of victory roared in Graf Gunthar's breast. Despite the numberless hordes of the enemy, they had no stomach for battle. Middenheim might yet be saved.

Then, as quickly as the prospect of victory danced before his eyes, Graf Gunthar saw it snatched away. His men had pursued the fleeing skaven deep into the Eastgate district, towards the great theatre of marble and alabaster that marked the cultural heart of the city. The once glistening walls were foul with soot and blood, the statues toppled, the glass dome shattered and smashed.

The wanton, savage destruction was cruel enough, but crueller by far was the deception that had brought the avengers here. As the cavalry charged into the wide plaza before the theatre, hordes of skaven erupted from every quarter. No alleyway or side street failed to disgorge a chittering swarm. From cellars and sewers, the beasts emerged, from wrecked homes and ruined towers they scurried. Out of the defiled halls of the theatre, a great horde of hulking armoured ratmen marched, cruel halberds and great axes clutched in their filthy paws.

At the centre of these armoured vermin, the ratkin carried a great palanquin fashioned from the smashed wreckage of a royal carriage. Gunthar recognised the heraldry as that of his chamberlain, von Vogelthal, and wondered what manner of death had claimed his old friend.

Lounging amid the cushions of the shattered carriage was a horrific skaven clad in armour that might have been fashioned from a thorn bush. He was a huge brute of a creature, his fur midnight-black. Heaped about the monster on his carriage were the spoils he had claimed as his own, a mad confusion of rubbish and treasure. Panes of glass rested beside bolts of cloth, sacks of grain were sprawled across a pile of swords. The carcass of a fresh-slain sheep lay at the warlord's side, its hide peeled back that the ratman might nibble at its innards like a gourmand with a plate of sweetmeats.

Even from a distance, Gunthar could see the evil glitter in the warlord's eyes as the creature stared at him.

For an instant, as the trap swung closed behind them, silence gripped the plaza. Gunthar saw the skaven turning uneasily towards their hideous overlord, their bestial bloodlust cowering before their terrible king. Even the snipers fell silent as they waited for the attack to begin.

The rat-king lifted his nose, sniffing the air, drinking in the scent of fear wafting up from Gunthar and his soldiers. Then, his lips peeling back to expose clenched fangs, the warlord brought his claws crashing together.

In response to the signal, the skaven hordes set up a deafening chorus of squeaks and shrieks.

An avalanche of fur and fangs closed upon the surrounded men of Middenheim.

Carroburg
Pflugzeit, 1115

For those within the Schloss Hohenbach, the spectre of the plague remained an omnipresent threat. Despite the horrible curative their Emperor had procured for them, despite the isolation of their palatial hermitage, despite everything, they were ruled by fear. Daily, rising from the city below, they would hear the dirge being rung by the temple bells. From the parapets they could see the processions of corpse-carts in the streets, the proliferation of white crosses upon the doors.

It was an affront to the might of Emperor Boris, a slight against his supreme authority. He had delivered these people from the plague, yet the plague refused to abandon its prey. Like a wolf just beyond the firelight, it circled and snarled and snapped.

Emperor Boris, with cruel deliberation, decided to remove the wolf from the castle gates. One afternoon, when the bells below had been particularly active, he gave orders. As a fortress designed to command the River Reik, the walls and towers of Schloss Hohenbach were littered with catapults. The war machines had been poised to lob death and destruction upon any ship so brazen as to flout the sovereignty of Drakwald. Now, at the Emperor's command, the siege engines were removed, redeployed so that they might visit destruction upon a much different victim.

Encouraging a festive air among his guests, Emperor Boris led the great men of his Empire onto the battlements. Von Metzgernstein's *Dienstleute*, supplemented by those Kaiserknecht and palace guards who formed Boris's own retinue, manned each of the catapults. A great brazier of smouldering coals stood ready beside each machine and nearby were bales of straw drawn from the castle stores.

Swaggering along the parapets, the Emperor addressed his subjects. 'We brought you here as a retreat from the tawdry concerns of commonality. Here you have feasted and revelled, savoured all the delights of the world. As your Emperor, We have treated you in manner as befits the friends of the Imperial throne. In the harmony of this refuge of royalty, We have allowed no discordant note, no blemish upon the rich tapestry of Our accomplishments.'

The Emperor turned abruptly, pointing at the clustered streets of Carroburg. 'This is an offence to the cultured tastes of you, Our most noble friends. It is a blight, a scourge upon Our delicate sensibilities.' The impish smile worked its way onto Boris's features as he turned back towards his audience. 'We will remove this outrage, and in the doing offer to Our loyal subjects a spectacle such as none of you have ever seen.'

At a gesture from the Emperor, the soldiers manning the catapults loaded bales of straw and hay into the bowl of each engine. Other soldiers brought kegs of pitch and, employing long-handled brushes, painted each bale with the incendiary. After the men with the pitch withdrew, a lone knight advanced with a blazing torch. Gingerly, the warrior leaned towards the catapult and ignited the material loaded into the bowl.

Boris raised his hand up high. For a moment, his eyes glanced over at Erna. He could see the unspoken appeal written on her face. He grinned at the woman's temerity. Since her capitulation during the masque, he'd found her far less interesting. Whatever charm she'd exerted over him had been rendered impotent. He knew she had broken at last to his will. There was nothing else to interest him now.

Savagely, the Emperor brought his hand slicing down. In time with the gesture, the arms of the catapults snapped upwards and hurled their flaming missiles into the air. Boris's guests rushed to the edge of the walls, watching in rapt fascination as dozens of burning missiles descended upon Carroburg. Like fiery rain, the incendiaries came crashing down, exploding into little fingers of flame as they struck streets and rooftops. Wooded shingles and thatch ignited under the provocation, the fire quickly spreading among the semi-deserted neighbourhoods.

Again and again the incendiaries came raining down. The bells in the temples rang not with the slow notes of a dirge but with the rapid clamour of an alarm. From boarded homes and dilapidated hovels, the people of Carroburg rushed into the streets. Frantic mobs swarmed towards the river, gathering buckets, jars, pots, anything that might fetch water to oppose the flames.

Emperor Boris laughed at the peasants and their futile efforts, his jaded courtiers quickly warming to the cruel mockery. Wagers were soon placed on where each salvo would fall, the nobles watching with bated breath to see if their guesses would prove accurate. Jests were made over the pathetic fire brigades, the soldiers manning the catapults encouraged to lob their missiles wherever it seemed the peasants might turn back the flames. When a ring of flames began to close upon a stables that had been given over as a hospice for the sick, the nobles were treated to a parade of crippled humanity scrambling from the building, trying to hobble and crawl to safety before the fire could reach them.

Rare amusement this! Boris congratulated himself on this novel entertainment. Who but an Emperor could command such a performance? Who but an Emperor could afford to lay waste to an entire city? If nothing else had impressed his guests with the extent of his power, this would emblazon it upon their very souls! Once the spectacle was past, once the wonder and emotion had cooled into the reflections of cold reason, they would understand and appreciate what they had been witness to. He was thankful that the Black Plague had finally reached Carroburg. Without it, he might never have considered such a display of unrestrained power.

The conflagration quickly spread, entire districts blazing, the afternoon sky blotted by thick pillars of smoke. Before the gawking, jeering spectators assembled on the castle walls, Carroburg died.

Emperor Boris, tiring of the fiery display, turned from the battlements, seeking to find Erna. The woman's helpless disapproval would, he decided, still add a much needed spice to the banquet of Carroburg's destruction. He scowled when his roving eyes failed to find her. She'd retreated back into the castle, hiding herself away as she had when the nobles would feed the beggars. Boris chuckled at the absurdity. As though by not seeing a thing she could make it any less real.

He was debating whether to send someone to fetch Erna from wherever she had hidden herself when a note of alarm rose from the nobles on the parapet. Thinking perhaps he had missed some rare incident of unique tragedy, Boris rushed back to the battlements. He was surprised, even disappointed to find that his guests weren't watching the fire but had instead turned their attention to something close to the base of the castle wall.

It was then that the Emperor became aware of the sounds, sounds that perhaps had been present for some time but had been deadened by the applause of his guests and the din rising from burning Carroburg. The sounds were strange, a confusion of dozens of small bells that seemed to have been selected for their disharmony. Beneath and around the chaotic notes were the tones of many chanting voices.

But such voices! Boris felt his pulse quicken at the loathsome noise. They were shrill, scratchy voices – the squeaks of vermin trying to contort themselves into the patterns of speech. He thought of the reports from the southern provinces, the appeals for monetary and military aid against hordes of horrific ratmen.

The Emperor's guests pointed with trembling hands at a ragged line of sinister figures in tattered green robes. They were somehow monk-like despite the uncanny wrongness of their every step, the surging scurry in their gait that belonged to nothing human. It was from these figures that the eerie chant arose, and clenched in the furry talons of many of them were bells of every stripe and size.

Around and around the Otwinsstein the inhuman monks marched, filling the winding road with their pestiferous numbers. Every fifth monk bore aloft a metal censer fitted to a long pole, swinging it with crazed fervour overhead. The ball-like censers expelled clouds of grimy smoke, filth that was borne towards the castle by the winds sweeping across blazing Carroburg.

Emperor Boris heard the frightened mutters of his guests, the superstitious fears of men who now repented their mockery of the gods.

'We stand protected,' Boris called out to his guests. 'The

enchantment will shield us.' Even as he spoke, he waved soldiers away from the catapults, sent servants hurrying to ready bows and arrows.

'The magic will protect us,' Boris scolded the terrified men around him as he watched a noxious green fog slither its way up the castle walls. 'The gods are powerless to harm those who reject their power.'

Inwardly, however, the Emperor doubted his own words.

─< CHAPTER XX >─

Middenheim
Ulriczeit, 1118

The skaven horde closed in around Graf Gunthar's troops. The plaza rang with the clash of swords, the screams of terrified horses and the cries of dying men. Upon the roofs, skaven jezzails pelted the embattled soldiers, cackling viciously as warpstone bullets slammed through steel plate to explode inside human flesh. Mobs of scrawny slaves wrenched knights from their saddles, packs of clanrats thrust spears into horses and chopped down infantry with crooked swords and rusty bludgeons.

Before the pillars of the theatre, the Verminguard butchered their way through nobles and peasants, hacking them down with their wicked blades. At their back, Vecteek the Tyrant roared with sadistic mirth, relishing every scream, savouring the stink of blood in the air.

This night belonged to Clan Rictus and their despotic War-monger! Before dawn shone down upon Middenheim, the humans would be exterminated. A few, perhaps, might be taken back to Skavenblight, trophies of his supreme victory. Most, however, would die. The armies of Rictus were vast and hungry.

Vecteek hissed with satisfaction as he watched his Vermin-guard cut down a knight and his destrier, reducing man and animal to a mangled heap before they were finished. Yes, his triumph would send terror coursing through not only the foolish hearts of the man-things, but through the perfidious minds of skaven as well. Where other Grey Lords had failed, he would return in victory! All would bow to his tactical genius, his incomparable might as general and warlord!

Baring his fangs, Vecteek swung around as a black shadow dropped towards him from the charred roof of the theatre. The Warmonger's bronze mace in his paws, his foot kicked out, sending one of his palanquin's bearers stumbling towards the shadowy apparition. It was only when the cloaked figure sprang forwards and sent the bearer reeling against the side of the palanquin with a graceful drop kick that Vecteek recognised the fearful presence as his faithful retainer, Deathmaster Silke of Clan Eshin. Just to be careful, he kept the stunned bearer between himself and the infamous assassin.

'More man-things come,' the Deathmaster reported, his voice like the whisper of a knife. 'Dwarf-things too.' Silke lashed his tail in anger. 'Vrrmik betrays us!'

Vecteek snarled in outrage. Raising his mace he started to lunge at the Deathmaster. Silke, however, was one of the few messengers even Vecteek knew he couldn't destroy. Instead, he contented himself by smashing the skull of his hapless bearer. 'That tick-licking spider-pizzle!' Vecteek roared. 'Vrrmik-meat shall suffer much-much! Slow-die long-long!'

Other shadows dropped down from the roof, the menacing shapes of the Deathmaster's apprentices. Briefly they whispered into the ears of their master, careful to keep their gaze averted from Vecteek's enraged notice. The restraint he showed to Silke might not extend to themselves.

'Men and dwarfs come,' Silke told the Grey Lord, waving a paw towards the south.

Vecteek followed the gesture, whipping his tail in anger as he saw the assassin's warning play out. The ratmen holding that part of the Eastgate were scurrying into the plaza, streaming from the streets and alleys in a confused panic. Behind them, rushing after them like hungry cats, came the armies of both Middenheim and Karak Grazhyakh, the armies Vrrmik and his treacherous scum were supposed to be holding down inside the Wolfrock!

The Grey Lord swung around to demand Silke and his assassins do something, anything that might stave off the disaster. The cloaked killers were already gone, evaporated back into their shadows. Vecteek gnashed his fangs and looked around for Puskab, thinking perhaps the plaguelord might have some pox or contagion that would strike down the avenging armies. Like the assassins, however, Puskab had vanished.

Fortune was abandoning Vecteek, and with it went his allies. The Grey Lord quivered in fury, brought his mace slamming down into the skull of another bearer. His improvised palanquin crashed to the street as the remaining bearers fled.

Crawling from the wreckage, Vecteek sniffed the air, drinking in the scent of his fleeing slaves. He would find them and they would pay. So would Puskab and Silke and that mould-furred dung-slime Vrrmik! All of them would suffer the wrath of Vecteek's vengeance!

The Warmonger turned his keen nose towards the south, picking out from the riot of scents and smells the familiar scent of Middenheim's pup-king. The prince was certain to be leading these enemies. Therefore, if Vecteek was to prevent the collapse of his own army, the prince must die!

* * *

As he led his men into the plaza, Mandred's heart froze. Even their grisly march through the ravaged streets of the Wynd as they emerged from the temple of Grungni hadn't prepared him for the carnage unfolding before them. That embattled ring of men at the centre of the plaza and the verminous horde that surrounded them. He had imagined the host down in the Fourth Deep to be formidable, but they were nothing beside the legion of ratkin he now gazed upon.

The men in the plaza were in a hopeless position unless they could be relieved, unless Mandred's troops could fight their way to them.

'Wolf and graf!' The war-cry thundered from the throats of a thousand men. Even some of the dwarfs took up the cry, a show of solidarity that even in the bedlam of battle impressed the Middenheimers with the severity of its depth. It was no empty gesture, that adoption of the human cause. The humans had been ready to die in defence of the Crack; by joining the fight for Middenheim the dwarfs were promising to pass a grudge debt to ten generations of descendants should the city fall.

The dwarfs were sparing with words of gratitude. For them, deeds spoke louder than any words, and Mandred's decision to honour his oath and drive the skaven from Karak Grazhyakh even when his own home was threatened had struck to the core of what a dwarf valued: honour.

With the help of the dwarfs, Mandred's troops drove the skaven before them. The monsters died by the score as they wreaked a terrible vengeance. Revenge, however, wasn't the passion burning in the prince's heart. Rising above the heads of the men trapped in the plaza, he had seen his father's banner, the heraldry of the castle and the wolf which only Graf Gunthar could bear.

He didn't know if his father yet lived, but he did know that when those brave men had marched against the skaven, it was the graf who had led them.

Beside the prince, Beck cursed as the flailing body of a ratman fouled his sword and nearly dragged the blade from his hand. The knight looked around anxiously, observing that they were perhaps being a little too eager in their advance. They were striking deep into the skaven formation, but at the same time they were becoming separated from the bulk of their own forces.

'Use the edge, not the point,' Kurgaz Smallhammer scolded Beck. The dwarf hero had insisted on accompanying Mandred when they struck out for the surface. Many ratkin deaths would be needed to balance the murder of his brother Mirko. The theft of Drakdrazh, he claimed, was a grudge that no amount of blood could wipe away. Each skaven skull he smashed was a dirge to his brother and a vow that he would find the white vermin that had stolen his hammer.

Beck snarled at the dwarf. 'I know how to use a sword,' he snapped, tearing the blade free just as a ratman leaped for his throat. The brute knocked Beck onto his back, its claws raking his cheek. Before the thing could do any worse damage, Kurgaz's hammer came crashing down.

Beck blinked up at his saviour from a mess of vermin blood and rodent brains. Kurgaz shook his head at the knight. 'If you fight like one of them, you may as well smell like one of them.'

Mandred chopped the paw from his own adversary, the creatures behind it losing their appetite for battle when they heard the squeals of their maimed comrade. The prince struck the injured ratman across the neck as it tried to flee, dropping it in a quivering heap. The other skaven fled, struggling to wriggle past the press of warriors behind them.

'Beck! Kurgaz!' the prince shouted as he saw the nature of

those warriors. They were tall, black-furred skaven clad in imposing armour of plate and chain. Rending axes and murderous halberds were clenched in their paws.

Mandred's comrades rallied to his side, guarding his flanks as the Verminguard charged at them. Slippery, treacherous foes, the huge skaven married their bestial strength to the depraved tactics of the lowest street fighter. Mandred thought of his many mock-battles with his instructor, van Cleeve. The swordmaster would have been appalled at the feckless, vile methods employed by these monsters.

Kurgaz was nearly beheaded after a Verminguard smashed the butt of its halberd into the dwarf's groin, eliciting a shrill gasp Mandred would never have believed him capable of. Beck's left eye was an oozing mess of blood and jelly after a skaven jabbed one of its claws into his face.

His own turn came when a Verminguard was practically thrown onto his sword by one of the skaven's treacherous kin. Mandred's sword was wrenched from his grasp by the shuddering body impaled upon it. As the armoured ratman crashed to the ground, its betrayer moved in for the kill.

Its fur was even blacker than that of the Verminguard, its armour cast from some strange alloy and adorned with a riot of spikes. There was a stamp of such unreserved evil in the thing's aspect that Mandred reflexively recoiled from the ratman's approach. The monster's eyes glowed with an eerie luminance as it bared its fangs.

'Prince-meat,' the skaven hissed in debased Reikspiel. 'Die-die for Vecteek!'

The Grey Lord jumped at Mandred, bringing a huge spiked mace smashing towards the prince's skull. Mandred managed to throw himself to one side. Instead of having his brains dashed in, his shoulder was merely clipped by one of the spikes. Even that slight cut sent burning agony roaring through his veins. As Mandred reeled away, trying to fend off the skaven with nothing but a dagger, he realised the monster's weapon was coated in some loathsome poison. Vecteek didn't need to land a telling blow; even a glancing hit might deliver enough poison into his system to drop him!

Vecteek raised his muzzle, snuffling as he inhaled the smell of fear wafting from Mandred. The Verminguard had distanced themselves from the fight, concentrating on Beck and Kurgaz and the others trying to aid the prince. The ratmen seemed confident their overlord could settle Mandred on his own.

That display of contempt, executed by such lowly creatures, was a slight that made Mandred forget his weariness, forget the burning pain of skaven poison throbbing along his shoulder. Even the fate of his city, the rescue of his father were forgotten. All that was left was outrage.

Snarling like one of Ulric's wolves, Mandred dived at the gloating Vecteek. His drive brought him upon the monster almost before the fiend could react. He felt the mace slam against his back, felt the sting as some of its spikes pierced his mail. But he also felt his dagger slice against furry flesh, felt hot blood ooze down the blade.

Vecteek leaped away from the prince, snarling in pain. The skaven pawed at the cut across his forearm, hissing as black blood bubbled up between his claws. There was an almost human expression of disbelief on the monster's face, as though he refused to accept that anyone could be so bold as to strike him.

Mandred exploited Vecteek's distraction. Fighting against the pain that coursed through his body, he threw himself to the ground in a sprawling dive. Vecteek reacted swiftly to the prince, bringing the spiked mace crashing down. The blow narrowly missed Mandred, slamming into the paving stones and pelting him with chips that cut his face.

The ratman reared back to strike again, but his opportunity was lost. Mandred's dive had brought him to where a skaven carcass lay. Snatching the rusty sword from the dead paw, the prince rolled onto his back and thrust the point of the blade upwards at the same instant that Vecteek dived down upon him.

The point of the sword caught the monster in the belly, Vecteek's own impetus driving the sword through the spiked mail he wore. The skaven's fierce howl of bloodlust disintegrated into a pained yowl of agony.

Vecteek's foot raked across Mandred's face when he tried to drive the blade deeper. Instinctively, the prince flung his arms across his face to protect his eyes from the vermin's claws. The instant the grip on the sword was gone, the skaven staggered back, his own mace falling to the ground as he clawed at the impaling blade.

Squeaking in agony, Vecteek wrenched the sword free, his glowing eyes glaring vindictively at Mandred. For an instant, the wounded monster seemed determined to rejoin the battle. Then the hate-filled eyes widened, the bestial head whipped from side to side in frantic, erratic motions.

A keening wail of sheer terror rolled across the plaza, erupting from a thousand skaven. The scent of Vecteek's fear, the sound of their invulnerable tyrant squealing in pain, these had resonated through the senses of every ratman, driving black terror into their craven hearts. Moaning, bewailing their own imminent doom now that the despot was defeated, a wretched rout began. Wherever Vecteek turned his head, he saw the same thing. Hundreds of warriors throwing down their weapons, clawing and trampling each other in their desperate efforts to escape back into the streets. Men and dwarfs pursued the creatures, butchering them as they tried to flee.

The terror of his minions infected Grey Lord Vecteek. His eyes widened with fear. Whipping his tail at Mandred, forcing the prince to again shield his face, the Warmonger turned and fled, dashing towards the burned shell of the theatre.

Vecteek the Tyrant never reached the safety of the ruin. As he fled, a lone figure stood in his path, a blazing sword clenched in his mailed fist. Much of his speed and agility had bled out of the wounded skaven. When Legbiter came slashing at his head, Vecteek wasn't quick enough to escape the runefang's bite.

Bloodied, his finery reduced to rags in the long fighting, his wolfskin cloak dragging behind him, Graf Gunthar spat on the twitching corpse of Grey Lord Vecteek. A kick of his iron boot sent the vermin's head bouncing across the plaza.

The graf cast his eyes across the battlefield, nodding to himself as he watched the defenders of Middenheim pursue the fleeing skaven back into the streets. The battle was over, now the cleansing would begin.

From the corner of his eye, Graf Gunthar noticed movement. He watched as a man rose painfully from the ground. Until that moment, he hadn't realised that Vecteek's foe had been his own son.

Across the bloodied battlefield, father and son looked to one another. The eyes of the son were filled with love and adoration, exhilarated to find the father alive. The eyes of the father beamed with pride, exalted to know that his son had become the man he had always prayed he would become.

For a moment, the lords of Middenheim stood, not speaking, words too clumsy to convey what they would say to each other.

The moment ended as a sharp crack boomed from one of

the rooftops. A puff of smoke, a flash of flame and a slinking shape retreated into the darkness.

The graf cried out, threw up his arms as the warpstone bullet slammed into him, chewing through armour and flesh like a hot knife. The agony of his wound sent him crashing to his knees. From his knees, he pitched forwards onto the ground.

Mandred rushed forwards, cursing the pain that slowed his steps, that tried to drag him down before he could reach the body lying sprawled face-down on the cold stones. A tangle of soldiers and noblemen had already gathered around the graf, but the solemn circle parted at the prince's approach.

Sickness bubbled in Mandred's stomach as he stared down at the horrible hole in his father's back. He recognised the evil black bullet sizzling at the centre of the wound. It was such a bullet that had almost killed Kurgaz Smallhammer – the poisonous bullet from a skaven jezzail.

His hand trembling, the prince reached down and gently rolled his father onto his back. A gasp of pain shuddered its way from the graf's lips. Mandred's heart raced. The graf yet lived!

'Quickly!' Mandred shouted at those around him. 'Lift up the graf!' He hesitated for a second, wondering where they could take him. The Sisters of Shallya were below in Warrenburg. The alchemist Neist was dead. It might take days to stir any of the physicians of Eastgate from their hiding places, assuming any of them had survived.

The life of his father hung by a thread. There was only one power to which Mandred could appeal for mercy, the same power that he felt had delivered Middenheim from the skaven.

'Take him to the temple of Ulric!' Mandred ordered, praying that the Lord of Wolves would again lend his aid.

* * *

Carroburg
Sigmarzeit, 1115

The green fume crept up the walls of the Schloss Hohenbach, rising like some fog spewed from Khaine's black hell. The nobles, only moments before mocking death and plague, now trembled in terror, rooted to the spot in fascinated horror as the noxious cloud came for them.

Archers loosed volleys of arrows down into the fume, hoping to strike down the inhuman monks that menaced the castle. Blinded by the green smoke, the bowmen had to trust to luck rather than skill. Only a few pained squeaks rewarded their frantic efforts.

Emperor Boris recoiled from the battlements, retreating as the odious fog rolled up between the crenellations. Baron Pieter von Kirchof – the Emperor's Champion, the most famed swordsman in the Empire, the man who had offered his own niece to stave off the plague – was the first to be touched by the foul fog. Slow in withdrawing from the battlements, he suffered the caress of one of those ghastly wisps. The effect was both immediate and ghastly.

Von Kirchof's skin blackened, his face vanishing beneath a confusion of hideous boils. He took a few staggering steps, then collapsed, a wheezing, coughing wreck. Blood bubbled from his lips, gore dripped from his nose. In a matter of heartbeats, the man grew still, his body heaving in a final agonised gasp.

The Emperor's guests degenerated into a panicked riot, converging upon the door leading back into the castle as the fog swept up over the parapet. They stampeded the archers who stood in their way, trampled the bodies of peasant servants unfortunate enough to impede their escape. In their hour of death, the great and good of the Empire, the scions of culture and society, the paragons of government, showed their quality.

Boris, first and greatest of them all, anticipated the rout. First through the door, first to abandon the walls for the security of the castle, he slammed the portal closed even as Count Artur of Nuln came racing towards him. The Emperor could feel the count's fists beating on the heavy oak frame, could hear the muffled pleas spilling from his lips. He could hear Count Artur's entreaties become screams as the maddened rush of nobility crushed him against the unyielding door.

The Emperor shivered as the cries of the doomed hammered against the door. The green fog was boiling across the wall now, bringing its loathsome death with it. The vapour wasn't simply smoke and mist, but a concentration of the plague itself, a concentration so vicious that it did its deadly work not in days or hours but in minutes. The green monks had brought it to the castle, had brought it to smite the Emperor and his minions.

Boris retreated from the door. The impact of fists against the heavy oak had become weaker as more and more of those on the wall fell victim to the fume. It was a stout door, designed to repulse invaders in a siege. Even the strongest man would need something better than his fists to bring such a door down. But what good was a door against something without substance or shape?

Seeping under the door, glowing in the gloom of the corridor, the ghastly fog crept into Boris's refuge, almost as though in pursuit of the man who had escaped it.

Moaning in terror, the Emperor turned and fled. It was impossible! All of it impossible! Fleischauer's spell, the warlock's magic! He had been assured it would work, that he would be defended against the Black Plague!

The warlock had deceived him. It was a realisation that made the Emperor's stomach turn sour. As he fled through the empty passages of the castle, Boris screamed for Fleischauer. If he were to die, then he would demand an accounting from the feckless conjurer!

Boris found Fleischauer in the great hall. The warlock was lying on his side, prostrate before the pedestal. One of the enchanted leeches was clenched in his hand, but he would never draw its magic into his body. The man was dead, a look of such abject horror frozen on his face as to make even von Kirchof's agonies seem timid.

Lying atop the sprawled warlock, its toothless mouth slobbering impotently at his neck, was the tattooed thing, the violated husk of Sasha. It hadn't been left to the thing to visit any real harm upon its tormentors, but in some caprice of fate Fleischauer's mind had collapsed when Sasha fell upon him from the pedestal. The warlock's heart had burst from sheer fright.

Gazing in horror at the obscene vista, the Emperor fled once more. There was no pattern or motive to his retreat now, simply the blind panic of a man who feels the cold claws of death reaching out to claim him.

Through chamber and corridor, down stairs and steps, the most powerful man in the Empire raced to preserve even a few scant moments of his corrupt life. He passed the collapsed forms of servants and soldiers, their bodies disfigured by the attentions of the Black Plague. Within the whole of the castle, he alone yet drew breath. All around him were the marks of death.

Approaching the dungeons in his desperate flight, Boris at last encountered something alive. It was a creature that carried itself in crude mockery of human shape, a verminous abomination cloaked in the habit of a monk, the cloth unspeakably foul and tattered. From beneath the hood, the fanged muzzle of an enormous rat projected. Its whiskers twitched as it drank in the Emperor's scent, and its beady eyes glittered with obscene delight. Waving a disfigured paw that was bloated with pustules and lesions, the ratman summoned others of its breed from the stygian darkness.

Boris shrieked. His retreat before had been frightened. Now it was the product of madness. In his derangement, the Emperor fled back the way he had come, matching step for step as he tried to elude the ghastly ratkin.

Chance brought the Emperor into the little forsaken chapel of Sigmar. Rushing into the sanctuary, he slammed the stout door shut behind him. Sweating, the seams of his finery splitting as he dragged the crumbling remains of a pew against the portal, Boris did his utmost to block the entrance. The first pew was followed by a second, and then by a dusty tapestry he tore down from the stone wall and stuffed beneath the edge of the panel.

Panting, huffing from his exertions, the Emperor turned away from the blockaded door. It was only then that his panicked mind appreciated that he wasn't alone in the chapel. Two other survivors had found their way here: a noble and a peasant knelt before the altar.

'There are… things out there,' the Emperor stammered. He rushed to the noblewoman, turning Princess Erna around to face him. 'Vermin… Underfolk!' he wailed, imploring her to believe him. He wilted under the accusation in her eyes. She'd begged him not to bombard Carroburg and he'd been deaf to her pleas.

Unable to maintain her gaze, Boris turned to the peasant, gripping Doktor Moschner's arm in a desperate clutch.

'They're all dead!' he wailed. 'The Black Plague. The ratmen brought it. They mean to kill us all. We're next!'

Doktor Moschner shrugged free of the Emperor's hold. 'If we are meant to die, then we will die, Your Imperial Majesty,' he told Boris. He turned back towards the altar, raised his eyes to the hammer on the wall. 'Only a power higher than even an emperor can help us now.'

The Emperor cringed away from the altar, horrified by the fatalistic acceptance adopted by his companions and their retreat into the facile comfort of faith. All his life he had doubted and mocked the gods. To think they had real power, to believe that they truly governed the world around men – it was a concept as abhorrent to him as his own mortality. Yet, in this hour, was it not his own mortality that confronted him? Where would all his power, all his authority go if he were to die? What would be the legacy he would leave behind?

In his despair, Emperor Boris knelt down beside Princess Erna and Doktor Moschner. All through the night he added his prayers to theirs, when he wasn't confessing his many sins to the gods he had reviled all his life. Many were the vows he made, the oaths he swore as he beseeched Sigmar to spare him his life.

Every moment, the Emperor expected to hear his companions admonish him for his many crimes, waited to hear the ratmen scrabbling at the chapel door. Neither voice nor sound disturbed him through the long hours of darkness.

The vermin had too many victims readily available to bother about sniffing out the Emperor's refuge.

The survivors were too shocked by Boris's confessions to offer either comment or accusation.

There were some things too despicable even for the gods to hear.

* * *

Bright sunlight streamed into the chapel as dawn broke above the ruins of Carroburg. The first rays stabbed down, piercing through the shadows to illuminate the holy hammer mounted behind the altar. Despite the patina of dust covering it, the daylight shone from the bronze icon bolted to the hammer in an almost blinding brilliance. It was an instant only, then the sun shifted position and the blaze of light was gone.

The three survivors who had sat praying through the night rose slowly, their legs weak from cramps and impaired circulation.

'We've survived the night,' Boris observed, the words spoken in a timid whisper.

Erna shook her head. 'Is that a blessing or a curse?' she wondered, staring at the comet and hammer behind the altar.

'While there is life, there is hope,' Doktor Moschner offered. He started to move down the connecting passage leading to the great hall. He saw the fright that rushed into Erna's eyes. They'd heard the Emperor's description of what they might find waiting for them outside. 'Someone has to go,' the physician stated. 'Besides, I'm only a peasant,' he added, directing a glare at the Emperor.

Erna watched the doktor withdraw down the passage, creeping up on the barricade as though he were a hunter stalking prey. Timidly, he began shifting the pews Boris had used to blockade the door.

'We are alive,' the Emperor said, this time in a louder voice. His expression was no longer meek, but instead uplifted, the cherubic smile once more dominant. 'Even the gods don't dare kill Us.'

'Do not tempt fate,' Erna warned him. 'You made many promises, pledged to undo the crimes...'

'Crimes?' Boris sneered. 'An Emperor is the law itself. We can commit no crime!' He brought his bejewelled hands clapping together. 'We can use this,' he mused. 'If We act quickly, position the right people, We can fill the vacuum left by the ones the plague has taken. We can put Our people there, make the leaderless domains Our own! It might take a show of force to–'

A far different show of force came crashing down upon the Emperor's skull. Boris collapsed before the altar, blood gushing from his fractured head. Erna stood above the tyrant and brought the stone hammer crashing down a second time.

A third.

A fourth.

'Sasha and Fleischauer aren't in the hall. The ratmen must have carried them away…' Doktor Moschner's report trailed off as he stared at Erna and at the mangled heap sprawled beneath her. Both were barely recognizable as the people he had left behind. Erna's hair was bleached white, her face contorted into a fearful rictus. The Emperor had no face that could be recognised as such.

When Erna finally lifted her eyes from the man she'd murdered and saw Moschner, she let the heavy stone hammer fall from her fingers.

Doktor Moschner said nothing, simply advanced and tenderly led Erna away from the dead tyrant.

'We must leave this place,' the doctor declared. 'Go somewhere there are people. People we can tell this to.'

Erna stiffened, tried to pull away from his grip.

Doktor Moschner smiled at her and shook his head. 'You've done nothing,' he told Erna. 'His Imperial Majesty has expired from the plague. I am his personal physician. I should know such things. That is what I intend to tell people. If an idealistic young princess tells them otherwise, we will both visit the headsman.

'You've done what no one else was brave enough to do,' he

told her. 'Come, we must hurry from this place. There is an entire Empire waiting to hear that Boris Goldgather is dead.

'In dark days such as these, the people can use a reason to celebrate.'

—✦ CHAPTER XXI ✦—

Altdorf
Kaldezeit, 1114

An avalanche of fur and fangs, swords and spears, the skaven crashed into the Altdorfer battle line. Men died upon the points of rusted spears, were dragged down by verminous claws, or slashed and stabbed with blades of every description. In that frenzied charge, the speed and ferocity of the ratmen, the bestial bloodlust pounding through their brains, took a butcher's toll of the untrained peasants. The few clusters of seasoned warriors, the templars and the groups of soldiers, were spread too thinly to blunt the murderous impact of that initial charge.

The skaven revelled in the slaughter, trampling dead and wounded beneath their paws. Many of these had been the same fiends who had marauded through the towns and villages of the south, depopulating entire swathes of country in Averland and Solland. They had seen first-hand the breaking point of humans such as these. Any moment, they expected the confused rabble opposing them to break and flee, to turn tail and try to escape. In that moment, there would be a real reckoning. Even the lowest skavenslave looked forward to a full belly after this day's work.

The ratkin soon found they didn't know their enemy at all. The humans held their line. Peasant after peasant was dragged down, mutilated by the ferocity of the skaven, yet for each that fell, another grimly stepped forwards to take his place. After that initial frenzied charge, the monsters found themselves locked in close combat with an adversary who refused to falter. Caught between the human battle line and the press of their own reinforcements rushing up from behind, the skaven lost the room to manoeuvre, their advantage of speed and agility negated. The fight became a test of muscle and endurance, qualities where men had the advantage.

The tide of battle began to turn. First around the knots of templars and soldiers, then across the whole of the perimeter, the ratmen began to die. Vengeful swords smashed verminous skulls, vicious bludgeons dashed rodent brains, cruel knives opened ratty bellies. Squeaks of fright sounded above the snarls of fighting men, at first only a few but then growing into a terrified din. The pungent stink of spurting glands washed across the battlefield.

Across the line, the imposing black-robed hulks of Sigmar's warrior priests shouted encouragement to the faithful. Swinging their warhammers, the priests splashed bestial blood across the paving stones, their voices raised in echo to the battle-cry of the Grand Theogonist. 'For Sigmar!'

The skaven host, only moments before an almost elemental force of unstoppable destruction, broke before the stalwart valour of the defenders. Initially, only a few ratmen turned, but their panic spread like wildfire through the packed vermin. The craven nature of their slinking breed subdued the feral bloodlust of moments before. Wailing and whining, the skaven began to flee.

'Run them down!' a bold warrior priest shouted, swinging his hammer overhead to draw the eyes of his compatriots to him. 'Run them down!' he repeated, rallying those close to him to the pursuit.

Before the priest could chase after the fleeing skaven, a sharp crack sounded from the window of a building overlooking the square. A few keen-eyed men saw a flash of flame and a puff of smoke, a glimpse of the lurking jezzail hidden inside the house. None, however, could fail to see the gory effect of the ratman's shot. The priest's bald head exploded like a melon, leaving his headless corpse to flop to the ground.

More shots cracked from the buildings as other jezzails fired into the defenders, seeking to blunt the impetus of their pursuit. The snipers targeted mounted knights and shouting priests, the plumed helms of Imperial officers and the ruffled collars of nobles. It was a concentrated effort to eliminate the commanders, to slaughter the leaders behind the human opposition. The skaven were only too familiar with the kind of rout that would result should their own teeming swarms be deprived of the malefic threat of their chiefs.

Again, the vermin failed to understand their foe. Instead of blunting the attack, the cowardly sniping only evoked a dull roar from the charging humans, a savage cry of rage and indignation.

Then an opportunistic jezzail-wielding sniper, perhaps more calculating than others of his kin, fired at the glowing priest standing upon the steps of the Great Cathedral. The report of the shot seemed to somehow ring out above the din and clamour of battle, reverberating through the ears of all in the square. On the steps, the Grand Theogonist's body was thrown back by the impact, blood flying from the wound. Knocked against the huge doors, his body slumped against the twin-tailed comet carved there, Gazulgrund's arms drooped, the bulk of Thorgrim hanging limp in his hands.

All eyes turned to the doorway, man and skaven alike appreciating the enormity of that single shot. A hush fell upon the battle, both sides watching with bated breath, one with eagerness, the other with dread. After the hideous havoc wrought by the other jezzails, there were none who doubted that the Grand Theogonist would fall.

Gazulgrund defied their expectations. Pushing himself away from the door, his body surrounded by a nimbus of light, he strode out to the edge of the topmost step and raised Thorgrim on high once more, hefting the immense mattock as though it weighed nothing. 'For Sigmar!' he roared, his voice like the bellow of a titan.

A mighty cheer sounded from the defenders, drowning out the shrieks of terror that rose from the ratmen. The skaven were now thrown into complete disarray, fleeing in a crazed crush of furred heads and scaly tails. Awed by the divine aura of the Grand Theogonist, the jezzails didn't dare fire again, but quit their sniper nests with obscene haste.

As the skaven scurried back into the streets, abandoning the square and their siege of the temple, it seemed the battle belonged to Altdorf. Then, from those skaven trying to flee southwards, there sounded a new note of terror. The beasts began to scatter, many of them turning and trying to dash through the very ranks of their pursuers. A moment later, the reason for such abject desperation made itself known.

Great sheets of green flame shot out from down the street, incinerating those skaven who had not yet fled the avenue. Dozens of men were caught in the vicious blast, their bodies bursting into flame as the fiery green vapours engulfed them. Behind the fires, two wagon-like machines were dragged into the square, burly ratmen working the nozzles of hoses to spray the caustic demi-fluid across any who tried to approach the street they guarded.

The fire-throwers made no effort to advance, nor did the armoured warpguard who assumed positions on their flanks. Their orders didn't include capturing the temple or killing the humans. Those tasks were being left to the warpcaster.

Shortly after establishing their perimeter, the vanguard of Clan Skryre heard the crackle of Sythar Doom's voice barking orders to his warp-engineers. A moment later, the ground shuddered as the siege engine arm was sent crashing against the crossbeam.

The crystalline sphere hit high upon the face of the cathedral, flashing with ghoulish luminescence as its malignant energies vented themselves against the façade. Sculptures withered in that burst of corrosive power; gargoyles were sheared from their moorings and sent plummeting to the plaza far below. Glass melted, dripping down in grisly streams that marred the once unblemished marble. It was a terrifying display, but far less than Sythar Doom had hoped for. The Grey Lord's whiskers twitched as he wondered if, just perhaps, some divine power did defend this man-thing temple.

Irritably, the Warpmaster snapped fresh orders to the crew of the warpcaster. He hadn't failed to notice the shining aura emanating from the Grand Theogonist. They would put the power of this man-thing god to a real test – by unleashing the might of the warpcaster against something far less resilient than marble and stone.

Adolf Kreyssig dug his spurs into the flanks of his destrier, sending the great warhorse bolting down the narrow street. The animal's steel-shod hooves stove in the verminous bodies of the skaven that blocked the way, crushing them beneath its bulk. His sword licked out, slashing right and left at the ratkin who snapped at him in their dying agonies or who thought to clamber up into the saddle with him to escape the destrier's stamping hooves. Behind him, a squadron of Kaiserknecht and mounted Kaiserjaeger slaughtered the maimed monsters he left behind.

It was a desperate gamble, risking all in this frantic effort to relieve the siege around the Great Cathedral. Given his own choice, Kreyssig would have tried to hold the Imperial Palace, a structure that had been built for defence, not worship. The choice, however, wasn't his own. Bitterly, he reflected that it had been he himself who had allowed the decision to be taken from him. By seeking to control and exploit the Sigmarites, he had caused their faith to regain much of its faltering prominence among the peasants of Altdorf. He had used Sigmar to rally the people. Now he had to back his wager. If they lost the Great Cathedral, then they would lose everything.

Kreyssig struck out with his boot, kicking fangs down the throat of a lunging skaven. The brutes they encountered now were less organised, more frantic than the packs of looters they had seen up on the hill. It occurred to him that these might be refugees from the battle unfolding around the Great Cathedral, that against all reason and odds the Sigmarites had somehow turned the tide.

Then his gaze was drawn skywards by a bright flash of light. Kreyssig saw the sphere crash against the temple wall, watched in mute fascination as the very stones began to corrode beneath the unleashed energy. His hopes of only a moment before were dashed. Some of the skaven might have quit the field, but others were still on the attack and they had brought with them some unholy weapon.

'We must hurry,' Baroness von den Linden called out from behind him. It was uncanny, the horsemanship she displayed, urging her slender mare to feats that even a destrier would balk at. Further evidence of the witchcraft at her command. Witchcraft, she seemed to think, was no longer a thing to keep hidden.

Kreyssig frowned and urged his own mount further into the swarming press of skaven. Half a dozen of the beasts crumpled under his lunging horse, two others fell beneath his sword and still the path ahead was engulfed in vermin. 'We'll never get through!' he cursed. There were other streets they might try, but that would mean falling back, retracing their steps to the Imperial Palace. The idea of turning his back to the ratmen made the flesh between his shoulders itch, almost as though it felt the point of a skaven spear pressing against it.

Baroness von den Linden shook her head. 'I will save this city,' she vowed in a voice that was like a razor. Once again, Kreyssig felt the deathly chill of magic in the air. The witch's eyes faded into pools of amber light, her crimson hair flowing about her in a spectral breeze. Thrusting her hand forwards, she pointed at the ratmen.

The witch's voice rose in a keening wail, a sound that had in it the shattering of glass and the shriek of quenched steel. It was a banshee cry that sickened the comparatively dull ears of men. To the hyper-keen senses of the skaven, it was an aural torment, a scourge that set them squeaking in agony. Wracked by pain, clamping their paws over their ears, the ratmen turned and fled, hacking their way through their own kin in their desperate rout...

When they had ridden from the palace, Kreyssig had contrived to remove all the other prominent leaders from the effort to reach the Great Cathedral, sending Duke Vidor to coordinate his fragmented army, dispatching Grand Master Lieber to the river and warning Arch-Lector von Reisarch to keep inside the fortress lest the ratmen claim all the hierarchs of the temple in one fell swoop. He hadn't been able to resist the baroness's demands to accompany the group, however. It had been enough of an ordeal just to get her to keep to the rear ranks. He knew that if they succeeded the leader of the charge would be adored as a hero by Altdorf. He would be that hero.

Now, however, he found himself pushed aside by the witch. Baroness von den Linden urged her mare down the road, her eyes still aflame with the power of her sorcery. The monsters didn't make any more attempts to scurry up the street, but instead decided the witch was more terrible than whatever they had fled in the square.

The plaza around the Great Cathedral was a chaotic scene. Ratmen swarmed seemingly everywhere, some intent on fleeing, others, cornered like the rats they so resembled, putting up a vicious fight. Corpses littered the square, the stones soaked with the red blood of men and the black filth of skaven. Upon the steps of the cathedral, his body aglow with an unearthly nimbus, stood Grand Theogonist Gazulgrund, his voice booming out in a paean of battle. At one corner of the square, a disciplined brigade of armoured skaven fended off the ragged assaults of peasants and flagellants. Assisting them in their efforts were two grisly, flame-belching contraptions.

In the street behind the fire-throwers, Kreyssig could see the palanquin of the spark-toothed rat-sorcerer. There was no mistaking that disfigured abomination. Towering behind the sorcerer was what looked like a clockwork catapult constructed on a monstrous scale. Even as he watched, the long arm of the machine sprang forwards, slamming into the crossbeam and flinging another sinister glowing sphere into the sky.

As the sphere came hurtling earthwards, Kreyssig was nearly blinded by a flare of brilliant blue fire close beside him.

Overhead, the orb exploded in a burst of similar brilliance, showering a dark miasma that crackled with green lightning onto the heads of the armoured skaven and across the bulks of the fire-throwers. The skaven wailed in agony and terror in the brief instant they had to grasp what had happened.

A third flare of blinding light, but this one wasn't silent as those from before. The crackling miasma that rained down upon the skaven sizzled on their armour, incinerated their flesh and ignited the combustible fuel that fed the fire-throwers. Green fire blossomed from the wooden casks, immolating the entire corner of the square. Hundreds of skaven were reduced to embers in the firestorm, the fire-throwers exploded into charred splinters.

Kreyssig looked from the skaven to the persistent glow beside him. In horror he beheld the body of Baroness von den Linden seemingly wrapped in a mantle of blue fire. The witch's hair and gown billowed about her wildly, caught in a tempest that was so confined that even the mane of her steed failed to suffer its touch. Whatever she had done to the sphere, there was no concealing her magic now. Hundreds of awestruck peasants and clergy were watching her as she calmly trotted her horse towards the flames.

Cursing under his breath, Kreyssig spurred his warhorse towards her. 'Are you mad?' he growled, trying to catch her reins. 'Everyone will see. Everyone will know!'

The witch pulled away from his approach. She favoured Kreyssig with that familiar coy smile. 'Let them see,' she said. 'After I save this city, not the Grand Theogonist himself will dare touch me.'

Rushing masses of peasants came charging across the square, eager to come to the aid of their miraculous saviour. Savagely, they cut down the few skaven who had escaped the holocaust. Somewhere, someone gave voice to a shout, a cry that became a frenzied chorus: 'The Lady of Sigmar!'

Kreyssig could only stare in wonder as the baroness rode towards the flames. He could see the skaven beyond that wall of fire, frantically trying to reload their catapult. He saw their spark-mouthed sorcerer threatening and shouting at them. The jewel-eyed rodent glanced back, flinching as he saw the glowing witch approach. Self-preservation overwhelmed his lust for victory. With a loud yelp, he leaped from his palanquin and scurried off down the street.

The skaven operating the catapult weren't so fortunate. Raising both her arms, thrusting her palms in the direction of the strange siege engine, the baroness invoked a spell of devastating potency. The orb being loaded into the catapult shattered as it was being set into the bucket. The rampant energies flashed into a blinding coruscation. Other flashes of light followed the first, one after the other, as steady as footfalls. The detonation of the first sphere had caught the ones behind it, igniting them inside their wooden boxes.

Kreyssig could only marvel at the devastation, the utter decimation of the skaven. With her magic, Baroness von den Linden had broken the back of the skaven assault.

As he was considering what that meant, what the chorus of shouts from the mob might mean, Kreyssig was suddenly seized and pulled from his saddle. He crashed to the ground, landing on his side in a painful sprawl.

He expected to feel the fangs of a ratman at his throat; instead, he saw a man in the hooded habit of a monk looming over him. 'You brought the witch here!' his attacker accused. 'You brought her here to deceive the people with her sorcery! But Solkan is not fooled so easily...'

In those murderous tones, Kreyssig recognised the voice of the witch-taker. Once before the fanatic had tried to kill him. Then he had been thwarted by his own penchant for ritual and the timely intervention of the skaven. This time, Kreyssig knew neither factor would sway the killer's hand.

Instead, rescue came from the most unexpected source Kreyssig would have imagined. As Auernheimer brought his sword arm up to deliver the killing blow, he was himself struck from behind. The witch-taker crumpled, the back of his skull shattered like an egg. Bits of the Solkanite's brain dripped down the jewelled haft of Thorgrim. Grand Theogonist Gazulgrund stared down at the man he had just rescued, a strange look in his gaze.

'You rescued me,' Kreyssig said, not daring to move while the priest held the mattock over him. The nimbus of divine energy was fading from the Grand Theogonist, but there was still a terrible power in those eyes.

'It was the will of Sigmar,' Gazulgrund said. 'You brought relief to the temple. You saved the house of Sigmar from profanation.'

The priest's voice was far from grateful. Kreyssig felt his spine tingle when he noticed that Gazulgrund's awful stare wasn't directed at him. He was looking past the prostrate Protector. He was looking at the cheering mob surrounding Baroness von den Linden. Listening to those blasphemous chants.

'I saved you because you are the only one who can do what needs to be done,' Gazulgrund said. 'You are the one who can save the people from delusion.'

Kreyssig guessed what the priest expected. His answer was a sneer. 'She is my ally and my mistress, why would I side against her?'

The Grand Theogonist impiously kicked the corpse of Auernheimer. 'As long as she lives, you will never be free of such fanatics. The cult of Solkan, the Inquisition of Verena, even the zealots of my own Temple. They will not abide such overt witchery. They will not rest until it – and those tainted by it – have been destroyed.' He gestured with Thorgrim at the cheering mob. 'Today the people cheer, but tomorrow they will remember the holy manifestation of Sigmar. A true miracle leaves its mark on a man's soul. Sorcery, even employed benevolently, leaves only nightmares.'

Gazulgrund's shoulders sagged, the great weight of Thorgrim causing him to hunch over. Whatever sacred power had briefly manifested within him was draining away. Still there lingered that terrible power in his eyes, in his voice. 'Choose your side well, Protector. You may either profit by what has happened here today, or become a victim of it.'

Kreyssig watched the priest slowly withdraw towards the temple, his last words echoing through his mind. He turned his head, studying the mob, seeing them cheer and praise Baroness von den Linden. To them, the witch was nothing less than a living saint, a miracle worker. The Temple of Sigmar wouldn't dare refute such beliefs because to do so would be to admit that sorcery had succeeded where the power of their god had failed.

No, the Sigmarites wouldn't dare act against her now.

Middenheim
Ulriczeit, 1118

The Ulricsmund had been spared the worst of the skaven assault. The Teutogen Guard and the wolf-priests themselves had proven more than the pillaging verminkin wanted to contend with. With their tyrannical leader rampaging across the Eastgate, the ratmen had simply bypassed the Ulricsmund to find easier prey.

Avoided by the skaven, the district had become a sanctuary for the people of Middenheim. Refugees clustered in the rectories and barracks, filled the gardens and sacred grove. The sanctuary of the great temple itself was packed with ragged groups of humanity, noble and peasant alike. In the face of annihilation, distinctions of blood and breeding had been forgotten. Westerland burghers sat beside Talabecland farmers, Middenland foresters huddled against Drakwald craftsmen, all united in their despair and fear.

That sense of doom had started to lift when messengers arrived describing the rout of the skaven horde in the East-gate. Dread descended once more when Prince Mandred came marching into the temple, battered and bloodied, looking as though he had clawed his way from his own grave. Behind the grim prince, Grand Master Vitholf and Beck carried the body of Graf Gunthar between them. A sombre procession of dwarfs and men followed after the graf, the banners they carried not held aloft in triumph but lowered in a gesture of mourning.

Among the refugees gathered in the temple were those who had left the Middenpalaz, sent to the safety of the Ulricsmund before Graf Gunthar embarked upon his desperate sally against the skaven. When they saw their liege lying lifeless in the arms of the knights, a great wail of agony rose from the royal retainers and servants.

Only one among the palace refugees had eyes for son rather than father. Lady Mirella stirred from her bench, her heart breaking when she saw the anguish on Mandred's face, the crippling pain in his every step. She started to rise, to rush to the prince, to offer him what relief it was in her ability to bestow.

'He will not welcome a friend right now,' Brother Richter spoke into her ear. Mirella turned towards the Sigmarite, hurt and confusion in her eyes. The priest bowed his head, and then continued in a sympathetic tone. 'He seeks a miracle. Comes here to beg before his god. Do not intrude upon his sorrow.' Richter gazed sadly at the sombre procession making its way towards the altar. 'The last ember of hope must burn itself to ashes.'

Tears were in Mirella's eyes. 'Why?' she asked Richter.

The priest's gaze became distant, his voice a mere whisper. 'Because it is on the anvil of pain that the gods forge heroes.'

Mandred was only dimly aware of the multitude crammed into the temple. The sound of wailing, the sobs of despair and alarm, these reached him as though from a great distance. Even the altar and the Eternal Flame seemed hazy and indistinct. When Ar-Ulric came bustling down from the pulpit whence he had been addressing the assembly, the prince could discern only an old man in wolfskin robes, his mind incapable of reconciling the sight with his memories of Ulric's high priest.

There was only one thing that was real to the prince. That was the near-lifeless body being carried behind him. In his mind, he thought he could hear the beating of the graf's heart, a dull drum-like rhythm that grew weaker with every breath. His father's fate was all that mattered to him now. Not Middenheim, not the people, not even the poison rushing through his own veins. Again and again, as he limped through the sanctuary, he begged the gods to take him and spare his father.

If the gods heard, if Ulric was listening, they gave no sign.

'Your grace,' Ar-Ulric was speaking, clutching at Mandred's arm. 'You are injured!' The old priest turned, shouting across the temple, for the first time in his long years forgetful of decorum within the sanctuary. He shouted for those wolf-priests versed in the healing arts, for the handful of herbalists and doktors who had trickled into the Ulricsmund amongst the other refugees.

Mandred pulled free from Ar-Ulric's grip, continued to hobble down the aisle. He would reach the altar, abase himself before Ulric, offer that last flicker of his own life in return for his father. Nothing would sway him from his purpose.

Vitholf and Beck spoke with Ar-Ulric as they passed him, bearing the graf towards the altar. Mandred knew they were talking about him, explaining that grief had disturbed the mind of their prince. They enjoined Ar-Ulric to get his healers and to likewise bring some of his Teutogen Guard to restrain the prince. As servants of Ulric, they were beyond the prince's authority, a duty which bound both of the knights to follow Mandred's commands regardless of the madness behind them.

There was no anger in Mandred's heart when he heard his subjects speak of him in such manner. They were concerned that he was neglecting his own welfare. In their minds, they had already abandoned Graf Gunthar to Morr's gardens of death. The prince would not.

The altar loomed before him. Mandred dropped to his knees, pressing his forehead to the floor. An inarticulate sob wracked his abused body as he cried out to Ulric. There were no words in it. There was no need for them. Ulric knew what Mandred prayed for and what he was prepared to offer in exchange.

A shriek pierced the solemnity that had fallen upon the temple, soon followed by other cries of fear and horror. Mandred raised his head just in time to see the cloaked shapes that dropped down from the beams overhead. Verminous voices chittered in obscene delight as three black-furred skaven lashed out with dripping blades, cutting down wolf-priests and refugees with abandon. Mercilessly, the monsters fought their way towards the altar.

Deathmaster Silke and his apprentices, the master killers of Clan Eshin, had come to avenge their dead overlord and reclaim the honour of their murderous order.

Silke slashed down a knight who stood in his way, leaping over the sprawling man and lunging towards the altar in a seamless blur of lethal fury. His apprentices followed after him, keeping the way clear. One of them was borne down when he was set upon by Kurgaz Smallhammer, the dwarf's brawny arms driving his warhammer into the beast's spine. The other parried Grand Master Vitholf's blade, struggling to hold the knight back.

Mandred rose to meet the Deathmaster. His weakened grip would never have drawn the sword hanging at his side, the blade Beck had given him as they withdrew from the Eastgate. The skaven assassin was beyond the swiftness of the most hale and hearty man. Silke would fall upon him before his hand even closed around the hilt.

A ragged, bleeding figure flung himself between the assassin and his prey. Exhibiting a sudden spark of vitality, a burst of unguessed strength, Graf Gunthar pulled free from Beck's arms and propelled himself into Silke's path. The Deathmaster's sweeping blade hewed across the man's chest instead of finding the neck of his son. The ratman blinked in disbelief at the unexpected intrusion that had cheated him of his intended prey.

In that instant, while Silke freed his poisoned dagger from the collapsing body of Graf Gunthar, Mandred freed his own sword from its scabbard. A brilliant light blazed from the edge of the blade as it was drawn. No common sword had Beck given to the prince, but no less a weapon than Legbiter, the runefang of the Teutogens!

Deathmaster Silke cringed before the enchanted sword. All skavendom had lived in terror of Warmonger Vecteek, and here was the sword that had killed that dreadful tyrant. An emotion that the Nightlord of Clan Eshin had tried to torture and burn from the glands of the Deathmaster returned to assail the ratman's pounding heart. Fear, so long rejected and denied, came flooding back into Silke's body.

The surviving apprentice saw the change in Silke's posture, the bristling of the assassin's fur, the weak flick of the killer's tail. Nartik's lips curled back in a snarl as he saw fear overcome his hated master. In a contemptuous display of skill, Nartik ended his duel with Vitholf, springing past the grand master's guard to slash the muscles of his sword arm and leave the limb hanging limp and useless at his side.

Before another opponent could close upon him, Nartik dashed towards the altar where Silke was turning to flee from Mandred. Chittering malignantly, Nartik dived at the combatants. His poisoned blade flashed out, slicing through flesh and bone.

Deathmaster Silke squealed as he crumpled to the floor, the tendons in his leg slashed by Nartik's blade. The treacherous apprentice glared at him for an instant, then went racing away, dodging past men and dwarfs as the fleet-footed killer made good his escape.

Mandred ignored the fleeing Nartik, intent only upon the sprawled Silke, the slayer of his father. The prone assassin lay limp and helpless as the prince stabbed down with Legbiter, driving the sword at the vermin's back.

In a blur of motion, Silke rolled aside before Legbiter could strike him. The Deathmaster's motion continued in a reverse twist that caught the edge of the blade in his cloak and wrenched it from Mandred's weakened hands. At the same time, the skaven's paw came sweeping out from beneath his leather tunic, flinging a clutch of ugly black throwing stars into the prince's body.

Mandred crumpled atop the monster, sprawling across Silke before the Deathmaster could twist away. Every speck of his being cried out in pain, the venom tipping the edges of the stars adding to the poison already in his veins. Mandred was deaf to the misery of his flesh, hearkening only to the misery in his soul. Fiercely, he forced his hands to close about Silke's throat, willed his numb fingers to tighten, to crush the life from the inhuman murderer.

Deathmaster Silke flailed beneath Mandred's strangling hands. Twisting and rolling, the skaven threw his attacker to the ground, yet still the hands would not release their terrible grip. The ratman's claws raked the prince's body, his fangs closed upon his shoulder, yet still Mandred wouldn't relent. All the strength in his battered frame was focused into the fingers clenched about Silke's throat.

Men were rushing to help the prince now, shouting and roaring at the skaven pinned beneath him. Kurgaz kicked his boot into the side of Silke's head, trying to force the skaven to loosen his fangs. Desperate, the Deathmaster twisted from his tormentors, rolling himself and the prince across the floor. Their bodies glanced from the altar, bounced across the patch of bare earth beyond it.

A gasp of horror rose from every man, woman and child gathered in the temple as the two struggling combatants rolled into the blazing fire of the Sacred Flame.

For an instant, the flame burned brighter, blinding the panicked observers. Then they could make out the shadowy shapes of Mandred and Silke lying within the pillar of fire. The prince's hands were yet wrapped about the ratman's throat, even in the midst of the Sacred Flame.

As the stunned assembly watched, Silke's body began to

disintegrate, charred into ash by the spectral energies of the fire. Soon there was nothing left of the Deathmaster.

Silence dominated the temple as the remaining combatant emerged from the midst of the Sacred Flame. Where the fire had obliterated Silke entirely, it hadn't so much as scorched the tattered cloak hanging from the prince's shoulders. When he stepped from the flame, Mandred's step wasn't the limp of a cripple, but the steady march of a conqueror. There was no blood on his face, no wounds marring his body. An almost ethereal glow burned behind his skin, slowly fading as he approached the stone altar.

It was Brother Richter who was the first to find his voice, the first to cry out in recognition of the miracle they had all witnessed. 'Hail the Wolf of Sigmar!' the priest shouted, his words booming like thunder within the crowded temple. The cry was taken up by the multitude, shouted with the passion of a delivered people towards their saviour.

Only Mirella was silent. She alone looked beyond the miracle, looked beyond the triumphant saviour. She looked at the man himself, the man who didn't hear the cheering voices, the man who didn't look at the jubilant throng.

Mandred stared down at his father's corpse sprawled before the altar. As he gazed into Graf Gunthar's cold eyes, he felt a bitterness boil up inside of him. Why had the gods refused his prayer? Why him and not his father?

The answer seemed to shine in his father's dead gaze, in the beauteous peace that had settled upon his face.

The son's prayer had been rejected.

The father's had not.

Mandred looked up as he found Beck approaching him. The knight bowed and offered him Legbiter once more. Solemnly, the prince took up his sword, the sword which was now his right to bear as Graf of Middenheim. Holding the

Runefang aloft, he faced the cheering crowd and this time he heard their adoration.

'Hail the Wolf of Sigmar!'

Altdorf
Jahrdrung, 1116

Months after news of Boris Goldgather's death reached the Imperial capital, a festive quality lingered in the streets. The gigantic statue of the dead Emperor, a dwarf-crafted colossus that dominated the Königplatz and which had been funded by a special bread tax, had been pulled down and demolished by the citizenry, the rubble carted off and dumped into the Reik. For weeks, jubilant processions had marched through the streets of Altdorf burning dung effigies of Boris. Even now, ribald and scathing ballads about the last of the Hohenbachs were favourites in the city's taverns.

Adolf Kreyssig, Protector of the Empire, had deemed it politic to leave the peasants to their celebrations. His position was a precarious one. As a man of humble birth, he had no birthright to the power now at his command. It was only through the indulgence of the late Emperor that he enjoyed his position as steward of the Imperial throne. At the moment, the good people of Altdorf were happy to overlook that fact. Kreyssig had led them in the defence of their homes, had saved the city from conquest by the abominable Underfolk. To the commoners, he was a saviour.

Better than any noble, Kreyssig knew how fickle the mood of peasants could be. Today's hero became tomorrow's tyrant. Without the support of the Emperor there was no legitimacy behind his rule, only the clamour of the mob kept the Reikland nobility from casting him from the palace. He knew that the nobles would do their utmost to sow discontent among their peasants. Once the populace turned on him, it would all be over.

Kreyssig stalked through the cold halls of the Imperial Palace. Many of the paintings and tapestries had been stripped away, sold off to rebuild the depleted Imperial coffers. Diamond goblets, emerald chairs, an entire armoire made of polished amber, thirty-seven matching sapphire brooches, a cloak of gold leaf over leopard skin, a tub fashioned from pearl – the list of Boris's extravagances was as extensive as any dragon's hoard. Kreyssig knew he hadn't been able to sell the Emperor's luxuries for even a quarter of their worth, but at the moment bread and beer were far more essential than gold and silver.

'You needn't fret over the mood of the people,' Baroness von den Linden scolded her paramour as she joined him along one of the deserted galleries. The witch had adopted a lavish gown of imperial purple, a colour reserved only for an empress or an emperor's consort. Apart from the scandalous impropriety, Kreyssig was worried about the subtle implication, the implied threat to the nobles. If the baroness wore purple, then maybe the nobles would think he was sizing himself for a crown. At the moment, he didn't need the Vons thinking about such things.

'Let them think what they like,' the witch laughed, resting her hand in the crook of Kreyssig's arm. 'The peasants are behind you and they have greater numbers than all the nobles. The blinders are off now and men like Duke Vidor will find it difficult to put them back on again. The commoners have been awakened.'

Kreyssig frowned at his companion. 'Easy for you to say. They adore you as some divine instrument of Sigmar Himself. Even the Grand Theogonist is afraid of you.' He turned away from the mural he had been inspecting, a fifth-century piece depicting the Battle of Black Fire Pass. Once it might have been a priceless heirloom, but Emperor Boris had contracted vandals to alter the work so that Sigmar's face bore a closer resemblance to his own. Many of the paintings in the palace had suffered such destruction.

'Stefan isn't fooled,' Kreyssig continued as he walked with the baroness. 'He knows your powers owe nothing to his god. He knows there is witchcraft behind you.'

The baroness smiled. 'He may know much, but what can he prove? Can he make the people believe?' She laughed, a bitter spiteful note. 'Would he dare? If he exposes me, if he denounces me, what will that mean for his precious Temple? How will the peasants react if they know their homes were saved not by Holy Sigmar but by a heretical witch?'

Kreyssig led them down one of the arcades overlooking the extensive gardens, scowling at the great glass windows. Another vestige of Boris Goldgather's extravagance, and another that wasn't so easily traded to provide the essentials the city so badly needed. 'After the battle with the ratmen, the Sigmarites are more influential than ever before. They have resources beyond anything the other temples can match. The bread they distribute to their faithful has won them even more converts than your miracle in the plaza.'

The baroness stopped and glared into Kreyssig's face. 'And where have they acquired such resources?' she demanded. A faint glow crept into her eyes and a chill slithered into the air as she continued to hold her companion close. 'What have you been doing with the money Boris's hoard has brought you?'

'I need allies,' Kreyssig answered readily. He knew the witch could pluck the thoughts from his mind. There was no need to hide this from her. Not when there were other things in far greater need of secrecy. 'The Temple of Sigmar is the strongest in Altdorf. With them behind me, the nobles don't dare move against me. I provide them with the gold they need to buy bread, they feed all those who will bend the knee and swear upon the hammer.'

'You don't need them,' the witch declared. 'The people worship me and the Sigmarites don't dare do anything about it! I am the only ally you need.' Her tone softened, her expression lightened into a coy smile. 'Together, Adolf, we can rule the Empire. We can gather up all the pieces and make it greater than before. You and I, Emperor and Empress.'

Kreyssig walked on in silence for a moment, his eyes staring down the long corridor. 'That is a bold ambition,' he said.

'Tell me it is one that you haven't harboured deep down inside,' the baroness challenged him. 'A lowly peasant rising to become greater than them all.'

'You've been peering into my mind again,' Kreyssig snarled. He quickened his pace, marching down the arcade. Baroness von den Linden matched his angered step, her scandalous gown rustling about her velvet slippers.

'It can all be ours,' she told him. 'No one will stand in our way. Not Vidor, not Gazulgrund. None of them.'

Kreyssig stopped, resting his hand against a golden door set into the inner wall. Another example of Boris's excessive luxury. 'You make it sound appealing.'

Baroness von den Linden smirked and shook her head. 'As

though you weren't already thinking such things. That is why I took you in, healed your wounds. I saw the dreams in your heart.'

'Did you?' Kreyssig asked.

Something in her lover's tone brought a flicker of doubt sweeping across the witch's face. For the first time she was aware of a dissonance within Kreyssig's thoughts, a mental partition that resisted her.

Before she recovered from her surprise, Kreyssig tore open the golden door with his left hand and with his right swung the purple-gowned witch into the chamber beyond. Frantically, he slammed the door shut behind her, fearing every instant that she would unleash some spell against him.

The baroness shouted at him from behind the door, but the first shout quickly faded into an inarticulate shriek of horror. The witch had realised what room she was in.

One of the most expensive of Boris Goldgather's luxuries had been the construction of an indoor apiary, that he might be provided with fresh honey even in the deep of winter. Dwarfcraft and magic had gone into the building of the chamber, with pipes behind the walls to maintain a constant temperature and beds of enchanted flowers that never lost their bloom. A dozen hives, each in a box of crystal and gold, resided in the apiary to indulge the late Emperor's sweet tooth.

The apiary was one of Boris's extravagances that Kreyssig hadn't demolished. He had a use for it. A use he was now putting into effect. He remembered the enchantment Baroness von den Linden had placed upon herself, a spell that offended insects and frightened them away. He also remembered that she'd said ants, with homes to protect, wouldn't flee but would instead turn and fight.

As for ants, so with bees. Even through the thick door,

Kreyssig could hear the angry buzzing of the insects as they rose from their hives. He heard the terrified screams of the witch as the swarm descended upon her, a stinging tide of rage. In her panic, the baroness forgot all her magic, all the spells and conjurations that might have saved her. All the cold discipline, all the manipulative cunning, all the careful plotting and politicking, none of it served her in that final terror.

The muffled pleas, the desperate entreaties that became less articulate as venom swelled her flesh and terror assailed her mind – Kreyssig savoured each one. He felt a thrill course through his hand as he felt the witch's impotent fists pounding at the door, nails scratching uselessly at the golden panel.

'It wouldn't have worked,' Kreyssig said, pressing his mouth against the door. He could hear the impact of bees against the panel as they struck at the witch, knew that for each insect that missed there would be many more that would strike true. 'You are a Von, after all.' He heard a dull moan from inside the chamber, felt the door shake as a body slumped against it. He stepped away from the door, a regretful expression on his face. 'And I am but a lowly peasant.'

Kreyssig turned and marched back down the arcade. He'd have Fuerst brick up the apiary. With Boris gone, there wasn't any reason to squander expenses on year-long honey. After the room was sealed, no one would ever find the body. Baroness von den Linden had simply vanished, walked off into the mists of legend like Sigmar had done. It would be something to elicit mourning but not unrest among the peasants. The Temple of Sigmar wouldn't be connected in any way. The conditions of his arrangement with Grand Theogonist Gazulgrund would be satisfied. Removal of the witch in exchange for the Temple's support. He might, of course, have used the Grand Theogonist's daughter to sway him, but as it happened, eliminating the witch had suited his own purposes. The baroness thought she could control him; in her eyes he would never be anything but a peasant. He just couldn't afford such an attitude so close to the Imperial throne.

Not if he would make it his own.

The orison the Sigmarites had taught him had served to conceal his intentions from the witch right until the last. He must remember to thank Stefan – Gazulgrund – for that bit of assistance.

Kreyssig paused, glanced out through the windows and towards the distant spire of the Great Cathedral. Something Fuerst had told him, an unsettling bit of trivia he'd heard a few of the dwarf goldgrubbers discussing. It was tradition for the Grand Theogonists to adopt a dwarf name, but the one Stefan had chosen was unsettling.

Loosely translated, it meant 'the Death God's hammer.'

Skavenblight
Vorhexen, 1118

Supreme Warlord Vrrmik of Mors settled into the coveted Twelfth Throne, that chair adjacent to the empty seat reserved for the Horned Rat himself. The symbols of Rictus had been removed, relegated to the lower position Vecteek's successor had assumed. Vrrmik bared his fangs as he glanced at the simpering Kreptitch. He was a twitchy, nervous piebald ratman typical of the underlings the Warmonger had surrounded himself with. Any warlord of too great an ability was quickly eliminated from the ranks of Clan Rictus; it was one of the ways Vecteek had preserved his own position. Now, however, his plan was suffering from the resultant lack of leadership.

Too much of their power had rested in the paws of a single skaven.

There had been many changes in the Shattered Tower. The Verminguard had been expelled from the fortress, replaced by a mixture of Clan Mors stormvermin and Clan Pestilens plaguevermin. The shared responsibility for safeguarding the Council of Thirteen had been a concession the Grey Lords had accepted with qualms. Happy to be rid of Vecteek's troops, they weren't so keen on allowing a single clan to assume the duty. In the end, it was decided to pit Mors and Pestilens, the two most powerful clans, in the adversarial role of dual protectors.

Even as Vrrmik congratulated himself on seizing the Second Throne, he couldn't help but have a flicker of anxiety when he thought of the plague monks. Arch-Plaguelord Nurglitch might be content with a lesser seat, but he now effectively controlled three votes on the Council. Poxmaster Puskab Foulfur, progenitor of the Black Plague, had been the first of his disciples to acquire a seat on the Council, killing Worm-lord Blight Tenscratch of Clan Verms and assuming his seat. Now another of the plague monks, a plaguelord named Vrask Bilebroth, had gained a seat on the Council, acquiring the position forfeited by Warlord Manglrr Baneburrow of Fester. There had been many twitching whiskers at the unusual transfer of power, but with Clan Fester entering the Pestilent Brotherhood and becoming little more than a thrall clan to the plague monks, there was little difference whether Manglrr kept his seat or handed it over to his masters.

Grey Lord Vrask had risen to prominence after the ill-fated expedition by Seerlord Skrittar, bringing a copious amount of warpstone back to Skavenblight to enrich the coffers of Clan Pestilens and dragging the once powerful Clan Fester along with him like a bat on a leash. The same mysterious expedition had decimated Clan Mordkin, forcing Warlord Nekrot to invest in new breeders to accelerate the repopulation of his strongholds. However, the most pronounced difference, the thing that probably did more to aggrandise the position of Clan Pestilens than even a hoard of warpstone and a third seat on the Council, was the death of Seerlord Skrittar.

The most defiant and outspoken of Nurglitch's adversaries, Skrittar had been viewed with a mixture of religious awe and superstitious terror by the rest of the Council. Even the decimation of the grey seers, the loss of twenty-four of the most skilled of the Horned Rat's prophets, had done little to reduce the fierce reputation of Skrittar. His death in the human lands of Sylvania, however, had cast the entire Order into doubt. The new seerlord, a grizzled half-blind creature named Queekual, was a sinister figure of few words and fewer friends. Since rising to the Council, he'd been content to sit, listen and observe, like some black spider at the centre of its web. None of the Grey Lords knew what the new seerlord might be planning, but none of them desired to become his pawn.

Vrrmik glanced across at the hunched shape of Queekual. It had already been suggested to him that the grey seers be removed from their traditional occupation of the Twelfth Throne, that the dogma of Clan Pestilens had been proven the true path of the Horned One. The flattery of such a suggestion, that he was now in a position to abuse his power in the same manner as the despotic Vecteek, was somewhat diminished by the realisation that such an act could only earn him powerful enemies. There was a reason why the question hadn't been put to an open vote in the Council. Nobody was sure how much of the grey seers' power had perished with Skrittar.

No, the white-furred warlord reflected as he preened his whiskers, now wasn't the time to upset the already disordered ranks of the Council. Now was the time to marshal their forces, to secure the gains they had already made on the surface. To plan their future campaigns.

And to see which of his hated rivals Vrrmik could arrange a violent demise for on the field of battle. Vecteek should have some company in the Horned Rat's belly, after all.

Wissenland
Nachexen, 1119

A hairy, dishevelled shape clad in furs crept out into the bright light of a new morning. It straightened and stretched as it quit the narrow forest cave that had been its shelter. As the shape unfolded amidst the greenery of the clearing, it resolved itself into the figure of a man.

Erich von Kranzbeuhler rubbed a calloused hand across the thick mat of beard that covered his face. After six years, he imagined he might be able to impress a dwarf with his facial hair. His effect upon the ladies might be less profound.

The outlaw knight shook his head. There was only one lady he was interested in impressing and for all he knew, she was dead. Coerced by her father into a despicable marriage with Adolf Kreyssig, Princess Erna had failed to assassinate her husband. What vengeance the sadistic brute might have visited on her was too terrible for him to contemplate. If only he'd managed to kill Kreyssig in the sewers beneath the Imperial palace so much might have changed.

Thoughts of the sewers did nothing to ease Erich's mind. He couldn't forget the ratmen, those ghastly creatures that had first attacked him, then saved him. More than saved him, they had helped him escape, to keep Ghal Maraz out of the hands of Boris Goldgather.

At the time he hadn't understood. Now he did. The skaven hadn't helped him. They had tried to help themselves. With Ghal Maraz, any count in the Empire could declare himself Emperor and plunge the whole country into civil war. The skaven had depended on just that, to further weaken the lands of men so they could rise from their burrows and conquer the world. Already the vermin had claimed vast swathes of countryside, decimated cities in Wissenland and Solland. How much greater would their assault have been if the Empire had been decimated by war as well as plague?

Erich was thankful he'd encountered Arch-Lector Hartwich after his escape from Altdorf. The priest had given him important advice concerning Ghal Maraz and the terrible damage it could do in the wrong hands. He'd suggested Erich hide the hammer and keep it safe until the time was right, the time when men were most in need of a symbol to lead them.

For six years he had been waiting, leading a hermit's existence in the wilds of Wissenland.

The knight stirred from his musings, sighing as he watched a young doe limping her way into the clearing. The animal stared at him as she approached, drawing to within a few paces of him before lowering her head, almost as though bowing before an altar.

Erich lifted his eyes skywards. 'This isn't what I would call sport,' he complained aloud.

'Nor is it meant to be,' a voice intoned from the trees. Stepping into the light was a tall, powerfully built man dressed in buckskin, the hollowed head of a bear masking much of his features. The exposed skin of his muscular arms was leathery and scarred, the beard spilling down his chest twisted with burrs.

Haerther, the half-wild priest of Taal, had adopted the role of guardian of Erich when the knight was sent to him by Hartwich. It was only through the aid of the Taalite that Erich had managed to survive so many years of isolation beyond the frontiers of civilisation. He was grateful to his benefactor, but there were times when he resented some of Haerther's peculiar attitudes.

'I meant that I would prefer to hunt my own game,' Erich explained to Haerther. He glanced over at the injured doe. 'This way, I feel ashamed.'

The priest glowered at him. 'Are you ashamed to be alive? Think of all the creatures that have surrendered their existence to sustain you this far. All the plants that have been uprooted, all the birds plucked from the skies. Your life is their gift to you. To shun that is an abomination.'

Erich flustered at Haerther's reprimand. 'I just mean that it would be better to give the poor creature a chance.'

The priest nodded. 'I understand, but you must know this little one has reached her end. She has gone lame in her rear leg and would soon fall prey to another predator. I have spoken to her and explained that you are in need of sustenance. She understands.'

'Couldn't you… I mean with all your knowledge…'

Haerther frowned. 'That would be to violate the great cycles that Taal placed to govern all the wild things. No, her time has come. Take her gift to you. You will have need of your strength.'

Erich blinked in surprise. In six years it was the first time Haerther had ever said something that might allude to the future. 'Something has happened? You have heard something?' Haerther had brought him news before, had told him of the attack on Altdorf and the death of Boris Goldgather. Always such news had been accompanied by an admonition to wait, to bide his time. This time, Erich could sense, it was different.

'You must share your prey with the hunter who would have caught her,' the priest said. As he spoke, Erich was shocked to see a great white wolf stalk out from the trees and march purposefully to Haerther's side. The priest scratched the beast behind its ears.

'After you have eaten, we must discuss what has been happening in the north,' Haerther explained.

'The time is coming when Ghal Maraz will be needed to rekindle the hope within men.'

ABOUT THE AUTHOR

C L Werner's Black Library credits include the Space Marine Battles novel *The Siege of Castellax*, *Mathias Thulmann: Witch Hunter*, *Runefang*, the Brunner the Bounty Hunter trilogy, the Thanquol and Boneripper series and *Time of Legends: The Black Plague*. Currently living in the American south-west, he continues to write stories of mayhem and madness set in the worlds of Warhammer and Warhammer 40,000. He claims that he was a diseased servant of the Horned Rat long before his first story was ever published.